BOOK ONE IN THE STONE PACK SERIES

# *forbidden*
# LOVE

# HARPER PHOENIX

# ACKNOWLEDGEMENTS

When I started writing this book many years ago, I never thought I would get to the point where I would be thanking people who helped me achieve my dream of getting this story published.
So, to my husband, thank you for giving me the chance to achieve my dreams and always believing in me. For sleeping, despite the light from my laptop and the incessant tapping of the keys while I sit beside you in bed. Thanks for your patience and often doing my job as well as your own. You are my Forever and Always.
To my kids for understanding and accepting when I spent so many nights at my desk to get this crazy story done. I love you!
To all of my family. Thank you for believing in me!
To my friends who read and loved this story in its early stages—you know who you are! You gave me the encouragement to continue. I will always be thankful for that!
To my group of Beta's most of which were new to this just like me! You rock, thank you for all the hard work you put in and the amazing feedback you gave me!
To the angel sent from above! Your help and guidance helped me so much! I cannot thankyou enough Sarah Ellis! You Rock!
To my Editor, Claire Allmendinger of Bare Naked Words for making this story readable and pretty!
To Jo-Anna Walker of Just write creations for designing my kick ass cover! And for making my words pretty in every form!
To everyone who encouraged me along the way. Thank you!!
And thank you to you, the readers for daring to peek into my imagination!

# DEDICATION

For my Nanna. Always in my heart.

# *prologue*

## *Devon*

### *Aged five*

**D**ADDY TUCKED ME INTO BED and kissed me goodnight as I heard the door slam downstairs. He stiffened—that's how I knew he was sad again. Mommy had been gone since breakfast, and daddy missed her. I knew because he cried when he thought I wasn't looking. I didn't like it when daddy cried. It made me sad. I'd drawn him a picture, of him, and me without mommy. I was cross with her because she always made daddy cry. Mommy's shouldn't do that.

Daddy always told me I was clever at drawing things, and he always smiled big when I showed him a new picture. I liked to draw him and me because we were the same when we changed. Mom wasn't—she was different. Mom said I was different too, but I liked being the same as daddy, I didn't like being the same as mommy, and she would get mad. They argued about me a lot. I often heard them when they thought I was sleeping. Tonight–after daddy settles me in bed I hear them shouting. I sneak down to sit on the step, three down from the top because number four creaked.

'You have to allow her room to choose!' Mom shrieks.

'I always allow her to choose, I never force her one way or another, she does it herself. You are being ridiculous as usual,' Daddy shouts back.

I sit with my hands on my ears, but I can't block it out because I can hear everything. Daddy says we can't tell anyone how well I can hear because I'm special. I can hear everything. Other children can't hear like me, and it's a secret. Other children aren't allowed to run in the forest either, only I am, with daddy and sometimes mom comes too when she isn't angry with daddy. It hurts a lot when I change, but I like my wolf, and I like it when she plays—it's fun. I am always careful, just like daddy tells me. My wolf knows what to do and how to be good just like daddy shows me. But sometimes it's hard when mom comes too because I don't like my kitsune. Mom is a kitsune, and she says I should be too. But I like my wolf—I don't like my kitsune. I tell her but she doesn't like it, and she always blames daddy. I don't like mom very much sometimes either, but daddy does. He loves her very much. I love daddy. He's always nice, and we have fun, and he takes me to kindergarten and the park. He reads me stories and shows me things on the map—where I was born, where I have lived and where we could go next. We have a game, and we have pins on the board. I have lived in nineteen houses already. Daddy says we can visit every state and live in every city. Mom doesn't like that either. She says she wants to go home. I like this home, but mommy says it's not hers, and she isn't happy. Mom starts to shout even louder.

'I've had it with you. I'm done. I'm leaving, and I wanted to take Devon!'

'If you want to leave then go right ahead, but you are not taking her with you!'

'What would be the point anyway? You've ruined her. If I hadn't have gone through the labour, I would swear she has no kitsune in her. That she isn't even mine!'

'GET OUT,' Daddy yells. I hear glass smashing and some loud bangs, so I run back up the stairs and sit on my window seat. I like it there because I can see the forest behind our backyard.

'I'll be back for her when she's old enough to know better!' I hear mom yell over more banging. Then the noise stops, and I see mom in her kitsune form running from the back yard. I'm not sad. But I know daddy will be.

# chapter ONE

## Devon

**Present Day.**

AFTER A HELLISHLY LONG FLIGHT with the last leg sat by an asshole that really couldn't take a hint, I was more than ready to dump my shit and crash. The jetlag was already screaming through my body like a hurricane in an alley. I'd been up since the ass crack of dawn and had done nothing but travel since. I'd crossed time zones and lost a whole night's sleep, arriving in the wet and windy UK the morning after I'd left Phoenix. Which made me feel like shit. But dad insisted I take four flights instead of one direct. For safety's sake. As always.

I could tell by all the bewildered faces as I got out of the cab that I wasn't the only new face on campus. There were people dotted around sporting t-shirts with slogans such as 'Lost?' or 'Ask me a question' and 'Here to help.' I really didn't want to get in line and ask where I needed to be, so instead I walked around aimlessly for a while until I had to admit defeat and get in the damn line to ask the question because I had no clue where I needed to be.

The nerdy guy who walked me to my dorm reeked of fear. Maybe this was his first gig as a 'helper' or whatever he was. He kept throwing me a half smile whenever I caught him gazing my way, and then he uttered, 'So, if you want, I can give you my number, and if you need a guide…'

'Umm thanks, but I'll be okay.' I felt instantly guilty as he turned beet red and almost ran right into the glass doors. I watched as people laughed and instantly felt like a huge bitch. I rode the elevator to the third floor and found my room number.

I took a moment before inserting the key. This was huge. My dad had finally released me from his protective bubble. Well, more like kicked me out if I'm being totally honest. He booked my plane tickets so fast and had my bags practically ready before I'd even completed the application. To say he was in a hurry to get rid of me was an understatement. I was used to moving—we did it regularly, but I'd never done it alone. It was so unlike my dad to let me go further than school and home without him. However, this time he insisted. I'd grown accustomed to what I thought was my dad's paranoid behaviour, that before we were 'found out' we had to move, so I never argued. I just went to the next destination—our next chapter.

So although this was a lone venture I was more than happy to run with it. I wanted my own space, my own life. Time to finally find myself.

As I pushed open the door my first thought was *shit what the hell have I done?* The place was tiny. How the hell was I going to cope being cooped up in this shoebox of a room? And my roommate hadn't even arrived yet. I was used to lots of space, open plan living. Fair enough we never spent long in each place, but it was always big wherever we went. My second thought was, *to hell with it I only have to sleep here.* At the mere thought of sleep my eyes felt heavy, and as I rubbed at them, they felt like I'd brought half the Sonora desert with me. Shit, I was an asshole when I didn't get enough sleep. And the nerdy guy was proof of that. So I unravelled the new comforter and pillow pack from the bed and threw myself on it. I don't even think more than a few minutes had passed before I was out. Bliss.

I wake to a new scent in the room, I sit up bolt upright and fall backwards straight on my ass. I don't quite hit the floor because I fall into an open suitcase right by the bed.

'Shit, I was doing my best. I'm so sorry. I really have been sooo quiet. You were like completely comatose. You actually scared the bejesus outta me. I was like 'oh my god is she dead?' but then you started to snore, it was actually quite cute—' aaannd she goes on and on like that. I tune her out while I climb out of her luggage, detaching some Velcro shit from my ass.

'—Oh my god I don't even know your name, I'm Maiya by the way,'

'Devon.' I put my hand in hers and shake. Maiya doesn't stop grinning. She reminds me of the Cheshire cat from Alice in

Wonderland. The resemblance stops there though. She looks like she just walked right out of Adolf Hitler's fantasy of what an ideal race should look like. A little bit Danish and very much a blonde goddess.' She has gorgeous long blonde hair and big blue eyes, and a nice body on her too. Long legs, slim build, good tits and ass, all the things that any guy would go for, if she stopped talking long enough for them to appreciate it. Maybe that's what guys want in a girlfriend? Personally, I prefer not to say too much. Keep to myself and stay in the background. Unseen.

Growing up, trying to keep under the radar and go unnoticed was difficult at times, but it was something I got used to. We moved around all the time, and I never really made close friends. I never met any friends I was sad to leave behind because I was never around long enough to care. It was tough as a little kid, but I grew used to the life. I'm still well educated, and I mix with regular people. But I have a huge secret to hide, and that was the one and only sacred rule I could never ever break. It has been drummed into me since before I could remember.

'Never, ever, show your true self to anyone.'

I remember, once in kindergarten, I drew a picture of dad and me. I'd shown the teacher, and she called my dad in and raised her concerns with the principle. To a five-year-old me, it was an innocent picture of my dad and me in wolf form, sharing a rabbit. I had even labelled everything to make it easier. They didn't see it that way, though. They thought it was disturbing. I guess the blood and guts I'd drawn and coloured in would give that impression, as well as the teeth tearing through the rabbit. I've always been good at art. But I never drew another picture like that one again. The school thought I should be monitored and maybe referred to see a psychiatrist because I was showing a darker side. My dad took me home, and we packed up our stuff and left the state. It wouldn't be the last time that happened either.

Realising Maiya has asked me a question, I apologise.

'That's okay. I'm going out with friends soon. You're welcome to come along. If you want to obviously?'

'Thanks, but I still have a tonne of paperwork to get to the office, and I haven't even looked around yet.' I also needed to look for a job, I think.

Maiya is looking at me like I had two heads.

'You do know what time it is?' She giggles and snorts. I shake my head, trying and failing to find my phone and check the time. 'It's half past nine. At night. Nothing will be open on campus except the club.' She giggle-snorts again.

'Shit, I slept the whole day?'

'Like I said, you were comatose. So, now you have nothing to do, you wanna come along?' Well, crap, I really didn't have anything better to do.

'I guess I could get ready real quick.' Maiya lets out an excited squeal, which to my ears sounds a lot like a dying rabbit. This is gonna take a lot of patience.

Turns out we have a neat little bathroom. I drag my ass in there and shower real quick, leaving my hair. I'm not a real girly-girl so never really pay attention to fashion or makeup, but seeing Maiya in her get up, I realise I really needed to step up my game. I look in the mirror at a bleary-eyed me. Long, wavy dark brown hair—not curly but not straight either and a huge pain in the ass to keep a handle on. I have equally dark brown eyes, full lips, and good cheekbones, or so I've been told.

'I don't know what to wear?' I confess. My closet is seriously lacking in the 'night out' section. I dress for comfort and obscurity on a day-to-day basis. I turn from the mirror to find her rifling through my luggage. Seriously?? I'm about to snap her head off. But instead, I step back and take a breath. After all, she is trying to be helpful. Even though having someone encroach on what's mine goes against all of my natural instincts.

'Wow, you have some nice stuff, Devon, but we *need* to go shopping if you wanna go out regularly.' She smiles in a way that makes me think she is full of shit. She hates my stuff and wants to shop for a whole new closet. I laugh at her inability to lie.

'Really? Hoodies and joggers don't do it for you?' I ask dripping sarcasm, making her giggle-snort again as she pulls out a pair of black skinny jeans.

'These, though, these will work!' she declares throwing them my way. Then she starts rifling through her closet and pulls out a fire-engine-red halter-neck top, which doesn't look to have any support for tits and clearly doesn't have enough material to hide a bra inside. The whole back is none existent.

After an awkward twenty minutes of Maiya introducing me to tit tape and helping me get the top to fit securely and fasten over my ample puppies she declares she will never wear that top again because I look way better in it than she ever did. I barely put on any makeup, just brush my hair through and scrape it back into a ponytail. I do however slap on some bright red lipstick to finish off. While I do that, Maiya also digs out a pair of killer heels for me that match. I am so lucky that we wear the same shoe size, otherwise, it would have been sneakers.

After some more preening and doubting myself, Maiya takes charge and tells me I look stunning. I actually feel great too. I soon master the art of walking in heels, and we are good to go. On the way, I discover that she is indeed of Danish heritage, which explains the stunning blonde hair and blue eyes, but she was born and bred here in England. She told me the name of the place, but I can't remember what it's called, just that a television programme was filmed there. It's the middle of nowhere, and they still have steam trains. Maiya asks me all sorts of personal information, but she seems happy with my short answers. She now knows I've travelled from Phoenix and I grew up with a single dad, and I'm eighteen. So is she, apparently. That made her do a little happy dance and squeal a real lot. But I can't help but like the girl. She has a constant smile.

Maiya introduces me to a group of friends she's met during something I had missed that day. It feels strange being out in a group, but they are all really nice and easy going. It doesn't stop my nerves, though. I'm panicking in case I say or do something stupid or inappropriate.

'Okay, let's get mortalled,' Maiya squeals and drags me along to the bar. I follow behind her. I feel uncomfortable and awkward. The music is so loud that my hearing is tampered, and the stench in here of booze mixed with body odour and perfume makes my stomach turn a little. Maiya must sense my unease because at the bar she lines up four shots—of what I'm uncertain—it's green with some brown liquid on the top.

'On three! One... two... three.' She downs one and slams the glass onto the bar before doing the same to the next. I'm behind by one, but I catch up quick, downing the disgusting shit just like she did.

'What the fuck was that?' I ask screwing my face up. I can hear the smile in her words when she answers,

'That was your first 'shit on the grass'!'

'Say what now?'

She cracks up laughing at the look on my face. And I'm not surprised. Who the hell orders anything called shit on the grass? Well, apparently Maiya does.

'It's their shot of the hour. They have all kinds of weird and wonderfully named shots. When it's the shot of the hour, it's only a pound a shot, so we need to get on it.'

I nod my approval—she doesn't need to know it's my first time drinking. We head back to the table after another round of shots. This time, I beat her, slamming my second glass down while she's only just picking up her second. Practice makes perfect and all that. We carry on like that, and I am totally tipsy when it's my turn to get the drinks in. I slide past Maiya's friend, Mike I think his name is, and push his hand off as he grabs at my ass. He's been flirting with me since we got here, throwing stupid lines out like, 'Was your dad a boxer because you're a knockout'. Lame. Totally not happening any time. Ever. But I smile and move away politely. My dad would be proud, must be the booze calming my usual temper.

## *Jared*

I stand to the side of the dance floor—Howard on my right, Brad my left—watching the females pumping and grinding, getting their groove on. Brad's head bobs to the baseline and Howard's foot taps along with it. They look relaxed, but I know damn well they know where all the threats are, all the exits and all the best strategies to protect me and their pack. I know that one wrong move and they'll have my back. I never had to worry about that.

Kristen was hanging around, annoying as always. I'm scanning the room for a willing woman to sink my dick into for the night, when I'm taken by a female scent floating through the air, filling my nose like a fucking assault, stopping me mid-thought. I shake my head trying to clear it, but fucking hell it's fine, and it's calling out to me like a fucking sirens call.

I'm scanning the space for its source but moving forward my buddy puts his hand out to stop me. My frustration flares. I need to find the source of that scent. It's consuming me already. I need to find that female. I move forward on impulse. Irritated at the hand still pushing against my chest, I glare into Howard's eyes, and he removes his hand. Good call. I make my way through the crowd, toward the scent driving me. I know there are eyes on my back, watching my every move, but I don't care. Bingo. I see her. She's fucking beautiful. Black jeans cover her long legs, a pert ass, and a red top that screams fuck me, which shows off a pair of amazing tits—like flesh coloured hills wrapped up like a motherfucking gift. I watch as she stands from her seat and glides toward the bar. I shake my head trying to shake the feeling that's come over me. My dick's throbbing to its own beat in my jeans as I watch her make her way through the crowd. I'm going to cut her off at the dance floor. And then... I don't fucking know what I'm going to do. I just need...

In a split second, she's on the floor, and some cock-sucking fucker has his paws all over her. I have to dial it back a notch before I kill the bastard. I wade through the crowd, clearing a path so I can get to her. Pulling her up, I shove the prick back down. He is fucking lucky. The pure need to hold her outweighs everything else.

# *Devon*

I'm drunk. Yep. As soon as I try and walk on these stupid heels, I almost face plant. *Come on Devon, one foot, now the other. That's it,—you've got this.* I push my way through the masses on the dance floor, trying and failing to get to the bar, past women dancing around their purses and men with arms like Stretch Armstrong, touching wherever they can reach. I'm groped and pinched and getting seriously pissed off. This is the problem with men, and why I have issues keeping my secret. A human woman would slap their hand away and be overpowered by them. Me, I could lay the asshole out cold with a good swing, and that there lies the problem. I'm curvy but slender, keeping myself in good shape, and I shouldn't be any match for a man bigger and broader than me. So I have to hold back. I growl low in frustration as I push a wandering hand from my tit. I'm having trouble enough walking straight without this idiot mauling me.

'Seriously?' I glare at the idiot who's still insistent on groping me—like I would find that sexy.

'Come on, gorguuusss, you know you want a bit of this.' He slurs and thrusts his hips while he grabs his cock. Uurgh. I roll my eyes, praying for patience as I shove him a little harder than I should. As the idiot goes down, he grabs for my wrist to keep himself upright, and the weight of him, along with my already drunk ass on stupidly high heels, takes me to ground with him. We fall in a heap, and I hit my head on the floor. But before my brain even registers the pain, I'm being hauled up by strong arms, and my nose is being assaulted with an amazing scent. A scent that sends heat pooling between my legs. My face is mashed up into his neck, and he is sooo divine. I could die happy right now. I hear him growl out something and it takes a minute to register. I step back in his arms, and I can only stare as I take in my saviour. Tall, dark hair and beautiful piercing green eyes—a five o clock shadow covering his jaw, and eyelashes any sane woman would pay a fortune for. I'm pulled into his side as his face morphs into anger, directed at the idiot still on the floor.

'No. Means. Fucking. NO. Dipshit,' he growls out through gritted teeth. His eyes, like saucers glaring at him. The idiot's mouth is flapping like a goldfish out of water, and his hands are outstretched trying to ward him off. I giggle. I can't help it.

'I didn't know she was taken, man. I'm sorry, I don't want any trouble.'

I would normally kick his ass and tell him he has no right even if I am single, but when I open my mouth to speak, dark and handsome's grip on my wrist tightens, and his eyes widen as he glares me into silence.

'Well, now you fucking know!' He prods the idiot in the ribs with his foot before he drags me off. Like he owns my ass. He stops his dragging and turns to face me. Something shifts in the air as I stare, incapable of anything else. His piercing green eyes stare back, as he looks through me like he sees my soul. The pull between us is intense. His face is impassive, but he exudes power. I can feel his will settling over me, like a hidden force. Even at my full height and on killer heels he still towers over me. His eyes are so intense as the muscle in his jaw twitches. It's impossible to take my eyes off him, but I refuse to be taken in. By sheer force of will my stubbornness takes over, and even if I want to kick my own ass for doing it, I pull away from his grip. He follows and as I get to the bar his arms encase me, pinning me to the wooden panels. My back to his front, I can still feel that energy thrumming between us. Can feel his hot breath on the back of my neck as he stoops to speak in my ear.

'Why'd you run?'

My breath hitches, as his voice flows over me like silk on my skin, making my body sizzle. Heat rushes to my vagina, and it turns into the Niagara Falls as my body betrays me.

My nose drinks in his arousing scent. He presses himself up against me, and I can feel the hard contours of his body, and the unmistakable hardness of his cock, which is currently nestled against my ass. It sends a shiver through my entire body, leaving goosebumps in its wake, and exciting me further.

'I know you're aroused; I can smell it.'

Jesus Christ, my body melts with pure heat. Any hotter and I will just be a gushing vagina on the floor. I need to get the hell away.

In a bid to get free, I press myself further into the bar, trying my best to escape his huge-ass cock. I don't want to speak because I can't form a sentence in my head, let alone formulate the actual words. Then he rolls his hips, pressing himself into me further, at the very moment the bartender asks for my order. On a squeak, I do my best to answer fluidly, and I order some test tube shots in various flavours, which are currently the shot of the hour. My mouth is suddenly as dry as toilet paper. I turn into him, my hands full, with the intention of walking away. His body language screams sex, and I want to scream 'Please fuck me,' right back, but I'll be damned if this arrogant bastard—no matter how he affects me or how hot he is—is getting any satisfaction from me. He bends his knees in order to draw my eyes to his. I hold my chin in the air and face him. *Can he tell I want to rip off all my clothes a lay myself out like a turkey on Thanksgiving?* I feel a tremble at my knees—he makes me want to submit. To lie on the ground and be taken. There is an air about him, and a power he yields over me. I need to snap the hell out of this and get a move on.

'Excuse me, please,' I mutter with a lot less vehemence than I intended. It is a pathetic effort, and I know it. His brows knit together in confusion. I try to move his arm with my elbow, but he's a solid wall of muscle, and I soon realise no one will move him unless he expressly wants it. I pull the stopper from a test tube with my teeth, and I drink it down, desperate for some courage, some will, to deny him. *God, I wanted to deny him, Right?*

'Come with me.'

It isn't a question. He takes the shots from one hand and replaces it with his, lacing our fingers. A feeling of electricity and warmth spreads from where we touch. With no choice but to follow, I go with him. Tugging at his hand, I try to get free as he draws me through the crowd, to the corner where Maiya is sitting with her friends. *What the hell?* He puts the shots on the table and gestures for me to do the same. I do. Maiya is looking at me expectantly from the far end of the table, but all I can do is gape. With no clue what is going on. None.

'She'll be fine. I'll get her home safely,' he tells her. I try to release his hand, but his grip just tightens until I think the circulation will be cut off if I don't stop struggling. So I give up, and he pulls me along behind him.

We leave the club and walk a short way. He doesn't speak to me at all. It's unnerving, but I also feel exhilarated. There's a need—a hunger that I've never experienced before. I want to be ravished right there, he affects me in such a way. *God damn it!* He may be sexy as hell, but there is no way I will be used like that. Never. Not ever— even if I want him. Really, really want him.

He stops suddenly and pulls me into the doorway of a closed building. With my back up against the wall, he releases my hand and places a bottle of water into it. *Where the hell did that come from?* 'Drink that.'

'No, I will not' I snap, clenching my hands into fists. I feel excited at denying his command. He throws his head back and laughs. It's such a sexy sound, and it sends waves of heat directly to my core. It's a deep baritone sound that comes right from his gut, and when he laughs his eyes light up, and I can see his perfectly chiselled face smiling in the light from a street lamp nearby. He uncaps the drink and sips a small amount before offering it to me again. This time, I take it and take a drink.

'Finish it. You're drunk. You need it.'

I glare at him and purse my lips. 'I am not drunk!'

'Yes you are. Now finish it, or you'll wake up with a shitty head tomorrow.'

'Sorry, dad.'

He laughs again. 'I'm sure as fuck your dad wouldn't have you pressed up against a wall ready to...' He stops and shakes his head. 'Who are you?' His voice is a tease to my ears, making me melt more with each word. But I am not giving in to him.

'Who the hell are *you* more like? And what's wrong with you? Ever heard of a chat up line? Or maybe asking a girl to dance?'

He looks at me as if I've slapped him. Which only spurs on my belligerent onslaught. 'I mean, who walks up to someone and is all...' I do my best impersonation of him, 'I can tell you're aroused I can smell it.'

'You are, and I can,' he says a little abashed. 'You wanna go back to dance?'

I snort back a laugh. Making him smile.

'I *need* to be inside of you.'

'Excuse me! Back the hell up.' I shove at his chest and am met with two solid pecks. A little growl escapes him. Under my touch, I feel the warmth of his skin and that electricity zinging through my veins. His scent emanates stronger with his arousal. He doesn't budge.

That fact that he's a werewolf was evident as soon as he got close to me in the club, but this is all new to me, and scary. I've only ever known my dad. I'd never mixed with any other wolves.

Before I can give it any more thought, his lips crash over mine, and I fall in.

# chapter TWO

## Jared

THE NEED TO FUCK HER is overwhelming. I lick at her lips, willing her to open for me—she does. My dick is solid as I fuck her mouth with my tongue—slipping in and out, her mouth moulding to mine. I swallow her moan as I slide my greedy hands around her waist and up her back, wanting to feel her—touch her everywhere. I hold the nape of her neck, tilting her head to exactly where I want it. Unable to resist, I glide my free hand to cup her ass and squeeze. Fuck me, what a sexy ass it is. The feel of her under my hands is incredible. I want to take her right here in the doorway. Lifting her into my arms, I deepen the kiss. Fuck, she tastes so good. The hint of apple and mint lingers on her tongue. Her scent is delicate and soft while screaming passion and heat. Her hands go to my hair, and she grips me, holding on, while the kiss deepens still, becoming almost aggressive. She likes it rough. Noted. I'm about ready to cream my pants when everything comes to a screeching halt because she bites my fucking lip. Hard. Not a sexy nip. No, a back the fuck off now, before I kick you in the balls, type bite. She draws blood, and then she shoves me away or at least she tries to. I drop her to her feet and back up a step, trying to rid my head of the horny haze I'm in.

'Back off,' she warns, panting. I hold my hands up in surrender and prop myself up against the wall to the side of her. Shit, moving away from her wasn't easy. I'm so fucking hard, and my body needs to do some catching up to my brain. My dick is eager and willing, but my brain screams *too fast, idiot.* I can't speak, so I just hold my hands up while I catch my breath. *Where the fuck did she come from? Why is she here? How is she here, and I didn't know?*

'I need to get back to my room, it's late.' She straightens herself out, and then she walks right past me. Fuck me and my impatience. Fuck. As gently as I can I take hold of her elbow, she stops but doesn't turn to face me. Shit, I *really* don't want her to go.

'I'll walk you back.' Was that even my voice? I sound like I've had a forty a day habit all my life. I can almost see the cogs turning as she thinks about it, and I'm half expecting her to refuse. She doesn't though. Thank fuck. Because she didn't have a choice. I was taking her, whether she liked it or not.

I walk her back to her room without any problems, following her earlier scent, which still lingers. I can't help but stare at her. I take in those big brown eyes, her full and now swollen lips as her tongue slips out unconsciously, and her hair as the breeze blows a stray strand into her face. I'm desperate to run it behind her ear, but I stop myself— instead, I rake my hand through my own hair, giving it a tug at the roots. *What the fuck has gotten into me. Where did she come from?* Coming at me like a fucking steam train, knocking the shit outta me. I never chase females or women for that matter. I've never needed to and wouldn't even if I did. They come to me, giving up what I need, and I never let them stick around afterwards either.

'Do you live on campus too?' she asks pulling me from my thoughts.

## *Devon*

I caught him staring at me as I asked, no hint on his face of the arrogant prick who'd picked me up at the club. His mask had fallen away. But no sooner had I noticed, the shutter came back down. That tenderness I thought I saw quickly disappeared.

'No, we live just outside of town.'

'We?' I suddenly feel insanely jealous. As if I have any right to be. He doesn't answer, and my mind is left reeling. *You've literally just met the guy. Jeez, get a grip.*

'What's your name?' he counters ignoring my question completely.

Pouting about the whole 'we' situation, I think about giving him a fake name.

'Devon,' I go with the truth. He offers me his hand.

'Jared.'

It suits him. It sounds masculine and powerful, both of which ooze from him like he wears them as cologne. He's commanding, and he makes me want to submit and obey. Both of which are crazy and never going to happen. We have a silent, almost uncomfortable, journey in the elevator, and then I'm digging my key out of my purse to unlock my door. I stumble, still inebriated. He takes my purse, hands me the key, and leans up against the wall, radiating sexiness, watching as I push the key into the lock. *Get your head straight, damn it.*

'Thanks,' I stutter out like an idiot. His brows rise in question. 'For bringing me back.'

'Anytime.'

I smile that awkward smile when you don't really know what else to say. My brain is drink-addled and firing off all sorts of scenarios in my head—like being taken up against this door or having his head between my legs while he eats out at Niagara Falls. Not at all helpful in the slightest because let's face it, I don't want to talk. I want him to fuck me right there in the hall.

'Bye, Jared,' I mutter, quickly pushing the door open and almost falling in. I brave looking back as I close it. I think he wants to say something and even wait for a beat of a second, but he turns away and leaves. 'Argh!' I stamp my foot in frustration. I need to get a vibrator for times like this.

Falling onto the bed, I stare at the ceiling—all of my energy sapped from that passionate mouth fucking he gave me. He made my body do and feel things I'd never experienced before. Now that he's gone, there is a throbbing ache left behind. My pulse is beating a staccato in my clit as if punishing me for walking away from him. I'm breathing deeply to calm myself, and hell if I can't still smell him— it's as if he never left, his scent lingering all over me. The need for him is still coursing through me, and it's left me feeling cold and lonely now he's gone. Annoyed at myself, I decide the best thing is a shower. I gather my things to take in, and I change into my robe. A rapping on the door makes me jump. I know who I'm going to find there. But I can't stop myself. I open the door.

He stands, filling the frame, his arms wide, and his hands gripping the frame at both sides. Jesus Christ, he is *HOT*. Our eyes meet and something passes between us, the electricity purring through the small space separating us. My nipples harden with every hitched breath. I want him—need him at that moment. I have no idea why my body reacts to him in the way it does, but the desire for him is almost painful. Fuck it. I'm past caring. The whys are irrelevant, what is important at this moment is me being under him. I need him. Now.

As if reading my mind, he growls, and comes at me, picking me up with his perfectly sculpted arms, his fingers splaying and cupping my ass. My legs instinctually wrap around his waist, and our mouths meet, crashing together like waves on a beach. He skilfully closes and locks the door without missing a beat. He has me on the bed, beneath him in a matter of seconds. His fingers tantalising as they move up and down the back of my thighs and then back to my ass. He sits back on his haunches, arousal written all over his face, and he pulls the belt on my robe like he's unwrapping a gift. It falls open, leaving nothing to the imagination. I lay bare in front of him. His eyes greedily take everything in. He takes my nipple between his finger and thumb and squeezes, making me whimper as he brings his mouth down on mine. He rains down kisses along my jaw, my throat, and along my collarbone, leaving a sensation of fire in their wake until he reaches the swollen peak and sucks my nipple into his mouth. *OH MY GOD.* He encases it with warmth as his tongue flicks, and his teeth graze it, tugging. A long moan slips from my lips, rivalling any porn star. He feels so good. Shamelessly I arch into him. I can feel the hardness of his cock, and I want it. I need him inside me. He expertly takes the other nipple in his mouth, leaving no part untouched. His arms wrap around me so I am pressed into his hard body. My brain seems to be shorting, all the sensations I'm feeling, overloading it. Abruptly I am left feeling cold and wanting. Again. He stands, covering me before adjusting himself in his jeans. I realise through my sex-addled haze that Maiya is in the hall, rummaging through her bag. Embarrassed, I tie the belt of my robe tight, shaking my head in an attempt to clear the fog. *What was I thinking?* I don't know where to look when Maiya finally gets the door open. Jared's eyes never leave mine, even as Maiya moves around him, I can feel them boring a hole into me, as I avoid his gaze.

'I'm sorry if I disturbed you guys,' Maiya slurs. Jeez, how much can a girl drink in a couple of hours? The stench of alcohol is overpowering.

'Jared was just leaving,' I tell her, feeling my cheeks burning hotter and hotter. Any minute now I'm going to burst into flames. Maiya lies on her bed fully clothed and passes out in seconds. Jared turns his head momentarily in her direction before his eyes are back on me. Through heavily lidded eyes he watches as I stand from the bed and try to step around him to open the door, but he pulls me into his embrace, and I melt into him once again. His lips slide over mine, and he opens the door without breaking the kiss and pulls me into the hall, tugging on the belt of my gown. He pushes me up against the wall, his body hard against mine, pressing in all the right areas. My head is a mess. I ache for him. For more. I have never wanted something so much in my life, and at that moment I am willing to give him everything right there in the hall. I'm dry humping him like a dog. Trying to get the pressure from his cock against my clit. We're interrupted again by a group of Chinese students. He steps away from me, breaking the kiss and I can see the torment on his face just as I feel my own. Leaning up against the opposite wall he scrubs at his face with his hands. Hands that had made me feel so much sensation only minutes ago. He runs one through his hair, keeping his eyes everywhere but on me, as if looking at me is painful. Then he leaves. Just leaves. Walking down the fucking hall leaving me aroused and embarrassed. Shit. I don't move for ages, worried I might disintegrate into a pile of ash from the fire raging through my vagina. What the hell just happened? *What the hell was I thinking?* My first night here and already I've made a complete ass of myself. *Fucking A. Devon. Fucking A.*

I slip back into my room unheard and gather my abandoned toiletries which are still on the floor, I spend the rest of my waking hours trying to get rid of his scent before I fall back into bed unbelievably still tired. Ignoring Maiya's ridiculous snoring, I sleep. And dream of Jared.

# *Jared*

Leaving Devon's building, I find Howard waiting in the car park under a street lamp, his arms folded across his chest. Disapproval all over his face. I grin, shaking my head. The idiot has probably been standing there the whole time.

'You look like you've just chewed a fucking wasp,' I tease him. Howard doesn't answer. He doesn't need too. I know what's on his mind. He never changes.

I feel torn. On one hand, I feel like a total fucking sleaze for leaving the way I did. But on the other, damn, I feel fucking elated. I can't stop the smile creeping back onto my face despite the massive case of blue balls I'm leaving with. Just the thought of her makes me hard again.

'What the fuck was that?' he asks me. I don't know what his problem is—he never cares where I stick my dick normally. Why start now?

'The fuck you talking about?' I stop walking and wait for his answer.

'What about Kristen?'

'Don't give a fuck about fuckin', Kristen,' I answer like a petulant kid.

'You can't just ignore this.'

'Who said I am? You don't normally give a fuck when I bang other chicks.'

Howard shakes his head, twisting his lips up in annoyance and rolls his eyes.

'I *saw* her—saw how *you looked* at her. I've never seen you pursue a female, *ever*. Chances are, Jared, you're not gonna go through with it with her on the scene.'

'What are you talking about?' I ask the question, but I know. Know exactly what he's talking about. I want her, like, fuck I don't even know. I just know I need to be inside her. Badly.

Being the alpha's son sucks donkey balls. Big time. But I know I have to step up. 'It won't change things,' I promise. I'm trying to reassure myself as much as Howard. I'd never felt like I did with Devon, with any other female. It was like her scent called out to me, to my very soul.

My blood boils at even the thought of any other male touching her. I crank my jaw shut and grind my teeth together. Trying like fuck to get that image scrubbed from my brain. Nah, I was going to be the only male from now on. I had to be. Couldn't have it any other way.

I didn't sleep, couldn't. All my thoughts were back in that dorm room with Devon. What would I have done if we hadn't been disturbed? Was I seriously asking myself that? I knew damn well what I would have done, and it's just as well I didn't. I did a lot of thinking, toing and froing between what I had to do and what I wanted to do. Howard's words echoing around in my head. I am going to be the alpha soon, and what kind of example am I setting if I can't follow orders? The pack has to come first, even over my own feelings. But would it hurt to see Devon again? Maybe I just needed to get her out of my system? Then I'd be able to think straight. After all, I hadn't officially made any commitments yet.

By the time the sun comes up, and after barely any sleep I have decided that I have to stay away from her. I'm certain I can't fuck her and not go back for more. So I'm staying the fuck away. How I'm going to do that, I'm not sure, but I have to try.

The next few days pass so fucking slowly. I don't leave the house. Can't. Because if I do the temptation will be too much. I know I will find myself back at her door. I still have a fucking hard on at the mere thought of her. The little noises she made, her hands on my body, her tits—fucking perfect little mounds with dark nipples hard for me. Fuck, I need relief. Stroking one out on my bed like a pervert at the images ingrained in my brain. Fuck me. This is what I've resorted to. But I can't even think about putting my dick anywhere near a pussy that isn't Devon's. And that makes me fucking mad.

## *Devon*

Maiya decides it's time for me to get out. Her patience has worn thin. I've locked myself up in my room from sheer embarrassment for the last couple of days. Maiya, bless her heart, has been keeping me well stocked with food and drinks. Today she's having none of it and has dragged my ass out, deciding we needed breakfast, I wanted a healthy breakfast, but after being out the night before, Maiya was craving what she called 'greasy café food.' I can tell where the name came from as soon as it was put on the table. It consists of a huge plate full of eggs, bacon, sausages, baked beans, and tomatoes with fried bread and an excess of grease. I order a bagel—I just didn't have my usual appetite—and even that feels hard to swallow. My head is elsewhere, the feelings I have for Jared are so confusing, and I just can't shake them. Why has he affected me in such a big way? I'm dreaming about him when I sleep and fantasising about him when I'm awake. Gah, it has to stop. It is getting me nowhere, and on top of that I needed to change and go for a run, it isn't healthy for a werewolf to be cooped up inside.

I make the decision after forcing my bagel down, that when I leave the café, I won't think about him anymore. At least for the rest of the day. Yeah, that doesn't work, it lasts about five minutes. Everywhere I go, I can smell him. So I keep looking for him, hoping to find him around every corner. *Jesus Christ!* Maiya turns to look at me abruptly.

'What? What's up?' she probes. Frowning, I shake my head in question.

'Nothing, why?'

'Well, usually when someone yells, "Jesus Christ," something's up? Yah know, it's like a big hint?' *Oh shit.*

'Sorry, I was thinking out loud, I didn't realise!' Maiya's eyes widen and her chin juts out and a look on her face that says, 'yes and?'

'It's nothing. I can't even remember now.' Her eyes roll at my vague answer.

The rest of the day passes quickly. Maiya drags me around all of the student crap going on for orientation week, and time passes relatively fast. I feel lucky to have met Maiya. She's been so good to me despite my bitchy mood the last few days. If I were her, I'd have stopped talking to my miserable ass already. Checking my phone, I realise I've missed a call from my dad. I listen to the voicemail.

'Hi, it's only me—Dad. Just checking in, I hope you aren't too jetlagged. Call me.'

I text a quick reply. Sorry didn't hear the phone. V busy here. Lots of ppl. Lots to see. Classes start in two weeks. Caught up on sleep. ☺ Don't worry will call you tmw. Love you <3

Maiya is going to hit the club again tonight. I'm invited, but honestly, I don't feel like it.

'You look like you *need* a drink and a dance, are you sure you don't want to come?'

I consider it for a second, but I stick with my original plan.

'Nah I'm just gonna curl up in my pj's and watch crap TV on my laptop.'

Maiya pouts and blows me a kiss.

'Your loss. There is so much hotness to choose from out there—you shouldn't brood over one guy. You should just go and find yourself another one.' She shimmies her ass out of the door, making me laugh, and then pops her head back into view. 'If you change your mind, you know where to find me!' I shoo her away and download the first season of friends.

# chapter THREE

## Jared

I'M GETTING FUCKING CABIN FEVER. Howard and Brad have paced the floor outside my room the last few nights, and they're driving me fucking crazy. I've had enough. I swing the door open so hard it goes through the stopper and hits the wall with a bang. I don't give a shit.

'Just fucking go out, will you? You're doing my head in. I'm not going anywhere, so you can quit with the fucking pacing.' I have no idea what either of them says in response, and I don't care, I just want them gone. Eventually, I win out, and they fuck off to meet up with the rest of the group at the club. And I finally have a clear space to think in.

My decision to stay away from Devon just isn't gonna fly. I'm restless, angry, and everything fucking irritates me. I'm permanently ready for a fight. It's no good. I have to see if getting her out of my system will work. Maybe that's all I need to do. Then I can go back to life as normal.

Decision made. I take my motorbike and intend to be back before the others even get home. I park up and ride the lift to her floor. I stand for a minute outside of her door. What if she has a boyfriend? Fuck me; I can't handle that shit.

I know she's home. Her scent is strong, sending all the blood in my body straight to my dick. Jesus, I want to break the fucking door down. My head is seriously messed up. I know this cannot be a one-time deal and I haven't even gotten inside her yet. I need to get the fuck out of dodge. I turn away and walk back toward the lift. Fuck me.

## *Devon*

Jared's all too familiar scent wafts into my room, and I know he's in the hall. I can't help but get excited. My heart rate goes through the roof, and I feel hot and bothered. I stand with my ear against the door and wait impatiently for him to knock. Then his familiar rap on the door sounds. EEEEP. I almost squeal, then realising I'd not re-applied any makeup or done anything with my hair after my shower, I panic. I must look like a hot mess. Shit shit shit. I scrape my hair into a loose band and wrap it up into a messy bun. I have no time for anything else. The fact that I'm in flannel pj's with penguins on, and a fluffy robe and slippers, is tough. At least I've actually showered today.

I open the door so it's only just ajar, enough so I can see him. He can only see my face and a smidge of the fluffy gown, which he'd become accustomed to the last time he'd been here. He looks all sex-god-like, just like he had the last time I saw him. His emerald green eyes are almost glowing in the dim lights of the hall. He's looking at me through lidded eyes—his head bowed and those long luscious lashes framing the green. Every part of my body heeds to him. Only my mind is being a stubborn ass, determined not to get into it with him again. Ever. But here he stands, in blue denim jeans and a white t-shirt that hugs his muscular body in *all* the right places. That already familiar feeling of the air becoming charged between us is strong.

'I shouldn't be here.'

He almost sounds like he's in pain. It wasn't exactly what I was expecting, but, okay.

'So why did you come?' I ask through the small crack in the door. He scrubs his face, clearly uncomfortable.

'Are you, do you have—Fuck.' He scrubs at his face again. 'Are you fucking anybody?' he growls it out like he's angry. *Really?? That's what he asks?* I'm stunned to silence. Shaking my head because I don't trust my mouth, I shut the door. I stand there with my back against the door, dumbfounded at his nerve. The door opens, propelling me forward. I turn on him.

'Hey!' I yell, but he keeps coming. 'Get out, Jared.' The arrogant asshole is back. How dare he? He walks me backwards until I have nowhere else to go.

'Just answer the fucking question.'

'No.'

'No, you aren't or no you won't answer the question?' He's visibly shaking.

'Just get out.' I try to shove him back toward the door, but he doesn't budge an inch. I scream in frustration and hit out at his chest. I'm used to being in control of my body and my mind, but around him? I just am not. No, I wasn't fucking anybody. But I didn't have to tell him that. I'm so angry. Angry with him for being here and having the gall to ask me that, and angry with myself because even as he stands there in all his arrogance, I want him in every way possible. I am so fucking aroused. And it's obvious that he is too. Fuck. I need this over and quickly before I offer myself up on a plate.

He grabs my wrists, halting my half-assed attempts at making him leave. My breath hitches at his skin on mine. His eyes are lidded, and his pupils dilated. My attack is forgotten—my breathing quickens. I stare into those green eyes and time seems to stand still. He pulls me into him—our bodies touching in every place possible. His hand slides around to the small of my back, and he crushes me against him. His head bows as he leans in. I think he's going to kiss me, but instead, he just lingers there, giving me the option. Take it or leave it? Like an idiot, I jump in. And god it feels so fucking good. He kisses me with such aggression like he can't get enough. I'm tearing at his clothes, desperate for more skin—our tongues sliding in and around like a choreographed dance. Human guys have never had this effect on me. Was it a wolf thing? Or was it just him? Would I want to jump the bones of every werewolf I came across? I doubted that. But at that moment all I wanted to do was get beneath him. The door was locked, my gown untied, and I was on the bed in seconds. Just like last time. He must have had lots of practice. That unwelcome thought invades my mind. I don't want to think. I don't want to do anything other than surrender to the feeling and emotions I'm experiencing being with him. His hands are under my pj's, exploring. But I want him naked too. I tug at the hem of his t-shirt, and he lifts his arms so I can take it up over his head. He is gorgeous. I stop and stare for a second. His body is perfect. He doesn't give me long to take in the view before he's on me, taking my mouth and fucking it violently with his tongue. He tastes divine. He starts fumbling with the buttons on my pj's, but they're too delicate for his big hands. I push them away and begin unbuttoning them, but he's impatient, and yanks the two halves open. My buttons pop off and land all over the floor. A growl rumbles up his throat as he latches onto my nipple with his mouth. My hands go to his hair, fisting handfuls, holding his head to my body as he expertly sucks and nibbles at me. OH.MY.GOD.

'I need to know,' he mumbles against my breast. Oh, for fuck's sake.

'No one,' I clarify, my voice breathy and barely audible. He rears up above me. Then comes down hard, taking my mouth with his. I can barely catch my breath, but then he stops. No. No. Not again! Looking up at him, I can see he wants to say something, but he's unsure of what to say or maybe how to say it. 'Just spit it out already?' I'm flustered and eager to finish what we've started. I don't want to wait a second longer.

'Are you a virgin?' he blurts. Oh my God! I laugh hysterically and shake my head. I see a spark of disappointment cross his face, and I'm eager to remedy that.

'I've never been with a wolf,' I confirm. I'm not sure if that helps or not, but he is greedily kissing my mouth while I fumble with the buttons on his jeans. I don't get very far because he grabs my hands and pins them above my head. I panic a little at being restrained, but when his mouth finds my hard and sensitised nipple again, that fear subsides. He uses his tongue expertly. Tracing the contours of my body, and then licking at my navel, which sends shockwaves straight to my clit. With one hand holding my wrists, he kneels and pulls my pyjama bottoms down, while I lift my ass to make it easier for him. Leaving me in only my panties, he groans and then his mouth meets my core through the already wet material. The heat from his mouth spreads over me. I want to touch him, press him closer. I buck a little, trying in vain to get what I need. He stops and looks up at me,

'Keep your hands there,' he orders. 'And spread your legs wide for me.'

I do as he asks. He rips my lace panties down the middle with little effort at all. Leaving me with two pieces of useless material clinging to each thigh. Then his mouth is at my core again, this time with no barrier. I'm mewling. It feels so good. The heat from his breath coupled with the hot sensation of his tongue makes me almost come for him right there. His thumb goes straight to my clit. He rubs and flicks until I'm a writhing hot mess beneath him. I grip the pillow so hard, I tear it. I climax on a moan, but he pushes me further until I can't take anymore.

'You get what you need, baby?' I can hear the smile in his voice—he's pleased with himself. 'Tell me what you want?' he asks huskily with need.

'Please… I want more.' I feel the nub of him pressing against me. He feels burning hot against my sensitive lips. He's taken me to a high already. One I never thought I was going to come down from. But this? I need to feel him inside of me, all of him. Arching my back, I try to push him in. He chuckles.

'You want my dick inside you, baby?' I can tell by his knowing voice, that he's fucking teasing me. He knows he has me at his mercy. Well, I can remedy that. Releasing the pillow, I grab his cock in my hand and angle him to my opening and push myself over him. He allows me that bit of control. His eyes close as I encase his cock with my heat. Taking in only an inch of him at a time, I'm stretched and tight but oh so wet and ready for him. He groans as I tease him, working him in, deeper and deeper, a little at a time. Slowly, until I have as much as I can take at this angle. 'You're so tight, fuuuck,' he groans out. I begin working my hips, but the angle is awkward. He spreads his hands over my hips and lifts me until I straddle him. He connects us again, and as I move, he works with my rhythm until I feel him swell inside me, getting impossibly bigger. I'm teetering on the edge, so close. 'Come for me,' he growls as his thumb connects with my throbbing clit and that's all I need to take me over again. He explodes inside of me. His cock kicking out his orgasm, as I milk him for every last drop. His teeth grind together, and his eyes close tight as he thrusts out his orgasm. It is the most intense sex I've ever had. I flop over his chest—both of us sweating from the vigorous workout. We stay there, connected for a while before I have to dash off and clean up in the bathroom.

I sleep so well. And waking to the sight of Jared's bare chest was fan-fuckin-tastic. The covers are caught frustratingly at his waist, his hand slowly but rhythmically stroking my arm. I don't want to look up—don't want to ruin the moment, but he senses the change in me.

'Morning,' he says in that gorgeous gravelly voice that makes me want to fuck him all over again. Stretching myself out I push my feet out to push the covers down ever so slightly, revealing that special v at his hips. My mouth waters at the memory of what we'd done several times. Then the realisation hits me. I have a roommate. SHIT BALLS.

I leap up and check her bed. It's empty. Had she come back? Had she been embarrassed and left? Oh god, what an idiot.

'Your roomie never came home if that's what you're worried about?'

*Oh, thank God.* I nod, running my hands through my hair, which is cascading over my shoulders now. At some point, throughout our hot-as-hell sessions, I'd lost the bun. Feeling a little self-conscious after leaping up, naked, I collect the robe from the floor and slip it on.

'You know that looks better on the floor right?' I laugh at his cheesy line. Which makes him smile too. His smile is genuine, and it lights up his eyes. He looks relaxed and content. But I'm not sure what to do with myself. I've never spent the night with anyone before, always leaving after my needs were fulfilled. What does he want from this? Was I just a fuck? Noticing the shreds left of my panties, I flush red and bend to collect them. He chuckles, and I feel his arms come around my waist, my back to his front, his fingers expertly loosening the belt. His hands come up to the sides of my throat, and then he grips the gown at my shoulders, allowing it to slip off and hit the floor. He pushes my hair to one side and over one shoulder while his mouth, tender and warm, sweeps across my other shoulder, and up, caressing my throat. His tongue flicks out and spreads heat throughout my body, igniting every nerve ending. He moves across my jaw deliciously. One hand at my waist, the other across my navel with splayed fingers. I want him again. God, I need him again. But I know what it's leading to, and I have to save myself the heartache when this is all over. It needs to stop. But his naked body pressed up against my back is delicious, and the feel of his hard cock pressing up tight against my ass. God help me, I have to stop this.

'Jared.'

'Hmmm?'

I turn to look at him, his hands resting perfectly on my hips. I rush my words out. 'I know this was a one-night thing, and I feel a little embarrassed. I've never actually spent the night with anyone. I don't know what's normal in this situation.'

He steps back from me, a look of confusion clear on his face. 'Is that what this was for you?' He gestures between us, his cock bobbing from its weight at his navel.

'Well, I guess. I just assumed that's what it was for you.'

'You assumed?' He's scowling at me, and I can see his shutters coming back down, the arrogant Jared is back.

'Yeah.'

He steps further away. 'That's exactly what it fuckin' was.' He's grabbing his clothes from the floor aggressively and jerkily putting everything on.

'Jared, I didn't—' He puts his hand up to stop me, and I'm so unsure of myself at that moment that I put the robe back on, and as he's putting his boots on, I slip into the bathroom to avoid any more awkwardness. Coward.

'Thanks for the fuck,' he yells through the door. I squeeze my eyes closed against the unexpected pain his words cause.

## *Jared*

I can't get out of there quick enough and stepping out of the lift I walk straight into Howard. I don't have time for a lecture and the look on his face tells me that's all he is good for. He walks up with a deathly glare that would make any other wolf quake in his boots, zeroed in on me.

'Fuck you, Howard.' I stalk past him and into the car park. I throw my leg over the Harley, stuff my head into the helmet, and kick her off. In my peripheral vision, I see Howard jump into his truck, in pursuit. Fuck you. Instead of going home I pull into a Weatherspoon's pub. It's only early in the day but fuck it, I need a drink, and they serve it all day. I stalk to the bar and order a double JD straight up. I knock it back and order another. Howard strolls in like he's the dog's bollocks.

'You drink that, and you won't be riding home.' God, why doesn't he just shut the fuck up? Everyone knows that I can knock back ten and not stay wasted, my body burns the shit up like water. I feel the effects only temporarily. Only if I drink fast enough will I get to that place I crave, and I'd still be sober within an hour to ride my bike home. I ignore him and knock it back. Gesture for a refill. Get another. Drink it. And gesture again.

'That will be five, dipshit. I guess you're walking home.' I scowl at my buddy but don't speak. I hate him right then—hate every fucker. They can all go and fuck themselves. I down my fifth double, and glare at him again. *Come on. Make me stop.* Slamming the glass on the bar, I gesture again and get another refill. For a minute I think Howard is going to try and tell the barmaid no. But he just smiles at me instead. It sets my teeth on edge. It is a cocky holier-than-thou smile that tells every fucker he thinks he is better than them. Well, fuck you. One after another the JD goes down. Burning a white-hot heat all the way down to my stomach. If I think it will make me feel better, I'm a bigger dick than I thought because all it does is send me into a fit of self-pity. That drunken haze I'd craved so badly hits me hard. But my mind keeps going back to how she'd felt. How good it felt to be inside her. How I want, more than anything, to be there again. And then her words hit me like a fucking freight train. *I know this was* just *a one-night thing.* What an idiot. The self-pity turns to anger, then rage. I stumble off the stool as I try and fail to launch the glass at the wall. Instead, it falls at my feet with a dull thud as the heavy bottomed glass hit wood. I kick it and miss. Howard pays my tab and follows my lead out of the door. I stalk over to my bike, stuff the helmet on, and fumble for the keys in my pocket. As I pull them out, Howard's hand whips up and snags them.

'I'm not even arguing, Jared. Get in the truck.'

'Give me my fuckin keys.' I go to grab them from Howard's hand. And miss.

'No, get in the truck. Brad can come for your bike.' I sway, and Howard goes out of focus. I blink, trying like hell to right my vision. Can't. Shit.

'Fine, but this little ditty,' I gesture between us, 'Isn't fucking over.' Who the fuck did he think he was ordering me around like he was the alpha? Who the fuck do any of them think they are, following me around and telling me what I can and can't do? Fuck him, and fuck my dad. Fuck Kristen, and fuck *her.* Especially her, and her one-night fucking *thing.*

I kick the door to the kitchen open and throw my helmet to the floor, storming through the room, ignoring the silence that meets me and the stares as I tear through, slamming the inner door, and stamping on every step like it was my enemy's head. When I finally get to my room, I slam that door too and throw myself on the bed. Sleep takes me, and I welcome it.

## *Devon*

Jared's lingering scent is all over my bed, and it fills the room. I groan, throwing myself onto the bed and screaming into my pillow.

This had not been the plan. Dad had said because of our secrets that I couldn't maintain a relationship with a human guy. Yet, I also can't have a relationship with anyone like me because we hadn't mixed with any. So I had fulfilled my needs and bolted every time, not caring how they felt afterwards. It had made me resent my dad at the time. And now I've finally met someone like me, someone who makes me feel things I've never felt before, and I've messed it up. I just didn't know what the hell to do with him. One minute he wanted me, and the next he was thanking me for the fuck. If I thought about it, deep down I'd hoped like hell that it would happen again. That it was the start of something great, but I had to open my mouth and mess it up. I was scared of being hurt I guess. But after the way it had ended, I knew it wouldn't be happening again.

The way he worked my body, though. The way he'd made me feel... he definitely knew how to please a woman. The thought of him pleasing other women in the same way he'd touched me, turned my stomach. *No, no, stop!* The mere thought of it mortified me, causing my stomach to roll. I rushed for the wastebasket, losing the contents of my stomach.

# chapter FOUR

## Devon

IT HAS BEEN FOUR DAYS, and there is no sign of Jared, but lots of Ben and Jerry's ice cream and bad TV in my pj's. Maiya wakes me up, and glares at me with her hand on her hip, tapping her foot. I cover my head with the comforter hoping she will go away.

'Get the hell up. We're going shopping.'

It takes me a while, but her constant whining and nagging at me wins out. So, in the end, I decide what the hell. I take my credit card and decide that some retail therapy is just what I need. We go to a mall, not that far away. I buy some gorgeous new lingerie, some new outfits, and shoes for nights out, which after shopping today I intend to have plenty of. We have lunch out at an all-you-can-eat Chinese, and then we have our nails and eyebrows done at a beauty parlour. If Jared isn't interested, I sure as hell will show him what he is missing.

That night, I hit the club again. I wear a black fitted skirt which finishes tastefully just above the knee, and a low cut V-neck cream silk top, which plunges down through my cleavage. Only a small gold chain is holding it together across my boobs. Maiya introducing me to the miracle that is tit tape has opened up a whole new range of wardrobe options for me.

After a few drinks, my confidence begins building. Making my way to the bar I'm cut off and pulled onto the dance floor by a guy I'd been chatting to earlier. He is grinding himself against my ass as Pink blares out about her wandering fingers. With a drink-fuelled confidence, I move up tighter against him, grinding my ass against his bulging crotch as he holds my hips, giving myself over to the music completely. As the music changes, I make to leave the dance floor, but he grabs my arm,

'Where are you going? We're just starting to have a good time.'

I smile and gesture to the bar. 'Ahh come on, darling, don't leave me hanging.'

He is half cut already and stumbling a little. I make to move again. 'I won't be long,' I lie with no intention of returning to him. He eventually lets me go reluctantly and tries to follow me. But I weave in and out of dancing bodies and lose him. At the bar, I order a long island ice tea and wait while the guy makes the cocktail. I sense Jared before I see him—that familiar scent, the air pulsing, and the feeling that only he gives me. Turning, I find him standing to my side, scowling. He has one foot and his elbows pressed up against the bar with his back to it, he leans down to speak into my ear.

'Did you have fun?' He nods toward the dance floor. The arrogant façade is back and oozing from him. Prick. At that, a blonde to his other side turns from the bar, handing him a drink with a killer smile, her legs almost to her armpits and heels to match. Striking would be an understatement, and she makes it quite clear that she is familiar with him. Her hand is sliding up his inner thigh while he stares right at me. Waiting, wanting a response. I want to take that perfectly manicured little hand of hers and break it. I want to pull her perfect blonde hair from her head. I visualise doing just that, and I feel sick. Glaring at him, I've clearly given him the reaction he'd wanted. Not sticking around for my drink, I make to leave, only to be stopped again by the idiot from the dance floor. He steps into my space as I cut through the dancers. My temper is running thin, and I need to get away. Now.

'Move,' I growl out through clenched teeth.

'Ah come on, darlin', don't be a cock tease.' I grab him by the scruff of his shirt, my patience at an all-time low.

'FUCK OFF! NOW!'

Surprised at my strength, he stumbles back as I shove him, and he falls on his ass. I don't go back to the table where Maiya and her group are. Instead, I walk out through a side exit and lean up against the wall to calm down, counting to ten and taking in some deep breaths only to get a nose full of Jared's scent mingled with another wolf's. Great.

I see them before they saw me, but I know he knows that I'm there. He's standing, looking up the alley toward where I'm standing in the shadows, his arms crossed, and his friend is approaching me at Jared's request. His nostrils flare as he comes to stand in front of me, and his face turns up in disgust.

'Shit, Jared, you fuckin' marked her!'

'Watch your fuckin' mouth,' Jared roars at him. The guy flinches, and grabs me by the wrist, trying to drag me back toward the door they've come through. But I wasn't going. Digging my heels in, I refuse. Turning, he twists my arm up my back and begins frog-marching me up the alley. *Oh hell no!* I throw my knee forward and up, gaining momentum, and I kick back and catch his knee hard. He stumbles, taking me to the ground with him. I didn't understand what the hell is happening, but I wasn't being taken anywhere. He falls hard, me on top of him and he twists, unintentionally pushing my face into the dirt as he scrambles up, pulling me up with him,

'Quit fighting, he just wants to talk to you,' he growls into my ear. I grab for his short hair, his eyes going wide as I yank on it.

'Fuck you.' I swing with my free hand and punch him. He stumbles back holding his jaw and taking the opportunity, I run. Straight into Jared. He picks me up, sweeping my legs from under me, while I push at his face with my hands. 'Put me down,' I snarl. His answering chuckle only makes me angrier.

'Don't fight, I'm not gonna hurt you, I wanna talk to you, that's all.'

'Fuck you, put me down NOW.' He can't defend his face because of how he's holding me, so I take full advantage of that. Clawing at him and grabbing at his face, he grunts as I connect a punch but it was half-assed at best, and he barely responds to it at all. He walks around some corners, and I find myself in another doorway. Again, hemmed in by him. He lets my legs slide down his body to the ground. I'm scared but at the same time, excited by him. My body immediately betrays me, my brain screams to get away, yet my body melts at his nearness. His face is bleeding from my attack, but the look on his face is both pained and affectionate.

'I'm sorry,' he mumbles. 'For all of this. I never meant to piss you off, and he shouldn't have put his fuckin' hands on you either.' His hands come up to my cheeks, wiping away the tears I hadn't realised had spilt over, with his thumbs. All I could think about was the blonde touching him.

'Who was the blonde?' I blurt out. Of all the things to ask in this situation, my jealousy wins out. He doesn't answer, and I watch as he swallows, unsure of how to answer. A look flickers across his face. He's about to lie. I don't want to hear it. 'Why are we here, Jared? What do you want from me?'

Our eyes meet, and I freeze in place.

'Do you feel it? When we're close?' So he feels it too? I can't deny it. I know exactly what he's talking about. My body wants him, *needs* him in a way I can't explain. The air is palpable between us. Like we're connected in some way. I can feel his presence even before my senses kick in. And he can obviously feel it too. 'I know you do,' he says. His hands travel down my arms until he holds my hands in his. 'I shouldn't be here. I shouldn't be with you, but—'

'Is she your girlfriend?'

'No.' he bites the word out as if he's angry I asked.

'Then why, Jared, help me understand? Why shouldn't you be here?'

'She's not my girlfriend, alright? And I don't know what the fuck is going on. I can't stop thinking about you. When I sleep, I dream about you, and when you're near me...' he shakes his head, his hands leaving mine to pull at his hair. 'You're driving me in-fuckin-sane.'

Well, I wasn't expecting that.

## *Jared*

I've put it all out there. I want her so fucking bad it hurt.

'Me too,' she says.

I exhale in relief. I dip my head to hers and kiss her, and the world falls away. I hold her to me, her soft to my hard. I can feel her taut nipples against my chest. She gives herself over to me as she responds to my kiss, letting my tongue slide in, against hers. But then I feel a shift in her, and she pulls back. Her eyes are full of heat, but there is something else. Shit. I need to apologise for leaving the way I did.

'I was mad.' I can't find the right words. 'Fuck, not mad, hurt. I was hurt when you said it was just a one-night stand.'

She looks stunned. 'I was embarrassed, Jared. I thought that's all it was for you!'

Her body language—arms folded across her chest, foot tapping—clear signals that she's pissed.

'That night.' I rub at my face. 'I've never felt like that before.' I hope, and silently fucking pray she feels the same way. Because this is way out of my fucking comfort zone.

'Who is the blonde?' she demands. Fuck me, I'm laying it all out, and she's only interested in the one fucking thing I do not want to discuss. I blow out a frustrated breath,

'It's complicated.' What the hell else am I supposed to tell her? The truth? How can I? She ponders on my answer for a second. I can see the indecision flash in her eyes. Then she decides it isn't good enough.

'Be honest with me?' She pleads. *Just say it, just fucking tell her.* I just don't know how to start. What to say. It's complicated just about covers it, what else can I say? I shrug my shoulders, like the prick I am. Total fucking dick move. I know it, but what else can I do?

'Okay, fine.' She pushes passed me. I don't try to stop her. But I follow her at a safe distance, just so I know she's safe. When I see her light turn on, I watch as she closes her curtains. I slip into the shadows so she won't notice me. Brad turns up then. I catch his scent on the wind before he sneaks up.

'What's going on, my man?' Howard had clearly had enough for the night and sent Brad instead. I don't answer—just start walking back to the club. 'Whoa, quiet down there, Mr fuckin' Chatty pants.' Ever the comedian, I have to smile. Brad keeps my pace and socks me in the arm. 'You gonna talk or do I get to beat it outta you?'

Shaking my head, I throw my hands up in the air. 'I don't fucking know, Brad, I'm going out of my goddamn mind.' Brad stops and puts his hands in his pockets,

'I don't know what to say, t'yah man. Maybe just speak to your dad?' He shrugs his shoulders, knowing damn well that's a lost cause,

'He won't fucking listen, why the fuck I ever gave in and agreed is beyond me. I don't know what I was fuckin' thinking.'

'Jared, you've always put the pack before yourself, maybe you need to think about yourself for a change?'

My head whips up at that. Could I actually do that? It was just bad luck that my father was the alpha and I was the alpha heir. Sometimes, I love being a leader. It's in my blood, and it comes naturally, but now, I feel suffocated, closed in like an animal in a cage. I need some time alone, a break, to give my head some space.

'You're right. Listen, buddy, I need some time to think. I'm gonna disappear for a couple of days, give my head some space.' Brad starts to backpedal then, stuttering and starting to protest.

'I didn't mean you should fuck off somewhere. I meant like choose who you want. You can't just disappear? He'll go apeshit.'

I know what my father will do, but I need this if I'm going to commit the rest of my life to a female I barely tolerate, let alone like. I need a clear head to rationalise why that's a good idea. I need time to decide if I can put myself through that for the good of the pack.

Because right now, my head and my heart are on the same page, and that is with the female I've left to walk to her dorm room alone, not with the one my father has chosen.

# chapter FIVE

## Devon

WHEN I WAKE UP THREE days after seeing Jared in the club, I decide to get a grip on myself. I get a shower and go out, making my mind up to just ignore him if I see him around. There are all sorts of things going on at the University for fresher's, so I make my way through the crowds and wander around all the market stalls—there is everything from jewellery to cupcakes. I'm taken by a small art stall, which also has a collection of used books for sale. Deciding I need something to occupy my mind I peruse them all. I usually read on my Kindle, but you can never beat the smell and feel of a real book. Each one that catches my eye seems to be a romance. And I am NOT in the mood for that. I decide, in the end, on a serial killer's story. Myra Hindley. That sounds disturbing enough to keep my mind off of Jared. I pay for it and wander on. I'm passing a small sweet stall when I get the feeling I'm being watched, and looking around I notice a guy watching me. He's a kitsune, good looking—not Jared good looking—with blue eyes and scruffy blonde hair. He doesn't look away, just stares right at me. Unsure of what to do next I smile in acknowledgement and carry on walking. Weird.

I leave the market area and head on toward a café bar. I order a latte and wait for it to arrive while reading the first chapter of Myra Hindley's story. It's not long before blue-eyes walks through the door. I sigh as he comes over and sits opposite me in the booth, uninvited. What is it with guys at the minute? He sits there, exuding confidence. Resting his arms wide on the back of the sofa he grins an Oscar-winning smile. It's perfect but for a slightly crooked tooth, and the curve to his nose is a tell-tale sign it has been broken at least once.

'Oh, by all means, sit down,' I say with as much sarcasm as I can muster. His smile quirks up at the side of his mouth.

'I don't need permission.'

I lift an eyebrow in question, a little surprised at his self-assurance. Maybe it is the kitsune in him? I've barely had any experience with kitsunes so from this meeting, and my mother, of course, I'm lumping them all together and assuming they are all assholes.

'Oh?' I question. He shakes his head slowly. He looks menacing now.

'I do what I want, when I want, with whoever I want.'

Jesus Christ, do I attract them? I get up to leave because honestly, I don't have the energy for another asshat.

He grabs for my arm. 'Hang on, Devon.'

I turn back in shock at my name on his lips. 'Look, do whatever you want, with someone else, I'm not interested.'

His grip tightens minutely before he lets go. I walk away. Shaken, I stand outside the café, unsure of where to go. I don't want to go back to my room, but the weather is rubbish, so I don't want to mill around aimlessly either. I text Maiya, asking her to meet me. I don't want to be alone. I'm astounded at the fact I've managed a whole eighteen years without bumping into another wolf or kitsune besides my parents, and in less than ten days I've come face to face with three.

Maiya comes out to meet me. We make a couple of stops at various bars. We are well into our afternoon drinking when I catch the scent of Jared's brawny friend. He stands a distance away but doesn't come over. He holds his pint up in acknowledgement when I catch his eye. He is just what I don't need. Fantastic. Maiya finishes her drink and shakes her glass at me,

'You're slacking,' she giggles. I smile and down my drink in two gulps.

'I think you forget—I'm a lightweight when it comes to drinking.'

'Only one way to remedy that, come on next pub.' I look over to Brawny and give him a dirty look as I pass. I hope from that, he understands just how I feel about him and his cheating asshole friend. We end up in a quaint little English pub. There's an open fireplace in the middle of the room lit with a roaring fire, the pictures on the wall sport brass frames of men in red coats on horseback. Everywhere I look, there are more brass ornaments, horseshoes and other trinkets dotted around. I'm lost at all there is to see, my eyes going from one thing to another. Maiya, noticing I've stopped, comes back, tugging on my arm. She laughs. 'I was having a full on convo with you. I turn around, and you're gone. Made me look like a right loon.' I'm still mesmerised by this pub. There are beams on the ceiling, and none of the walls are straight or smooth. It's like something you'd see in a painting. The windows are so small that there's barely any natural light, and the bar has glasses hanging above it. The only other customers are a couple of old men in one corner and a small group of younger guys playing darts in the far corner. Maiya gets the drinks in, while I sit at a small round table. I knew I was wrong to trust Maiya when she brings back two glasses of amber liquid and two shots.

'What are those?' I point.

'That is a red bull,' she tells me pointing to the larger glass, 'and this is a Jägermeister.' She lifts the two shots and drops them into the larger of the glasses. 'And that is a Jägerbomb.' She grins like the Cheshire cat. My glass is fizzing when I lift it to my mouth.

'Mmm.' It tastes delicious.

'Good, right?' I nod my agreement. And take another sip, just as Brawny comes in. I groan internally. The last thing I need is another round with him. Hopefully, it's just a simple coincidence that he's come in after me. My hopes of that are soon dashed when he lifts his phone to his ear, as Maiya leaves for the ladies.

'She's here, yeah, in The Crown, yep no problem.' He's come over and sat on Maiya's stool while he speaks. I gather my jacket and bag and make to go after her, wanting nothing to do with him. He stands and goes to grasp at my arm, but thinks better of it, as I glare at him, daring him to touch me again.

I walk into the ladies. Maiya is also on the phone.

'Yeah, we're in The Crown, you should definitely come.' I want to interrupt her and tell her that I want to leave, but I don't have the heart. She continues talking while applying her lipstick and plumping her hair. She rolls her eyes and makes the universal sign for 'talks too much' with her hand. I smile, shaking my head because Maiya is the queen of talking too much. I tidy up my own hair and makeup while I wait. When we're finished preening, and her conversation is over, she divulges the details of who is coming out to meet us for our 'afternoon session' as she calls it. I'd almost forgotten that Jared's brawny friend was at our table, but was quickly reminded when I found Jared propped up against the wall opposite the ladies' room. I groan out loud. As I stop, Maiya walks into the back of me, jostling me forward.

'Shit, sorry.' She giggles like a schoolgirl. Jared is stony faced and has asshole written all over him. Despite being the most gorgeous guy I've ever laid eyes on, his mood is obvious. And it's clearly directed at me. Maiya gets the hint that I'm staying and she sashays her ass all the way back to the table, where brawny is still sitting.

'What do you want, Jared?'

He stands up straight and comes over to me, pushing his nose into my hair and cupping my face.

'Just you.'

My vagina has its own little party, and my stomach does flips at his words. But I will not give in.

'Looked to me like you were doing just fine with your supermodel blonde.'

He growls at my answer, clenching and unclenching his fists.

'She isn't important.' Nice.

'Well, I'm not into screwing around with a guy who has a significant other so—'

'Fucking hell. Will you give me a break?'

'Oh, *I'm* sorry. I didn't realise *I* was the one being unfair here! *You* came to *my* room, fucked me, *then* you complained about *me* calling it a one-night stand when *clearly* that was the case because you have a *girlfriend*!' I bite out, almost growling the last few words at him while I poke at his chest. He rests one foot up against the wall, looking resigned.

'Can we talk?

'So talk?' I snap.

'Are you drunk?'

I don't want to answer that. So I look on in defiance.

'Can we go somewhere private and talk?'

'Why, Jared? What is there to talk about? You have a girlfriend. The end.'

'Devon, please?'

God, he's killing me.

'Fine,' I concede. He leads me through a doorway, and we come out into another room with a pool table in, the light is still bad, and it has the same type of décor as the main room, but we're alone. I don't trust myself being alone with him because my body seems to have a mind of its own and acts of its own accord around him. But I certainly don't want to be second best to another woman. So the quicker we get this talk over the better. I walk over and perch myself on the corner of the pool table.

'Okay, talk,' I snap with my arms folded tight across my chest. He comes over to me slowly. Stalking me like a predator with its prey. I can see a slow-burning lust in his eyes that no doubt mirrors my own. I can't help but want him. It's like an inbuilt need. My body needs his. The minute we crossed that boundary it was like nothing else would ever compare. His hands are on my thighs, his green eyes boring into mine. I'm lost to him. I jump sucking in a deep breath as Niagara Falls once again fills my barely-there panties.

'Whoa, back up, this needs to stop.' He doesn't move—just presses his fingers into my thighs.

'Jared!' I warn.

Again he doesn't move. His mouth is almost on mine. Just a little more—an inch, that's all it is. I lick my dry lips in anticipation. That pushes him over the edge. His lips meet mine in a soft embrace. So delicately. His tongue is willing my mouth open for him. My hands move to his hair as he crushes me against him. He moans into my mouth as my legs come up and around his waist like a desperate, needy slut-bag. My boobs are pressing up against his hard chest. My body recognises his and as if it has a mind of its own, goes on autopilot. My brain is clearly giving way to the moment.

He ends the kiss, leaving my lips tingling, and now we've started my body objects to the sudden change of plan. I shake a little sense back into myself. What the hell is it with him?

'I need you to hear me out,' he says. 'Please don't run again. Just listen to me. I need to explain everything.'

I come back down to earth with a bang. Shit.

'Okay.'

'So the female you saw me with...' He's clearly uncomfortable talking about her, but I giggle at him calling her a female. Then straighten my face as he remains serious. 'It's a pack thing.' When my eyes widen, and my brows shoot up, he knows I'm clueless. 'In your pack—' I put my hand up to stop him.

'Wait a minute. I don't have a pack, Jared. I was an only child and my dad raised me. I've never met anyone else like me until I met you.' Now his brows shoot up.

'Whoa, you never met any other wolves? How did you...'

I shake my head at his change of subject?

'The blonde, Jared? You were saying?' He sucks in a deep breath,

'Right, yeah erm... In my pack, my father is the alpha, but soon I'll take over as alpha. And as the alpha's son, I have certain responsibilities. One of those responsibilities is making sure my bloodline continues to be strong. I had until I was eighteen to choose a mate. If I haven't chosen by then, my father chooses for me.'

Wow, this is the twentieth century, right?

'It's the way it's been for centuries.'

'Hang on, how old are you now?'

'Twenty.' it takes a second to digest, but then the penny drops.

'The blonde is your father's choice? Like an arranged marriage?'

'Yes, this is what I was trying to say. It's complicated, but I've already been on the phone to him. I can't be with her Devon, not when...' He runs his fingers through his hair. 'I can't explain it.' He laughs nervously, his eyes never leaving mine, his fingers back to caressing my thighs. 'You... It's like nothing I've ever experienced before. I haven't eaten or slept properly. I can't stop thinking about you. I'm driving the rest of them crazy. I don't even see Kristen. I know it's not fair to her, but I just don't, she can walk in a room and turn every man's head, but not mine.' So she has a name. Kristen.

'Does she know about me?' He nods. His face is pained.

'When we,' he stumbles over his words before starting again. 'When we were together, I umm, I kind of—' he sighs in frustration '—I couldn't help it, it just happened.'

'What? You, kind of what?' For god sake spit it out already.

'I marked you. I didn't know it was happening, but I knew I wanted to and it just kind of happened.'

'Say what now?'

'I've marked you as mine.' He looks quite pleased with himself. I'm still confused and a little taken aback. 'It's not meant to happen the first time. As far as I know, it's meant to happen when you choose your life mate—when you fall in love.' *Shit on a stick.*

'How? I haven't seen any mark? I don't feel any different— what's changed? I don't get it?'

'You smell different. My scent is all over you and to any other wolf, male or female, they'll know that you're mine.'

'I'm *yours?* You say it like I'm property.'

He grins. Actually grins.

'Well, it's kinda like you are, once you're marked, all males know that if they touch you, they pay.'

'You have got to be shitting me? First of all, you don't fucking own me, and second, even if I *wanted* to be marked, which I *don't,* who gives you the right to lay claim on me?'

'Don't act so surprised. Surely it happens in your pack all the time?'

'I just told you I.DONT.HAVE.A.PACK.'

'But you know how it works right?'

'No, Jared, I'm fucking clueless when it comes to your shitty caveman ways.'

'Devon…' he scoffs

'Don't fucking *Devon* me. You did this, and I have no idea what it means. You can't just claim someone. I'm a human fucking being!'

He stops pacing and stares at me

'No, Devon, you're a wolf, and this is our way. You should fucking know this. How can you not know this?' He pulls at his hair, frustrated. I stop and let it sink into my head. It doesn't take long for my thoughts to return to the blonde. Of all the things I should be thinking about right now. He has laid claim to me and my brain is still stuck in jealousy mode. Fuck a duck.

'So she knew that night when she was all over you? She knew about me?' He nods.

'She knew when I got home that I'd been with another wolf, and she realised it was you at the bar, yes.' *When he got home?* They *live* together? Fuck me sideways.

'Can't imagine she was too happy about that?' I ask. He shakes his head looking like a guilty little boy. I wasn't too happy; how dare he mark me as his when he hadn't run it past me first. When he already has a mate. Oh, shit a brick. Hang on a fucking minute. 'Have you marked *her* too? And you *live* together?'

'Fuck no, have you not heard a word I've said? I never wanted *her*. I accepted that's what was gonna be 'cause I had to. It was a duty to my pack, to my father. But that all changed when I met you. I marked *you*. It's not a choice I made, although I would have made it, it just happens when…' He takes a deep breath. 'Well, I don't need to explain it 'cause you know.'

'When you fucked me?' He cringes at my words. Well, let's call it what it was.

'If you have to call it that, yeah, but that's not what it was for me. I was hoping it was more than that for you too but…' His words creep into my soul, and I start to thaw.

'It was, Jared. I was right there with you, but it was *one* time. I just didn't—' He puts his fingers to my lips, silencing me. A moment passes as I fall deep into the depths of his green eyes. His lips meet mine, and our tongues entwine. The kiss is gentle but carries the weight of a mountain. I am *his*. And no matter how wrong I know it is, I want him.

'It's gonna be more than once,' he says against my lips. And I know it will be. I'm his anytime-anywhere. I'm like a moth to a flame. A prostitute to a punter. A stupid fucking girl, screwing around with a taken man. Thinking with my Niagara vagina.

'Yes.' I groan out against his lips, the tenderness turning into a burning desire, his lips crushing mine. His hand pushes under my skirt and past my panties, his fingers expertly finding my slick folds. He moves down my throat with his kisses, nipping at me with his teeth. As his fingers slide home, he growls deep in his chest. I'm ready to come apart right there. But I hear the door creak open and see Brawny standing in the doorway.

'Don't move,' Jared whispers against my ear. 'What?' he snaps, turning his head toward the door, where Brawny stands, completely unfazed.

'Just checking on you, J.' The guy doesn't move and waits for an answer. It's killing me. Jared doesn't falter, moving his fingers inside me, stroking over the sweet spot inside. Making me groan.

'I'm fine, Howard, and I'm *busy*. We'll be back when *I'm* ready.' Wow, that voice. His dominance is so clear, so sexy when it isn't directed at me. I'm wet and needy, as he turns back to me, his lips meeting mine in a vicious exchange. I roll my hips shamelessly into his fingers, desperate for more. 'You're soaking, tell me what you want, baby.'

'I need you.' The words come out on a moan. I don't even sound like myself. He pushes his face into my neck, one hand fisting my hair as his other works away inside me.

'If I do that, everyone will know when we leave here. Are you good with that?' I don't give a flying fuck. I need him—it's agony. I need him there now.

'Yes, pppplease,' my words are breathy and desperate. 'Nnnneed you.' I'm squirming under the building orgasm. His answering chuckle breaks me. The wall comes down, and I come for him. My toes curl in, and my legs are jerking out of my control. I bite down on his shoulder to stem my scream.

'That's it, baby.' He lets it subside and then he's there again. His fly unzipped, he slides himself in slowly, carefully, his hands on my hips as he deliciously slides inch-by-inch inside of me. I can't fit him entirely, not like this, but he feels amazing. He pulls me forward, laying me on my back, his hands on my hips as he powers into me, for his pleasure and mine. He's exquisite. He's *mine*.

How long we are in that room, I can't be sure. But we leave and find Howard looking mighty pissed off—leaning up against the wall in the small corridor between the two rooms. He's clearly heard *everything*. And if he could smell Jared on me before there is no mistaking it now. Howard's lips twist in a disapproving way. Jared slaps him on the back.

'Devon, this is Howard, one of my pack members, and one of my best friends.'

I look up at him.

'Yeah, we've met already, remember?'

Howard rolls his eyes. He clearly dislikes me. Well, the feeling is mutual, dickface.

'Howard's problem is, he takes his job too seriously, don't yah, Howie?'

I like this Jared. Fun, loving, and carefree. He has his arm slung around my shoulder, and we walk back through to the bar. The night has completely done a U-turn. I was out trying to get Jared off my mind and instead… Pfft who cares? This is right. We feel right. Apart from the giant elephant in the room. But right now I am not going to think any more on that. Not tonight.

He drops me home along with Maiya and the promise that I will see him again the next day. I decide it's best to give my dad a call that night and wait for Maiya to fall asleep. I'd sent and received a few texts, but it was about time I made an actual call. We got all the usual crap out of the way, then I broached the subject.

'So I met someone.' Silence. 'Dad?'

'I'm here, Devon. Tell me about him?'

'Well he's a lot like *you,* dad,' I'm hoping I don't need to spell it out because although I think Maiya is asleep, I'm not a hundred percent sure. Again I'm met with silence.

'Devon, are you alone?'

'Maiya is sleeping.'

'Okay, Devon. Just answer me the best you can. When you say he's like me, do you mean as in personality?'

I laugh. 'No, dad, I mean literally like you.'

He makes a strangled sound. 'I knew this was a bad idea.'

I frown, pissed at his reply. 'Why is it? Because I've finally met some people like me? Who accepts me as I am? Who I don't have to hide from?' I try to whisper, but my temper is barely holding out.

'Devon, listen to me.' My dad's tone is serious. 'When you say people? How many?'

'He has a pack.' I cringe at my words and look over to Maiya. She's snoring. Phew. 'Dad, I don't get it? Why are you so upset about it?'

'Devon, does he know about you?'

'Know *what* about me?'

'For god sake, Devon. About what you are. What your mother is? Have you told him?' Jeez, calm down. What's wrong with him?

'No, I haven't. Why? What's the big deal?'

He doesn't say anything.

'Dad? Will you answer me, Jesus, you're acting like someone fucking died?' I inwardly cringe as I realise I'd just cussed at my dad. But his lack of reaction has me even more worried.

'I really didn't want to tell you like this.'

'DAD?' I can't bear this, 'I'm going to put the phone down now unless you start talking.' I was so frustrated, and it reflected in the way I was speaking to him. I would never normally do that. Ever.

'Devon, listen to me. When your mother and I first met, it was a while before we realised how, shall we say, different, we were. We saw each other regularly, each of us thinking the other was merely human.'

'Yeah, yeah. I know this story.' They got serious and then started to notice the signs in each other around the time they needed to change, and eventually they talked about it. And although they were different, mom a kitsune and dad a werewolf, they decided that was fine. Until she decided otherwise.

'The thing is, Devon, your mother is the daughter of a high-ranking member of her skulk. And she was forbidden to leave. She was meant to mate with a member of her group and her sons and daughters would be then mated to other high-ranking members.' I listened now intently. I had never known this before. 'Because I'm a werewolf, your mother and I were forbidden to be together. My pack wouldn't accept her, and your mother's skulk tried to take her back— to keep her away from me. They tried everything to force her back at first. But she was already pregnant with you by then so we ran. They would have killed you for being a crossbreed. And me for mating with your mother.'

'Is that why she left?' He didn't answer. I feel sick. In that short conversation, my whole existence is shattered. Everything I'd known was a lie. I shouldn't have even been born? I was a mongrel. And my mom left because of me.

'Devon, there's more. I need you to listen carefully…'

But I zone out for a while, in shock, trying to digest it all. The phone in my hand slips away. I can hear him calling my name frantically. Oh, my God. What am I going to tell Jared? Would he still want me? He's the next alpha. How could he? He would have to abide by pack law. I disconnect and drop the phone. It starts ringing again immediately. I silence it and put my pillow over my head. I cry until I fall asleep.

# chapter SIX

## Jared

I ARRIVE HOME TO FIND my father sitting at the kitchen table. *Fuck me*. He's accompanied by his usual goons who all try to look important standing behind the alpha. He's sitting at the head of the table. I have a lot of respect for my father. He brought me up in a very strict environment. I lost my mother at a young age, and I guess my dad did his best for me in the way he knew how. But he was never like the other dads I knew in the pack. He never played football or fished, or went to any matches with me. It was all about the pack. I grew up knowing how important pack life was. My father just never knew how important it was to love someone. I never had that kind of connection with him. It was a relationship born of respect and rules. Not love. That was just how we were. I never expected anything more from him, until now.

I'm acutely aware that I'm walking in reeking of sex and booze, and I could kick myself. I'm in a fantastic mood, and I don't want to come down from that, but this little ditty is going to change all that. Guaranteed. Howard stiffens at the sight of his alpha and immediately goes to sit to his right at the table. I greet my father and try to walk right on through the kitchen as if his presence was as natural as the sun coming up each morning. No such luck.

'Jared, sit.' I've only made it to the fucking door, and my good mood plummets to my boots. I sit at the opposite end of the table, slumping in the chair with an 'I don't give a flying fuck attitude.' My father is pissed. Real pissed. I know because I've learned over the years to notice the small signs. On the exterior, he looks as cool as a cucumber. But he has tells. His nostrils flare, and he has a small tick in his jaw that you can see only if you kn0w to look for it. And he grinds his teeth. The average person, they probably won't hear it. But for me, it is as loud as a nut cracking at Christmas. And that only means one thing. He is going to lay down the law and put me in my place. Or so he thinks. I have other ideas. As my father begins his speech about alpha duties—the one I know by rote. I zone out. My eyes glaze over, and my thoughts go to Devon. How she felt, how she tasted, how she sounded beneath me. Fuck, I want to be back there right now. Without thinking, I get up from the table and follow my feet up the stairs. Howard catches me half way up.

'What the actual *fuck,* Jared? Your dad is fucking *raging* in there, and you just walk away from the fuckin' *ALPHA*? What's gotten into you?' His voice is almost high pitched it's comical, he tries to tug on my arm to take me back, but I pull my elbow from his grip and walk on,

'Fuck it, Howard. I don't even care anymore.'

Howard's eyes go as wide as saucers, and I chuckle. Whatever. I throw out my hand, dismissing him, and walk the rest of the way to my room. It isn't long before the door opens. I say opens. It almost comes off the fucking hinges—no knock. My father stands there, filling the doorway. His calm exterior is slipping a little as he takes in my carefree sprawl on the bed. I don't speak. I just lay with my hands tucked under my head and my ankles crossed. Staring at the ceiling.

'I see you've been with her, despite my orders against it.' It wasn't a question, so I don't answer. I just roll my eyes in my father's direction and then back up to the ceiling. Whatever dickhead. 'I will give you today, Jared, and I hope she is now fully out of your system because my choice still stands and you *will* do as I say.'

I sit up then, looking my father straight in the eye. 'No.'

I don't know what's funnier, the shock on his face or the fact I'd actually said that out loud. To my father. Not many live to tell the tale when he isn't obeyed. But I'd made my mind up, even if Devon didn't want me, I wanted her, and I couldn't change that. I didn't want anyone else. Ever. And I was not going to mate with Kristen.

My dad seems to fly across the room, but I don't flinch. He's a fierce wolf, one to be feared. One who *is* feared by many.

I was scared shitless too, until I outgrew him, and outmatched him. I knew I could take my father if necessary. I won't because I have respect for him as the alpha and as my father. But this is a sticking point I'm just not willing to move on. So either he will have to back down on his decision, or he will have to find a way to force my hand. The latter wasn't working out so good for him, so he'd come down to do it in person. The fact that Devon's feelings for me had been confirmed tonight only held me in stronger stead. I was not budging. Not even an inch. My father will hopefully accept that and respect me for making a stand. After all, I am the alpha heir. It's in my nature to lead, not follow. I watch as my father's face goes from pissed to shocked, and then there is a flicker of something else—fear? Respect? Before it finally settles on amused. I haven't moved from the bed, and I'm in a vulnerable position with my alpha standing above me, but I don't care.

'Are you sure this is the female you want?' my father asks to my surprise.

'Absolutely certain.' I didn't hesitate. He snorts in disgust.

'And she wants you?'

I nod.

'Well I can see that nothing I say is going to change your pig-headed mind, but know this, you will be punished. You cannot and will not defy me and get away with it. I am your *ALPHA!*' he growls out the last word.

I inwardly flinch but don't show weakness. There's silence for a moment, and I don't take my eyes off of him, maybe he's deciding my punishment and is going to dole it out here and now. And what about Devon? Is he allowing it? Is he calling off the mating to Kristen? I have so many questions I need answering. 'You may have this female,' he says, and I let out a breath. Thank fuck. 'But, the mating to Kristen still stands. You will follow my orders, and you will produce great heirs. That is the way it will be.'

I stand from the bed and go toe to toe with him. I have at least four inches on my father, and I outweigh him easily pound for pound.

'I won't mate Kristen, and that's the fucking end of it. You think you can make me? Try it.' The indecision on my father's face at that moment is clear. Does he challenge me head on, or does he accept my choice and make like he made the decision? Time seems to stretch while I wait. Then my father gives me a nod, turns and leaves my room. What the fuck does that mean? I pale. What the fuck have I just done? Faced my father—my alpha, down, practically challenging his position. Shit, I wasn't ready to be alpha yet, but I just came damn close. Is this how it's going to be from now on? I feel like I've just let something loose—like I've just opened Pandora's fucking box. Did I do the right thing? I knew sure as shit it was wrong to mate Kristen. But I'd just disobeyed my alpha for a female I barely knew. I could be cast out. Turned away from all I knew. Is she worth that? The answer is easy, though. Yes, she is worth all that. I know it in my gut.

# *Devon*

The next morning comes around way too quickly. I have to register and fill out all the relevant paperwork dealing with finance, and various other boring bits regarding being an international student. I walk around in a daze, going through the motions, Maiya at my side the whole time, guiding me through it. She decides a coffee break is needed. I welcome the caffeine, but I'm not up for chatting, she seems to get that, so we each sit with our own thoughts.

'Umm, you gonna get that?' Huh? I look at her, startled from my thoughts. 'Your phone? It's ringing.'

I look and realise my phone is moving as it buzzes across the table. I shake my head at her. I'm not in the mood to speak to my dad. But no sooner does it stop, then it starts again. I stare at the screen, which reads 'Home'. 'Oh for god sake.' Maiya snatches the phone from the table and answers, 'Devon's phone' in a high-pitched girly voice. I listen as my dad asks where I am. 'I'm Maiya—her roommate—she's gone off to register this morning but left her phone charging while she went. Can I take a message?' My dad asks that I give him a call when I get in. 'No problem I'll pass that on.' Maiya hangs up and relays the message. 'It would have rung all day, at least this way you have some slack. So, you wanna talk about it?'

I shake my head. I do want to talk about it, but not with Maiya, and certainly not with my dad. In the end, she lets it go, and we head back home.

I seriously need to think about changing soon. I'm very irritable and can feel my mood changing. Over the years I've learned that I can go about three weeks without changing, but my mood and general health are better if I don't wait that long. Doing the math, I realise it has been two weeks. No wonder I feel so angsty. A little recon is required to decide where I can change safely. I will go as soon as it gets dark. It's handy having the choice of Kitsune and wolf because in a town like this if a fox is noticed, it won't look so out of place. Whereas a wolf would be best unnoticed. I preferred running as a wolf, though, and I'd always favoured that side of me.

Maiya seems to understand I want time alone and doesn't complain when I blow her off.

The woods around campus are calling out to me, so I go to check them out. The sounds and smells of the forest, although not the same as back home, give me goose pimples. The normally dry, crisp smell of back home is moist and damp smelling here, but it's still so alluring. Excitement thrums through my body, the energy of my wolf coming to the surface as I walk deeper, telling me I'm home and it's time. I have to fight the urge to change there and then. I have to battle hard against it because the thought of running with no feelings about anything else— just to run and hunt—I need that. My body almost goes with the change, and I have to fight to keep control. I want it so badly and to fight against it is painful. On my knees in the throes of battling my change, I get the sense someone else is there. I snap my head up, and my senses go on high alert. It is blue eyes, and he is close. And coming closer. I can hear the crunch of his feet over the leaves on the ground. Gathering myself, I stand and run in the opposite direction.

'Hey, where you going in such a hurry?' Shit, I really am not up for another round with this jackass.

'Home,' I sneer, the venom in my voice evident. He catches up and falls into step by my side. Fantastic. His hands are in the pockets of his leather jacket, but he is giving off menacing vibes, which isn't good, I just don't trust this guy, maybe it is the kitsune side of him, I'm not sure. Maybe I have mommy issues and won't trust another kitsune again. I decide the best thing to do is keep him talking while I walk back to civilisation.

'What are you studying?' I blurt lamely making him laugh.

'Come on you can do better than that?' He cocks his head with a snide grin on his face. 'I'm not a student, but I think you already know that.'

'No, why would I know that?'

He laughs again. It's a cold laugh that carries malice.

'You really are a prize, Devon.'

Shit. I stop walking. I stand stock-still, staring at him. *How the hell does he know my name?* He's still grinning, and he is very intimidating. And he knows it. 'Tick tock tick tock,' he says. I finally find my voice I'm about to ask who the hell he is, but thankfully a group of students comes into the small clearing we are now standing in, and he turns and walks away. My head is spinning. What the fuck?

'It won't be too long, Devon.' I hear him shout through the trees. Before I know it, I'm sprinting. *Holy shit, what the fuck is going on?* Passing the student support buildings, I decide on a caffeine boost because I need a clear head and want to be somewhere public. Parking my ass in a circle booth, I order a latte with an extra shot of coffee. I'm toying with the idea of ringing my dad and running this whole mess past him, but that would be a bad idea. One because he would make me leave and go back home at the first sign of trouble. And two, I'm not speaking to him yet.

If this kitsune knows who I am, what does he want? Does he actually know who I am? Or just my name?

I sit there just mulling everything over in my head. Time passes, and I'm not sure how long I'm sitting there when I feel the familiar tingling that tells me Jared is near. I catch his scent at around the same time he comes into view. All my problems seem to melt away at that moment. He is so gorgeous, and my mouth waters. He walks up, sinfully sexy, and sits next to me, taking my shaking hand, which I hadn't noticed until that moment. His face changes from happy to see me, to something in between fear and confusion.

'What's wrong?'

My eyes sting with that familiar burning sensation as they begin to fill, and the tears start to fall. Unable to answer, I just shake my head. He pulls me into his arms and onto his lap, and he holds me there. The coffee has gone cold, but another appears, piping hot, along with cake and a coffee for Jared. He urges me to eat, but I just can't bring myself to. He feels so good against me, but I feel so guilty. I shouldn't be enjoying his embrace. I need to steer clear of him. He needs a proper mate, not a fucking mongrel. I need to go home. I can't stay here and not have him. It's the only way. I have to, for Jared's sake. This had already gone way too far.

I struggle against his strong hold trying to get up and leave.

'Devon, talk to me?' he says as he cups my face in his hands, rubbing his thumb across my cheek. I wanted to nuzzle against him, feel his warmth, but I can't.

'I have to go home.' I tell him. His alarm shocks me. It's obvious he realises I'm not talking about my room.

'Like fuck you do!' His voice is firm, commanding—he doesn't like not having his way.

'Jared, I'm wrong for you.'

'Fuck that! 'he interrupts, but I carry on speaking over him.

'And you need to do what is right by your father. You can't be with me, Jared. I'm not right for you.' His hands slam down in fists onto the table, making me jump.

'Who the fuck has been in your head? Kristen? Howard? Who? Tell me *now*, Devon? Because I'm not listening to this shit. WHO?'

He's scary when he's angry, but I love that he's willing to fight for me. I can't answer him. I can't give him what he wants. Sobs escape each time I try to speak.

'Come with me.' he pulls me up, throws money onto the table and guides me by my arm to his car. 'Get in.'

I do as I'm told, resigned to the fact that he isn't going to drop this until he gets the answers he wants from me. He slams the door behind me after buckling my seat belt and gets into the driver's side. He takes off without another word. We're driving for about a half hour, and we don't speak the whole way. His jaw is clenched so tight, the muscles twitching as he grinds his teeth. His knuckles are white from his tight grip on the steering wheel. He's scary like this but sinfully sexy.

A lovely white house comes into view at the end of a dirt path. He pulls around the back and before he gets out he sits for a moment, clenching and unclenching his jaw. I still can't speak. I don't want to. I don't want to open the floodgates and have to tell him everything. I can't bear for him to hate me. He gets out of the car, slamming the door, and he stomps all the way around to open the door for me. He reaches in and unbuckles the belt and roughly helps me up out of the car. He unlocks the door to the house and pulls me inside. So this is where he lives. We enter straight into a kitchen. It is old looking but beautiful. I'm looking around when he pulls me from my reverie.

'Talk,' he demands.

Definitely not an option. I shrug my shoulders because honestly, I don't know where the hell to start.

'Do you want to be with me?'

*Oh, Jared of course I do. I want nothing more. But how can I?*

My answering sobs and the nod of my head buys me an embrace and a kiss to my forehead.    'Baby, please. I can't fuckin' bear this.'

This isn't right. I *need* to tell him. I take a couple of deep breaths as he lifts me onto the worktop. His hands cup my face, his eyes telling me that he would hold the world on his shoulders for me. Gathering my thoughts, I start and stop, the words running around in my head, trying and failing to find the right ones. He stands, waiting. It seems like an eternity has passed before I'm ready to speak aloud.

'It's not you Jared. It's me.'

His eyes fill with irritation.

'Don't you dare use that fuckin' line on me, Devon. Whatever this is—whoever this is, it stops now. You're *mine*, and you're with *me*. And I am *yours*. You said that was what you wanted? What the fuck has *changed*?'

His eyes are full of tears as he chokes on the last words. He is desperate. I am desperate. I love him. How that can be, so soon, I don't know. But I love every fibre of his being. I'm sure of that. I reach up to hold his face in my hands, and he stills, his body trembling. He kisses me, tenderly, so soft like he might break me. His tongue slides against mine so delicately, and he relaxes against me, lost in the kiss I'm so eager to give him. Tears streak down my face as I greedily kiss him back. Wanting him more with each lovingly-given stroke of his tongue. His hands slide under my blouse, as his fingers slip around my back and deftly undo my bra. He cups my breasts in his palms and gently squeezes. Somewhere, a voice in my head is screaming to stop this. But I want him so badly. He's undoing the buttons of my blouse when my conscience finally kicks in. His mouth is at my nipple.

'Jared, stop.'

He stills, his hands unmoving. His eyes close, the pain clear on his face. He stands up straight. I begin re-buttoning my top, and he turns away and rests his hands on the table, giving me his back. I go to him, my hand going to his shoulder.

'Don't.' He chokes the word out.

My heart breaks. 'Jared, I need to explain.'

He turns then and glares with his arms folded across his chest. 'Well fuckin' explain then, 'cause you're fuckin' killing me here.'

Where do I start? How do I start?

'I'm not a full-blooded wolf.' I just blurt it out. He frowns down at me.

'Don't bullshit, Devon, I'm not an idiot.' He's hurt and angry.

'Jared, my mother isn't a wolf, only my father is.' I can see he's thinking because his lips quirk up a little when he's thinking. It's cute.

'Okay, it's not the norm to mate with humans, but it happens. This doesn't have to be a problem, Devon. My dad, he'll come around to the idea, he doesn't even have to know about that.' *Wait what?*

'Your dad isn't okay with this? With us?' He purses his lips flat.

'No, not yet, but he will be, he'll have to be.'

Right there is just another reason why I am bad for him. I groan and prop myself against the table end. He reaches out to me then, but I hold my hand up for him to stop.

'There's more, Jared, a lot more, and you may not want me here when I'm finished.'

'Try me.' he says in a smart-ass tone like I could say anything and he wouldn't change his mind. I pull out a chair, he follows suit and sits next to me, turning it so he looks directly at me. *Just do it, Devon. Get it over with.* I take a deep breath and throw it all out there.

'My mother isn't human either.' He cocks his head, and I can see he's trying to work it all through and he can't figure it out. 'She's a kitsune, Jared.' I fiddle with the hem of my blouse, desperate not to meet his eyes. The silence is deafening. Resting his elbows on his knees, he scrubs at his face, and still he says nothing. The silence stretches on, and I can't take it anymore. I grab the bag I dropped and snatch my cell. I dial for the local operator. 'Could I have a local cab number please?'

'Would you like me to put you straight through?'

'Yes, please.' I have my back to Jared. I can't face him. As I'm put through to the cab firm, he takes the phone from my hand and disconnects it before giving it back.

'You just gonna leave? Is that it?'

He looks broken. Defeated. I don't know what to do, or what to say.

'I thought that's what you would want?'

He shakes his head at me. But he says nothing, his face showing no emotion. I feel uncomfortable just standing there. I can't meet his eyes, afraid of what I'll see there. I want to go. I can't bear this. As I look up, I notice the change, the angry flicker in his eyes. And it's directed at me.

'This is so fucked up. Who sent you? Do you work for that cocksucker trying to take what's ours? Did you get a guilty conscience? Suddenly decide that now you've suckered me in you'd just fuck off now your job's done?'

I'm shaking my head violently. He is so far from the truth, but I can't speak for crying.

'Save the tears, *sweetheart*. You got me good, really fucking good.' He spits the words at me. He's so angry, so cold. I reach out to him, pleading. I need him. He doesn't meet my eyes, but he steers me toward the door, throwing me out.

'Jared, I didn't know.' I sob desperately. 'My dad never told me. I swear to you.'

He slams the door behind me. I hear him clattering and banging about inside, breaking things in temper. I clutch the phone in my hand and dial again for the operator. By the time the cab comes I've walked up the dirt drive and met the cab at the roadside. He takes me back to my room. I'm in no mood for small talk, so I avoid the lift and take the stairs. I'm so desperate for a change now, so I drop my stuff in my room, switch my phone off and change to gym clothes and sneakers, while Maiya looks on wide-eyed and questioningly. She obviously worried at my state. But I can't talk, not right now.

'I'm going for a run.' It isn't a lie. Just a small omission of the full truth.

## *Jared*

I'm sitting at the table when everyone gets home. My hands are bleeding, and I no doubt look a fuckin' mess. I don't give a shit.

'What the fuck happened?' Brad asks. I don't look up at him. They're all staring wide-eyed around the room,

'Jared?' It's Zoe. 'Who did this?

Shit, Jared, are you okay?' Brad comes back into the room. I hadn't even noticed he'd left.

'Nothing's missing. It's just in here that's a wreck,' he announces. They think someone else has done it. I don't explain, instead, I get up and go to the bathroom.

'Jared, let me see to your hands.' Zoe again. I wave her off. I'm not capable of throwing any words out there just now. I'm still fighting the tears. I have that fucking burning in the back of my throat, and I need to make myself scarce. Sitting on the toilet lid, I let it all out like a pansy ass motherfucker. Gradually, they all come and knock on the door. But I don't want to see or speak to anyone. When it's Howard's turn again, the asshole tells me either I speak to him, or he will speak to my fucking dad. Dickhead. I let him in.

'What the fuck, Jared?'

I start washing the blood from my hands and pulling the shards of glass from my knuckles. My world has just bottomed out, and this asshole is demanding answers,

'Fuck you, Howard. I don't owe you any explanations,'

'Well, you sure as shit owe me something. Let's start with why you totalled the fucking kitchen?'

'Leave. Me. Alone.'

He stands, defying me, staring me out in the mirror. I roar out my frustration and shatter the mirror with my fist. And he still stands there. I turn my rage on him. He's on the floor, taking hits when Brad comes in and hauls my ass up and into the hall. I was done anyway. Still covered in blood I take my ass to bed.

Howard knocks on my door a while later. I'm calm now and ready to talk to Devon. I should have fucking heard her out. I shouldn't have reacted like I did.

'You ready to talk?' He's bruised and has a split lip, but it is already healing.

'Everything is fucked up, Howard.'

He doesn't ask for an apology, and he hears me out. I tell him what happened, what Devon had revealed to me, and I make it very clear how I feel about her. He listens and the whole time doesn't say a word. The question now is, will he have my back or will he go to my father, his alpha? We both know what he should do, but I'm hopeful that he is with me on this. He looks torn. Like someone is messing with his moral compass.

'I'm only going to say this once, Jared, and I won't admit it to your father. But as your friend, if she is what you really want, then no-one needs to know she's—' he pauses, clearly thinking of the right word, 'different,' he finishes. Relieved I let out a long breath.

'This stays between us right?'

He nods, agreeing. Now I have to right a wrong.

I leave through the kitchen and realise just how bad it is. The girls are still cleaning shit up, and Brad is trying and failing to repair the wooden doors. I keep my eyes on the floor.

'Leave it, get take out. I'll have someone come and fix it. I'll make some calls tomorrow.' Brad follows me out to the car. 'Wait up, man,' he calls.

I turn and face him. I'm sorry for all the shit they are having to deal with, but I'm not up for a lecture. 'Listen, man. Whatever has you all chewed up—I'm here. I've got you. Just so long as you know that, 'kay?' He claps me on the shoulder.

'Appreciate that, Brad.' I trusted all my pack mates with my life, but with this business, they have to choose between my father, and me, and that was a big ask. He was their alpha, and it was huge to expect them to agree with me over him. If I could help it, I wouldn't have them make that decision. So as much as it pained me, it would be a secret that only Howard and I would bear.

# chapter SEVEN

## *Devon*

I GO DEEPER INTO THE forest than I had earlier in the day. There's no trace of anyone else around, so I find a tree, undress and hang my clothes over a branch discreetly, so no one wandering around will come across them. If ever I leave my change to chance, without making a decision beforehand, the wolf is always dominant, and she is the more powerful of the two and the one I always favoured. I'd never shared that information with my parents. I was always worried about hurting mom's feelings. *Pfft—shame she couldn't have thought that way about me when she fucked off.* I crouch and feel the first tingles of my change. It's painful and exhilarating all at the same time, and it gives me a sense of freedom. When I become one with my wolf, it always feels as if I have been locked away, and I'm then being set free.

To run through the forest unhinged is amazing. The sounds and smells are all unfamiliar to me, but they call to me all the same. Here it's damp and misty on my fur. It smells clean and fresh. And full of prey. Rabbits begin thumping their hind legs in warning as I stalk closer. Darting from side to side they run, and I chase. Not from hunger, but for the challenge. I love a challenge, and nothing can beat the chase. Whipping through the forest at speed has me hungry in no time at all. It is time to pounce. I kick up my speed and watch as the rabbit I have in my sights darts from side to side, trying to evade me. I kick up another gear and out-smart it. I feign left, and it goes right just as I planned. It squeals as I clamp my jaw around it and the sound makes my mouth water. I snap its neck. A quick and clean kill. I'm settled down with my meal when I sense someone close by. I have my nose deep in the rabbit, but I can hear someone—branches snapping a distance away. I swivel my ears, listening intently. There it is again. I snort, clearing my nose. Jared. Jared is coming. It's early evening now, and there is barely any light in the forest. I stayed put but on alert. The rabbit still between my forepaws. The sound of his feet stop, and I hear the unmistakable sound of his change. The wrenching sound your throat makes as the pain almost makes you hurl. Then nothing. My ears are swivelling one side to the other, my hackles raised. Unsure of what to expect, I'm scared. Why has he come?

Then I see him—he stands at the edge of the small clearing. He's big, as black as night and he has the same piercing green eyes. He's a dominant wolf—that much is obvious in his gait alone, as he walks over to me. I rise, allowing a small growl to escape me. He returns it with a growl of his own. And bares his teeth. I lay down submitting to him. Looking up, I see his eyes are strong, taking every part of me in. He lays beside me then and begins lapping at my muzzle, cleaning me of the blood. I lay very still until he's finished. He yips at me and throws his head over his shoulder beckoning me to go with him. I follow. Still uncertain. We run a while, and my fear eases, until he rounds on me, sniffing at my rear, and licking at me. I clamp my tail between my legs. Making him growl and prod at me with his muzzle. I sit in defiance, unsure of what he wants. He rubs himself up against me until all I can smell is him. Then he's licking me, cleaning me all over. I don't know how to respond to this behaviour because I've never experienced anything like it before, so I just remain still. We lay together in the dark. I feel warm and content and eventually, I fall asleep.

I wake in my human form, not sure how I've gone through the whole change without waking because I'd never fallen asleep out of human form before. I have always changed and dressed after a run. I was butt-ass naked and cold, except for the solid heat at my back. Jared. His arm is wrapped around me, possessively.

'Morning,' he says with a smile on his face as I turn to look at him. I'm so confused, but I smile. I can't help it. He's also butt-ass naked and very much aroused. That alone makes me lose focus on what happened between us, at his house. The length of him is pressed teasingly against my ass and lower back, reminding me of just how big he is, and how much I need him inside me. He turns me onto my back,

'Jared—' I begin

'Shhh, don't.'

He holds his weight above me with his arms and pushes my legs wide to accommodate him. He kisses me. It feels raw and full of emotion. I realise then that he's crying. I lose myself in him. The kiss says so much. All the words I wanted to say.

'I'm so sorry,' he says, pushing his arm underneath me and rolling me so I straddle him. 'I was a jerk. I'm so fucking sorry, will you forgive me?' He sits up so our chests are touching and kisses me again, with a desperate hunger. I can't speak—he won't let me. He's keeping my mouth busy with his own. I push away breaking the contact and instantly miss it.

'Jared, this doesn't change what I am. We can't be together. Your pack won't allow it.'

He pulls me to him. My pert nipples, so sensitive as they brush up against his pecs.

'It's too late for that, Devon,' he says, kissing my throat, my jaw and then he hovering over my lips. 'When you left yesterday,' he closes his eyes against the pain of it. 'I didn't know what to do with myself. I felt like a piece of me had died.'

'But I di—'

'Just hear me out, please?' he coaxes. I nod. 'Devon, I *want you*, every part of you. I don't care what others say. I wanted you before I knew about that part of you and nothing has changed. You're still the same. I still want to be with you. I *need* you, Devon.' Oh my God. Could we do this? Could I have him?

I can't speak. Instead, I kiss him, tasting him, sliding my tongue in teasingly. He growls, and latches onto my bottom lip, the pinch of pain sends vibrations all the way to my core. His hard cock is pressed up against my abdomen. I fist him in one hand and milk him. His answering moan spurs me on. I want to please him. I want him to know that I'm worth it. I move off him.

'Stand up,' I demand. He does as I ask with a smirk on his face and I kneel before him, licking my lips before I take him as deep as I can into my mouth. I suck on him, licking the head as his pre-cum glistens for me. I lap it up. Hollowing out my cheeks I hold onto his ass while he fucks my mouth. I feel him harden and lengthen, his orgasm close. I grab the base of his cock and cup his balls while his orgasm wracks through his body. My greedy mouth takes all he has to give me. Milking him of every last drop. He doesn't soften, but I let him go and sit back on my haunches. He comes down to my level, kneeling before me, kissing me hard. I can sense the excitement coursing through him. No doubt because he can taste himself on me. Inside me.

'Am I forgiven?' he asks, breaking our kiss. I laugh, and he lunges at me. I'm on my back in no time at all, and he's inside of me in a matter of seconds.

'You're not spent?' I giggle.

'Not even close,' he growls as he powers into me, making me scream out with the pure delight of feeling him reach the very end of me, over and over, hitting that delightful spot. He seems to know my body so well already. He lifts my legs, my ass coming off the floor. Only my shoulders and upper back resting in the dirt. My legs are on either side of his head—he's even deeper this way. He feels so good. Rough or gentle it doesn't matter. I need him in any way I can get him. He is *Mine*. He speaks to me in the throes of my orgasm. I can't be sure what he's said, and at that moment it doesn't matter. I tremble all over, the orgasm taking hold and wracking through me, going off like a bomb inside of me. He rides it out until I'm more than sated and he's come for the second time. He cuddles me into his side.

'Jared?'

'Hmmm.' His reply is lazy and contented, making me smile. That's exactly how I feel too.

'What did you say to me before?' I lean up on my elbow, suddenly aware of how incredibly hard and scratchy the floor is.

'Nothing,' he says, grinning. I poke him.

'You said something to me, now spill,' I demand, prodding him again.

'Ooh, keep doing that, and you know where it's going to go?' I poke at him again. I can't resist, and he leaps on top of me,

'Behaviour like that,' he says pinning my arms above my head, 'will get you well and truly fucked.'

'Really?' I ask wriggling beneath him. The hard ground is forgotten. I truly doubted he had anything left in the tank. I was wrong. He slips himself inside me, and he feels so deliciously right.

'I asked, what have you done to me?' he whispers in my ear. 'I can't be without you.' I hold him tight to me like my life depends on it.

'I feel the same way,' I tell him as he nuzzles into my neck.

'I love you, Devon.' My breath catches, and I melt beneath him. Whatever has happened to me and my emotions has hit him just as hard. I thought I'd been stupid to think I loved him so soon, but clearly, we are in that boat together.

'I love you too.' He stills, even his breath hitches to a stop. He pushes up holding his weight off me as his green eyes meet mine. His lips quirk in a half smile before he takes my mouth with his.

We lay completely and utterly spent. I'm dozing against Jared's chest when he suddenly stiffens and stands bolt upright—he pulls me up behind him. There's someone here.

'Fuckin hell, Howard?' Jared snaps. He's trying his best to keep me behind his bigger form and away from Howard's eyes. I feel vulnerable and a little violated. How long has he been there? Has he watched us? Howard comes striding forward from where he's standing. 'What the fuck are you doing?' Jared demands, although not in as sharp a tone as I would have used. Howard shrugs his shoulders.

'My job! When you don't come home, and stay out all fuckin' night without even a word, after you totalled the fuckin kitchen yesterday, I get worried. Not just 'cause we're tight, Jared, but 'cause yah fuckin' dad would rip me a new one if anything happened to you on my watch. Bet you didn't think of that while you were fucking her?'

Jared moves so quick I barely see it. He has Howard on the floor by the throat. Howard's hands go up in surrender and his eyes go down before moving my way.

'Don't fucking look at her,' Jared growls out. He gets up off him. 'Gimme your jacket.' Howard sits up and shrugs out of his jacket, handing it over. Jared gives it to me, and I'm so grateful for it. I slip it on, covering myself sufficiently. Jared, however, is still gloriously naked. I bite my lip to stop the girlish giggle that's desperately bubbling up my throat. He is so authoritative even when he's naked, and it stirs me up inside. Getting up, Howard walks over to the tree he'd been propped against and slings a bag at Jared's feet.

'Brought these just in case.'

'Thanks. I'll be home soon, and I'll see you there,' Jared tells him dismissively. Howard leaves without his jacket or another word. Jared looks up at me as he pulls the contents from the bag. I answer his smile with one of my own. 'Nothing like being caught with your pants down,' he says grinning.

I laugh, and he launches a t-shirt at me.

'I don't think I can handle you wearing another man's jacket,' he says. I shrug out of the jacket and put the t-shirt on. It's white and rather large, and although it clings to my nipples, it does nothing for my figure at all. We walk through the forest, towards our clothes. We find his first. They're damp from the fog, so I hold out no hope for mine.

'Yup, just as wet,' Jared announces as he pulls my sweats and tank top from the branch above him. 'You'll just have to do the walk of shame in that,' he says lifting the hem of his t-shirt.

I snatch my clothes from him laughing. No way I am walking through the campus as I am now, not a chance. I slip into the damp pants, but I keep on his tee. The fact I have no underwear on doesn't slip his attention either.

'Mmm, you always go commando when out for a run?' he asks with his eyebrows wagging up and down.

'Yep, no point in over complicating things.'

'Noted,' he says with a wink. I bite my bottom lip at the growly sound he makes. Realising that at the rate my vagina turns into Niagara Falls—the entire time I'm around him—I should really reconsider the no underwear when going on runs. I feel like a horny school kid. Slipping on my sneakers, I hold onto him for support. When I'm ready, he holds my hand and walks me back to my room. It's still really early in the morning, and no one is around. As we get into the elevator, Jared pulls me to him. 'I want you to come back to the house with me.' That little quirk of his lips does things to me.

'Okay,' I agree without really thinking it through.

Jared tells me to pack an overnight bag, so I pack accordingly. I leave a note for Maiya, explaining that I am staying out overnight and tell her to text me if she needs me because I don't want to wake her. Jared has conveniently left his truck parked in the lot near my building. He'd obviously come looking for me and found my trail in the woods.

We arrive at his house, and I realise I haven't given any thought to the fact that Jared has house mates or more to the point that Kristen, the woman scorned, could be one of those people. Fuckety fuck. The last time I was here hadn't been a nice visit. But we had been alone, so when he takes my bag and holds out his hand for me to get out of the truck I'm a little surprised to see the kitchen full of people. I hesitate and Jared notices.

'Just be you,' he tells me. But I'm not sure if that's good enough for them. They're his pack, and I've encroached on their turf—Kristen's turf. I hold his hand tight, squeezing for him to stop.

'Jared, I'm not sure this is such a good idea, maybe…' I stop walking. He turns and pulls my hand up to his lips and kisses my knuckles. I really don't want to walk into that room, but he more than convinces me that it's worth it. *Suck it up, Devon.* We walk into the kitchen, or what is left of it. *What in the hell had happened?* If I was hoping for a discrete entrance, I was shit out of luck. *Everyone* stops what they are doing and looks our way. *Oh, shit a brick.* Jared squeezes my hand in reassurance.

'Devon, this is Zoe.' A girl with dark curly hair sitting at the dining table, waves at me with a stunning smile. I smile back. 'This is Brad,' he points at the only black guy in the room. His hair is in cornrows, and his smile is so warm it shows in his dark eyes too. 'You should totally stay away from him,' Jared teases,

'Don't listen to him, Devon, he's just jealous of this,' he says lifting his shirt and flexing with a huge grin on his face. Jared punches him in the arm, and I laugh, feeling a little more at ease. Brad is a stunner—his body is perfectly sculpted. He clearly works hard to keep it that way. But I remember Jared's body and he has nothing to be jealous about.

'Logan and Imogen.' Jared points to a couple at the stove, Imogen's smile for me puts me even more at ease. They both have gorgeous long blond hair and blue eyes, but Imogen's are a piercing blue. They remind me of the sky on a really clear day. Logan smiles genuinely before going back to what he is cooking on the hob. Howard sits at the furthest end of the table. He smiles as Jared points in his direction. 'You've already met Howard,' he says with a smirk. I nod in acknowledgement to him, not really feeling much like smiling at Howard but not wanting to be rude either. 'So what's cooking?' Jared asks of Logan, as he steers me to the table,

'Bagels, with bacon and cheese, pancakes and we have porridge and croissants,' he answers. Jared turns to me,

'That okay for you?'

I'm a little embarrassed that he hasn't even asked if I could join them. 'Jared I don't want to put anyone out,'

He laughs at that. 'They *always* make enough to feed an army, and that's after we've had seconds.'

I look to Imogen for confirmation.

'We need to keep all of these fed it's not an easy task.' She smiles.

I feel instantly at home, although I think that's partly due to Kristen's absence, and the fact that she isn't mentioned either, which I'm very grateful for. I don't want to come across as a boyfriend-stealing-bitch, nor do I want to rub it in her face. But, I'm not about to give him up either. We eat and it's delicious. It's so nice to eat with people who have an appetite as big as my own, and not have to pretend I've eaten enough. They're all so welcoming toward me. We laugh, and they all poke fun at one another. It's immediately obvious to me that Imogen and Logan are an item. They're so in sync with one another. Howard laughs with the rest of us, but I notice he's a bit more reserved, and he watches everyone.

By the time we've all finished up, my coffee cup had been refilled at least four times. I feel really comfortable. I've had an effortless conversation with everyone except Howard. The day passes by quickly. Zoe and I speak about going on night's out, and some killer heels she wants to show me, so when she asks me to go up to her room to show me, Jared encourages me to go with her. Surprisingly, I don't feel at all awkward, without Jared there as my anchor, like I expected. Zoe is so easy going and I feel like we get along just fine. We go through her entire 'partying' closet. She has some amazing outfits, and the shoes she was telling me about are to die for. Made from what looks like a delicate belt that wraps around the foot and ankle in a silver grey material with tiniest of rhinestones. They're stunning. I've never really been one for fashion but they are so gorgeous I can't even say what I want to say. I'm gaping like a fish out of water.

'I know right? How gorgeous are they?'

'They're so nice.' That's all I manage. How lame.

'I had to work for three months before my dad coughed up and gave in. He said no pair of shoes should cost more than a car. I disagree obviously.'

'More than a car?' I squeal out. She laughs at my reaction slapping me on the back.

'I love expensive shoes, what can I say?' she shrugs. 'Whoever I mate with will have to have the means to keep me in that habit.' She laughs.

Over an hour later, I make my way down the stairs to where I'd left Jared. Halfway down, I run into Howard. He looks at me with disgust. Shit, I thought we were past that.

'You should leave him alone and go back to where you came from.' I knew he didn't like me very much, but that was a slap in the face.

'What does it matter to you?' My tone's clipped and stern. I'm upset, but I'll be damned if I'm going to show it.

'What matters is *him* and this pack. You don't belong here.' He comes so close I'm pressed against the wall, but I keep my chin in the air. He isn't intimidating me. I won't let him.

'If Jared agreed with you I wouldn't be here and since it's his decision and not—'

'It's the *alpha's* decision,' he growls in my face 'and the more you cosy up to his son the more pissed he is gonna be, and it's *Jared* that will pay for it.'

'What do you mean?' His face twists in disgust at my question.

'You're completely clueless, aren't you? Just go home and leave Jared alone.' Someone rounds the corner at the top of the stairs making him take a step back from me. I'm still in shock at his outburst.

'Come on now, Howard, play nice.' Brad pushes between us and loops his arm through mine, guiding me the rest of the way down the stairs. I can feel Howard's eyes boring a hole in my back the whole way down.

'What's his problem?' I ask as we turn the corner at the bottom.

Brad just shakes his head. 'Another time,' he whispers.

Jared comes into view then. He looks breathtaking as the sun streams through the windows, and he leans one arm above his head against the side of the French doors. Brad leaves my side, and I go to Jared. He doesn't turn, but he knows I'm there. His body reacts in much the same way as mine does in his presence. I slip my arms around his waist and hold him, my face to his back. I really have it bad. In the short time I've been gone, I hadn't realised until now just how much I missed him. And at that moment I would be happy never to leave his side again.

His hands rest on mine at his waist. I kiss his shoulder blade. He still doesn't turn. I look on at the view he's so taken with. The woods around their home are beautiful and inviting. I can see why they choose to live here. It looks beautiful as the sun begins to set. The trees are so tall and dense and so green, even at this time of year. I would have expected the leaves to be sparse but instead, the forest is bold and full of life. Beautiful. We're alone in a kind of sitting room I think. There are bookshelves filled with beautiful looking books, of all different kinds, and a red wing-backed leather chair sitting not far from where Jared and I are standing. Around the room, are other chairs of similar likeness and in the centre of the room a really large coffee table made from solid wood, which looks like it's seen many years of service. I move from Jared to look at the bookshelves, wondering if I'll find anything of interest. The books are sorted by genre and then sorted by author and size where possible. I lose myself there for a while before I notice Jared, now studying me, from where he stands. I smile at being caught enjoying one of my favourite things in life. His lips quirk in a small smile, but it doesn't reach his eyes. There's something wrong.

'What's wrong?' I move back toward him. He takes a deep breath and moves to sit in the chair. And still, he doesn't speak. 'Jared?' He looks at me, and I can see the pain in his eyes. 'Jared, please?' He scrubs at his face. Something I was learning he did when he was nervous or unsure.

'My father has been in touch.' His tone makes my heart sink. It's defeated. Oh, fuck.

'Tell me?' He looks into my eyes, and I want to crawl inside myself because I know what's coming. This is about me. This is what Howard meant. I stumble backwards and fall on my ass. He's picking me up before I even realise I've hit the floor. He holds me tight.

'It's okay,' he says, but it isn't.

'Jared, what's happened?' He takes another deep breath as he lifts me up into his arms and squeezes me so tight I think my ribs may pop. He's stalling. I pull away.

'Jared?' I snap so impatiently my own tone shocks me. He wears a pained look that I hate to see in his eyes.

'Do you have to stay? Here I mean?'

*Oh, my God.* I hadn't expected that. My heart breaks right there in front of him. But I steel myself against the pain. And put on my best snarky fuck-you voice. 'No, I don't, I'll get my things.' I make to walk away. But he grabs my arm pulling me into him.

'Devon, shit. I didn't mean it like *that*. Fuckin' hell. Come here.'

I fall into his offered embrace. Desperate for him, and I hold back my sob.

'*We'll* leave together, go elsewhere, the problem is I don't know where yet.' I realise exactly what he's telling me then.

'Jared, why? What has your father said?' *This can't be happening?* I can't be responsible for him leaving his pack. 'Tell me why we have to leave—is it because of me?' He takes a deep breath and sighs.

'As the alpha, he's told me that I either obey his orders or I'll be cast out.' My gasp is answer enough. I have no words. His own son! He's going to cast out his own son. I'm angry. At that moment I want to rip into him, to tell him what I think of him. How dare he treat his own son this way? What kind of father is he? The shitface bastard.

'He'd do that to you? His own son?'

He nods. 'The pack comes first. We can leave together, but we go today. He's only given me until tomorrow night to make the *right* decision before he makes it for me. I'm not sticking around for that.' he spits. Oh shit. My eyes are wide, and I think I forget to blink.

'He knows what I am. Is that why?' Jared shakes his head, but he doesn't answer my question.

'Devon, just think about what I'm asking of you for a minute! I don't want to make you do anything you don't want okay? You need to know that going nomad isn't easy. It will be real fuckin' hard, but we'll be together. Think on that for a while. I'll be right back. I just have a couple of things I need to do.' I nod. I did know. That's what my dad and I had done my whole life. It was really hard, never staying in one place for too long.

He leaves the room, leaving me standing and gaping open-mouthed at the forest outside. How had this day gone from waking in the woods and being so happy, to this, in a matter of hours? I didn't need time to clear my head or think things through, there was only one option, and that was Jared, he had to come first. He either left with me and lost his pack, his station in it, and all he's ever known. Or he let me go.

Decision made. I open the French doors, and without looking back, I leave him.

# chapter EIGHT

## Devon

IT BREAKS MY HEART, BUT I can't allow Jared to leave everything behind. My life has been sheltered from it. I won't be losing anything. I will only gain. But he will be losing a whole way of life just to have me. I can't let him do that, not for me. I'm running blind—the tears so thick and fast I have no way to tell where I'm going. The sobs wrack through me. I'm a mess, but I have to keep going. I need to get distance from him. I briefly prop myself up against a tree. I have no idea how long I've been running, but my chest is hurting so much, it feels like I have a fire inside. I take some heaving breaths and swipe at my face, clearing my eyes for only a second before more tears replace them. I want to run back to Jared and tell him that I've made a huge mistake. I want to run away with him and tell him that all will be okay. But I don't want that for him. It's selfish. I will not let him do that for me. The forest has become dark now, and I'm still no closer to a road. I have no clue of which direction I need to go. I have to get a grip, or I won't be able to change.

I hear voices in the distance. People shouting my name. I listen hard and run in the opposite direction. Crying so hard has hindered any chance of using my sense of smell, so I rely solely on my hearing and sight, which are also at a disadvantage because I haven't managed to rein back the tears. I know they will follow my scent easily, so I know I have to stay well ahead of them until I have the opportunity to jump in a cab or take some other escape route that presents itself.

I stop and listen every so often, the shouts getting further away. I run flat out, my body aching for the change, it's screaming that I can go faster, listen harder, as a wolf. But I don't have time to change now, and I can't afford to leave my clothes behind. Stopping to listen, I finally catch the sound of what could be a road. I climb the branches of an oak tree so I can check on my direction. I stumble and trap my leg between two sharp branches, and manage to cut the palm of my hand while trying to pull my leg free. I have a gash on my leg, and it stings like a bitch. I jump down and make my way toward the road. I tear the bottom of my t-shirt and wrap it around my hand to stem the bleeding. There isn't much I can do about my leg except try and walk it off. Finally, I can see the road through the trees. The relief of finally arriving there overawes me. I limp towards the bush separating me from it, and start to push my way through, but I'm grabbed and pulled through by strong and all too familiar hands.

'Get off me!'

Howard's grip on my shoulders doesn't ease up. He yells for the others to come.

'You told me to go?' I growl out. 'You told me to leave him alone?'

'Not like that. Are you an idiot? Did you think he wouldn't track you down?'

I shake my head, staying where I am, sulking at being caught, and then Jared walks up. He's understandably upset and angry. It radiates from him. Howard walks away and leaves us both alone, and I scowl at his back. I know I'm going to have to explain myself and not sure how to start. Jared doesn't speak at first. He props himself up against a tree just glaring at me. I feel about six inches tall. His face—stony and annoyed, speaks a thousand words.

'It's not what you think,' I start with the lame excuse.

'Oh really, please fucking enlighten me?' he spits with such sarcasm it makes me cringe.

'Jared—' He cuts me off

'Just tell me one thing. Did you ever *really* want to be with me at all?'

I can't speak for a second. Did he believe that?

'Jared, I *do* want to be with you, more than anything, but it's selfish, and I can't let you sacrifice everything for me.' I'm shaking. He doesn't say anything, and the silence drags on. He covers his face with his hands. I'm aching for him to say something, anything. I go to him and take his hands in mine. 'I'm sorry I ran, I just didn't know what else to do, you were going to throw your whole life away.' He grips my hands tighter then, painfully so.

'Isn't that my decision to make?' he growls. 'I've committed myself to you. I can't change that. I can't stop wanting you. I've marked you, and you keep fuckin' running away.' His voice cracks a little.

'You threw me out remember? That wasn't my doing. Don't forget that!' Anger bubbles up inside, and I prod at his chest. 'Don't you dare put that on me, Jared. Yes, I ran just now, but it was for *your* benefit, not mine.' I'm on the verge of screaming. He grabs the hand I'm prodding him with.

'I said I was fuckin' sorry!' he growls, pinning me to the tree. Then his lips are on mine. It isn't a nice kiss. It's a display of his dominance, but I don't submit. I won't be treated like that. I shove at his chest.

'Don't treat me like one of your bitches, Jared. I'm not a part of your pack.' Shoving him aside, I stomp off.

'Fuuuuck,' he shouts, and I hear him coming after me. 'Devon,' he shouts before he catches me and spins me to face him.

'What??' I stomp my feet like a toddler and fold my arms. I look at him, eyebrows raised in question.

'We're not done—' He takes my hand. '—We are at least going to talk about it.'

'Jared, I won't come between you and your family. You're going to be the alpha of your pack. I may be naïve, Jared, but I think that's pretty important.' I carry on walking.

'Devon, stop, just stop fuckin' walking away!' I do. 'Come back to the house with me? Please.' I owe him at least that.

'Okay.' He definitely wasn't expecting me to agree. He stutters a little, but then clearly decides it best not to rock the boat and just takes my hand and leads me with him. He walks us through the forest, with no problem at all, unlike my bungled escape run, and it takes next to no time to get back to the house, proving what a complete idiot I had been. I follow him obediently. We don't speak at all. We bypass everyone, and he takes me straight to his bedroom. It's big. A huge wooden bed takes up one end of the room. There is an en-suite bathroom, and it has its own dressing room. It's painted in black, white, and red. A real bachelor pad—the furniture is really tasteful, though. I don't know exactly what I was expecting, maybe flat pack furniture and beer cans. He catches me checking it out.

'This isn't how I planned to bring you to my room for the first time.' He's fidgety, and it's obvious he doesn't know what to do with himself. I sit on the edge of his bed as he paces in front of me. 'Devon?'

I look everywhere but at him. I'm scared if I look into those green eyes I'll be lost to him, and I'll waiver. I need to stay strong and do this for him. He needs to see that it's for the best.

'Look at me?'

I obey just like that. I can't help it when his voice takes on that tone. I'd do anything he asked of me. 'I won't let you leave me again.'

What do I say? I want him more than my next breath, but I want him to have a life. I don't want him to be cast out and leave all he knows behind, just for me. I'm not worth that. He deserves to have a real life mate, one who can give him children, werewolf children, not mongrels like me. I'd had a really hard time growing up, and I'm only just understanding why. He knows nothing else but pack life, pack law, and pack community. I can't give him any of that. I pull on the DIY bandage and fiddle with it.

'Jared, I'm not right for you,' I say on a hiccup, which turns into a sob. He growls from deep within his chest.

'Tell me how you're not right for me? Explain to me why I marked you the first time we slept together? Explain if you are *not* the one for me, how that happened? Because it doesn't, it *can't,* unless it's meant to be.'

I'm stunned. My mouth moves, but no words come out. I look like an idiot with my mouth gaping. I didn't know any of this. How are we wrong? It doesn't feel wrong. It feels like everything clicks into place when I'm with him. It does feel like it's meant to be. It's outside influences that make me doubt it. It doesn't come from me. It isn't how I feel. He looks at me his eyes pleading, the anger now abated. He looks desperate. Broken. Hurt.

'But I'm a mongrel,' I whisper. For the first time in my life, I feel ashamed of what I am. I'm heartbroken. Jared kneels in front of me. He takes my hands from my face and holds them in his own. Tears roll down my cheeks.

'Don't ever say that again.'

'It's true.'

He shakes his head.

'Who says so? You're not a fuckin' mongrel,' he chastises, quietly but assertively, his voice both loving and calm.

'Your father doesn't want us together, Jared. We can't just ignore that.'

'Devon, he'll come around eventually. He'll have to unless he wants to lose me.'

'And if he doesn't?'

He shrugs his shoulders.

'Then that's his fucking loss.'

My phone begins an incessant buzzing in my bag that has somehow found its way to his room. I ignore it but it doesn't stop and eventually Jared hands my bag to me, and I fish it out to find my dad calling from his cell. *Weird he never uses it.* I look to Jared in apology.

'Go ahead.'

'Dad?'

'Devon. Thank God. I've been calling you for days now.' Shit a brick. I haven't spoken to him since our spat. 'Did your roommate give you the message? I've been worried sick—where are you?'

'Whoa, slow down. I'm fine. I've just been really busy and had a lot to think about, you know? I'm sorry I didn't call you back.' I can hear lots of people in the background and a woman speaking over a tannoy system. It sounds a lot like an airport. 'Are you going on a trip?'

'Err, actually I've just landed. I was so worried, and I couldn't just sit at home. I thought something bad had happened.' Oh, shit on a stick.

'You're *here?*'

Jared's pacing again.

'Yeah, I just landed, and I have a reservation at a hotel not far from where you live.'

'It really isn't necessary, dad. I'm fine. You can get on a flight back home.'

'I didn't travel all this way for nothing, Devon. I at least want to see you—to speak to you face-to-face, about, well, everything.'

'About me being a mongrel?' I snap. I hadn't realised just how angry I still felt with him. But the fact that Jared was pacing before me—making life-changing decisions about something he should never have to do all because of my parents' selfishness just accentuated my anger.

'Devon Hathoway. Don't you dare say that.' I laugh and use as much sarcasm as I can muster.

'Why dad? It's true. I'm just saying it like it is.'

'It is not!'

'You know what, I'm over it. I'll call you tomorrow.' I disconnect the call. Jared gapes at me like I'm some kind of alien. 'What?' I snap, his eyes widen, and he shakes his head.

'Seriously? Your dad has flown half way across the world because he's worried about you.'

'SO?'

'And you don't think maybe you were a little harsh?' That gets my back up.

'Harsh was when he decided he would bring me up in an all-human world. Make me hide who and what I am—making me believe all was normal in my world. And then he ships me off half way across the globe after never allowing me any sort of freedom whatsoever, throws me into a situation where I finally meet someone like me, and then I find out we can't—shouldn't be together! Because of my parents. He lied to me—*that's* harsh!'

I'm ranting. I'm so flipping angry. At my dad, Jared, and at myself. I throw myself onto his bed, pushing my face into his pillow and I scream it out. He strokes my back—it's soothing and just what I need. I relax into his deft hands. Between his father and mine, I've had enough. I'm so tense. I rarely feel like this so soon after a change. His hands go from soothing to firm, as he starts kneading the knots in my shoulders.

'Mmmmm that's good,' I mumble. He chuckles and it makes me tingle inside.

'How about just for tonight we forget about everything? About everyone else? Huh?' I make an attempt at nodding. 'I'll take that as a yes?'

'Mmm hmm,' is about all I'm capable of. His expert hands are working miracles. He removes my t-shirt without me even getting up off of the bed, and he unclasps my bra and works my whole back. I'm sleepy and so relaxed. I feel his lips touch my shoulder blade. They're so soft and warm as they glide up my neck and back down again. He kisses down my spine, the small butterfly-like touches sending shivers right to my core. His hands go to my hips and around to my stomach, where he undoes my pants and wiggles them down my legs, with no help from me. My panties are next—he stops when he gets to them. I think waiting to see if I'll protest. I don't. Obviously.

He takes them down painfully slowly—I think he's offering me a chance to change my mind—either that or he's a complete tease. When his hands go to my butt, and he massages my lower back and ass, it's so sensual, so intimate, that I almost come. Niagara instantly starts flowing. He works on every part of my back, then my arms, followed by those beautiful butterfly kisses. He works my legs one by one and then his fingers are at my core. I'm wet, ridiculously aroused, and he knows it. He groans out as he pushes a finger inside, finding out just how wet I am for him. He leans over and kisses my cheek.

'You okay, baby?'

My reply is breathy and weak. 'Yes.' I'm eager for him, wanting more. He's still fully clothed. He moves away from me but doesn't stop moving his fingers inside me. Teasingly. He lifts my ass, so it's pointing upward, and then I feel his tongue. Deliciously lapping at my clit. Oh, my god, I'm gonna come. Pleasure radiates throughout my whole body. A white-hot heat. I tremble with it, biting my lip so I don't scream out. I don't want everyone hearing me. The orgasm wreaks havoc through my body, sapping me of all energy. He carries on relentlessly, finger fucking me and licking at my clit. I try to pull away only to be held in place. I can't take anymore. I come again, screaming out his name. To hell with everyone hearing me. He releases me then, pulling me backwards onto his lap, and he holds me. I nuzzle into his neck, breathing in his scent. I don't care about anything beyond this room right then. I want to stay here. Forever. He rocks me in his arms. I'm so tired. He lays me down on the bed, covering me with his duvet.

'I'll be right back.'

'Don't leave me,' I plead. And he laughs, shaking his head.

'I'm just going to the fridge. You need some water.' He's right, my mouth is so dry, and I'm so tired I can barely move.

'Hurry back,' I tell him as he kisses my forehead.

'Always.'

We spend the best part of the night talking and really getting to know each other better. I already feel like I've known him my entire life.

'Tell me about pack life?' I ask. Jared smiles at my question as he turns to face me, propping his head on his hand,

'What do you want to know?'

'Everything. How you grew up? What was your life like? Who was your first kiss? I want to know it all,' I tell him honestly.

'My first kiss? Seriously?'

I nod. 'Mmmhmm, all the deets.'

He laughs, and it's such an awesome sound after everything I've put him through tonight.

'Okay, so I'll start at the beginning. I grew up in Ranmore Common. It's a small place in Dorking, Surrey. It's where my family have always lived and worked, and obviously where my dad—the alpha—is based. But our pack spans for miles across the country, and believe it or not, although we are a just a tiny country, we have the strongest, most influential pack in Europe.'

'How is that even a thing? Like how can you gauge it?'

'Well, it's kinda in the genes. Well, at least in the Stone genes, and with each new generation that's born, we mix them with equally strong genes, so each alpha is as strong if not stronger than the last.' My heart sinks a little at his revelation, and he must notice the change.

'And the next generation will be the strongest yet, because their baby mamma is strong and beautiful, not to mention stubborn as fuck.' I giggle and slap his shoulder. He comes back with a poke to my ribcage, making me squeal.

'Okay, okay. I surrender,' I tell him on a giggle. 'Tell me more?'

'Okay. So the pack is well known for being able to, um, to handle ourselves.'

'Meaning?' He looks awkward and tries to kiss me, closing the subject down. But like he said, I'm stubborn as fuck. I peck his lips and settle back down for the rest of his story. 'Carry on?'

He huffs out a breath and rolls his eyes at me. 'Baby, my dick is hard, and he's a needy fucker when it comes to his pussy.'

I pout. I really want to hear the rest of this story, but I can't disappoint his 'needy dick' especially after he ate out at Niagara Falls. 'Okay, so hold that thought because I want to hear the rest, but I have a question for Mr needy dick.'

'Shoot.'

'Where does he wanna go?'

'Mouth or pussy?' he asks wagging his eyebrows at me. I blush, stupidly because he talks like that, I should know by now. So I just nod.

'Say it?'

'What?' I ask, knowing damn well what he wants me to say,

'Mouth or pussy.'

I purse my lips and roll my eyes,

'Oh, baby, don't roll your eyes at me 'cause I'll have to punish you for it,' he says grabbing my hands and stretching them up above my head, before biting down on my neck, leaving his mark. I squirm under him as he moves to nip along my shoulder and down to my nipple.

'Say it!' he demands again. When I don't, he bites my nipple making me moan—some punishment. I'll keep quiet all night at this rate. He flips me so quick I don't see it coming, and he slaps my ass hard. And it stings like a bitch. 'SAY IT!' he tells me again. This time his voice holds the tone I'm certain he uses when he wants things done. That alpha tone that says 'don't fuck with me' and it works. Not only do I want to say it but my vagina starts to scream, 'I volunteer as a tribute.'

'What do you want? Mouth or pussy?' I ask almost breathlessly. He strokes my ass and lays on top of me, spreading my legs apart with his knees,

'I always want your pussy, baby, but maybe I'd like your mouth first.' He lifts my ass off the bed and plunges balls deep inside of me. I'm not expecting it, but I'm more than ready for him. I guess he can't wait. He fucks me hard and fast like he's been starved of sex. God, I will never tire of this. Sex with Jared isn't like anything else. Nothing compares, not even close. Just his kiss alone has me gasping and panting like an addict for more. He's just that good.

*Devon*

AFTER A SHOWER, HE COMES back to bed, where I'm still sprawled on my stomach.

'Baby you look tired.'

'Oh no, big guy. Not so fast. I want that bedtime story.'

'Like I said, stubborn as fuck!' He grins. 'Okay, where was I?'

'We were talking about how you gauge the pack being the best.'

He laughs

'I never said the best. I said the strongest.'

'To-mate-toe, to-mart-toe,' I say, shrugging my shoulders.

'Okay, So we are just well known for handling our business, and for not tolerating bullshit.'

'So people are scared of you? Or you're just amazing businessmen?'

'Both.' He grins. 'Obviously.'

'So what business is the pack in?'

'That's a story for another day, but I will tell you that we have fingers in lots of pies and when we do something it's never half-assed. My dad will only agree to take on a job if he knows with a hundred percent certainty that whoever is doing the job can do it well.' I accept that he doesn't want to say much more on that subject, and I understand why. I'm not a part of the pack, so I'm not in a need-to-know position. I move on.

'What business do you want to be in when you finish here?'

'I want to set up an engineering company when I'm done here.'

'Wont that be a little hard if you are the alpha?' He nods his head

'Well, I didn't expect to be the alpha anytime soon. Anyway, the way things have been going I'm not even sure what's gonna happen.'

My heart plummets once again and fills with guilt. If it weren't for me, none of this would be happening, and I feel so bad.

'Baby, don't do that,' he says, stroking my face. 'I've told you, with you is where I want to be, pack or no pack. I chose you. So your stubborn ass needs to accept that as a done deal, besides, my dick and his needs where your pussy is concerned, is a major fucking addiction so… stop with the guilty face,' I giggle, but my heart still feels heavy.

'I can put it simpler for you, my dick plus your pussy equals one happy Jared. There, see? I'm good with the math,' he says, winking. 'My dick *minus* your pussy, equals one majorly unhappy motherfucker, with a serious withdrawal problem. Shall I continue or do you get the picture,' he asks with a deadpan look on his face. 'Now it's my turn to ask a question. Where are you originally from?'

'Well I was apparently born near the blue mountains in Oregon, but I don't remember them. I've moved so many times I've lost count. I guess I now know why. He said the kitsunes would have killed us and his pack wouldn't accept me,' I tell him, shrugging my shoulders as I fight back the tears. 'So we moved every couple of months—at least that's how it felt. I still managed to graduate high school though—I just didn't make friends. I tried when I was really little, but I just didn't fit anywhere, and then when I learnt to adjust and mingle, I didn't bother with friends because we would only move again anyway.'

'Fuck that must have been hard?'

I nod.

'I can't imagine how your dad felt too.'

I feel guilty and vow to check in with my dad first thing.

Morning comes around all too soon. I wake to the gorgeous sight of Jared sleeping beside me, on his front, one arm above his head and the other stretched out across my midriff. I watch his back muscles twitch and contract. Not wanting to break the moment, I stay just like that. I don't want to face the world and start a new day, but nature calls and I have to move. I lift his hand slowly, so I don't wake him. I move from under him and climb off the bed as delicately as I can. Jared's eyes fly open, and he sits up as quick as a snap.

'I'm just going to use the bathroom,' I whisper. 'Go back to sleep. I'll be right back, I promise.'

''kay' his sleepy voice is sweet and sexy all at once. He lies back down and watches me walk naked to the bathroom. I hurry, wanting to get back to him as quickly as possible. Checking myself out in the oversized mirror, I push my fingers through my hair and tidy myself up a little. I find Jared propped on his elbow, his head in his hand, as he watches me saunter back to his bed.

'This is how I want to wake up every day.' He reaches for my hand and pulls me on top of him. Giggling, I straddle him, kissing him, morning breath be damned. His hands find my ass as his arms wrap around me. I want this too, every day, waking to the sight of him. I move to the side of him, propping myself up just as he had. He mirrors me, his head in his hand. 'You okay?' He isn't sure, I can tell.

'I'm good, you?' I smile, and he instantly relaxes.

'I'm great.' He grins at me, his bare chest a tease to my eyes. And his arms. Oh those arms. His muscles twitch as he holds himself up. I could die happy right now with this arm porn alone. I reach out and fist his cock. He's already semi hard. I move closer to him and get into a rhythm. He halts my movements, though, pushing me onto my back, and kissing me. It begins slow and tender, his tongue stroking mine, before becoming desperate and rough with each stroke.

'Only one place I wanna be right now, and that's inside you.'

Well, who the hell can argue with that? He slides a finger into me easily—I'm gushing at his mere words. He groans as he adds another. I'm lost to him, and we haven't even got to the good part yet.

'So fucking ready for me.'

I nod, I'm always ready for him.

It's lunchtime before we make any attempt at getting out of bed. Sheer hunger, driving us. We both have huge appetites and missing breakfast is not a normal part of either of our days. But the need to be together, alone, outweighed it all.

Brad had come hammering on the bedroom door,

'Sorry to interrupt your sex fest but lunch is ready and since we all know what you were doing at breakfast...' he sniggers like a teenager at his own joke. Making me snicker.

'Ready to eat?' Jared asks. Am I ever.

'I'm starving.'

We get ready. It takes us longer than it should have because we stop at every given opportunity to kiss and put our hands on each other. I find it just as sexy putting clothes on Jared as I do taking them off. Before we leave his room he picks me up, my legs instinctively wrapping around his waist, and he kisses me hard. Reaffirming everything I feel for him. Jared leads me by the hand to the kitchen, and we walk in to a round of applause. I turn pink with embarrassment. Jared just laughs it off and takes a bow. I cannot believe he just did that.

'We wondered if you were ever gonna leave your bed,' Brad chimes in. Jared smacks him on the back of the head, as he leads me to sit at the table.

'Anything I need to know about?' Jared asks of everyone at the table,

'Nada,' Brad answers. 'Nothing to report.'

'Good, what's cooking?'

It smells so good.

'We have, mashed potatoes, roasts, and rabbit stew.' Mmmmm. Everyone helps themselves from the pot. There is crusty bread and dumplings too. Jared serves me up a bowl before himself. I'm grateful. I'm not comfortable enough yet to help myself.

Everyone is so easy to get along with, and the conversation flows effortlessly. Howard is absent which helps. And I'm still yet to meet Kristen properly. I've just finished my bowl of stew when she walks in. Fan-fucking-tastic. Jared puts his hand in mine. She's dressed in clothes she's clearly worn to go out the night before, and she reeks of sex. Her barely-there skirt leaves nothing to the imagination, and her tits are un-tastefully bursting out of her top. She leans in, right between Jared and me, and snatches up a piece of bread, making damn sure her cleavage is all he can see.

'Hey, guys have I missed much?' No one says a word. It's so uncomfortable. You could cut the tension with a knife. Then she puts her hand on Jared's shoulder and squeezes.

'Nothing new, Kris, all's good in the world,' Brad pipes in cheerfully. Trying and failing to lighten the tension.

Kristen strokes Jared's hair before he shrugs her off, and I have to choke back a snarl. Which comes out like a grumble. She hears it. Of course. Everyone does.

'Oh, hey, I didn't notice you there.' Bitch. Jared is squeezing my hand. And keeping me seated. I want to wipe the stupid grin off her face. Jared leans over and kisses me, lingering on my lips, his hand at my cheek. Letting me know I have nothing to worry about. When I open my eyes, everyone is looking my way, and I just catch a glimpse of Kristen's back as she leaves the room. I feel uncomfortable again— like I'm intruding. I stand, and Jared stands beside me, his face pained and unsure.

'I'm just going to get my stuff together. I'll be right back.' I smile and make my way up the stairs. I'm half hoping I won't see Kristen, yet a bigger, bad-tempered part of me really hopes I'll bump into her. You know that saying 'be careful what you wish for'? Kristen is standing right outside Jared's bedroom door. I almost falter in my step, but I'll be damned if I'll let her best me. I walk directly to her and make to open the door, ignoring her existence. As I go to close the door, she sticks her foot in it and pushes her way in, uninvited. I bare my teeth and snarl. It's new to me. It's something I've always had to dial back so it's not as menacing as I'd like.

'Bitch, please! You sound like a lost puppy. Oh wait, you *are* lost, you've wandered onto *my* turf.' I'm not sure who attacks first. But I swing my fist and knock her on her ass. Then I'm jumping on top of her, banging her head against the floor, gripping her hair tight as I do. She swings a right hook, splitting my lip and claws at my face before clinging to a handful of my hair. But I have the upper hand. I punch her over and over in the face until I'm dragged off. Jared holds me by the arms as Brad shoves Kristen back and tries to remove her from the room. I struggle against him but have no chance at all of getting away.

'Let me go!' I yell, but his grip only gets tighter.

'This isn't over, bitch,' she screams at me. Oh, I'm finishing this right now! I fly for her again, but Jared holds fast, pulling me against his chest. I'm panting hard, adrenaline coursing through my veins. I want to rip her head off, but he holds me tight, with my arms pinned behind me. I realise my legs are free, so I take full advantage of that. I kick out, using Jared's strength to my benefit. I catch the back of her head with my foot and manage to knock Brad off balance at the same time.

'Anytime!' I scream back. Kristen struggles against Brad but gets nowhere. She's screeching as the rest of the household come hurtling toward us. Jared pulls me into him and closes the door behind us. He lets me go, and I run at the door trying to get back at her. He plants himself in the way but doesn't speak—just watches as I pace up and down. I'm so fucking angry. I don't think there is even a word to express how angry I am. Who does she think she is? Jared stops my pacing and wraps his arms around me.

'Are you hurt?' I shake my head against his chest. He lifts my chin and wipes the blood from my lip, then puts his thumb to his mouth and licks it off as his brows lift in question. 'You sure?'

'I'm fine, just very pissed.'

'I'm sorry, baby.'

'Have you screwed her?' His jaw hits the floor. He doesn't answer. Just looks at me, the discomfort all over his face. Fucking fabulous.

# chapter TEN

## Devon

'LL TAKE THAT AS A yes,' I choke out. Pain. In my chest. My heart. Even the words feel painful as I speak them. I push him away from me and stomp around the room collecting my stuff—violently stuffing things into my bag. I need to get away from here right now.

'Devon,' he pleads. 'You can't punish me for something I did before I met you.'

'You *lied* to me. You told me you didn't see her. You told me you hadn't slept with her.' I scream in his face. I want to punch it.

'No, Devon. I *never* lied to you.' He snatches the bag from my hands and stands in front of the door. 'I've never lied to you. You asked me if I'd marked her, I said *no*. I told you I don't see her because I *don't*!' He speaks in an eerily calm voice, but I'm way too mad to realise he's angry too.

'Oh, but you saw enough of her to fuck her?' He throws my bag across the room and grabs my arms, almost shaking me as he does.

'Okay, how about we go over *your* sexual history while we're here, see just how many mistakes *you've* made huh?'

I slap his face. He glares back as anger flashes clear in his eyes, but I'm not done.

'*You* made me believe there was nothing between you, other than your father's wishes. *You've* let me come here on *her* fucking turf and sleep with *her* man.'

'I was never *hers* and never fucking will be.'

'So what was it, Jared? A means to an end? A fuck buddy until something better came along? Is that my fate too? When you get bored, you'll move on, and let me stick around long enough to see it?' He cringes, hiding his face in his hands as he moves to sit on the bed.

'This is so fucked up. How did we even get here? Kristen is a first-class bitch and trouble is what she does best. Why are you letting her do this?'

'That isn't what this is about Jared, and you know it.'

'What do you want me to say, Devon, huh?' He looks broken. 'I'm *sorry* I fucked her, *once,* a long time ago. I'm sorry I didn't tell you about it, but *fucking hell*, I didn't think you'd want to hear it. *I* sure as fuck wouldn't. And it's not something you just drop into a conversation.' He stands now and halts my pacing. 'Devon, listen to me.' He holds my hands and lifts my chin until our eyes meet. 'I want *you, only* you. I don't want anyone else, *especially* Kristen.' But his words don't penetrate because I've already put up my barriers.

'Jared, this is just another reason why we shouldn't be together. Your dad wants *her*. It's for the best that we just call it quits now.' I'm so emotionally spent that I feel numb. My feelings for him are in a compartment, and I've built a wall around them. I have to otherwise this is going to tear me wide open. Not an option.

'You can walk away just like that?' he asks. He's angry and hurting, but I don't answer. 'You're it for me—you know that right?'

How can I know that? How can I trust that that's the truth? I can't get caught up in any more emotion. I can't risk it, so I just look through him. He laughs, but it's humourless. Bitter. 'But if you don't feel the same, I can't fucking make you.' He leaves the room, slamming the door behind him.

## *Jared*

As I walk away, I feel like half a man. My hands are shaking, and my throat feels like it's closing up, making it harder to breath. All I can do is swallow, trying like fuck to clear the lump in it. I walk right out through the kitchen, ignoring everyone. I can still feel the tension in the room. I want to run. I start stripping my top and unbuttoning my jeans as I stalk to the tree line. I drop my jeans in a heap and go with the change. It takes me immediately, and I let the wolf take over. Not caring. I just want the escape. The thrill, the freedom—I crave it. And right now, in this frame of mind, it's the best thing for me. I run flat out. I take no time to adjust after the pain of the change. I just take off the second my paws hit the ground. I can hear the rabbits scurrying desperate to get away, but I have no interest. The ground cracks and breaks under me as I rip a path through the forest floor. I run until there are no more trees then I circle back, not slowing down at all.

# *Devon*

As Jared leaves, I collapse in a heap against the door and let my emotions rip. I cry until I have nothing left. Literally. There are no more tears, no sound. Just pain.

It is time to get off this emotional rollercoaster. I pull myself together and dig around in my bag for my phone. It's still switched off. Booting it up I think about what I want to say. It beeps immediately with messages, but I ignore them all. Scrolling to Jared's name I text him in desperation.

I'm so sorry. I love you. Please come back to me.

He doesn't reply. I wash my face in the bathroom, and I wait. Maybe he isn't going to reply. Maybe he's done with me this time? About an hour passes, and I decide I'm not getting a reply, so I have to leave. I'm gathering my bag when the door flies open, and Jared walks in like a man on a mission, scooping me up in his arms, his lips find mine in an unforgiving kiss. When he pulls back, he's shaking, and his eyes are glazed with tears.

'I'm so sorry, Jared.'

'I won't lose you.'

His lips crush mine so hard it hurts. His hand fists in my hair as he drops us on the bed. There's no romance. It's just raw, aggressive passion driving him. He's taking ownership, marking his territory, and reaffirming it. I understand. I want that just as much. I want to stake my claim. He's inside of me quickly-so quick we haven't even undressed properly. As he pushes himself inside me, balls deep, I bite down on his shoulder to stop my scream. I wasn't quite ready for him, but it feels so right as he thrusts into me. It's almost savage, the sense of urgency clear. He isn't doing this for my pleasure or his own. He's satisfying a need. A need we both feel. The need to be claimed. This time, I smell his marking scent—so strong it seems to fill my every fibre. Such a beautiful, masculine scent, like nothing I could even compare it too. I don't know how I missed it the first time. Holding his weight above me with our eyes locked he comes with a roar so loud I'm sure the whole house hears. It's so intense. He kisses me then, so soft and tenderly, a complete contrast to what has just gone down between us.

Everything I feel for him is echoed in the way he kisses me, and the look in his eyes. If there was any doubt that he was mine before. It's quite clear to me now. He is *mine*. All of him.

# *Jared*

We fall asleep after I fucked her senseless twice more. Brad knocking on the door wakes me up. Luckily for him, Devon doesn't wake, even when I detangle our bodies. I want to go out to Brad because I don't want him seeing Devon like this. Only I see that. *Mine*. Pulling my jeans on, I open the door. He grins as I blink the sleep from my eyes, pushing a hand through my hair. I need a fucking haircut and soon.

'Hey?' he greets with a shit-eating grin on his face.

'Sup?' I question since he's knocking on my door.

'Nothing, man, just wanted to check in an' shit.'

'Huh? What the fuck do you want?' He woke me, and he just wanted to 'check in an' shit?' Seriously?

'About earlier man, Kristen is downstairs acting like that shit never went down, and I just wanted to know how you wanna proceed with that? Because although that shit was hot! Like off the fucking charts HOT, I'm guessing you don't want a repeat? Unless you do? Then I'm all over setting that shit up,' he said, his grin getting even wider.

'You guessed right first time, dipshit.' I shove him playfully. 'Gimme a minute. I'll sort it.'

'Okay, boss man,' he says walking down the hall. Fucking boss man. I'll kick him in the ass next time he says that shit. I close the door to find Devon sitting up in bed, looking all mussed with that just fucked and sated look. It makes my stomach flutter and my dick stand to attention.

'Hey, boss man.' She smirks.

'Yeah that's right, remember that,' I tease, pushing her down and tickling her until she's out of breath from laughing so hard. It's so testing having my hands on her body without mounting her like a horny fuckin' kid. That's all I want to do. All the fucking time. I get serious though because we needed to talk this shit through. So I sit on the bed and pull her into my lap.

'Look, baby, we need to chat about—'

'Kristen. Yeah, I gathered.' I flatten my lips and nod. Please let this go fuckin' smoothly.

'Promise me, Devon, that you won't fly off the handle? You gonna listen to me?' She crosses over her heart with her finger and smiles up at me. Cute as fuck. Now or never. 'Okay, so I told you about the pack and where we come from yeah?'

'Yep.'

'So this place.' I gestured around me. 'Has been in the pack since before I was born, and it's used for everyone of university age. We all attend here. We don't go anywhere else.'

'Why?' she asks genuinely interested.

'Pack territory, and it's close to home.'

She frowns now.

'I get that, but what if you wanted to go somewhere else? Like to live?'

'Well, nomads do that. They float around from place to place but don't affiliate with a pack. Me, I'm affiliated, so if I were to go to Uni elsewhere, out of our territory, I'd be handed my ass or worse, for being on someone else's turf.'

'This is so confusing.'

'Okay, lemme get to the point. All of us were sent from our homes in Surrey to come here for however long our degrees take.' She's still listening intently, but I haven't gotten to the crux of the matter yet. And I'm hoping like fuck she sticks around to hear it all. 'So we have a choice to either come here and study or stay home and get jobs within the local community. I want to get my degree and then earn a living with my own business like I told you.' She nods and gives me the odd, 'mmm hmm.' Okay, so far so good. Here goes.

'We *all* have to live here, together.' I'm cringing inside waiting for her to blow. But she doesn't. Instead, she just sits there. Not saying a word. I try to gauge her mood. Can't. Shit. Then she stands.

'Just need a sec, okay?' She beats feet to the bathroom, still gloriously naked. I get up to follow, but she closes the door. FUCK. I hear her bang about a minute and then she growls out a noise. Frustration? Then the door opens, and she has her poker face on again. No sign of emotion. Nothing. Double fuck.

'Carry on,' she says deadpan. I'm about to, but I bite my tongue. I need to tread carefully here. Really fuckin' carefully.

'Remember you promised you would listen?'

She clenches that beautiful jaw and nods as she climbs back into my bed, pulling the covers up to her chin. I could stop this right now and just fuck her back to contentment. I'm a coward when it comes to upsetting her. But I push on.

'You know I'm willing to go anywhere with you?'

'Yes Jared, but you can't leave everything else—'

'Devon, don't get all worked up over that again. I'll see what my father says, but if he doesn't agree then I have no other option—'

'But—'

'Devon, listen. It's irrelevant right now. What I'm trying to explain is that I can't just send Kristen away.' Her face is still void of emotion. Her only tell that she is pissed is the slight tick in her jaw as she clamps her teeth down tight. I try for a handhold. No response, so I just grip hers in mine.

'Okay, well, I guess I won't be staying over anymore then.' She half smiles, half curls her lip. Great. Fan-fuckin-tastic. No way am I not having my female with me. NO WAY.

'Fuck no, that's not gonna work for me. I want you here with me.'

'Well I'm not sharing air with *her*, so while she's here, I'll be staying in my room.' You have got to be shitting me. Now I'm pissed. There's just no reasoning with this female. I clench my jaw tight so I don't snap, and take a breath in through my nose and count, one... two ... three... while I pace in front of her. At ten, I feel a bit better. This female will be the end of me, I swear.

'Listen—' That's as far as I get. She's on her feet and in my face like she's about to gimme a beat down. If she wasn't snarling in my face, I could appreciate her gorgeous body an inch from mine.

'No, *you* listen, Jared. I'm not going to be that girl. I won't do it. As much as I want to punch her right now, look at it from her point of view?' I had, and I felt bad, but she doesn't know Kristen like I do. She's a conniving scheming bitch.

'Kristen couldn't give a flying fuck about me, Devon. She never wanted me. She wanted status in the pack. So don't feel fuckin' sorry for her like you've come in here and stole her man. It was never like that. She knew where I stood way before you came on the scene, but she stuck with it because of where it would get her.'

'So *you're* telling *me* she hasn't got *feelings* for you?' Would she ever let this fucking go? I snarl in frustration, turn and punch the wall my guts burning up inside. I'm so fuckin' angry. Why won't she just listen?

'NO! ALL SHE CARES ABOUT IS THE ALPHA-FUCKING-FEMALE STATUS!' I snarl back in her face—the sound reverberates around the room. Devon sits back down, covering herself, her lips in a pout, which looks damn sexy, and goes some way to calming my temper. I want to fuck the angry right out of her.

'That make you feel better?' She motions to the hole in the drywall. I don't answer. It didn't, and she knows it. 'So, she's power hungry?' I nod. I don't want to snap again, so I keep quiet. 'And she has no feelings for you whatsoever?' The way she says it makes it quite clear she doesn't believe that for a fuckin minute. I sigh, frustrated with this whole thing,

'Nope.' A one-word answer because I'm pissed the fuck off.

'Okay.' I'm stunned. What the fuck? Did she just concede? Fuck yeah. Progress.

'Okay, what?' I'm sceptical.

'Okay. I'm not convinced, but okay.' Fuck me she did, she just conceded. Score to Jared. If I could high five myself, I fucking would.

'So you'll stay?' She gets up and heads to the bathroom. Naked. Throwing me a sultry look over her shoulder.

'I didn't say that,' she says swaying her hips in a come-hither-and-fuck-me fashion. I'm up and through that door like a starved man. I kick my jeans off as I push her up against the shower tiles, hands above her head and kick her feet apart. I wind her hair in a twist and pull her head back, exposing her neck to me. I bite down leaving my mark on her skin. I lap at her, curling my tongue as I work my way around her neck and shoulders, before twisting her head and taking her mouth with mine. I will get my way, and this is how I'll get it. My free hand roams from her tits to her stomach, hips, and thighs, and she moans as I brush against her clit. I press ever so lightly there and feel her shudder. No. Not yet. Smiling to myself as she squeaks in protest. I'll teach her to fucking tease me.

'Jared,' she pleads. I take her mouth again and bend at the knees, pushing my dick under her ass to rest against her slick pussy. All the while unrelentingly fucking her mouth with my tongue. I stimulate her clit with my dick over and over again. She's making little mewling noises, desperate for me to bring her to climax. But I don't. I slide inside her, and she groans in relief. I pull right back and pull her ass out further away from the wall. Now she's bent at the waist, ass in the air and hands holding her up against the wall. Fucking beautiful. *Mine.* Using her hips as an anchor, I sink in deep till my balls hit her clit. I slam in again and again, but as I feel her walls start to strangle my dick I pull all the way out.

'Jared!' she shrieks like I've slapped her. I chuckle. This is too easy. Any minute now.

'Jared... Please...'

'What do you need, baby?' I know full well what she wants.

'Fuck me damn it!' So fucking sexy. *Mine.*

I ram myself in to the hilt again, and she quivers under my hands. Pulling out again she makes that mewling sound, and I almost cave. I push back so slowly it nearly kills me.

'You gonna stay with me, baby?' I ask just as I slide back out. This is torture.

'Yes…. Yes. God, I'll stay. Please, Jared….' I fuck her hard and have her crying out my name until she can barely stand. Hook. Line. Sinker. Mine.

I carry her back to bed and lay with her in my arms, a smile firmly on my face.

A knock at the door a while later has me up and dressed again. Howard stands on the other side this time.

'Had a call from your dad. He said he'll be coming up the day after tomorrow. He has some business he needs to settle first. He tried to ring you, but I guess he couldn't get you on the phone.' Huh. Strange. Two day's grace. Guess he's waiting me out.

'Okay thanks, man, 'ppreciate that.' Howard nods in his sullen way before he turns to leave. But stops and looks back to me.

'You coming down for dinner?'

'Yeah, we will do, what time is it?'

He checks his watch

'Five. Imogen said should be ready in about an hour. Kristen isn't in. She headed out about a half hour ago.'

'Probably for the best.'

He agrees and leaves. I sit on the edge of the bed watching Devon sleep. Each breath she takes makes her chest rise and fall, meaning her tits are constantly on the move. Stunning. I watch as her dark nipples, soft from the warmth, rise and fall just slightly with each intake and exhale. I could watch her all day. I can see her heart beat at the pulse in her throat. And her dreams behind the flicker of her eyelids. When she sleeps her fingers twitch like she's playing an invisible instrument, and her full lips—swollen from my kisses—make a pout. I want to kiss her again as my eyes fall on the mark I've left. My mark. And I'll put them all over her body.

# chapter ELEVEN

*Devon*

I WAKE TO MY PHONE buzzing on the carpet, but I don't want to move.
'Devon, it's your dad,' Jared says in a worried tone.

'Shit, I completely forgot to call him back.' With everything else, it was the last thing on my mind. I had cut my dad off and hadn't spoken to him since. I threw myself back on the pillow. Jared passed me my phone just as it started to ring again.

'Hey, dad, I'm—'

'Are you okay?'

I assure him I'm fine and nothing bad had happened to me since he'd called the day before. 'Don't you dare do that again, young lady,' he scolds. 'I've been worried sick by your thoughtlessness.' Jared gestures for me to calm down and take it on the chin. I blow out a deep breath and bite my tongue, allowing my father to rant. 'Where are you now. I want to see you.'

'Well, I'm busy just now, Dad, can we make it a little later on?'

'No, we cannot, Devon. I expect you to meet me within the hour. There's a small Italian restaurant not far from my hotel.' He went on, giving me all the details, and I reluctantly agreed to meet him there. I showered quickly and started to get my hair sorted. Jared came in and put his arms around my waist, kissing me before he stripped to get in the shower.

'Will you come back here afterwards?' he asks as I watch him wash. God, he is so hot.

'If you want me too.' I smile.

'Yeah, I do. I don't want to be away from you any longer than I have to,' he tells me. I think about that. I didn't really want to leave him either. Maybe it was time for Jared to meet my dad?

'Come with me?' I ask. He steps out of the shower with a dubious look on his face.

'Uuh, you think that's a good idea?'

'Why not?' I can't see why taking Jared would be a problem, after all, he's accepted me as I am, and wants to be with me regardless. My father would have to accept him too.

'Well, the fact I've marked his *only* daughter and haven't even met him could cause a problem. I doubt he'll like that very much.' I don't see the big deal, but clearly, in Jared's eyes, it is a big deal.

'It's like getting married without asking your father's consent. It's huge, and as soon as he gets a whiff of you he's gonna know, so I guess the question is, do you think he'll deal better if I'm there? Or would it be better if I'm not?'

I giggle. 'Are you scared of my dad?' I tease.

He doesn't laugh. Instead, he gets real serious. 'I'm not scared of much, Devon, and I can handle your father. I just don't want to complicate things for you—for us, but if you want me there, I'll be there.' He stands naked in front of me, towel drying his hair. I can only stare. His muscles twitch and tense. I put my hands around his waist and squeeze his ass, making him laugh. He cups my face in his hands and kisses me. It deepens quickly, and as he lifts me up onto the vanity, my legs go around his waist. My hands are wandering, and I grip his cock. He steps back from me then, chuckling and taking my hand away.

'Whoa. If I'm gonna meet your father, I'm not gonna go in there like a cocky kid who's just fucked his baby girl. I want to be a bit more respectful than that.' He kisses me, placating me. I stick out my bottom lip in protest, and he latches onto it, laughing.

'Speaking of marks…' I point to the huge hickey at the juncture of my neck and shoulder with a what-the-hell-were-you-thinking look on my face. Jared's grin just gets bigger like he's proud. He kisses the mark then meets my eyes in the mirror,

'Mine,' he says before heading off to get dressed. He makes my stomach flutter so hard when he acts like that, all dominant and caveman-ish. We finish getting ready together. He takes his time choosing what he's going to make his first impression in even though he assures me that no matter what he wears or says, all my dad will notice is the fact Jared has marked me. He says nothing else will register. If that's the case, then I'm hoping dad won't react too badly at Jared being there.

After bailing on the rest of the guys, Jared drives us to the restaurant. He parks in the lot and takes a deep breath.

'The calm before the storm?' I ask he rolls his eyes my way.

'I'm really nervous actually. I've never felt like this before.'

I kiss him, just a peck on the lips, to reassure him. 'You'll do great.'

'I just hope he likes me.' He grips the steering wheel with both hands and takes another long inhale. 'Okay, let's do this.' He taps the wheel.

Jared, like a proper gentleman, comes around the car and helps me out. He laces his fingers in mine, and we walk into the restaurant together. I spot my dad towards the back and give him a wave as we walk over. My dad is red in the face and looks like he may breathe fire. Jared's step falters a little, but he holds his head high and keeps walking. Squeezing my hand slightly, he whispers, 'I told you, he looks really fuckin angry.'

My dad is mad, really *really* mad. He stands as we get to the table. I lean in to kiss his cheek, but he isn't looking at me. No, he's glaring at Jared. In an I'm-gonna-kill-you-any-second-now kind of way. Awkward.

'Jared, this is my dad. Dad, this is Jared, who I've told you about.'

'Apparently not everything,' he grits out through clenched teeth. Jared nods to my dad.

'Mr Hathoway.' He doesn't offer his hand, which is probably for the best since I want him to keep it attached to his arm. Jared pulls the seat out for me, and I sit, hoping that we can all sit around the table like adults. As Jared sits beside me, I'm looking at my dad, but he doesn't take his eyes off Jared. I feel so uncomfortable, and I squirm in my seat. Jared thankfully doesn't stare back—and being a very dominant wolf, I know that must be really hard for him. But instead, he looks at me with affection and puts his hand on my thigh. I'm not sure if that's a good or bad move, but I appreciate it.

'So,' I squeak out, 'I'm starved, shall we have a look at the menu?' They're large leather-bound booklets, and for a moment Jared and I hide behind them, Jared mouthing to me, 'I told you.' He raises his eyebrows as much to ask 'what do you want me to do now?'

I mouth back, 'You're doing great, I love you.' His face says it all—he's so nervous. I laugh and snort a little, trying to hold it in, which in turn makes him smile.

'Are we ready to order?' the waitress asks eyeing Jared appreciatively. I order for my dad because he seems to have lost the ability to speak. I rush and order myself a chicken linguine. It is the first thing on the list. And then I look to Jared to get his order. Dad is still glaring, and he's looking from Jared to me and back again. I guess that's an improvement, if only slightly. Jared offers to go to the bar, asking what my dad wants to drink. He gets a mumbled answer of white wine. And he leaves. My dad turns on me immediately.

'Jesus Christ, Devon! I didn't even think you were—' he blows air out through his nostrils as he clenches his jaw '—well, active!' I look everywhere but at him. This is not a conversation I want to have with my dad. Jeez. I want the ground to open up and swallow me. 'He's *marked* you!' It comes out like a whisper-sob. I cover my face with my hands. *Please make this stop!* 'Do you have any idea what that means for you? Have you even thought any of this through? Did he discuss it with you first?' No, it was a surprise to us both. But I wasn't going to tell my dad that.

'You've only been here for three weeks!' I take a deep breath, trying to fathom an answer when Jared places a long island iced tea on the table in front of me. He gives my shoulder a reassuring squeeze.

'May I?' he asks me. I nod. I'd rather poke my eyes out and cut my own ears off than continue this conversation. Go for your life. I had no clue what to say anyway.

'Fill your boots,' I tell him, my face beet red and my hands shaking. He takes a couple of breaths calming his nerves, and then he looks my dad straight in the eyes. My dad shifts a little in his seat. Until that moment, Jared has not asserted his dominance at all, keeping his eyes low out of respect for my father. Now. It is obvious. Almost palpable in the air. I feel a little sad at seeing my dad squirm under Jared's authoritative stare. But Jared is respectful and makes my heart melt even more.

'I'm sorry you had to find out like this. I meant no disrespect to you.'

My dad clears his throat and cracks his neck, clearly nervous at the change in Jared.

'I *have* marked your daughter, but Devon is completely able to make up her own mind about me, and I would never take that from her.'

My father shifts again in his seat. He doesn't look Jared in the eye as he speaks,

'Well you say that now, but—' Jared cuts him off,

'There is no but, Mr Hathoway. Devon is her own person, and she is free to choose her path, with or without me. I would never force her.'

'But, if she left—'

'It would kill me, yes, but I want her to be with me of her own volition, never because I have forced her will.'

'Do I have your word on that?'

'*Dad!*' Jesus Christ. 'I'm right here?'

'You have my word, Mr Hathoway.' If my dad were a bird, he would preen his feathers at that moment. He seems to straighten up and have an air of confidence he hadn't had only moments before. Jared squeezes my hand. I have no clue what they are talking about really. Jared has never spoken of forcing me to stay with him. But I put that away for a later conversation. Right now we need to move past this. My dad seems satisfied with Jared's answer. He lifts the bottle Jared has placed on the table and begins filling his glass. He looks over at my glass, which Jared has brought for me. It is a stemmed glass with lemon, and an umbrella protruding from the top.

'What on earth is that?' he asks me directly.

'Um, huh, it's a cocktail.' Dad doesn't say anything, just looked at me disapprovingly. Jared widens his eyes in apology. He wasn't to know dad still likes to treat me as a child. Which is why he is having such a hard time dealing with Jared. Our food comes. Dad is on his third wine, Jared his second lager shandy, and my dad has even ordered me a second cocktail. Things are definitely starting to relax. Then dad pipes up with the questions again,

'So, how do you feel knowing Devon has a kitsune mother?'

I almost choke on my mouthful. But Jared doesn't flinch.

'If you're asking if it changes how I feel about Devon? It doesn't,' he says flatly. Then my dad pipes up again, clearly with an alcohol-fuelled confidence.

'Does it not bother you at all? What about your pack?'

'I won't lie to you Mr Hathoway. I was surprised when Devon told me, and I'm not going to tell you that it didn't upset me because it did. But when it sank in, it didn't matter. I couldn't walk away. Who says that we can't be together anyway? I love her, and I think it's safe to say that she feels the same way about me?' He looks to me then and squeezes my hand. I have a huge smile on my face. My dad is trying his best to work Jared out. I can see the cogs turning behind his eyes.

'And your pack?' my Dad queries. I look to Jared, unsure of what he's going to say.

'Part of my pack are here with me as we're all attending university together. Devon has met them all, and they get along.' Okay so, not a total lie, but not the whole truth either. Was it good enough for my dad? Apparently not.

'So they know of Devon's parentage?'

'No, they don't, and I see no reason to change that either.'

'So you plan to live as if she is full blooded?'

'Yes.' Jared had stopped eating placing his cutlery down, his hands on either side of his plate. He looks relaxed, but I know different. The muscle in his jaw is twitching minutely. A sure sign he is getting annoyed.

'And what if someone finds out?'

Jared looked him in the eyes.

'I would do whatever necessary to protect Devon and to be with her. If we can't live among my pack or she doesn't want to live among them, we will leave. It worked for you didn't it?'

My dad looks uncomfortable.

'It was very hard for us over the years, and having being brought up as you have, to then go it alone will be extremely tough. I've done my best for Devon but had we been able to live with my pack, I would have chosen that. They cast me out because of her mother.'

'I appreciate that, but it can be different for us. Devon isn't just kitsune, and she can lead a life as a wolf. No one has to know.' Jared had obviously given all of this thought. I knew he was willing to leave his pack behind because he had already asked me to leave with him. By the end of our meal Jared and my dad seem to be getting along great. We are all set to leave when my dad asks if I will go back to the hotel with him and stay the night. He wants to spend some time with me before he flies back home.

'I suppose I should really be asking you, Jared? I know how territorial a bonded male can be.' Jared makes a funny sound in the back of his throat, which sounds like a half-strangled scoff. I look at them both wide-eyed. Shocked that my dad had just asked for my boyfriend's *permission* to stay with his own daughter. I mean seriously what the hell?

'I'm good with that,' he tells my dad.

'Oh, well, now we've covered what I can and can't decide for *myself*, maybe I should get a permission slip just in case?' I look at them both, annoyance clear on my face. I think Jared actually blushes.

'Devon,' my dad splutters. 'I'm not saying you can't decide for yourself. I'm just respecting the fact that you're a marked female now.' Talk about a complete turnaround.

'So you think that makes Jared the boss of me?'

Jared laughs and tries to hide it with a cough.

'Baby, calm down,' he coaxes. 'He didn't mean anything by it.'

I level him with a stare. He puts his hands up in resignation. 'Baby, do you wanna spend the night with your dad at the hotel before he goes home?'

'I'm going to the bathroom, and I'll think about it while I'm there.' I stomp off like a spoiled child. Of course, I will go back with my dad, but I won't go because I'm 'allowed'. Hell no.

Saying goodbye to Jared feels worse than I expected. I really don't want him to go. I want to climb in the car with him and go back to bed with him. But I owe my dad some dad and daughter time. It's the least I can do since he's flown all this way and I've acted like a total bitch.

We enjoy a bottle of wine in the hotel bar—something we'd never done before. We have a lovely night. We talk a lot—about mom, our life, his life after the pack, and how he'd felt when mom left. As a kid, I hadn't really picked up on his pain. He'd done an amazing job of shielding me, and I told him that. He gets emotional, and by the time we go up to bed, I feel like we've opened up a new chapter in our relationship. I resented my dad as a child growing up, always making me hide myself never allowing me to stay in one place or make friends. But after speaking to him at length and being completely open with each other, I came to the realisation that he had it just as hard as me. He'd never dated, never met another woman he could spend his life with, and all of that was because he was protecting me. I was the reason he'd never moved on to join another pack. And I had given him nothing but shit for it. I felt so ashamed of myself, but he showed me nothing but understanding.

I text Jared before I slept,

Goodnight, miss you already xxx

I got an immediate response,

I shudda said no! Miss you too xxx

I sleep really well after our long chat. I never expected to be in this place with my dad, and I'm actually really sad to see him go the next day. His plane leaves at lunchtime, and we are up early so that he can make the three-hour trip to the airport. I wish I could take him, but instead, I wave him off and call a cab. I decide to go straight over to

Jared's, eager to see him after spending the night apart. I text him but don't get a reply. Maybe he is still sleeping. Even better, I can climb in bed, and he can wake up to me.

The cab pulls up around the front, and I hop out and walk around the back to the kitchen. I stop dead in my tracks. I'm stunned. I cannot believe what I'm seeing. Jared is in the kitchen and Kristen is wrapped up in his arms, her head in the crook of his neck. I'm trying to process what I'm seeing when he kisses the top of her head affectionately. I squeeze my eyes shut. Pain, like I've never felt, crushes my chest, and I can't breathe. I run as far and as fast as I can. My body is quivering, desperate for the change but I can't stop. I can't afford to take the time to change, and I don't want to have to come back for my stuff. Ever.

I'm crushed. That bastard. I wipe away the tears streaming down my face. That's the last time. The last time I ever cry over him. My heart is broken. No, not broken, shattered beyond repair. He fucking lied to me, and he played me.

# chapter TWELVE

## *Devon*

I DON'T KNOW HOW I got home. I don't remember the walk, or how I got myself into bed. But I wake up sobbing. The sound is like a dying animal is clawing its way out of my chest. Maiya is standing over me with a look of pure fear on her face in a red bra and panty combo. At any other time, I would have laughed. I mean who wears that to bed? But I have no control over myself at that moment. I feel broken, my body aches for something I can't have. I'm like a junkie who's run out of crack. As I wrap my arms around my knees, Maiya sits next to me, pulls me into her embrace and just holds me. It's just what I need, but I can't tell her. I can't speak. I'm a hot mess of snot and tears. We don't say a word—she gets it. I'm so grateful for that. I'm in no state to chat. I stay there for a while and wallow. When I wake again, Maiya is still there, and I know she has questions. I pull myself together enough to explain.

'It's over. He has a girlfriend.' I burst into another fit of tears, and she wraps me in her arms.

'Ssssh. It's okay, huni. Everything will be okay,' she soothes

'I can't believe he would do that to me?' I sniffle.

'Oh, huni. Listen, men are assholes. Karma is a bitch, though, and let's hope he gets cock rot.'

'Cock rot?' I laugh as I wipe my nose.

'Yeah, cock rot, and let's hope it fucking falls off.'

I giggle at her anger on my behalf. She's thrown on a t-shirt now, but she flashes her ass as she bends to grab a glass from beside the bed, which makes me giggle harder, I can't stop. I'm bordering hysterical. I can't breathe. I'm holding my stomach because it hurts from laughing, then I'm not laughing anymore. Unwanted tears stream again. Oh god. Jared. I feel empty. Half of a whole. I cry myself to sleep as Maiya holds me.

When I wake, it's morning. Twenty-four hour's post-Jared. The curtains are closed, but the daylight streaming through the cracks tells me I've overslept. I have my first intro classes today and a shit tonne of paperwork to do.

'Heeeey, sweetheart.' Maiya speaks to me like she's trying to ward off a tiger. 'How're ya feeling?' Like a fucking wrecking ball swung and hit me in the chest, but I don't say that out loud. Instead, I force a smile

'Mmmkay,' I mumble. I get up on shaky legs. I actually feel like a train wreck. My body hurts everywhere. Who knew this shit could have a physical effect on your body. I shower and feel a little bit better for it. But I have the worst headache, and I feel like crawling right back into bed. Maiya has other ideas though. Handing me clothes, she lifts her brows, daring me to argue.

'So I took the liberty of switching your damn phone off,' she says handing it to me 'I hope you don't mind. I thought you could use the sleep, and since it never stopped with the constant ringing, well it was pissing me off. I mean who the fuck rings constantly for hours? At night?'

I shrug. 'I guess I'll find out.' I turn it on and wait. A minute passes before it pings so frequently it's like one continual drone. I have a hundred and forty-three messages and a hundred and twenty-seven voice mails. All but one is from Jared. But he hadn't come over. That says it all really. He's too busy with his fiancé, mate, or whatever the fuck she is. He clearly thinks a phone call will suffice after stringing me along in his little game. I'm such an idiot. I switch my phone back off, get dressed, not caring what I wear. Maiya manages to make me look half decent with her choice of outfit though, so I'm not a complete wreck. We go to the student café, but I can't eat, and I barely touch my coffee either. I'm so grateful for Maiya right now. Without her, I would be completely alone. She's proven to be a great friend in such a short space of time.

'You're a star, Maiya. You know that? Thank you so much for putting up with me. I know I must be driving you insane right now.'

'Don't be ridiculous. Men are dicks, and we have to stick together—that's what friends do. Hoes over bros.' She laughs, snorting at her own joke. Maiya begs me to stay out and keep busy for the rest of the day but honestly I don't feel like going anywhere, so after classes, she comes back to the room with me. That night I just want to sit in and veg, wallowing in my own self-pity. I tell Maiya to go out, but she is a total legend and brings in a pint of Ben and Jerry's ice-cream and instead of heading to the club, she gets her pj's on and watches crap TV on my laptop with me. We giggle and chat about anything and everything, and I go to sleep feeling a little easier.

Forty-eight hours post Jared. I still feel crushed. I decide to try and make an effort, just for Maiya's sake. So I drag my ass up to get ready for class. From the bathroom, I hear a knock at the door. Well, I say a knock, it's more like someone is beating the door down. I'm halfway through brushing my teeth when Maiya opens up. His scent hits me immediately, and I feel sick. I want to see him. I'm desperate, like an addict who can't stay away.

'Devon isn't here, *asshole,* now fuck the hell off.' I hear her squeak and know he's pushed his way through the door and past her. Maiya is hollering all kinds of obscenities, but he's clearly ignoring her. It's time to face the music. I open the bathroom door. Maiya is looking dismayed and upset. 'I'm sorry,' she mouths at me. I shake my head and place a hand on her shoulder to reassure her it's okay. I can do this, I tell myself.

'It's okay.' I smile.

'You want me to stick around?' she asks while glaring daggers at Jared. I shake my head. Jared is glaring at me, burning a hole into me. He is so difficult to look at in his denim shirt and black muscle-hugging jeans. I don't make eye contact until Maiya leaves the room. Jared sits on my bed. His fists clenched on his thighs. His jaw is twitching as he clenches and unclenches it. I sit opposite and put my poker face to good use. He still hasn't uttered a word. I face him, and our eyes finally meet. And I am gutted all over again. We sit in silence. I wait him out. I want to hear what he has to say. If he's even going to tell me? It feels like hours before he finally growls something out through gritted teeth. I look up at him confused.

'What?'

'I said why the fuck haven't you been taking my calls?' He's mad, like really fucking mad. At me. Ha. Well, that makes two of us.

'How about you tell me. JARED?' I sneer at him, my lip curling up as my anger takes hold.

He stands and before I know it, he's kneeling in front of me, his hands gripping my face. Our eyes meet, and at that moment I want him and hate him all at once. I want to scream and shout at him. I want to beat his beautiful head in, and I want to kiss him within an inch of my life. I'm so messed up it's crazy.

'I'm sorry,' he starts. All his anger has abated, and his words drip with sympathy. And I want to do is plug my ears and shout 'lalalalalalalala'. I don't want to listen. I don't want to hear that he doesn't want me. 'Baby, listen to me. I had to go home real quick. There was an accident, and I was needed.'

'What?'

'I tried to call you as I was leaving. I text you. Fuck, I even rang the dorm security. I came back because I was fucking worried out of my damn mind.' He pushes his hands through his hair in frustration.

'Why?' I ask him honestly. I mean why bother? Why not just cut me loose? His jaw clenches again as he looks at me,

'Why? The fuck? WHY?' His tone is angry, but he's stuttering his sentence as if he's trying and failing to hold back his words. His face is all scrunched up like he can't understand what I'm saying to him. It's really quite simple. He paces in front of me. I don't look at him. I can't, I'm waging a war inside my own head right now and looking at him will throw me over the edge.

'Give me one fucking reason why I shouldn't have worried? Why I shouldn't have come back?' I don't answer. I just sit there because what I want to say is on the tip of my tongue, but it makes me sick to the stomach to think of it, let alone say it out loud.

'You know what, Jared, just go,' I plead. 'I don't even know why you bothered to come. If there really was an accident, I'm sorry. But if this is some kind of play in your game of 'let's head fuck Devon' then know that I'm done.' I put my hands up in surrender, my eyes blurring with the tears. Jared grabs my wrists and pushes me up against the wall, hands above my head, pinned. He crowds into my space, his nose a whisker from mine. His eyes aglow with anger and lust.

'What the fuck did you just say to me?' My legs are like jelly, and my head is pounding. I'm done. I can't—won't—do this to myself anymore.

'I said, I'm. DONE.' I enunciate each word, so there's no question. His jaw clenches and an eternity passes while his eyes bore a hole in mine.

'You're done? Just like that? No reason? No explanation, nothing? Just fucking done?' I laugh. It sounds like a hiccup, and again the words won't com., I can't even say *her* name, without bile rising up. 'No... You don't get to say that to me. NO!' He presses hard against my hands before he lets go and begins pacing the room again. How fucking dare he. He was supposed to be with me, but all the while he was there with *her*. Playing the happy couple. And he's pissed because I'm done being second best? He needs to leave and not look back. I can't do this again. I heave in a breath and before I know it the words spill out.

'I came by the other day. I jumped in a cab when you didn't reply to my text. I assumed it would be okay because why the hell wouldn't it be okay for your *girlfriend* to stop by at your house right?'

I have his attention. He stops pacing and folds his arms across his chest, his jaw clenched tight, holding back any words that may interrupt my tirade. 'Right?' I ask again, he nods. So we're playing like that? 'So you can imagine my shock when I walk up to the door to find you with your arms wrapped around *her*, as you kissed her.' He frowns. Fucking frowns like he's confused. That's fucking it.

'GET.OUT. NOW.' I don't even want to hear what he has to say. I can imagine what lies are going to come out of his mouth. His confusion morphs to anger as he thinks over what I saw, as he realises, then I see recognition dawn on his face. He knows what I saw.

'Baby, you're putting two and two together here and coming up with fucking five.' Gaaaaahhhhh, Really?

'No, Jared, I think *you* are putting one man with two women and coming up with *'That's okay by me'*. Well, it's *not* fucking okay by *me*!' I scream at him as I walk over to the door and try and fail to open it fluidly like I had planned. Instead, I stumble and lose my grip on the handle before I manage to compose myself enough to open it correctly, and I gesture for him to walk the fuck through it. He doesn't move a muscle. Shitballs.

'Just a fuckin' minute. You're telling me you've got your knickers in a fucking knot over what you saw in the kitchen?'

Knickers in a knot? What the hell?

'I *saw* you *kiss* her, Jared. I fucking *saw* you,' I scream but as I'm standing with the door open, I suddenly realise this is no longer private, so I slam the door again. I can just imagine everyone down the hall snickering behind their doors at the poor girl who isn't enough for her boyfriend. I head into the bathroom, but he follows and fills the doorframe with his imposing, sexy, albeit angry, self. *Look away. Look away now before your panties melt off. Jeez.* Even in this sorry state, he has my body ready and willing. *Get a grip.*

'What did you *actually* see that day? Hmm?' If he thinks I'm going to lower myself to describing it. No way. Ugh ugh. He moves closer. I back all the way into the tiny room until I have nowhere else to go. 'Answer me.'

I close my eyes and suck my lips over my teeth, pressing them together in defiance like a toddler, shaking my head. 'Okay, Devon, you won't tell me what you *think* you saw—'

'I *know* what I saw,' I correct him.

'I'll tell you what you fuckin' *saw*! We were *all* in the kitchen eating breakfast. My phone rang. It was my father. Calling to tell me there had been a car accident. That one of our pack had been killed. What you fucking *saw* was me breaking the news to Kristen that her uncle was dead.'     I'm stunned. I'd seen him being affectionate and kissing the top of her head. In my mind, it was two people embracing each other in a way a couple would. I hadn't thought for a second that it would or could be anything else. Fuck me on a freight train. I'm a total bitch. One hundred percent fucking bitch-in-a-basket. I can't look at him. I'm so ashamed of myself right now. I'd let the green-eyed monster get the better of me, and I let my thoughts blow what I saw out of proportion. If it had been anyone else, I would have walked in and asked what was wrong. But it was *her*. I feel sick. I'm relieved. How sick is that? I'm relieved someone died. What kind of person thinks that way?

'I'm so sorry,' I tell him. He runs his hands through his hair, blowing out a huge breath. He shakes his head and walks out of the bathroom. I follow. He turns to me, and his anger is shining brightly in his eyes.

## *Jared*

'What are you sorry for Devon? That you accused me of cheating? That someone I care about died? Or that you had me so worried fuckin' sick that I left while the arrangements for his funeral were being made?'

Her face pales and she sinks to the floor, face in her hands. I hadn't meant to say all that shit, but it comes rolling out like verbal diarrhoea. I want to cut my fucking tongue out as soon as the words are spoken. Instead, I just stand there. Not saying a goddamn thing. More than anything, I want her touch. I need it. But I'm so fucking mad at her I'm not sure I could be gentle. I've been outta my mind. Ringing her damn phone every second I could. Not able to give Garret the respect he deserved because I didn't have my head in the game. I nearly left against my alphas orders twice, and finally left with him on board only because his threat to disown me didn't work. I was leaving, no matter what. So he gave his permission. I knew damn well he gave it to save face.

I was ready to be alpha and his orders over me were becoming less and less impossible to ignore. He was failing to bend my will. No, *had* failed to bend it. He knew it was time to step down. But he wanted me to follow his final order first. That was where we'd left things. I wasn't going to push it while Garret's body was still warm. It wasn't right. So I would face that argument another day.

My female is on the floor in a heap sobbing. I need to make this right. I suck up my anger and pick her up, cradling her in my arms. Her tears smell like salt on her skin, and her arms come up around my neck. Thank fuck for that. I breathe her in, kissing her face, her eyes, her nose. I smooth her hair over and push it behind her ear. Finally, her eyes meet mine, and I'm done for. My dick has been at half-mast since I walked in. But now? Solid as steel behind my fly. Uncomfortably hard. My mouth finds hers, and I don't want to talk anymore. I don't want to hear anything she has to say. I just want to feel. I want her to show me how she feels. No words necessary.

# chapter THIRTEEN

## Jared

IT'S LUNCHTIME WHEN I FINALLY let Devon get out of her bed. If she weren't hungry, I would have kept her there all day. I needed our connection to stay strong, and being inside her seemed to cement that for me. My dick didn't want to break for lunch. He seemed to want to be all up in there permanently. Which I was totally okay with—except I needed to feed her. So while she went and showered, I stayed in her bed. Otherwise, my dick would take over, and we'd never get any food.

We still had shit to discuss. Shit, I really didn't want to broach right now. Like why the fuck she didn't trust me, and the fact that I need to go back home for Garret's funeral. We have tonight though so I'll address it later. Now, I just need to be with her—to show her that she's it for me, and I need to make sure I'm it for her too. I feel like I can't breathe without her. Like my body can't physically function without her. It's crazy, but I now know what being a bonded male feels like. My body sings when she's near, and when I'm inside her, fuck me. It's like nothing I've ever felt with another female. It's like having one long orgasm from the minute I slide inside her. Then when I do come. It's fucking euphoric. I hope to fuck she feels that too because, shit, when she told me she was done, it took all I had not to break down, get on my knees and beg like a fucking pussy, for her to change her mind. I need her. I want her to need me right back. I can't handle anything less. Nothing else will cut it. So how the fuck, do I make her feel the same way? I know one hundred fucking percent that she's all I want, and I won't ever look at another female. Does she feel the same? Do I have to worry about other males? She doesn't trust me. Is that because she doesn't feel this bond? That she doesn't need to be with me, near me? Fuck me. This shit is difficult. I'm all in. Every fucking last piece of me. Now she needs to get on the same page and fast.

## *Devon*

Jared seems quiet over lunch. He's brought me to a little American diner where they have all the classics. I'm in my food element as I order a second helping of fries after my burger and then a stack of pancakes too. I know I need to start a conversation about me stupidly accusing him of cheating. But how do I start? I mean I've said sorry a million times already, before, during, and after our makeup sex. But he's still off. He keeps reaching for my hand in between mouthfuls. That has to be a good sign, right? I sigh. I just don't know what I'm doing. I've never had a relationship before, let alone felt anything as intense as this does. I want to tell him how I feel but the words just don't come. And I'm scared. I don't want to get hurt. I'm so worried that I'll let him all the way in and then he'll leave me because of his loyalty towards his pack. And I've not given him any reason to stay with me. I've left him and accused him of cheating. Oh, my God. I'm such an idiot.

I brush the back of his hand with my fingers in a small circle. His eyes snap to mine, and I want to kiss him so badly. I shuffle closer to him—leaning across the table between us. He does the same. But he doesn't close the distance like he normally does, nor does he take control. He leaves it all up to me. I need to let him know how I feel. This is how we work best. No words. As his mouth opens to mine, I want to climb across the table and crawl into his arms. I want to feel that connection thrum through my body. I want the feeling that only he gives me. Where the entire world around me falls away and only he remains for me. Him and me. Together. Our tongues are dancing to their own tune, and I'm vaguely aware of our surroundings, but I don't care. I feel him swipe the table and then his hands are under my armpits, and I'm crawling across the tabletop. Our kiss deepening still, I sit, straddling his lap. And I feel every inch of him beneath me. I want him. Now. Our food is completely forgotten. Only we exist in this bubble.

That is until I hear a clearing of a throat and a quiet, 'Excuse me.' I pull back from Jared's lips, but my eyes linger as his tongue swipes his bottom lip. I pull mine between my teeth and exhale through my nose. I can feel his arousal, and I think mine is pretty evident in the air because his nostrils flare and his eyes dilate ever so slightly. The waitress trying to get our attention is standing just in my peripheral vision with a coffee pot in her hand.

'I'm sorry, but this is a family place, so umm, if you want to umm... Fornicate, you'll have to leave.'

'I'm sorry—' I start to tell her as I climb off Jared's knee. She has a huge grin on her face like she just got the gossip of the century.

'We're leaving,' Jared says immediately cutting off my apology. He stands, lifting me all the way off him and dropping my feet to the floor. He throws some cash on the table and takes my hand, pulling me behind him. I look back at the waitress in her red dress and white checked pinafore. She has a grin so wide I can't stop giggling. Jared pushes me up against the wall at the side of the building.

'I need inside you,' he mumbles against my lips as he laps at my mouth, willing me to open for him. He licks his way inside and our tongues tangle, vying against the other. This would be a beautiful moment if only we weren't pushed up against a café wall in broad daylight.

'Not here,' I pant into his mouth. 'Not for all to see.'

'No. No one gets to see you come but me, I need to get you home, female, and I'm gonna fuck you until you're so sore you can't sit down without thinking about my dick inside of you.' OMG Niagara just overflowed into panty territory. His lips clamp down over mine again as I melt into a hot mess and practically dry hump his leg. We fucked like rabbits not even an hour ago, and I'm riding his leg like a junky craving her next fix. How does he do this to me?

He breaks the kiss and drags me towards his car by my hand. I follow dutifully, panting behind him. He opens the passenger door and lifts me into the seat then bends his neck forward and is kissing me again like his life depends on it. If we carry on like this, we'll get arrested for public indecency. But as his tongue glides around mine like he owns it, my hands wander to the back of his head and pull him in even closer still. He groans into my mouth, and my hands wander further and further until I reach the button of his jeans. I'm at a point now where I don't care who sees. I want him naked, and I want him now. I try for just that. He pulls back, chuckling at me, and shakes his head.

'Patience, baby.' I suddenly realise that the lot isn't empty and we are, in fact, not alone. Oh, fuck a duck. I feel a blush rise through my entire body, and it lights my face up like a belisha beacon.

'Jesus Christ, Jared,' I mumble while I cover my face with my hands. People are staring. *Kill me now.* He saunters around the car like he's king shit and gets in, smiling so hard his face must hurt.

'What are you smiling about?' I ask, still mortified at what I just did IN PUBLIC! He looks at me and winks as the car roars to life, grin still in place.

'Just love that you can't get enough of my dick, baby,' he says so cockily, I'm sure if we were walking he would be strutting right about now. I quirk a small smile, unable to hold it in.

'I do love your cock,' I tell him, only half messing. I do love his cock after all. He laughs. 'Say it again.'

I look at him in question.

'Tell me what you love.'

'Your cock!' His jaw clenches and his eye twitches as he puts his foot further down on the accelerator,

'Fuckin' love it when you talk dirty.' Oh? Well, I'm sure I can do better than that.

We pull into Jared's house, and he barely has the engine off before he's at my door and lifting me out into his arms. He kicks the back door open after unlocking it and strides with purpose through the kitchen and to the stairs. I wriggle out of his hold and slide down the front of his body. He backs me up to the wall. I'm a couple of steps above him, so we're on a level. My mouth is against his, and he slams into me. I moan, we frantically start to undress each other but don't want to part our lips. We clash teeth and tongues in an effort to stay connected, but I don't care. His fingers find my now soaked through panties, and I almost come apart.

'Fuck me, Jared.' His eyes flash with lust? Need? He rips my jeans and panties down my legs together, and he pushes me down on all fours on the stairs. Then he's inside me. Fucking me so good. So Good.

## *Jared*

I've had her in every position and everyplace possible leading up to my room, and again in the shower, and I still want her.

'Baby, are you sore?'

'Mmhmm' is all the answer I get. Shit. Looks like my dick will have to wait, she's practically sleeping. Worn out. Well used and sated. I felt just the same until a minute ago when I pictured her strangling my dick from behind on the stairs, and then, fuck. I'm hard as steel. I try to turn away, so I don't prod her ass with it. But she wiggles into me and fuuuuuuuuuuuuuck.

I clench my teeth and try again. I need to go and jerk off in the bathroom. But she has her head on my arm and her ass all up on my dick. And he wants in. Pussy, ass, he doesn't give a shit. But she's worn the fuck out and needs to rest. I try for releasing my arm and damn it she wiggles that ass again. I groan out loud this time, unable to hold it back. She turns her head to look at me through lidded eyes. Gorgeous. And she grins. Her naked ass is still pressed up against me. My dick's like a heat seeking missile locked onto its target. But then he's called off in the last second. All that energy and pent up shit has to blow somewhere. Shower. Jerk off. Now. But that smile. Fuck me.

'You're hard again?' she asks sounding genuinely surprised.

'Well you're naked and your ass is—' something flashes in her eyes. Fear?

'Baby, it's okay, I know you're sore.'

'I'm not ready for that, Jared.' She looks embarrassed. 'I've never done that before.' Oh shit. She thinks I'm trying to get into her ass right now.

'No baby, I didn't mean... I don't want to fuck you in the ass. No. I mean I do, of course I do—why wouldn't I? But I mean...fuck—'

She starts to giggle. I'm such a pussy right now.

'It's okay,' she says, her hand going to my face.

'No, it isn't. Baby, I don't ever wanna do anything you ain't ready for okay? We go only where you are comfortable going? But just so you know, you have THE sexiest ass I have ever laid eyes on, and I would be a fool not to want to claim that. BUT—' I shrug. 'I can wait, and I have to say, it makes me even more fuckin' hard knowing I'll be the first and the last.'

I smile. I'm not sure if I've just made her feel better or worse. Maybe she doesn't ever want to go there? I can cope with that, I guess. I feel her fingers work their way down my chest, across my abs, and into pubic hair territory. Then she clamps her hand around my dick and starts to stroke me. My eyes are closed, and I'm enjoying the best fucking hand job. The covers are yanked back and then hot silky warmth. Annnnd I'm a goner. I'm grunting and moaning like a chick having an orgasm. Man, this feels fucking amazing. She glides to the head and lets me pop out of her mouth, and I groan as her hand takes over and her tongue works fucking magic, flicking and lapping at my bell end. Then she takes me deeper and fuck me, I'm gonna come. Already.

'Baby I'm gonna—Uuuuuuhhhh.' I try to stop her as my dick kicks out ready to explode into the back of her throat. But she only sucks harder and faster until I'm shooting off in her mouth and she moans, swallowing. I open my lids, and she's looking up at me while she takes every last drop. My dick is still kicking up in her mouth. I've never seen anything so sexy in all my life. I pull out of her mouth with a 'popping' sound, and she licks her lips, catching the small amount that has overflowed. *MINE*. I can't take my eyes off of her. She is perfect. *Mine*. I pull her up and kiss her within an inch of my life. Then she settles with her head on my chest, and she goes to sleep. I relax and listen to her breathing. Thinking about what I'm going to say about leaving in the morning. And how to ask the question about trust. I'm not sure if I should ask, or if I should just let it go. I don't know what's the best way, I've never done shit like this before and I sure as shit never cared what anyone thought before. But the thought of her not trusting me hurts. I don't want her to feel that way about me. I let her sleep for an hour before I wake her up.

'Wake up baby. I wanna take you out.'

'You do?' she cracks her lids just a little, and she looks so damn sexy all mussed and sleepy

'Yep, first I'm gonna feed you. Then we can go to a club have a drink or two, and we can talk.' Her eyes snap open all the way. Worry is etched on her face, and she sits up real fast, clutching the quilt to her chest. My heart starts beating ten to the dozen at the change in her.

'What's wrong?' I ask.

'What do you want to talk about?' she asks. She's alert and completely awake now. Fuck. I'm shit at this.

'Nothing bad, baby. Don't look so worried.' She visibly relaxes, and I blow out a breath. Fucking hell. 'Devon, I've never done this before. I'm shit scared I do or say the wrong thing when all I want to do is make you happy, feel safe, you know?' That gets me a smile. Phew.

'Then you're doing just fine.' She clasps my face in her hands. 'I always feel safe with you, and I am happy, really happy.' I have a fuckin lump in my throat. I swallow it down, and I just kiss her. No words.

I take her to a small pub restaurant, and we order enough starters that the waiter asks if we're expecting friends to join us. Devon looks at me, worried,

'Nah, mate. I've got a big appetite, and my girl here worked me real hard today,' I tell him with a shit-eating grin on my face. Devon looks like she could sink under the table as the waiter throws his head back and laughs. Then she kicks me under the table.

'Owww.' I laugh

'I cannot believe you just said that to him!' But she's smiling.

'Why? True story.' I grin at her as she squirms a little under my gaze. Fuck me, if I'm not horny again. Jesus, I want to make sure she actually finishes a meal this time without me dragging her off like a caveman. This afternoon was fucking amazing, though. If I could keep her in my room and do that every day, I would.

# chapter
# FOURTEEN

## Devon

JARED AND I HAVE EATEN our way through most of the menu, and he's still asking for the dessert menu. He orders more drinks when the guy brings it over, and the waiter goes off to get them. When he comes back he orders cheesecake, knickerbocker glory's in two flavours and lemon meringue.

'Baby, do you wanna add to that?' I shake my head no.

'I think that's plenty.' I smile at the waiter. 'Thank you.' I tell him.

'Maybe a pecan pie too?' Jared adds looking at me in question. 'Yes, add pecan pie. I love a good pecan pie,' he tells the poor guy still looking at us in shock. But he scribbles it down on his little pad and goes off to place the order.

'He's going to wonder why we are eating so much.' I scold him, but he sits back in his chair and grins.

'Devon, the only thing going through his mind, is what you did to work up my appetite so much,' he says wiggling his eyebrows. I laugh. I can't help but worry about people questioning our appetite. I always just pretend to be full, but Jared doesn't give a crap. I suppose being a guy he can get away with it. And so what if people question? Their first thoughts on it were not going be, 'Oh, they eat so much they must be werewolves.' Of course they won't think that. Our desserts arrive. Jared is intent on sharing everything with me. So with two spoons we tuck in. I watch him as he scoops up mouthful after mouthful. It's clear he loves the deserts. He doesn't just eat for sustenance—he enjoys it. I am so relaxed about eating with him, that before I know it, we are down to our last bite of pecan. Jared scoops it onto his spoon and leans across the table feeding it to me.

'Open wide,' he says wiggling those damn eyebrows again. I laugh at his innuendo. But I open my mouth wide and accept the offered pie. I close my eyes and chew, savouring the flavour. When I open my eyes, he's staring at me.

'Do you know how turned on I am right now?' he asks, his eyes half closed, pupils dilated. I bite my bottom lip and shake my head, fixing my eyes on his.

'Seeing your tongue slip out and meet the spoon and when your eyes closed as you took it. Sexy as fuck.' His lip quirks up at the side in a sexy smile. Then his hand shoots up, and he's asking for the cheque.

'I'm ready to take you out—' He stops as his phone ringing distracts him. He checks it and looks to me in apology. 'I need to take it,' he says. 'Brad?'

'Hey, man. We're back and you ain't home, so we're coming to you. Where you at?'

Jared groans.

'Brad. I'm out with Devon. I'm heading back tomorrow. You didn't need to come back.'

'Fuck that. We wouldn't have stayed at all if we'd known you'd left. What's with that anyway?'

'I just needed to be here that's all.'

'Right. With no fucking protection? Great move, dickhead. Howard nearly had a full on panic attack.'

I can hear him laughing now. But I caught the seriousness in his tone. I've never known Jared be without his pack at his back, and I can't believe I missed that. He really did leave in a hurry because of me. The guilt hits me hard. What if something had happened to him, all because of my irrational jealousy? What an idiot I have been. He wraps up the call and tells me we are meeting up with them in a short while. He doesn't seem too pleased, but then our party had just been pooped so I guess he wouldn't be. I suppose I will have to get used to being around his pack all the time I'm with him. This was normal for him. My phone pings with a text. It's Maiya checking in.

Hey, bitch tits, how r u? You'd gone when I got back. U ok? I hit reply

Hey, hoe bag. I'm really good thx will explain EVERYTHING, promise

I expect ALL the deets!

I laugh as I put my phone away. I can imagine how that conversation will go.

We arrive at the club I first met Jared in, and we head straight for the bar, where we find Brad Howard, Zoe, Logan, and Imogen. They have the drinks order in the bag and Zoe heads straight for me.

'Hey, girl, we missed you.'

I pull a face and laugh. 'It's literally been a couple of days.'

Zoe laughs at my reaction. 'So I guess you didn't miss us at all then?' she says sarcastically. 'Here.' She hands me a drink. I'm not entirely sure what it is as I take a sip, aahhhh long island ice tea. It's amazing.

'Thanks.' I gesture to Howard who has clearly ordered and paid as he was still handing drinks back to everyone. I get a small nod of the head in return. Cock face. Zoe pulls me along, and I find myself being propelled away from Jared. I look back, slightly panicked, but he smiles big and lifts his pint letting me know he'll follow shortly. Imogen, Zoe, and I sit in a booth while we wait for the guys. They are huddled in conversation, still at the bar. Watching them makes me think back to the conversation Jared and Brad had, he'd said he was going back tomorrow. He must be going back for the funeral. I feel myself getting jealous of the fact Jared will be with Kristen, consoling her, comforting her. I should be disgusted with myself, but I can't help but feel that way. My gut twists at the image I see in my head, and I have to wrench myself from those thoughts. In a time of need like this, of course Jared will be there for her. I have to accept that and know that's all it is. But why does it feel so painful? What if he feels sorry for her and changes his mind? What if he agrees to mate her? Oh, my God, I feel sick. I jump up and head for the bathroom. Thankfully there's an empty stall as I push through the door. I head straight in and grasping my hair in one hand I hover my head over the seat. Public toilets are a phobia of mine. I don't let anyone know it, but I always clean the seat and never sit, always hover. I only ever use them in cases of emergencies. I would much rather wait and go to my own sanitised one. As I gather my hair, I feel the panic rise from having my head in a toilet someone's just had their ass on. Annnnd my stomach empties. I pull some tissue from the roll realising it only lets you have a small amount at one time. I throw the initial bit in the toilet—someone's had their hands on it while wiping their ass—and I pull a load from the roll dispenser. Wiping my mouth. I wait. Heave again. Wipe. Wait. Heave. I'm sweating, and my hair feels damp by the time I'm done. I wait a little while longer just in case.

'Devon, you in here?' Jared. In the ladies' bathroom! I roll my eyes and get up off of my knees and unlock the door. The bathroom is now empty. Huh, must have missed that during my puke sesh. Only Jared stands there with a worried look on his face. He comes straight to me and wraps his arms around me.

'You sick?' he asks pulling me in tight he brushes my hair back from my face and kisses my forehead. 'Come on, let's get you home.'

'I'm okay now. Honest.' And I was if I didn't think of him with Kristen or the germs I could have possibly ingested from that toilet. I would be fine.

'Baby, you just threw up. You're not fine.' He looks at me like he's chastising a kid. 'I'm taking you home, and I'll take care of you.' I really was okay, but Jared taking care of me was not to be sniffed at. I will lap that up like a spoiled princess, all with a smile on my face. I relied on no one, but I was slowly but surely beginning to fold when it came to this man. He ordered, and I obeyed. And I liked it.

I'm not sick again that night and when I wake in Jared's bed, a feeling of contentment eases me, I reach out for Jared, who is sleeping quietly. It's still dark out. I put my hand in his, and he instinctually entwines our fingers. I watch his chest rise and fall with each breath, and I eventually fall back into sleep myself.

My stomach, growling like an angry beast wakes me. I pat the sheets, unable to open my eyes yet. Jared isn't in bed. I snap my eyes open. Jumping up I check the bathroom. Nope. I'm pulling my panties on to go in pursuit when he saunters in with a tray full of food. He looks at me, disappointed.

'I can't feed you breakfast in bed if you're not in bed,' he chastises. His pout makes me giggle.

'I would have come to you in the kitchen.'

'I'm meant to be taking care of you—now get in the damn bed so I can feed you.' Oh, bossy Jared. How I love you.

'Yes, Sir.' I salute before climbing onto the bed. I'm still in his t-shirt, which I've decided I'm claiming as my own. I love wearing his clothes.

'Good girl.' He grins, winking at me. I blush as Niagara once again bursts its barriers and overflows in a hot liquid mess, in my panties. I can't help it—he is too damn sexy. And he knows it. He steps closer, clearly noticing my arousal in the air. Fuck me standing. He places the tray on the bedside table and takes the lid off a plate.

'I intend to feed you first.' He looks at me, and I blush some more—*how is that even possible?* 'Your stomach has been growling for near enough an hour. You need food, then, if you feel up to it, we can take care of your other needs.' He smirks.

'Smart ass,' I mumble, but my attention is soon taken with the smell of the eggs he's brought for me.

'Wasn't sure what you would feel up to, so I went with bland and safe.' He shows me scrambled eggs, dry toast, bagels, and preserves.

'I'm feeling absolutely fine now, thanks.' I gesture to the food. 'Will you eat with me?' He shakes his head.

'I had a quick bite downstairs while Imogen cooked your eggs.'

'Your pack is so nice. Jared—' I didn't get to say much more on the matter because he shovelled a huge fork full of eggs into my mouth. And we went on like that until I'd eaten the lot.

'How're you feeling now?' he asks putting the tray to one side and pulling me into his side.

'Better still now I've eaten, thanks.' He nods—his face is a little grave. I brace myself for whatever is to come.

'I have to go home. It's Garret's funeral this afternoon, and I have to be there.'

'Jared, of course you do. I'm just sorry about this whole mess. You should never have had to come back.' The guilt hits me once again. Fuck a duck.

'That's done with now, don't go there again.' His tone is soft, but it's not a request. I nod my agreement. I know I can't go with him, but I wish I could support him through it.

'Jared, take as long as you need. I'll be fine.' And I would be. I wouldn't fall to pieces without him. I came here on my own. I could manage. I have Maiya. Classes also. He sighs and nods.

'I know you will, baby, but I don't like leaving you.'

'And I don't like you leaving, but it's important right?'

He sighs again. 'It really is, yeah.'

I squeeze his hand.

'Then go, and don't worry about me.'

'Leaving you unprotected though. It goes against all my instincts.' He clenches his jaw.

'Jared, seriously. I'm not important enough to have security,' I giggle. 'And what do I need protecting from?' He just looks at me.

'Fucking men.' He smiles. 'Minute I'm gone they'll be lining up ready to take what's mine.' He's smiling, but I sense that he really believes this. Talk about putting someone on a pedestal.

'Jared, seriously, what do I need protection from? Nothing. So go and do what you gotta do.'

We get ready and say our goodbyes as he drops me back at my room.

Maiya is out. No doubt shopping again. As soon as I leave Jared I miss him so intensely my heart actually hurts. I keep myself busy by going over the syllabus for my Austin to Hardy module, and I do some reading. It doesn't seem like long before my stomach is growling again. I make my way to the shared kitchen on our floor and grab some super noodles. I can't find anything else quick or more substantial so they would do. Chicken flavour. I measure out the water put them all into a bowl in the microwave and nuke it for three minutes. Five minutes later I'm eating them at the table. A guy comes in shortly after. Surfer shorts on, no top. He isn't bad looking and obviously works out. His hair is mussed, and he looks like he probably just woke up. It's past twelve now. I smile as he waves his hand in a 'hi', but doesn't speak. He flicks the kettle on then rummages through the cupboards looking for something.

'Shit.' He turns to me. 'No coffee?' We do have coffee, well at least I did. I go to my cupboard get it out and hand it to him. 'Thanks, can't function without it.' I laugh with him.

'Me neither.'

'You want some?'

Actually, I did. 'Yeah, I will do, thanks.'

'Milk and sugar?' he asks with his back to me spooning coffee into two cups,

'Just milk please.'

'Ah sweet enough eh?' he says turning to look at me. I laugh.

'I guess. I just don't do sweet—' I was going to say coffee

'You do sweet real well, darling.'

Oh dear. He's flirting. The fact that he is half naked in an all-girls building clearly means he's just left someone's bed. That offends me. Not that I would be interested. Hell no. But have a bit of decency. Jesus. He sets the coffee in front of me and moves to sit next to me at the table, at which point I stand up.

'You have to leave so soon? I was hoping to get to know you a little better.'

'I don't think that's a very good idea. Maybe you should go on back to whoever's room you left just now. Bye,' I mumble the last word as he looks up at me, and he smiles.

'Fair enough' he concedes with a nod of the head, and a smirk on his lips.

As I get back to my room, my phone rings. It's a coffee shop not far from my room. Maiya had taken my resume in and saved their number to my phone. Maybe they had a vacancy and wanted to interview me. I close my door and look at the phone again. I'm nervous but hell I have nothing to lose.

'Hello?'

'Hi, is that Devon Hathoway?' A pleasant sounding guy asks.

'Yes speaking.'

'Hi, I'm calling from Coffee Planet. We have an opening for a trial today if you would like to come over. I've got your CV in front of me, and it seems you're qualified as a barista?'

'Yes, I've worked in lots of coffee shops all over America.'

'So? Trial today? Can you do it?'

'Umm, sure, I can be there in a half hour?'

'Great, I'm on my own so the sooner the better. Just come to the counter when you arrive. I'll be the one with no hair left.' He laughs and disconnects the call. Well, that was weird. Never had an interview quite like that before. I gather my clothes—I decide on all black since I don't know the uniform—and I grab a quick shower.

# chapter FIFTEEN

## *Devon*

WHEN I ARRIVE, I FIND the guy behind the counter. He has reddish hair and is built like a house. He's easily the tallest man in here. He sags visibly in relief as I introduce myself.

'Thank God. Please tell me you can work your way around these machines?' He points behind him. He has a queue almost to the entrance door, and I smile realising I've used these machines plenty.

'Just tell me where everything is, and I will get right on it.' Everything is within reach so no need for trips to the back. The fridges with everything I need are right there. We decide on a plan of action. He serves cake and pastries and takes the money, and I make the drinks. Before I know it, the queue has gone and an hour and a half has passed. It's two thirty pm already.

'I'm Wade, by the way, and you are awesome.' He comes and shakes my hand. 'My usual barista called me this morning to say he wouldn't be in anymore as he's moved back home.'

'Ouch,' I cringe.

'I know, right? Left me right in the shit. Anyway, after that performance, the job's yours if you want it?'

'Wow, thanks. I don't really know what to say?'

'Start with, 'I'll take the job?' I nod, laughing, still a bit gobsmacked. That was the easiest interview I'd ever had. I barely spoke to him or anyone else. It was great.

'I know you're a student so we'll work out what shifts you can do, but I definitely need you for the rest of the day and tomorrow if you can?'

'Umm, yeah. I guess that will be fine. I'll have to check my timetable for my classes next week though because they all start properly then. I've only had intro's at this point.'

'No problem. You help me, and I'll help you. Pay is minimum wage plus tips. There is always overtime, and if you let me know in advance, you can have time off too. It's easy going here. Do the work, and I'll leave you to it.'

'Sounds good to me.' I smile. The rest of the shift flies by and before I know it it's five thirty pm and another girl comes in to do the evening shift.

'Hey,' she says giving me her hand to shake. 'I'm Cammie. So glad he hired you so quickly.'

'Devon. Yeah, was definitely a strange interview.' I laugh.

'They don't always throw you in the deep end, but he doesn't do things like other bosses do. He says he gets a feeling and goes with it. That's how he hired me anyway. And now you. So welcome to the team. It's a madhouse.'

'Hey, Cammie!' Wade shouts over. 'Don't put her off she won't come back tomorrow.' We all laugh as I grab my purse. I check my phone as I leave and I have missed calls from Jared. Shit. I dial him, and he picks up immediately.

'Baby, you okay?' I don't even manage a hello. His tone is hard and worried.

'I'm fine. I've been working! I got a job!' He's silent for a second.
'I didn't know you wanted a job?'

'Yeah. I put out my resume when I first got here but got no replies, so I assumed there weren't any jobs. Anyway, this guy called me today from Coffee Planet and said I could work a trial, and he gave me the job.' I'm babbling. Jared has just buried a pack member for God's sake. I stop. Take a breath and ask him.

'How did it all go?'

'As well as can be expected. We're all going back to the big house now and having drinks in his honour. But when I couldn't get hold of you I panicked.'

'Jared, I'm so sorry, that was really inconsiderate of me. I should have text you but it all happened so fast and when I arrived it was as busy as Times Square—only everyone wanted coffee.'

'It's okay. I'm just glad you're okay. I can relax now. You can tell me all about your job when I get back tomorrow, okay?'

'Sure, but I'm working tomorrow too. Nine till five. I get a half hour break though?'

He sighs, it sounds like heavy breathing down the phone.

'I'll see you there then. Text me when you get home, and I'll call you before you go to sleep tonight.'

'Okay.' I sigh. 'Jared?'

'Yeah?'

'I really miss you.'

Again he sighs.

'God, I miss the shit out of you too, talk later yeah?'

'Bye.'

'Bye, baby.'

I can't stop thinking about Jared. I don't go out with Maiya, to her utter displeasure, but I want to be up and fresh for work tomorrow—not hung over and tired. After much pouting and sulking though, she finally relents and leaves me to go and party the night away. Not before I divulge all the details on Jared and me, though. I don't get off that lightly. Maiya is so funny when it comes to men. You would think after the way she called him out for being a cheat and rode my ass about finding a new one she would hate him. But no, he's all awesome again in her book because I'm happy. I'm sure the minute I wasn't happy she would be there to cut the crotch out of all his boxers and jeans though—she has my back.

I have a fitful sleep that night, and I toss and turn, unable to get comfy. When I do sleep, I have a nightmare. Well, not a scary as shit, Nightmare on Elm Street type, but a bad dream, and it's so vivid and real I think I'd rather have Freddy Kruger in my head, at least then I could kick his ass. This was torture. I stand at the sides, unseen and unheard, while Jared goes about his life. He has made the commitment with Kristen, and she has a swollen belly, full of his baby. They hold hands and laugh as they pass me. I don't exist in his world, and therefore he doesn't see me. They look so happy. Then I'm in a room. It looks sterile and like a hospital, but isn't. Kristen is giving birth, twins. Jared cries as his identical boys are born. I cry at my own misery. Why? Why would he do this to me? Why the hell do I have to see this? My own screaming wakes me. I sit up stiff in my bed, the vivid images still playing like a movie on repeat behind my eyes. Torture.

Maiya stumbles across the small space, clearly half asleep and still drunk, but she hugs me, albeit awkwardly—it's the thought that counts. She shushes me like I'm a crying toddler. I don't say anything, she means well and is too drunk to be of much of use. So I let her have this. And in a strange way, it's comforting. I check my phone: three am. Shit, I feel like I haven't slept at all. And honestly, I didn't want to go back to sleep if that's what I will see. No thanks. I'd rather scoop out my eyes with a spoon.

I've only been at work two hours when Jared walks in. The place is quite quiet at the minute, so I spot him immediately when the over the door bell rings. I squeal in excitement like a small child at Christmas and Wade my boss looks up from cleaning tables a strange look on his face, but I pay him no mind, all I can see is Jared. He's wearing a white tee showing off all the dips and rips in his arms and shoulders. Mmmm. And his jeans hang just perfectly from his hips. I lift my hand to my mouth because he is seriously drool-worthy and I don't want to embarrass myself at work. He strides straight toward the counter, which I am rounding like an addict. Jeez, I only saw him yesterday. I practically jump into his arms and suck his face. He chuckles against my lips.

'You miss me, baby?'

'Mmhmm,' I mumble back. My arms are wrapped around his neck, and he has me by the ass. Our bodies are crushed together, just like our mouths. I can't get enough of him—just when we are bordering on inappropriate he sets me down and holds my face in his hands.

'What time is your break?'

I sigh. Why do I need a job again? 'I'm not sure, yesterday it was around two o clock, but I guess it will be whenever it's quiet.' I shrug. Jared looks around the place, noting the small handful of people.

'Seems pretty quiet to me?'

'Jared, shush. It's like my second day. I can't go on break when I feel like it.'

'Why do you want a job anyway? Won't you have enough on with study?' He scowls noticing Wade now behind the counter. 'And who's he?'

I shush him again. 'That's Wade. He's the boss.' Jared doesn't look pleased, and he propels us forward to the counter. He sticks his hand out to Wade introducing himself.

'I'm her man,' he simply states. I internally groan and slap my hand to my face. OH MY GOD. He may as well have just pissed on me, marking his territory.

'Umm, okay. Good to know. Well, I'm Wade and just so you know, I'm gay.'

I want the ground to open up and swallow me where I stand.

'Good to know.' Jared just looks at him, and I can feel the testosterone in the room. Seriously?

'Wade, this is Jared, my boyfriend,' I say giving Jared a wide-eyed 'what the fuck was that' look. Jared grunts like he's pissed at him for hiring me. Holy shit balls.

'Well, since it's quiet, you can have a short break if you want? I'm sure I'll manage for fifteen.'

'Oh, wow. You sure?' I ask

'He's sure, come on.' Jared tugs at my arm until I dutifully follow like a lap dog. What the actual fuck has got into him. He pulls me along until we get to his truck, then he opens the door, turns, lifts me into the seat and closes the door, I wait until he rounds the front of the truck and climbs in the driver's side.

I turn in my seat to face him, not quite sure how I should play this. I don't give him a chance to get settled before I blurt out my feelings on the situation he just put me in.

'What the hell was that all about?'

He has the grace to look a little embarrassed about his behaviour. But he doesn't answer.

'Jared, what is your problem?'

He rolls his eyes and turns to me. 'Baby, I've missed you. Let's not do this now. Come over here and show me how much you've missed me.'

'Oh no. You are not distracting me with your body. Spill.'

He looks up at the roof of the truck and takes a deep breath,

'I don't like that he's your boss.' I shake my head in disbelief. I mean what the hell? 'Don't look like that. Would you like me spending my entire day being bossed by another woman?' He makes it sound sexual, and the image that jumps to my mind is not a pleasant one. No, I wouldn't like that, but this is not like that.

'Jared, you make it sound seedy. It's a coffee shop! I make coffee and clean tables. I'm not doing anything wrong here.'

'Why do you need to work?' Well duh, why does anyone need to work?

'Well, Jared. There's this thing called cash, and it makes the world go round. You earn it and then you spend it. Makes life a whole lot easier.'

'Smart ass. You don't need to work. I've got plenty.'

'Wow, I man, you woman,' I say in my caveman impersonation. 'You gonna chain me to the kitchen sink too?'

He glares at me. 'Devon don't be like that. You don't need to work. I don't want you to.'

'Ahh, so now we're getting to it? Why, Jared?'

'Just because. Okay?'

'No, not okay, Jared. Why?'

He pushes his hand through his hair and grumbles to himself in frustration. 'Because you are MY female, and I am supposed to take care of you.' Jesus Christ on a stick.

'Yes, Jared. I am YOUR female. But I like to earn my own money—what's wrong with that?' I whine, my voice getting higher by the second.

'I don't like it.'

'Well, gee. I'm sorry, NOT. I'm not accustomed to being handed everything I want or need, and I like to pay my own way, so deal with it! I'm working, end of story.' Jared looks at me, and I can see the frustration dancing behind his eyes. He's pissed. Real pissed.

'We'll see.'

I look up as he starts the truck. 'What are you doing? I've gotta get back inside.' He puts it into gear, and we take off, leaving a cloud of grit and dust from the car park. Oh shit.

'JARED TURN AROUND.' He ignores me clenching his jaw tight. I can just see the muscle there ticking with each clench. But I'm mad.

'JARED STONE. TURN THIS CAR AROUND RIGHT NOW. SO HELP ME I'M—' he brakes and laughs at me. That deep rumble sounds so sexy, and I melt a little in my seat. We've pulled over at the side of the road, about two miles down from Coffee Planet, and he turns in his seat, his face inches from mine. I close the gap. I can't help myself, and I find his tongue with mine, God, I have missed him so much. Then he's lifting me into his lap. My ass bumps the gearshift, but he isn't deterred. I straddle him. He deepens the kiss, and his hands roam—my nipples are pebbled and desperate for attention. And my vagina is in full overflow mode. I need him. I want to climb his cock and ride him right here. He has his hand in my hair, and he's tugging at the roots. His other is slowly finding its way into my panties.

'Jared, please…' I pant now, even more desperate. His fingers slide home, and I moan his name all breathy and needy.

'What is it, baby? What do you need?'

'You, Jared, please…'

'What exactly do you want?' he asks while kissing me up and down my neck and collarbone. He's maddeningly sexy, and I need him inside me.

'Your cock. Jared, give me your cock.'

'Say please,' he chuckles, and I'm beginning to get frustrated at him drawing this out.

'Jared, just… please,' I whimper,

'Okay, baby. Anything you want.' He reaches down between us and then his cock springs free. I can feel the heat against my damp panties. Thank god I wore a skirt today. I am gyrating against him— unable to satisfy my needs because he isn't moving, isn't helping me at all.

'Jared,' I pant thrusting my hips.

'Baby, what do I get if I give you my cock?'

'Anything. Anything you want, just please…'

'Anything?'

I'm too far gone to realise what he is doing here, and at that moment I don't care.

'Give up your job,' he says rubbing his cock over my clit, and it's like a bucket of ice water to my system. I stop what I am doing and slap his shoulder hard.

'You bastard, I should have known,' I say climbing off his lap and into my own seat. I'm sulking so hard right now. Sexual frustration is no fun and that combined with my anger at him is a recipe for full on bitch mode. I should kick him in his balls. I am actually mad enough to do that. But I don't, only for selfish reasons though and not because I don't want to cause him pain at this moment in time. Because believe me I do. Instead, I open my door and start walking back towards Coffee Planet.

'Baby, get in the car.' I ignore him. I'm wearing a full-on pout, and I am not backing down. He wants to use sex as a way of getting what he wants, or for punishment when he doesn't, well two can play at that game. In the end, though, I give in and get in the car. He takes me back without another word, and I continue with my shift. Jared sits drinking coffee and watching me for the rest of the day.

When my shift ends, I go in the back and collect my stuff. Jared is waiting by the door to take me home.

'I'm gonna stay at the dorm tonight.' He doesn't say anything but his jaw remains tight the rest of the journey. He pulls into my dorm car park and walks around to open my door, but I'm jumping out by the time he gets there. I hear him inhale a calming breath. Well, don't be an asshole and I won't be a bitch! I will make him regret doing that to me today. I will withhold my pussy. See how he likes it! The only way I am going to achieve that is by not sleeping in the same bed as him. Otherwise, I will give in, in a heartbeat. He comes into my room with me. I head straight for the shower while he waits. When I'm done, a towel wrapped around me, I step out only to find him naked and in my bed.

'What are you doing?'

'Getting comfortable in this tiny piece of shit bed.'

'Why?'

'Because I'm staying here.'

'Jared. I have a roommate in case you have forgotten, and I'm not supposed to have boys stay over.'

'Boys? No boys sweetheart. Just your man.' Gah, he is so infuriating! And sexy, and hot, and all things sinful. I find my most non-sexy pj's and get myself dressed. The look on Jared's face tells me he knows what I am up to. And much to my disappointment, he doesn't try a thing. Just lays there 'comfortable.'

'We not having food tonight then?'

'Why'd you think that?'

'Well, the nun's pyjamas kinda gives me the impression you're ready for bed?'

'Nope, I'm just all about the comfort. Where do you wanna eat?'

'I'm thinking steak?

Mmm, I could definitely do a steak.

# chapter SIXTEEN

## *Devon*

I WAKE THE NEXT MORNING, and I almost choke on my sexual frustration. Jared has cuddled me all night as if he knew he was torturing me. So much for my plan.

Jared drops me at work and says he will be in at lunch, and then back to pick me up when I finish. We eat lunch outside on the grass. Jared even brings a picnic blanket and feeds me strawberries. So sweet.

The rest of the day passes in a blur. We are so busy I don't even realise the time. I'm refilling a guy's coffee when he gets a bit too handsy. I don't say anything, just unravel myself from his arm, which he persistently wraps around my hip, trying to pull me into his lap. There are things I want to say, but I hold back. This is only my third day on the job, and I want to keep it. I'm just pushing his hand away from my ass for the third time as I fill another cup at the table just behind him when the bell above the door tinkles and I turn to find a stony-faced Jared storming toward me.

## *Jared*

I walk in to see some fucking stuck up asshole with his hands and eyes all over my woman. Mother fucker.

'I'll bury you, motherfucker,' I growl out through clenched teeth, lifting him from his seat. He squirms and says some shit, but I can't make it out. I want to put the fucker in the ground more than anything, but I step back and release his fucking poncy shirt, shoving him away from me, and he clambers, smacking into his chair. Everyone in the immediate vicinity gets up and moves away from me. Devon's shaking her head. It takes me all I have not to pound my fist into his face until he's unrecognisable. But the look on my girl's face tells me that's a bad move. So I watch as she saunters into the back to collect her stuff. I turn and face the bastard then.

'Touch what's mine, fucker, and you die. We clear?' The fucker nods his head, over and over, muttering some shit about not wanting trouble.

'Should have thought about that, motherfucker, before you put your hands on my girl,' I tell him. Seeing her come through the back door I walk toward her, but she walks straight past me and out to the car. I can't fucking win.

We don't speak all the way back. I've almost bitten my fucking tongue off twice so I don't fuck this up.

'What the hell was that for?' she whisper-shouts as we get through my bedroom door. I roll my eyes at her as I strip off my t-shirt and unbuckle my belt. I'm pissed, and she wants to shout at me?

'Get undressed.'

She looks at me with that cute angry pout, and I want to smile, but I'm still pissed at her. 'Get un-fucking-dressed.' I pull her to me and rip the top she's wearing over her head. She protests, but I don't hear it. My head is pounding with need. I have one focus, and that's to be inside her. Now. Still defying me, she stands hands on hips. Sexy as fuck in her pink bra and black jeans. Her lips forming words that I'm not hearing 'cause I'm too busy thinking about those same lips being wrapped around my dick. I see that look in her eyes, arousal. I smell it. She wants it just as much as me, but she's being stubborn as usual. She steps back as I advance on her, but she doesn't say no, and her body is screaming yes.

'Wait.' I stop immediately, Fuck, maybe I was wrong. 'Jared.' Her hands rest on my chest. 'Listen to me for a minute?' I let out a long sigh, my dick throbbing like a jackhammer against my fly. 'Will you?' I clench my jaw and nod my head. Sitting on the edge of the bed.

'Shoot,' I tell her. And she sits down next to me.

'Jared. I'm not sure what you think was going on when you walked in, but that guy was just being an asshole. He didn't deserve that.' Well, fuck that. Defending him?

'You. Are. Mine. *MINE*. And no one looks at you that way but *me*,' I yell as I thump my chest to drive it home. She stands, stamping her feet as she does.

'I'm not a fucking possession, Jared, and so what if he looked at me? Are you going to beat up every guy that glances my way?'

I'm seething fucking mad. 'He wasn't glancing at you! He was fucking you with his eyes. The motherfucker had his paws on your ass as I walked in. So don't fucking tell me he didn't want his dick in MY pussy! Is that what you wanted? Did you want him to fuck you? Is that why you're pissed?' I'm standing now, hovering over her. She looks up at me as her eyes fill with tears, shaking her head, she pulls her hand back, and before I realise what she's doing, it connects with my face.

'FUCK. YOU. JARED!' She's dragging her top back on and heading for the door. Shit.

'Fuck! Devon, wait,' I plead. 'I'm sorry.' I step into her space and pull her hand from the doorknob. She pauses there. I lace my fingers over hers and pull her into me, her back to my chest, inhaling my favourite scent in the world. Devon. 'I'm sorry, baby.' She turns in my arms, and I take her mouth with mine—our tongues and teeth clashing. My goal? Get inside my female and fast before she remembers I'm the asshole she's pissed at. I make quick work of her top and bra and latch onto her hard nipple, making her moan—music to my fucking ears. I push my jeans and boxers down while walking her backwards to the bed. I'm starkers and intend to have her the same way. I lay her down while my attention is on her other nipple. I slide her jeans and panties down in one, and she kicks them off her feet, just as eager as I am. Thank fuck. Pushing a finger inside her, I groan.

'Baby, you're soaking for me.'

'Only you.' She lifts her ass and pushes me deeper. I need to be inside her. I line myself up with her heat and push in hard.

'Fuck. Yes.' I savour the moment. The connection I've needed since she started withholding on me. I'm a desperate man, and I'm only realising now just how desperate I have been. I move slowly at first—each thrust a slow torture to my dick. But I need it this way because it's what she needs. She opens up her neck for me, and like a starved man I dive in, sucking and biting at her throat. She moans my name. Fuck yes.

'Harder, Jared.' I don't need to be asked twice. I go for my life. Lifting her ass to go deeper, I feel her clench around me. Her tight pussy is milking me for all I'm worth. I'm about ready to fucking explode when she comes hard. Screaming my name and clawing at my back. I feel the sting as her nails bite into the skin. I pump faster, her orgasm still in full flow as I go over the edge with her, hammering her as hard as I can. My eyes roll with the pure fucking ecstasy of it as I blow into her sweet pussy. I'm home. Our chests heave, vying for oxygen. I lay on top of her, holding my weight on my forearms. She's smiling, but I sense she's still annoyed. I don't pull out yet, instead, before she can start on a rant, I kiss her again. Slowly telling her everything I feel without words, and she lets me.

We decide after our marathon sex session that we'll join the rest of the pack for dinner. I'm starving after the workout she's given me. And I smell stew. One of Imogen's special recipes. It can't be sniffed at. Devon isn't keen on getting her ass out of bed after her long shift and then our workout, but I convince her that it's worth going down for.

Devon

After Jared fucks me within an inch of my life, I'm shattered but find myself at the table in the kitchen waiting to sample Imogen's famous chicken stew. Everyone is in, even Kristen. Ugh. I want to punch her stupid face. But I smile instead, and eat the damn stew. It's good, really good. Damn, it's delicious. Now I understand why Jared dragged me from a post-sex sleep. Wow. I look to Jared in appreciation. He nods lifting his brows,

'I know, right?' I mumble a reply around another mouthful, and he laughs, gaining the attention of the table. All eyes are on me as I shovel another spoonful into my mouth.

'Imogen, I think Devon likes your stew,' Brad hollers over to where she is slicing bread for the table, making her turn and look at me.

'Oh my God, this is so good, Imogen.'

She laughs at my muffled appreciation and brings the fresh bread over.

'I'm glad you like it.'

There is a rare silence as everyone tucks into their own bowls. All that can be heard is spoons clashing with the bowls and then Brad, true to form, breaks the silence. I've never known him keep quiet for long.

'So what have you two kids been up to?' he asks of Jared, and me but everyone looks on waiting for an answer. Brad looks pretty damn pleased with himself. Clearly, he already knows what we've been 'up to'.

'Ah, you know, the usual.' I try and blag a non-descript answer, and he almost spits his mouthful of orange juice at me as he chokes on his laughter.

'Is that what the cool kids are calling it these days?'

'Give it up, Brad. She's not gonna give you details, you pig,' Zoe singsongs.

'Nah, but Jared might,' he says wiggling his eyebrows and leering at me. Jared looks to me and then to Brad.

'Not a fuckin' chance, Romeo.'

'Okay, okay. I get it.' Brad shakes his head. 'So who's up for a group run tonight?' Jared looks at me and must decide from my shocked face against the idea.

'Nah, man. Not tonight.'

Brad whines like a child for a minute and then the girls join in. 'Aww, come on, Jared. We haven't had one in weeks,' Zoe coaxes. Jared leans in and whispers in my ear.

'Your call, baby.' I swallow hard, wondering what the hell they all do on a group run. Do they change together? Get naked? So many questions, but there's a buzz around the table and everyone seems up for it except me. Jared kisses me along my jaw, and then back up to my ear. He nibbles at my lobe before whispering again, 'You'll have fun either way, I promise.' I shudder at his sexy as hell voice. When I ran with Jared, we did have a lot of fun, but we were alone. Well, until Howard. Oh what the hell.

'Okay, let's do it.' I smile up at him. Brad didn't need Jared to confirm my answer. He was already whooping

'That's my girl,' Brad hollers with some more whooping.

Jared's face turns serious. 'My girl, asshole.'

'Oh, I know that, dick face. Just testing.' He winks at me, and I have to laugh. He flirts all the time, but I know he isn't ever serious. He's just being Brad.

# chapter
# SEVENTEEN

## Devon

BABY, DON'T BE SO NERVOUS, we do this all the time. Back home we sometimes run with the whole pack, so this is nothing,' he says it like it's a trivial thing and it grates on me. If I'm totally honest, I feel like throwing up right now. I don't know what the hell came over me agreeing to this so soon. I don't even know these people well, and I am going to be at my most vulnerable with them all around me. It doesn't feel like nothing. Jared moves toward me and feeling my hesitance his arms come around me from behind. We are in his bathroom, and I've been watching him in the mirror while I brush my hair. I'm stiff, and he notices. 'What's wrong?'

'Jared. I'm not sure this is such a good idea. What if I'm different?'

Jared shakes his head at me his lips flattened out in a line. 'Baby, it's fine if you are you are. But you forget, I've already seen you in wolf form, and you are just the same as everyone else. Well actually, that's a lie. You're hot as fuck—unlike the rest of them downstairs.'

I giggle and smack his arm. 'There's my girl.' He grins. 'Now move your sexy ass before I put my dick in you again.' He grinds his cock against my ass, and I groan, parting my legs invitingly. It's instinctual with him, almost automatic. He growls deep in his throat, which only turns me on more. He runs his hands up the outside of my thighs, and I flood my panties as usual. Just as he gets his fingers lined up with Niagara, there's a loud knocking on the bathroom door.

'Brad, you have shitty fuckin' timing man,' Jared growls out.

'I believe I have impeccable timing, Jared. If you two start 'that' we'll never fuckin get out of the house.'

I giggle. He is right after all.

We walk into the woods, hand in hand, some of the group in front and some behind us. I'm anxious as all hell. Jared is clearly aware because he is rubbing his thumb over mine repetitively, trying to calm me. Part of me is really excited to be doing this, but another part of me is screaming 'what the hell are you doing.' It's like a war waging inside, and I'm not sure which one is going to win.

'Baby, come here. You're shaking.' We're deep in the woods now, and the scents are amazing. I'm desperate for the change, and my body is trembling in anticipation. My wolf, eager to be set free. Jared pulls me in for a hug, and I embrace it, trying like hell to pull some positive energy into myself so I can relax into the change. The more you mentally fight it the more painful it will be. And my mind needs to get with the program. This is happening, and there is nothing I can do about it.

'What's the worst that can happen right?' I ask him, peeking up from his tight hold.

'Devon, listen. You are gonna be just fine. We'll have a great time. Just like before.' I nod in agreement. We really did have a great time. 'You ready, baby?' He pulls me over to a tree and explains that this is his patch to change. And everyone else will be scattered through the woods.

'I've seen Brad's ass once, and it's not a sight I wanna see again,' he tells me, laughing. I'm feeling so much more relieved now I know I don't have to change right in front of everyone. Phew. Jared starts to strip. I look around for a bit of privacy. I've never changed in front of anyone—not even my dad. It's private. Jared looks at me. I'm still fully clothed; he's naked in all of his beautiful glory.

'Don't go shy on me now,' he chuckles.

'I've never done this in front of anyone before. I'm not sure if I even can.'

'It's just me, baby.' Jared looks at me puzzled. For him I'm sure this is a normal, everyday occurrence, living with a pack. But this is huge for me. It's just Jared I tell myself over and over. He pulls me to him and begins undressing me, unzipping my jacket and pushing it from my shoulders, then pulling my tee over my head, lifting my arms up as he does. I bring them down onto his shoulders and pull him into me,

'Oh no, female. I know what you're doing,' he says against my lips. I slide my tongue along his lips in encouragement. He can't normally pass up an opportunity for sex, so maybe we could just lose ourselves in this and me changing will be forgotten, although the vibrations from my body alone are a big enough reminder. My body is desperate. I don't think I could stop it now if I tried. I step away from him and brace myself, taking a deep breath.

'I'm ready.'

Jared doesn't speak, he just grins. He allows me to slip behind the tree as I take my leggings and sneakers off. I get on all fours and concentrate, allowing the change to take over. The pain is excruciating but liberating. My muscles stretch and my bones dislocate under my skin. The all-familiar point where my chest is so restricted, and I feel like I'm suffocating, comes, and the short state of panic leaves me as my wolf lungs inhale deeply. It's thankfully quick today. But no sooner have I lifted my rear off the ground, I feel Jared's wet nose between my hind legs. I huff out and sit my ass down. He whines, which turns into a grumble, as he prods at my rear end, pushing me up and onto my paws. I take off running and hear him sprinting after me. If I could laugh in this form, I would.

I run into a clearing and come to an abrupt stop. All around me are the rest of the pack. I tentatively take another step forward. Another. And then I stop completely. A nervous feeling runs through me as everyone looks at me. I feel Jared nudge me forward as each member of the pack comes forward. First, comes Zoe. In her wolf form, she is stunning. She has chocolate coloured fur, stands at about my height, and her dark eyes shine as she looks at me. She bows her muzzle and rubs herself along my side. I'm unsure what I should do, so I do nothing. Next, comes Imogen. She is just as stunning as a wolf. Her light blond hair comes through when she changes, and her piercing blue eyes are just the same. Again Imogen goes through the same ritual, closely followed by Logan and Howard. Brad walks up and something about his swagger tells me he is going to start something—albeit in fun. Brad will be Brad after all. He bows his head and begins rubbing against my side. All of a sudden I feel his nose at my rear and instinct has me sitting down, but not before I let out a snarl. Jared is in motion before my ass hits the grass. He has Brad by the throat. Brad is belly up and whining in submission. A few seconds pass and no one moves a muscle. Jared lets him go, and he scrambles to his feet but doesn't stand. Instead, he stays in a laying position in front of me. Am I expected to do something? Is this an apology? Shit, I have no idea. Jared yips a small sound and Brad moves away, and then Howard is approaching. He goes through the same process that the others did. I notice then that they are all behind me in a semi-circle, only Kristen is left. She's looking none too happy at what is about to go down. As she steps forward, she looks like she is in pain. She doesn't bow her head like the others and then tries to walk past me to join them. I would have happily ignored her and moved on from whatever this was, but Jared has other ideas. He snaps his jaws and snarls, so loud everyone cowers. I turn a little toward him and see his teeth bared completely. He looks almost rabid. Kristen cowers under his glare, and she bows her head a fraction. Now for the rubbing—great. I feel her against me, not affectionate like the others. I get a clear pissed off feel from her. Ditto bitch. Just as she is passing my head, I feel a sharp pain at my ear. I whip around, and in no time at all, we are snapping and biting at each other in a flurry of fur and fangs. We're literally rolling around. Vying for the best position. I have a mouth full of fur around her throat, and she is beneath me now. I bite down harder and taste blood. All the while her hind legs are gouging the skin on my underbelly, as they pinwheel around. She's trying like hell to throw me off. And she has lost the use of her best weapon—her teeth because of how I have her pinned down. I hold on for as long as I can and just as I feel I can't hold her anymore she stops struggling. I immediately let go to find her submitting to me completely. Her legs are lax, and her neck is on show. Bleeding. Well, what do you know? I bested her. I curl my lip in a snarl, letting her know I'm not happy.

Kristen stays where she is, and Jared nudges me from the side and throws his head up in a 'come with me' gesture. I follow—leaving Kristen sprawled out behind me. The pack walk with us, surrounding us, in a kind of formation, I hear Kristen scramble to her feet, whining. Hopefully in pain. And she joins the group at the back. Bitch. I'm still no clearer on what just happened, but I can't think on it too much because when Jared lets out another little yip, the pack disperses in all directions. Leaving me alone again with Jared. He rubs himself along my body one way and then back the other side. He licks at my muzzle, and I feel that all too familiar arousal flow through my body. Shit a brick. I'm in wolf form, and I'm aroused. What the hell? I didn't even know this was possible. Jared must smell it. It's clear in the air, just as his scent is. He starts to get worked up like an excited pup, lapping at my face. His tail is wagging, and he seems to be very taken with my ass end. I'm excited—it's instinctual. I cannot help myself. I have a sudden urge to submit and mate.

My wolf has almost completely taken over my rational mind, when I hear someone approaching. Jared spins in a protective stance snarling toward the sound. I realise then that it's Brad. He's making a wheezing noise that sounds a hell of a lot like he's laughing. Pleased with what he's just interrupted. He throws his head back over his shoulder and yips at the two of us. Jared calms down pretty quickly, and we follow. We run through the woods, and I feel full of life with Jared at my side. I can hear the rabbits thumping their legs in warning all around me, and I hear all other signs of life cease as we get close, knowing we are predators. Brad keeps the pace, and we follow him easily, jumping boulders and huge tree roots, hopping over felled branches and dodging prickly bushes. We run like that for some time before we stop at a small stream. The rest of the pack is sprawled out with recent kills between their forepaws, tearing and ripping at their meals. Howard tosses a rabbit at my feet, and another at Jared. I follow Jared's lead, and when he settles in to eat, I do the same. I'm sated and feeling content when Jared comes over and cleans my muzzle, lapping at my fur. I return the favour, and when I'm done he rests his head over my back, and we lay there watching the rest of his pack fool about around us.

I've never seen a pack before, so their behaviour together amazes me. I could stay like this forever. I want to join in but a bigger part of me is still feeling reserved, and so I settle for watching. I go to get a drink from the stream and Jared follows. I watch as he bends his neck to lap at the water. He is such a stunning wolf. He is easily the biggest of all the males here and in my opinion the easiest on the eyes too. He is beautiful—his green eyes stand out from the dark colouring of his fur. He is so tough looking I'd have a hard time believing there's a wolf whom would dare to challenge him. I lose myself watching him, and he catches me. He saunters over as if he knows exactly what is on my mind, and he rubs himself under my chin and all over me. He is marking me as his and I then realise that that was what the rest of the pack were doing earlier—marking me as part of their pack.

Jared moves us to a spot where the stream narrows to almost nothing and I notice all the males heading to the section which leads up a small hill. It's quite a distance, but they stop on the crest of the hill. Zoe stands before Jared and me with a rock in her jaws. I watch not knowing what is going on. But Jared seems to have settled in to watch whatever it is. Brad and Logan both stand on the crest, Howard to their side. I watch as Zoe throws the rock upward and the second it hits the water the males are off sprinting toward us. Racing. Logan is a hair's breadth behind Brad all the way, and Brad wins literally by a whisker. They head back up to the top, yipping and bustling each other like a pair of teenage boys would. Then Howard lines up next to Brad. Racing the winner. And Logan stands watching at the top while Zoe thrusts the rock in the air again. This time, Brad is behind, Howard stumbles slightly and almost gives up his lead, but he recovers fast, and he beats Brad by a full head. Brad yips in our direction and Jared moves from our lazy spot. I watch his muscles contract as he pushes up the hill. It's possible I could be drooling right now. I watch as he lines up next to Howard. Knowing how fast Howard is, I have to wonder if Jared can beat him. The rock hits the water and in a matter of seconds Jared is back at the bottom—the winner. He's so fast that Howard didn't even come close. Wow. I jump up and rub myself all over him. I can't help myself. He is mine after all. He nudges me, and I come out of my Jared-loving haze and realise that the girls are now up on the hill.

First up are Imogen and Kristen. Kristen is easily the leaner and more athletic of the two, but does she have the speed? Yes, apparently she does, beating Imogen by a clear margin.

Next up are Zoe and Kristen. The rock is thrown, and Zoe has the lead easily, but she stumbles badly, and Kristen takes the advantage, practically bowling Zoe over in the process. Bitch. Kristen wins. I feel Jared nudge me again, and I am being beckoned by Imogen at the top of the hill. Oh, shit balls. I huff out a little and shake my head, hoping to get the message across, I don't want to race. I'm happy watching. He prods at me again and whines a little in an 'aw but please' kind of way. So I trot up there and stand beside the bitch, watching for Brad to thrust the rock in the air.

It hits the water, and we're off. It seemed such a short race when I watched the others but the end seems a million miles away right now. I'm in the lead, by almost my entire body—I can feel her hot breath at my rear. I'm suddenly yanked back by my tail. I yelp in shock, turning to find her jaws clamped on it. I turn—snapping and snarling at her, as we go at it for round two. I'm sick and tired of this little tramp. And it ends now. I've had it. I bite down on her ear and pull my head, tearing at the flesh. As blood pools in my mouth, I hear Jared growling. But I pay him no attention because I have one thing on my mind and that is to maim. I lose my footing and stumble, and she tries to get on top of me, but I'm up as quick as I go down, and as she clasps my foreleg in her jaws, I clamp onto her scruff and yank with all I've got. I feel a searing pain shoot down my leg as I throw her off but my adrenaline has kicked in, and my only goal is to hurt her and keep on hurting her. I yank again, and her teeth come loose, taking my flesh with her. I'm all over her, snapping and tearing at her fur. I will make sure she doesn't recover quickly from this. I tear flesh from her hind leg and move quickly to her rib area, where I bite again and again, moving the whole time so she can't get a grip on me again. The whole pack is surrounding us now as we circle each other. She's tired and flagging. I feel like I could go on all night. I'm hungry for more. I'm salivating at the thought of tearing her head from her body. I'm going in for the kill when Jared knocks me off course. I look at him in disbelief. How could he? Why would he want to protect her?

I turn and walk away. Only then realising just how bad my forepaw is. I lift it and carry my weight on three legs so I don't make it any worse. Jared follows me, but I'm pissed and injured and not in the mood. I want to be alone. I make my way slowly to where my clothes are. I want to change and get myself dressed before I have to deal with any repercussions about what I just did. Jared is not letting me go that easily though. He keeps prodding me and grumbling. I eventually give in and stop, sitting down as I breathe deeply. Jared is all over me, checking for injuries and he laps at my paw, trying to clean it. It stings like a bitch and I'm being impatient, but I want to change and take care of things. I try to move off, and he makes an impatient yipping noise and a low rumble in his chest. I huff out a sigh of frustration and sit back on my haunches. Resigned to the fact I won't be going anywhere until he's satisfied, I make no move to be affectionate while he cleans and checks my wounds. I am pissed. Despite my wolf wanting to reciprocate his attentions, I fight it because I'm so angry, and when I'm angry, I'm stubborn. So I sit with my nose in the air looking up at the sky.

My change is painful, and no sooner have I finished Jared is picking me up from the floor.

'Shit. Baby. This is bad. We need to get this stitched.' I pull my arm from his hands and ignore him. Struggling to grab my clothes, he pulls them down for me. I take them and stuff my legs into my leggings and my feet into my sneakers. It's difficult with my arm, but I'm being stubborn, so I don't give a shit how much it hurts. I'll do it by myself, thank you very much. My tee is an issue and Jared, realising he's getting the cold shoulder, is now leaning against the tree arms folded with a shitty look on his face. Making me even more determined.

'You need help with—'

'Nope,' I snap. I'm smearing blood all over myself trying and failing to get it over my head then put my arm through, so I try a different tactic and put my injured arm through first, then pull it over my head. I manage it, but I'm a hot mess. I harrumph at Jared and begin walking, in no mood to stick around. I'm going home. I am not staying to be berated for something she started. I get back to Jared's room—he's followed me the whole way, saying nothing. I start packing my bag, and he breaks his silence.

'The fuck are you doing?' he asks.

'What does it look like?'

'Well, looks a fuck-of-a-lot like you're packing your shit, for nothing, 'cause you're not going anywhere.'

I ignore him and carry on packing. Well, I say packing. I'm smearing my blood all over my clothes and stuffing them ungracefully into my holdall.

'Devon.' Nope, ignoring. Not giving in. 'DEVON!' I jump at the harsh and loud tone in his voice.

'Stop it, you're not going anywhere, and you need that stitching,' he says pointing to my arm. It's a real mess and still bleeding. He grabs my hand and steers me into the bathroom where he wets a cloth and proceeds to clean it. It stings, and I wince.

'Baby, I'm sorry, but it needs cleaning,' he says lifting me to sit on the counter.

'Maybe I should go and get a tetanus too?'

He gives me a 'don't be so stupid' look.

'Don't look at me like that, Jared. Who knows where that bitch has had her mouth?'

His eyes widen just a fraction. And I know why and can't help myself.

'Oh, that's right. How could I forget? I KNOW where she's been.'

'Fuckin' Hell, Devon. I'm sick of this shit.' He kicks the wastebasket over. 'How many times do we need to go over this? FUCK!' I look on at him in amazement. How can he make this about him?

'You know what, Jared. Fuck you.' I jump from the counter and move past him into the bedroom. The bleeding has stopped at least, with the cloth wrapped around my arm. I grab my bag and head for the door. As I open it, he slams it shut with his arm over my shoulder. He looks as if he's trying to show restraint. His jaw ticks, his eyes are closed, and his forehead is creased. He's past annoyed. Well, so am I.

'Let go of the door, Jared.'

'So you can run again? just 'cause the goings got tough?'

It's like a slap in the face. And my head snaps back like he's done just that.

'YOU.' I prod at his chest. 'You protected HER when you should have stood by me. She started that—'

'I WAS PROTECTING YOU!'

'Me?' I scoff. 'I had her handled. I didn't need protecting. *You* saved *her,* not me.' He cages me in with his arms. My back is flat against the door, and he growls in my ear.

'You are fuckin' testing me, woman.' Oh no, he didn't.

'Who the fuck do you think you are, Jared? Don't you dare pull that shit on me!' I shove at his arm, but all I manage is to hurt my own further. Jared drags me by my good arm and pushes me onto the bed.

'Who the fuck do I think I am?' he says calmly, but he's raging, leaning over me. I kick out at him, but he blocks my attempts. I'm so mad now I can't even see straight.

'I'm *your* male, and you are *my* female, and you will not fuckin' run out on me every time you get your knickers in a fuckin twist. You got me?'

I breathe in hard through my nose and grit my teeth. Jared pushes my arms above my head and puts himself between my legs. Holding me in place with one hand he grips my chin with his other. I see lust flash in his eyes as they meet mine. I'd be lying if I said I didn't feel it too. But then an image of him with her flashes in my mind, and I'm over it. I don't like feeling jealous—it's unwanted. But it's just not something I can switch off, especially when he pulls a stunt like that. I struggle, wanting to be free of him and that fucking image.

'Devon, Jesus Christ. Will you calm the fuck down and listen to me?'

'Why, Jared? Explain, why you did it?'

He frowns and shakes his head and pushes off me he drags his hands through his hair—something I've learned he does when he's frustrated.

'You really have no fuckin' idea how things work in a pack do you?' I raise my eyebrows. A sarcastic 'oh please' look etched on my face.

'Devon you can't just take someone out like that unless you have good reason, and don't fuckin' look at me like that, being jealous is not a good reason.'

'She started it, Jared!'

'Baby, you have me pegged all wrong here. I'm not trying to say you were in the wrong. Fuck, she deserved it, but I stopped you because of the consequences.'

'Well, the only consequence I see happening is her strutting her slutty self all up in my face because you saved her. How do you think that will look to her, Jared. Huh? Do you really think she'll be out there thinking, 'oh Jared saved me so Devon wouldn't get in shit?' Hell no. She's thinking right now that you still want her—that there's still a chance and that's why you saved her.'

He's pacing now, and my arm feels numb. I shake it a little, and the cloth comes loose. I have several gashes and all look like they need a couple of sutures, otherwise, they will heal badly. I don't care, though. I'm still mad.

'I'm going to get Zoe,' he tells me as he leaves the room. I jump off the bed to follow him, but he turns as he gets to the door,

'Do I need to lock the fuckin' door or you gonna behave?'

'Are you gonna answer me or are you gonna just leave?' He closes his eyes and takes a deep breath.

'I'm getting your arm looked at. That's my priority right now. THEN we will have this shit out, okay?'

'You gonna check on Kristen while you're gone?'

He growls at me and clenches his jaw.

'Just fuckin' stop, Devon. I'll be back with Zoe in a minute. Don't fuckin go anywhere... please.' He sounds tired and sick of all this. Well, that makes two of us. I lie on his bed and curl up with my arm on top. I must nod off because I wake up and Zoe is checking my arm out. She has a smirk on her face and keeps looking over to Jared, who's back to pacing.

'What's up with you?' I ask a smile in my voice. She shakes her head, rolling her eyes to look at Jared.

'You did a number on that little skank. She was in bad shape when you left.'

'Good.' I smirk a little too. Then she jabs me with a needle I didn't even notice her holding. It was like a sneak attack. 'Have you already patched her up?'

'Hell no. She can wait. She'll be lucky if I see too her at all after what she did to you.' I want to hug her so bad at that moment, but she has a needle in my skin so it would be a little awkward.

'Zoe, you're the best' I tell her grinning.

'Hell, yeah, bitches over stitches!'

I howl laughing. When I calm down enough, I ask, 'So does she need a lot of stitches?'

'Yep, she'll need a fuck load, and it'll be a damn shame if she heals before she gets em.' We giggle. I don't feel bad one bit and it's good to know that at least Zoe has my back even if Jared doesn't.

# chapter EIGHTEEN

## Jared

WHEN ZOE IS DONE, I'M hoping Devon has calmed the fuck down. I approach her when Zoe closes the door, trying to gauge her mood. Her arm already looks a lot better for being patched up, but it must still hurt. I'm raging at Kristen, and if it were up to me right now I would have happily let Devon take her out, but with the way my dad is being over the whole fucking Kristen and me thing, he would have seen it as Devon taking her out so his orders couldn't be followed. I couldn't have that. I wanted his consent, and I know damn well that if she'd have killed her without his order, the shit would hit the fan— even more so because she wouldn't have her own pack to back her up. He's already suspicious about her being here with no affiliation to a pack. We should have been contacted, told that she was coming into our territory. But that's how packs work, and she doesn't have one.

As I approach, her jaw is set as she grits her teeth. Okay. So still mad.

'Baby, don't do this. Don't let her come between us. Can we please just move past this?'

'That guy in the café—how did he make you feel?' she blurts.

I shake my head in confusion. Where the fuck is she going with this?

'What's that got to do—'

'Just answer the question, Jared.' I take a moment to choose the right words. One wrong one could send her fucking running again.

'I wanted to break his face, and make him regret even looking at you,' I sigh shrugging my shoulders. Her eyebrows raise, and she has this little pout on her face. It's cute, but it's smug as all hell.

'Exactly, Jared. You wanted to cause him pain when he had just made a small AND unwanted play toward me, so how do you think I feel, knowing that she wants you, and has HAD you and that she's meant to be with you?'

'Just because my dad wants it doesn't mean it's meant to be, Devon. Don't twist that shit.'

'My point still remains.'

She has a fucking point. If the boot were on the other foot, I would have killed that motherfucker dead the first time I saw him. I take a deep breath, resigned to the fact I'm not winning this argument because she is right.

'Baby, if I were in your situation, I would have killed him. I get that, I do. But in a pack, you cannot kill another pack member without facing the consequences. It just doesn't fly. There are rules, and we have to stick by them. If I were alpha, it would be a different story, but I have to answer to my father, and he is still unhappy about this whole business. If we want to make it work in the pack together, then we gotta play by pack rules, baby.' So far so good. She's letting me sit beside her on the bed, and as I reach up to cup her face she leans into my touch. Phew.

'I was so mad, Jared. I don't even know what I was thinking, to be honest. I got carried away, and I wanted to kill her,' her voice squeaks up a notch at the end like she's trying to hold back tears.

'Baby, I understand.'

'No, Jared. I would have killed her…' She looks a little pale like she might throw up.

'Devon, you okay?'

She jumps up suddenly and rushes into the bathroom and throws up. I follow and hold her hair back as she slaps at my chest, mumbling for me to leave the room. I rub at her back and ignore her. When she's done, I get a glass and rinse it out before filling and handing it to her as she rinses.

'You didn't need to see that. I'm sorry. I feel gross,' she says, wiping her mouth with the back of her hand.

'You sick?'

She shakes her head at me. 'No, apparently, almost killing someone, turns my stomach.'

I hadn't even thought about that. Shit. I have to keep reminding myself that she isn't like me.

'C'mere.' I push the seat down on the loo and sit, bringing her onto my lap.

'Baby, it's in our nature, and sometimes it happens. Don't beat yourself up over it, okay?'

'I was mad that you stopped me from ending a life, Jared—that's not normal.'

She was clearly not used to embracing her wolf side.

'Baby, I promise. It's not abnormal among wolves, and it will not be the last time you feel like that.' Maybe that wasn't the right thing to say because her face goes pale and harsh.

'Maybe not if I have to stay around that skank much longer.' She pulls out of my grip and stands to look in the mirror. She pushes her hair behind her ears then grabs her toothbrush and brushes for about five fucking minutes. I stay quiet. I'd only make shit worse, best to keep schtum. I wait till she's done and then follow her out to the bedroom. Is she talking to me? Or have we gone right back to the original argument? Fuck if I can understand how women's minds work! I'll just tread carefully and hope for the best.

'You ready to crash?' Maybe if I can just get her under the sheets, I can get her all relaxed and no longer thinking about Kristen.

'I guess so,' is her answer. I get naked and climb in the bed, patting her side with a smile on my face. She gets undressed, but it's far from sexy. She clearly needs some persuasion. In a huff, she undresses with her back to me, leaves her knickers on, and before I get a glimpse of her sweet little tits she throws my t-shirt on before she climbs in the bed and pulls the duvet up to her chin. Yeah, I'm still in the proverbial doghouse. I want to hold her so fucking bad, and I don't know what reaction I'm going to get. Ah well, I'm done playing this game. I shift closer and pull her into me. Her back to my chest, being careful I don't hurt her arm, I slide my arms around her so her head rests on my right arm and my left is over her waist. She doesn't complain. But I don't push my luck. I lay there with a hard on instead, sticking my ass as far out as I can manage so I don't poke her ass with it. Fuck, she might rip it off and feed it to me, the mood she's in.

I wake up to the light streaming in through the bottom of the curtains.

Devon's still sleeping. She's so fucking cute. She doesn't snore at all—she's that quiet I used to check her breathing when we first started sleeping together. Her face scrunches though, in a little pout.

We're still tangled up, and I want to kiss her lips, so fucking much. I'm worried that she might still be pissed at me. Ah, fuck it. I kiss her anyway—just a chaste peck. She stirs a little but not enough, so I kiss her a little harder, lingering this time. She moans and my dick stands at attention, ready to go to work. I lick at her lips, encouraging her to open up for me. I feel the change, and I know she's awake when her arms come up around my neck and she moans—all sleepy and sexy as hell. I push my tongue in, and she matches my eagerness. She isn't fully awake, but she's going with it. Maybe I'm forgiven. Or maybe she's just forgotten she's annoyed at my ass. Either way, this is happening, and I'm hoping that we can just start the day fresh. Forget all the shit that went down last night. Her legs wrap around my waist, and she starts grinding herself against me. Fuck, yeah. I push my hand in between us and work her clit through her knickers, making her whimper. God, I fucking love that sound. By the time she opens her eyes completely, I've got her knickers off, and I'm pushing inside her. I go slowly, knowing I haven't really had a chance to get her ready for me. I don't want to risk foreplay just in case she changes her mind and remembers she is pissed at me. I'm a fucking pussy when it comes to her. I slide in easily.

'Fuck, baby, you're soaked.'

She doesn't answer, just makes little mewling noises that turn me the fuck on. I can't keep the pace slow like I intended. I wanted to ease her awake and make love to her, but my dick has other ideas, my hips piston in and out in and out like a fucking teenager chasing his first orgasm. I can't get enough of her, and after lying next to her all night with wood, I am a desperate man. Devon doesn't seem to mind though—she's thrusting her hips up to meet mine, and we're in sync. 'God, I fuckin' love you, baby.'

She's panting now she's on the brink. I lift her leg at the knee, getting a deeper angle. A few more thrusts and she goes over, biting her lip to keep the noise down. Fuck that. 'Don't hold it in baby,' I grunt against her ear, barely able to get the words out myself. My dick is squeezed so tight as she comes. It's fucking beautiful to watch as her eyes almost roll back and her mouth drops open as the sweetest sound escapes her. Her pussy is milking my dick. The tightness has me growing even bigger as I'm about to blow. I grunt and thrust, grunt and thrust. The muscles in my neck and jaw go tight as I blow my load. The sound that comes out of me starts somewhere deep and keeps coming until I collapse on top of her. Fuck me, that was intense.

Our breathing is heavy, and our eyes lock. A smile spreads across her face.

'Good morning,' she says her eyes twinkling.

'Fuck, yeah it is,' I pant out. I kiss her, holding my weight on my elbows. Then I turn us on our side, not breaking our connection.

'Can we stay like this?' she asks. I don't think she's referring to our position, more about ignoring the shit storm we have to eventually face.

'All day, baby,' I tell her, and she squeezes my dick, tensing her pussy muscles. Knowing damn well what I was referring to. I growl, and it makes her laugh. I tickle her, and she squeals for me to stop. She's laughing so hard she can barely catch her breath—she's fucking beautiful. All the while, I'm still inside her, and before I know it I'm making slow, sweet love to her just like I'd planned the first time.

Our peace is broken though when Brad—being fucking Brad—hammers on the door.

'Stop what yo doin' 'cause I'm comin' in.'

'Fuck off.'

'No!' We both shout at him at the same time, which makes Devon start to giggle again. But obviously Brad doesn't listen, and the door flies open. He's in the doorway, bare-chested, flexing. Fucking flexing—posing like a body builder. I stare at him questioningly.

'What are you doing, fuckwit?'

'Just showing you a bit of healthy competition, Jared, that's all.'

I laugh at his stupid ass doing different poses and look around for something to throw at his head. The only thing on hand is my phone or a glass from the bedside table. Before I've made a decision on which would hurt the most, Devon launches her pillow across the room, and it smacks him square in the face. Brad composes himself, plucking a feather from one of his cornrows and has the audacity to look hurt.

'Devon! I'm shocked—who knew you could be so violent?' he says snickering. I feel her tense beside me, and her mood instantly plummets. Smooth move, asshole. Wrapping the top sheet around herself she gets up and goes into the bathroom. If looks could kill Brad would be dead. I glare fucking death his way. He suddenly isn't having so much fun as he catches my mood.

'Something I said?' he asks half-serious, half-not. I shake my head at him, pulling on some joggers. I walk over and prod him in his fucking chest.

'Nice, asshole. I've worked hard all morning to make her feel better about yesterday, and in one fuckin' minute you walk in and ruin it.'

'Why does she feel bad? Not like Kristen didn't ask for it...' I look up to the ceiling hoping to find some fucking patience.

'Because, dickhead, that was her first rodeo. She's never had a fight as a wolf, fuck, before yesterday, she'd never been on a group run. Why'd you have to open your big fuckin' mouth? What do you want anyway?'

'Oh, well fuck you too, cum splash. How was I supposed to know? You're always holed up in here, fucking or sleeping. I never know what's going on anymore.'

'Naaww. Is poor Bradley feeling neglected? I'm sorry, piss stain. I miss you too.' I tell him, wrestling him into a headlock and rubbing my knuckles along his scalp between his corn braids. He fucking hates it. And I know it. So it's something I always do. He fights me, trying to get his head loose, but I'm locked in and raring to go. Till he grabs my nuts. I soon let him go, and he's howling with laughter as I'm bent over double from the pain, and wanting to chuck up. Bastard. He'll pay for that when he least expects it. He turns to leave, then stops as I pick my head up from between my knees.

'Oh yeah, yah dad's on his way,' he says with a smile on his face. He clearly doesn't realise the seriousness of that fact.

'Fuck you, shit head.' I tell him. He turns, acting like he's pulling something out of his pocket, then flips me the bird like that's what he pulled out. I laugh. I can't help it. When he's gone, I close the door and tap on the bathroom door. The shower's running, so I know she's naked hot and wet. Just how I like her. I try the door. It's locked. Telling me to stay the fuck out. Fuckin', Brad. I lie back on the bed and wait. When she eventually comes out, she's dressed, and her hair is tied up. Ready for the day. As she picks her clothes up from the floor and stuffs them into her bag, I have to wonder if she's running again. When will this stop?

'What's the plan for the day?' I ask her, waiting for her to tell me she's leaving. She shrugs her shoulders.

'Nothing beyond going to work.'

'You're at work again today? I thought you had it off?'

'Well you thought wrong.' I close my eyes and take in a deep breath. No one told me finding your mate and falling in love was also mental fucking torture. I'm getting sick of this shit fast. It's like having Jekyll and Hyde for a girlfriend.

'What the fuck have I done now? Please tell me, Devon, 'cause I have no fuckin' clue! One minute we're in bed, happy as pigs in shit, the next I'm getting the cold shoulder and you're fuckin' leaving. What gives?' I stand in front of the door with my arms folded and a scowl on my face. This ends now. I'm not moving till we have this shit lay bare.

'I have to be at work, Jared, in...' she looks at her phone. 'half an hour.' Well, this was gonna take more than half a fucking hour, so sorry, shit outta luck.

'Oh no, you wanna walk out on me—you start explaining, 'cause you ain't going nowhere while we've got shit to sort through.'

'Jared?'

'Devon?' I say it back like a question. I'll play this silly game all day long. I don't give a fuck about that job. I don't like it anyway. Throwing her bag to the floor, she mumbles some shit under her breath. Not sure, but I think it was something like motherfucking men. And she stomps her way back to sit on the bed. Okay, progress.

'Jared, I'm not walking out on you. I'm going to work—there's a difference.'

'If you leave while we've got shit to sort through, that's you walking out.'

'Oh, so if we have a disagreement, the rest of my life has to go on hold until you're satisfied?'

'Don't twist my words,' I say that, but in reality, she's right. I know that's an asshole move, but I'm an asshole.

'Jared, I have to go to work. I don't want to be late.'

I can see she's put up her fucking barriers again. Her face is devoid of emotion, and it just sets to piss me off.

'You know what? We're not leaving this fuckin' room until you tell me what's crawled up your ass since you got up out of bed.'

'Jesus Christ, Jared, please can we not do this again?'

'Do what? Tell me what you don't wanna discuss, Devon!'

She sighs in defeat and puts her head in her hands.

'Jared, you don't understand how hard this is for me. It's a lot to take in. The pack the rules—the fact that I'm up against it before I've even started...'

I get on my knees in front of her.

'Baby, everything is going to be okay, I promise. You're not alone in this. I'm with you every step of the way. It's overwhelming right now because it's new, but it won't always be this way. Just please give it time—don't run.' I'm almost begging again. It's like I've grown a vagina, but fuck if I can help it. She annoys the fuck out of me, but at the same time, she makes me feel like nothing else even matters but her and me. I've gone soft.

'Jared, I know and it's not us, it's everything around us. I just don't want to feel like this. I hate it. I've never been jealous, and I've always had to keep my temper locked up, and if I'm honest it felt good too good to let it out. I don't want to be that person, Jared.' I take a breath and think about what I want to say next.

'Listen, baby. What you have just explained to me is your wolf side coming to the forefront. You and me, we're a bonded couple—feeling jealous will be instinctual when it comes to each other. It will ease over time I'm sure, but this is all new to me too, baby. I've never been in this position before either, and honestly, I feel like ripping every guy's head off just for being in the same vicinity as you. But, baby, I have to control it.'

Her eyes widen, and her eyebrows shoot up almost off her fucking forehead.

'Okay, so maybe I don't always control it so good—but I'm learning okay?' I smile. And her lips quirk up just a little at the sides, which turns into a full smile as I wrap my arms around her waist and pull her into a kiss, which turns into a fumble, and before long I have her under me, my hands under her top and in her bra. I pinch at her nipple, and she groans, pushing her pussy up into my already solid dick. I'm in mid grind when she gasps—not in a good way—and she starts pushing me up off of her.

'Shit, Jared. I'm late for work.'

Fuuuuuuuuck. I drop my head to her shoulder, disappointment all over my face. But I get up, adjust myself and pull her up by the hand. We walk through the kitchen and as bold as brass, Kristen is sitting there all beat up and swollen. While Devon's arm is already three-quarters of the way healed she looks like the whole pack took a swing at her. I don't spare her more than a scathing look as we say our goodbyes and I get Devon into my car. We don't mention what we just saw. Instead, I keep it light and tell her all about what I plan to do to her when she gets off work later that day. I leave her with a kiss, and I even apologise to her boss, 'Wade', about making her late. I give him a good enough description as to why. Just in case the 'gay' comment thing was just an excuse. I'm not convinced.

# chapter NINETEEN

## *Devon*

**W**HEN WE ARRIVE AT JARED'S, the drive to the rear of the property is already lined with cars. I look at Jared—he's gone very still at the wheel. His hands clenched around it. He closes his eyes and rests his head on it.

'My father's here.'

Oh shit. Jared looks pale. I'm fairly sure all the blood has drained from my face too. Before we have the chance to get out of the car, Brad comes to the passenger side and raps on my window. I press the button to let it down.

'Hey, Devon.' He greets me and then he looks right at Jared. 'Umm so your dad is here, and he's real pissed, just thought I would warn you before I left.'

'Wait, you're leaving? Why?'

'Alpha's orders, man. Sorry, we're all heading into town for a couple of hours.'

'Should I go too?' I ask them both and they answer in unison.

'Yes,' says Brad.

'No,' says Jared. If Jared doesn't want me to, I'm not going anywhere.

'Listen, man. I've got your back, okay? We all have, and I've said my piece. Not sure if it was helpful but I said it anyway. I hope it helps.' He shrugs his shoulders and gets in his car. The rest of the group come sauntering out of the kitchen then—all except for Kristen. I'm glad not to see her. Jared doesn't speak for a moment, and when they have all pulled out of the drive, he turns in his seat and grabs my hand.

'This could go really badly, and we'll have to leave immediately.'

I don't know what to say to him. I just nod and listen.

'If we have to leave are you okay with that?'

I nod again.

'This isn't about me, Jared. This is *your* pack—*your* father—this is about what you want.'

He starts to protest.

'Jared please, just hear me out? I don't want to put you in any position where you have to leave your pack, and I don't want to leave you either. I will do whatever it takes to make this right for you.'

He smiles then and squeezes my hand in his.

'I love you, baby.' He leans across and kisses me. A slow, lasting kiss that says he wants to do so much more.

I take a deep breath and using the same words he did when he met my dad, I say, 'Let's do this.' I'm smiling, but it's fake. I'm terrified. Jared helps me out of the car, and he walks me to the kitchen door. There are men sitting at the table, none of whom I recognise. And on the end is Kristen. Jared pushes the door open and walks in, his hand tight around mine as he pulls me to his side. He looks at a man at the head of the table, and I can see instantly that he is his father. Jared looks a lot like him, he has his broad build, his strong jaw and the same shape to his nose, his eyes and his smile must come from his mother though because where Jared has piercing green eyes and full lips, his father has blue eyes and thin, cruel-looking lips with a scar running down across them both. He has the same dark hair as his son—although it's peppered with grey now. I wonder then what his mother had looked like. His father looks at me. I bow my head in respect. Jared doesn't. I can see Kristen through the corner of my eye. She has a grin on her face. She's acting like a cat that has got the cream. A bruise is still evident on the side of her face, and her eye is still swollen. Good. I wanted to wipe that stupid grin right off her face. His father catches my attention. Standing, he gives me a smile, which I wasn't expecting and he holds out his hand for me,

'Harry Stone, and who might you be?'

I put my hand in his and met his eyes. 'Devon Hathoway, Mr Stone. It's nice to meet you.'

'Is it?' he says looking directly at his son. I pull my hand back and look at Jared also. I feel immediately uncomfortable. He meets his father's eyes, which terrify me. Mr Stone chuckles. It's a dark sound. Not a happy chuckle but rather, one of amusement.

'You are not alpha yet, boy. You will do well to remember that.'

Jared doesn't avert his eyes though, and the tension in the room thickens with every second that passes. It feels like an hour has passed before Jared speaks.

'Did you forget, in this house, on this land that I am alpha? *You* gave me that role.'

'That may be the case, but *I* am still *your* alpha.'

Jared nods, saying nothing more. His father gestures for us to sit at the table and Harry sits at the head of the table again. I'm closest to Kristen and opposite me are more men I don't recognise. They are all big and burly. They remind me a little bit of Howard. The palms of my hands feel slick with sweat. Jared doesn't let up on his grip, though. I sit awkwardly and look at him. Jared's gaze is directed at his father. He is waiting for him to speak. It is like a standoff. Had I been in any other situation I would have laughed at the absurdity of it. But it was serious, and what happened next was vital to our relationship and the rest of our lives. I keep my poker face firmly in place.

'So, Jared. I have heard some interesting things about your little bitch here.'

Jared's grip goes tighter on my hand, and his legs tense, to move to standing. I grip him hard and let him know I don't want him to argue over this—he is testing him. The only sound is Kristen, squeaking as she holds in a laugh. Her face has lit up at Mr Stone's insult. Jared's father obviously doesn't get the response he wants because he goes on. 'I've been told some disturbing stories. I'm sure you would like to bring me up to speed on what is correct and what isn't.'

He looks to me for an answer, raising his brows.

'Well, that all depends on what you've heard, Mr Stone,' I tell him bluntly, making him chuckle again. A dark, sinister sound that tells me he is going somewhere with this and this is just part of his game.

'Well then, correct me if I'm wrong, but I believe you have your grips into my son?'

My hackles go straight up. Kristen's pathetic little trill of laughter grates on me like a blunt saw on wood. Jared starts to answer, but I squeeze his hand, letting him know that I've got this.

'If by that you mean I have fallen in love with your son, the answer is yes I have. Why is there a problem with that?'

He doesn't chuckle this time. His face becomes very serious, and his neck lengthens as he pushes his face toward me.

'No problem,' he says shaking his head. That is a relief. I let go of a breath I was unaware of holding. Jared's hand squeezes so tight on mine I have to check his face for any sign of pain. He just looks angry. 'The problem is, my son has decided he can love *you*. It is very evident that he has marked you. Everyone in this room is aware of that. And there lies the problem.'

Jared stands then. 'Why?' He still holds my hand so my arm is stretched across the distance. 'I'm going to be with Devon, no matter what. If you cast me out, that's fine.' His father's whole body language changes—he had not expected that. He sighs loudly.

'This is why I *never* marked any female. Sit down, Jared.' He flicks his hand out gesturing for him to sit in the seat.

'Jared, I've been training you to take my position for some years now. You are a natural alpha. I wished for you to have a good female by your side.' Jared's lips went straight and thin, his jaw clenching. I squeeze his hand to help him calm down. 'I picked out a female for you. I thought that was settled?' Kristen leans back in her seat, grinning like a fucking Cheshire cat.

'Dad that was never settled, you knew that. I never wanted her, never had any interest in her at all.' That had to hurt. I peek over, and her grin has faltered. Ha! Bitch.

'That's not what Kristen tells me?' He raises his eyebrows at his son. Jared doesn't answer.

'Tell me. Did you or did you not bed Kristen?'

Jared blanches, but he remains silent. I inwardly cringe, so thankful that he'd already told me this. 'DID.YOU.BED.HER.OR.NOT?' his father demands this time.

'Once,' Jared bites out. 'And it was a fucking mistake. I told her that.'

Mr Stone looks to Kristen then, confusion on his face.

'Kristen? Is this correct?' she squirms under his gaze but doesn't speak. 'KRISTEN' he growls at her.

'No. He treated me like a mate.'

I feel sick. The room spins around me. I want to get up and leave, but as my legs tense, Jared holds my hand tight, turning to look at me, his eyes pleading with me. So I remain in my seat and hold my head high. It kills me inside. I want to run. Leave the room at least. I feel like an intruder. I do not want to hear about him with *her*.

'You lying bitch, Kristen!' Jared yells at her.

'Explain what Kristen is saying, Jared?' his father asks calmly. Too calmly.

'I've never led *her* to believe I wanted her as a mate. She's *lying*. I slept with her once, when I was drunk, and I told her it was a mistake right after and that it wouldn't ever happen again. I didn't treat her badly after that. We have to live here together. I didn't want any animosity, but I have never treated her like she was my mate. She wasn't, and never could be.'

'Do you have anything to add to that Kristen?'

I can't look at her. Jared scowls her way. She shakes her head. 'So what Jared is saying is the truth?' Jared suddenly slams his fist down onto the table making it shudder from the force of it.

'Do you *need* to ask that question? Do you take *her* word over *mine*?' He rises to his full height, his hands on the table. He stares his father down, anger radiating from him. A small yelp escapes me as he shouts down to his father. I'm worried what's going to happen next. Jared doesn't budge his position and his father, although he remains seated, is staring right back at Jared.

'LEAVE US!' his father demands. Everyone rises in unison. I'm not sure what I should do, Kristen hasn't moved though, so I'm not going anywhere. 'You too,' Mr Stone tells Kristen. She rises then, and I begin to do the same. Jared points without looking back, gesturing for me to sit back down. I hover over my seat, unsure, with my ass in the air. He puts his hand to my shoulder and pushes me back into my seat without a word, then he squeezes it affectionately before letting go.

'Well?' Jared gives his father the floor. Mr Stone's lips quirk up slightly as he's thinking about his answer. It isn't immediate. Instead, he takes his sweet time deliberating over an answer. It's almost painful to sit and watch this unfold before me. Jared's jaw is clenching and unclenching so hard I'm beginning to worry about his teeth. Finally, his father breaks the silence. And although I'm unsure of his answer, I'm so relieved that tension is over. I'm fairly sure I popped a few blood vessels on that wait.

'I am not in any doubt that you are telling me the truth, Jared, but this is not the only matter I wish to address today. If you do not want Kristen as a mate, I can choose another.'

'Come on, we're leaving.' Jared turns to me. I make to get up.

'SIT DOWN!' It's a command that I feel in the depths of my stomach. A command that I instinctively feel the need to obey—it's hard not to. But Jared is my alpha—if I have an alpha—not his father. Jared moves with me to the door.

'I'm sorry it's come to this.' He looks at his father. 'But I'm going to be with Devon, with or without your consent. I was hoping you'd be reasonable.' He opens the door, and I go through first.

'Jared!' He stops and turns to look at his dad. He has aged in that moment—I can see it in his face, hear it in his voice. He's lost the battle with his son.

'Let us discuss this.'

Jared blows out a big breath and looks to me,

'I'm with you no matter what,' I whisper. He takes us back to the table and pulls out my seat for me.

'Jared, I do not want to lose you as my alpha heir, or as my son, but this is a very difficult situation you have put us in.' Jared frowns, confusion all over his face. But I know what is coming. He knows. All this song and dance about Kristen wasn't important. It wasn't the issue at all. I was. He knows what I am. But how?

'Being the alpha heir is as good as having royal blood running through your veins, and you want to mate with *her*?' He spits the last word out as if it is something disgusting. Jared growls deeply. It's so loud the men on the other side of the door come in to see if their alpha is in trouble. He waves them off. Jared doesn't loosen up. He is so angry. And fuck me if I don't want to crawl up onto his cock right there, and ride him like a rodeo bull. Angry Jared is so HOT when he isn't mad with me. *Jesus H Christ, Devon. Brain in the game.* I squirm in my seat, a tad worried that my sudden arousal will be in the air.

'Jared, I understand you have feelings for the girl. I am not suggesting you send her away. Keep her, but you must mate with someone of true bloodline.'

Jared scoffs. He is visibly shaking, his anger undulating.

'I can *keep* her?' he bites out through clenched teeth, 'What, like a sex slave? As long as I make little alpha babies with someone else?'

'Exactly.' His dad sounds pleased like Jared has finally realised and is on board with the idea.

'GO.FUCK.YOURSELF!' Jared marches us out of the room and straight to his car.

He can't start it at first—he's so angry. He hammers on the steering wheel in temper while cussing everything and anything. Then he takes a deep calming breath and tries again. It roars to life. He drives us straight to a bar in the town. He doesn't say a word all the way there. He's way too angry to form words. So I just sit beside him and let him take us away. He parks in the lot at the rear of the bar.

'Do you want to stay in the car?'

No, I didn't. I wanted to go with him. I answer by simply getting out. He takes my hand, and he walks us fast and with purpose. As he pushes the door open, I catch the scents of his friends—his pack mates. The bar is not as quaint as others I've been in—this is more modern with more than one pool table and fruit machines line the back wall. The bar is a circle in the middle of the room. Jared walks us over to his friends who are playing pool at the back, near the fruit machines. And as I smile at Zoe everything seems to happen in slow motion. Yet it's so fast that no one can do a thing to stop it.

*Devon*

JARED FLIES OVER THE POOL table where Howard is taking a shot. He jumps back, noticing Jared at the last second. Jared's fist crunches against Howard's jaw and blood splashes up and all over them both. Jared hits him three times in total before he stops. No one moves in to stop him or to help Howard. They all just stand watching. I go to Jared's side and try to pull him to me. I don't know what the hell had just happened or why. He shrugs my arm off him and grabs Howard by the scruff.

'Why? Why did you tell him?' Jared asks him. Almost pleading with him. He is hurt, it's obvious.

'I swear I didn't tell him.'

'Then who did you tell?' he demands. Howard replies on a small whisper, almost incoherent.

'Kristen overheard us talking.'

It all fell into place then. Jared had obviously confided in Howard, his best friend, about me and what I was. Jared had assumed he'd told Mr Stone.

The security guy comes over, Brad and Logan are holding him off and telling him they had it all under control. The guy clearly isn't happy, but he lets it go. Just as well, the mood Jared is in, I don't fancy his chances. It isn't long before we are back in the car. Brad comes after us.

'If you're leaving the pack, I want the option to follow you, man.'

Jared nods.

'When we get sorted, you'll be the first to know.' He smiles then for the first time in hours. As we pull away, I wave at Brad, then watch as Jared's face changes from slightly relaxed to majorly tense in a second. He stops around the corner, pulling into another parking space.

'I don't know where to go from here, Devon?'

I know he isn't talking about right this minute but about life as a whole. He doesn't know what to do next.

'How about we check into a hotel tonight and go from there?'

His answer is to lean over and kiss me.

'Sounds like a good plan to me.'

We checked in at a swanky hotel. Jared refuses any money from me and pays for it in full. The first thing I do is run the huge bath and strip off. I shout Jared in. His eyes widen as he comes through the door, and that smile I love so much is spread across his face. I pull his top up and over his head—my hands greedily taking in all the ripples of his torso, as I move down to unbutton his pants. I slip my hands in, around the waistband, and push them down over his ass, leaving only his boxers. I stand back long enough to take in the view before I push them down too. He steps out of them and lifts me effortlessly into the tub before getting in behind me. He puts his legs on either side of mine, and I lay back against his chest with his arms wrapped around me. The warm water and bubbles slosh around us. It's heaven. We don't speak about anything that has happened—just savour the time together.

The light coming through the curtains wakes me. I reached out toward Jared but find the space empty beside me. I sit up to find him hunched over the writing bureau. He turns to face me as if sensing I'm awake.

'Hey, gorgeous.' He smiles at me as if I'm the best thing he's ever seen. Damn, he's sexy. I walk over to him, naked. The grumbling in his chest tells me what that does to him. He pulls me onto his lap. On the desk, he has a map and a notebook. He's been busy. Before I can look any further, he repositions me, lifting me effortlessly so I straddle him with my back to the bureau. I'm not complaining. He kisses me softly, and there is so much affection in every stroke of his tongue—every glide of his lips over mine. He tastes so good, and heat pools at my core. I want him, right there. He is aroused. His marking scent fills my nose, and I revel in it. I love that I make him feel this way. Love that he wants me as much as I do him. He deepens the kiss, tugging on my hair.

There is a knock on the door. He throws his head back and groans.

'That's breakfast.' He lifts me from his lap and reaches to give me a robe hanging in the closet. I cover up as he opens the door. Jared is topless, and the woman with the trolley practically swoons as she rolls it through the door, fluttering her lashes at him. I don't think she even notices I'm in the room. It grates on me, but I let it go. Jared pays her no attention. He directs her to place it by the small table, and he comes straight over to me, lifting me into his arms. The door closes behind her, but I barely notice because of the way he is kissing me. I tune everything else out. My stomach rumbles so loudly it makes him chuckle against my lips. The smell of breakfast has definitely made me hungry. I can't wait. I want him on the bed. Instead, he walks over to the table and chuckles again as I protest.

'You're hungry.'

'I'm horny,' I counter, pouting. He throws his head back and laughs.

'What kind of man takes advantage of a starving woman?' I stand and lean into him, pressing my whole self against him. He closes his eyes.

'Devon, I want to fuck you in more ways than I can count, but you are hungry, and I want to feed you. So sit that sexy ass down and eat—fast.' He chuckles as my eyes widened at his humour.

He's ordered a feast. We eat bacon and eggs, toast, pancakes with syrup, and drink copious amounts of coffee. He sits in the chair opposite me—his chest bare. I can hardly take my eyes off him. Gorgeous doesn't cover it. He's fucking godlike. And he wants to be with *me*. That part still astounds me. As far as I'm concerned, we are in a completely different league. Girls like me don't get guys like him. Jared though, is willing to leave everything behind for me.

'A penny for your thoughts?'

I blush a little, not really wanting to share what I was thinking.

'Just you, and me, us.' I shrug my shoulders,

'That's what I've been working on this morning.' He points over to the bureau. 'Places we can go to live. Or we could travel, or we could just stay put.'

I look on in confusion. How can we stay put? I thought that was decided and out of our hands. Jared explains.

'My father called earlier. He isn't willing to lose me or the pack members that are willing to leave with me.'

I gasp louder than I realised I had. He smiles. 'I have some good pack mates.'

'So what does this mean for us?'

'It means that if we want to stay in the pack, we can. But, if you don't want to, I'm with you a hundred percent?' I'm stunned. From the previous night, to this, in a matter of hours. I don't know whether I'm coming or going. I don't know what I really want to do either. I'm not used to living within a pack. I'm not used to their rules or their way of life. But Jared was a huge part of his pack, and if we stayed, he would one day lead it.

'Jared, I really don't know what it's like to live as a pack. I don't know what we would be missing—what *you* would be missing. I can't make this decision, it's not mine to make, it's yours.' He shakes his head rapidly.

'No, it isn't just mine. It's *ours*. I want you to be happy, wherever we are. And if that means leaving my pack then so be it.'

I love him so much I nearly burst. He will give up everything he's ever known, for me. I wasn't going to have that though.

'I know you would be happier surrounded by your friends.'

'Our friends,' he interrupted.

'And that is what would make me happy too. It may take some adjusting, but I want to fit in.'         He rolls his eyes.

'Like you don't already?'

So that was that. Jared spoke to his father again while I got ready. I could hear snippets as I let the water cascade over my head in the shower.

'If you treat her like an outsider, dad—' Jared must have been moving around. 'I don't want anyone else—'

Arrgh, it is frustrating to only hear a little bit. I have washed and rinsed my hair before Jared steps in behind me. His arms going around my waist and his lips finding the curve between my shoulder and neck as he pulls my body in to his.

Jared is insistent that I move into the house with him and his pack. I'm reluctant though because Kristen is still there. I know she's grieving, but after the stunt she pulled, I could happily finish what we started. So for now, I'm insisting on staying in my room with Maiya. Jared has other plans like seducing me into his bed at every opportunity. He thinks I don't know what he's doing when he has a beer late, so he can't drive me home. He's literally pulling out all the stops—he's relentless. He unpacks my bag each time I pack my toiletries, and he puts my shit in his cupboards, on his shelves, and in his closet. He really is determined.

I do love it here, but I don't love sharing air with her. I hate seeing her, let alone thinking of her with him—that she's had what's mine. It makes me murderous. And that atmosphere isn't good in any situation. But I still find myself at the dining table with her, despite my many efforts to thwart it. I can't even bring myself to give her my condolences. How evil does that make me? I'm even kind of glad she's hurting. Although I'm not glad her uncle died. From what Jared has told me of him, he was a great guy. I've expressed my sadness to everyone else. She is getting jack shit from me. I will simply ignore her existence.

'Hey, sweetness.' Brad chimes and kisses my cheek as I sit down, ignoring Jared's homicidal look. I giggle as Brad winks at me, making Jared even more furious.

'Calm down, big man. I'm not making a play for your girl.' This has become routine with Brad, he pushes and pushes Jared, but he is completely non-threatening. He's just a wind-up merchant.

'Put your lips near my female again, and I'll rip em off and stick em so far up your ass—' Hysterical laughter erupts as Brad pouts, doing kissy lips in my direction. You have to laugh. Jared pulls me onto his lap and kisses me hard. Laying claim. As if anyone in the room questions it. When he lets me up for air I notice Kristen looking my way, I smile. Yeah okay, it is bitchy but hell, I'm not above one-upmanship and I sure as hell have one up on her right now. I try to ignore her snarky comments all the way through dinner, and I find myself biting my tongue so many times I almost choke on it. But Zoe doesn't hold back after Kristen bitched her out.

'You have no room to talk. Just lately you fuck anything with a dick and a pulse, so don't you dare fuckin' comment on my sex life when you know fuck all about it,' Zoe shouts. Everyone goes quiet, as Zoe lays into her,

'How dare you! I do not fuck anything. In case you've forgotten, I was saving myself until *recently.*' She stares right at me. Oh hell no.

'You know what?' I stand. I've had enough. 'You should shut your cum catcher and sit the fuck down. We all know you come back reeking of a different man every morning. You wanna be a slut, go right ahead, but don't comment like the fucking Virgin Mary when someone else has a good time.'

Her eyes go wide, and she stutters. I sit back down and look around. Zoe is grinning so hard, and Brad is all red faced and making noises because he's trying to hold his laughter in.

The rest of the table, including Kristen, are gaping at me like I just grew an extra head. Then the slut herself has something to say.

'Who the fuck do you think you are, speaking to me like that? This is my house, my pack. *You* don't even belong here. You're a fucking outsider. A mutt—'

Jared moves so fast I don't see it. He's in her face and her mouth snaps shut.

'One more fuckin' word, Kristen, one more!' he growls. She stutters and starts to say something, but he holds his hand up to silence her. 'I'm not done talking.' She closes her mouth. 'I'm the alpha here—remember that. In this house, on this land, I AM ALPHA.'

She cringes at his tone. 'Devon is my female. So tell me, Kristen, what does that make her?' He uses a calm but intimidating tone. Her lips twist up as she fights back tears. Everyone is on their feet, obviously expecting another fight between the two of us. I stay sitting this time, waiting for her answer.

'Answer me, Kristen,' Jared demands. But again she doesn't speak. 'Okay, I'll remind you since you've clearly forgotten how this shit works. Devon is the alpha-fuckin'-female. That clear for you, Kristen? Or do I need to repeat myself?'

Tears fill her eyes and her lip trembles. I'm not sure if she's genuinely upset or if it's frustration. On the inside, I'm doing a little victory dance, but on the exterior, I'm a poker queen. Giving her nothing. Jared is clearly pissed that he still hasn't had an answer because he yells and I jump out of my skin. 'DO I NEED TO REPEAT MYSELF?' Kristen suddenly comes to her senses and answers, simply shaking her head before she leaves the kitchen. Everyone remains quiet until we hear her door slam shut upstairs. Then both Zoe and Brad double over laughing. Zoe is practically hysterical, and that makes everyone else laugh. They say laughter is infectious and in this case it really is. We are all laughing in no time. Except Jared.

'I don't even know why I'm laughing,' I squeal holding my side. It was hurting now, but it felt so good. Zoe busted laughing again.

'Cum catcher...' she roars out, tears streaming down her face. Eventually, we all calm down enough to finish our food. I really feel at home with these guys. After the episode with Kristen I decide that I really need to stay in my room tonight, and since all the guys are going out, I've told Maiya that I'll go to some sort of literature shindig at a local café bar. So although reluctant, Jared decides he will go out too.

## *Devon*

AFTER A GOOD NIGHT AT the bar, I'm glad to get back and kick my heels off. We've both had too much to drink, and all I want to do is get my pj's on and climb into bed. I don't even take off my makeup, I'm so beat. I text Jared goodnight, and he replies,

Miss you baby, sweet dreams x

I put my phone on charge and climb under the comforter. I'm so ready to crash.

Someone is in our room. It's dark and I'm still drunk, but I fight against heavy eyelids and open my eyes. More than one intruder…Hands grab me. It's a man. No, a kitsune. I kick out in every direction, trying to throw my attacker off. I bite at everything in the vicinity of my mouth, and I punch with everything I've got. I may as well be throwing cotton balls at him for the good it's doing me. I scream, but all my efforts are easily outmatched, there is nothing I can do to stop them. Darkness.

I come to, and I'm handcuffed to a bed. My arms are aching badly. Who knows how long I've been in this position? The cuffs are cutting into my wrists, and my right shoulder feels like it could be dislocated. I quickly assess the rest of my body, checking each part off in my head. Head fuzzy but otherwise fine, my face hurts badly, but I did take a beating. My left shoulder is aching but fine, my right arm, numb, other than the absolute agony of my shoulder. Wrists are bleeding from the cuffs, but the rest of me is intact. I sigh in relief. A noise in the corner gets my attention, and I try and fail to move away from it. I cry out as my shoulder twists at its awkward angle making bile rise from my stomach. I vomit, unable to keep it down.

'Hurts like a motherfucker doesn't it?' A guy says, stepping around to where I can see him. But I don't need to see him to know who it is. Blue eyes. The kitsune. I growl deep with all I can—a warning for him to stay the fuck away. But what comes out is more like the squeal of a dying animal. Not what I was going for.

'What do you want?' Again, I go for tough bravado, but my face must be a huge mess because what I said sounds more like 'Wah duuh yooo waaah.' I wanted to curl up and cry—what a fucking mess I'm in.

My body is trying to heal. I can feel it, but I'm so weak that I'm not sure it can. My mumbling makes him crack up, he bends over at the waist, laughing uncontrollably. Sick fuck. 'What the fuck do you want from me?' I scream. His laughter continues, only making me more desperate to get loose, just to ram his fucking head into the wall and shut him up.

'If what you're trying to ask is why you're here handcuffed to this bed? Well, it's a long story really, but the short version is because your parents went against nature, and fucked, making a little half-breed. And we decided that we could use a hybrid to our advantage. So you see, what I am doing at this moment in time is testing what you can handle—how far I can go before you break. How much you can take before the healing stops.' He steeples his fingers when he speaks. He sounds like a mad scientist, pleased with the results of his experiment. I glare at him through the one eye that isn't swollen closed and curl my lip up in a snarl. All I do is cause myself more pain. He doesn't react in any way. In fact, he comes closer, and then I felt the sharp jab of a needle as he smiles a maniacal smile. It is the last thing I see before everything goes black.

# *Jared*

I'm gonna tear the fucking town apart if someone doesn't give me something soon. How the fuck can she just disappear without a trace? Brad comes through into the kitchen where I'm pacing. He has his laptop in his hand.

'I've got all the CCTV footage from the campus.' He shakes his head, gritting his teeth. 'You're not gonna like it.'

I snatch the thing from him and put it on the table.

'Just fucking show me!' I bellow. Brad flinches but does as I ask. Howard comes into the room and stands over my right shoulder while Brad plays and replays the footage. A black van, with a fake plate, parks up in the small car park and four guys get out, all dressed in black garb. Not one of them shows their face. They fucking know where the cameras are. Then Brad fast-forwards about ten minutes, and we watch all four of them walk out, one carrying what looks to be a black sack. A fucking full sack with a dead weight inside. Jesus fucking Christ. I make him run over the footage again and again. There is no movement from that sack. Meaning she is either unconscious or dead. I refused to believe the latter.

'I need an ID on that van, and I need eyes on where it went. Now.' I clench my fists and try to focus. I let out a roar of frustration. Some bastards have my woman, and I have nothing. Not one fucking piece of information on who has her or where she is. I'm sinking, drowning in my head. Everything is meaningless without her. I have to fucking find her. I heave into the sink bringing nothing but bile up. What the fuck are they doing to her? Zoe hands me a glass of water. I swill my mouth, but I'm overwhelmed with emotion. I launch the glass and fall to the floor, and I cry like a fucking baby.

'Hey!' Howard shouts as he toe-prods me, 'Get the fuck up and sort yourself out.'

I stand and shove him away hard. 'Fuck you!' I yell at him.

'No. FUCK you! You've given up already! We're in there working our fucking asses off to find your female, and you're in here falling apart in a snotty mess. Wake the fuck up, brother.' He gets in my face, and I don't even care. He's right. What good am I doing her?

I find Brad in the study. He has every angle of the dorm and street cameras hacked and on the multiple screens in front of him. I start pacing. Our noses came up blank in the first instance, whoever took her wasn't a wolf, but they weren't human either. My guess was the fucking kitsunes. Had to be. They covered their hides, rendering all our usual ways of seek and rescue useless. So here we were, desperately searching in ways we weren't used to. How humans ever found anyone was beyond me. I feel myself slipping again when Brad suddenly points at the screen like an excited child.

'Gotcha, you bastards.'

I stop pacing and stare at the screen over his shoulder. He has the van—it moves along and then pops up on another camera, and then another. He has their direction and is now trying to narrow it down.

'I'm gonna get on the road and head in that direction. I'm taking my bike—it'll be quicker. I want you,' I point to Howard, 'to follow me up with the pickup. Bring Zoe—we may need her.' He nodded his agreement and beat feet to get organised. 'Brad, keep doing what you're doing, brother. I'm fucking hanging on by a thread here, and I'm relying on you.'

He doesn't stop what he is doing but gives me a dismissive wave over his shoulder. 'Go. I'll keep you posted. Wear your Bluetooth.'

I'm already out of the door and on my bike before I hear the garage door creak. With Brad in my ear, giving me directions, I full throttle my bike the whole time. I pull into a fuel station when Brad tells me this is as far as he could track them. I fuel up and grab an energy drink, and then I go for a walk around the place. They'd stopped here, so I wanted to try and catch a scent—something. Anything. All I could get was the same shitty fucking scent I got at her dorm. My ear bleeped.

'Tell me you have something brother?'

'Oh, I have something.'

# chapter
## TWENTY-TWO

## *Devon*

I WAKE UP TO A female in the room. I jerk up, lifting my head off the pillow. I'm tied up—my feet together at my ankles and my hands at the wrists. I can't change if I'm restrained. They'd thought this through well. My shoulder isn't so painful now, and my face feels less swollen. My head is really fuzzy though. I've been drugged. Fuck, he'd injected me.

The female was a kitsune. I don't know how I knew because I couldn't scent her like I could a wolf. I just knew she was. Something inside me recognised it in another. Just like the bastards that brought me here. I knew. It was like a light bulb moment—somewhere in my brain it screamed 'kitsune'. It was weird but until these fuckers had shown up and knocked me out I hadn't ever met another one, except blue eyes, and I knew instantly then too. Well, except my mother, but I can't remember ever having the same sense when she was around.

'Have a nice sleep?' The bitch asks, looking up from her magazine. She is slender and blonde, and pretty in a 'resting bitch face' kind of way. There is no kindness in her face at all. Her eyes are so brown they look black. I weigh her up while mentally ticking off all my body parts, making sure I am fully functioning. I'm not, but it will do. I'd rather take my chances with her than the guy.

'I really need to use the bathroom.'

Looking over the top of her magazine she narrows her eyes at me.

'Don't even think about trying to get past me, because you won't.'

I nod. She pulls me up by the rope around my wrists. It smarts a bit, but I don't show it. 'I'm gonna untie your feet so you can walk your own ass to the toilet. Try anything and I'll kill you. Are we clear?'

I nod again. Yeah, we're clear, bitch. Untie me, and I'll kill *your* ass. I walk stiffly behind her, my legs protesting a little to the sudden activity. She yanks on the rope, and I nearly fall into her. I get to the bathroom and find I really do need to go. She closes the door, and I sit on the toilet—no time for cleaning it—taking in my surroundings and weighing up my options. No window—so no escape. Weapons? Not even a fucking toothbrush. I tried to wriggle my wrists out of the rope. No chance. I am wondering if I can actually wrap my arms around her neck and choke her out—when she rattles the door.

'You've got ten more seconds.' I don't make a sound. And count one… two… She bursts through the door in a panic. Ha, her mask has fallen, and she fights to put it back, but I've already seen the fear of losing me on her face. So I now know she isn't in charge.

'Hurry up, bitch.'

Lucky for me I'd been kidnapped in my pj's, so I don't need to fiddle with zips and buttons. I pull them up best I can and walk like a good little girl from the bathroom. The idea of choking her is still in my mind, but she yanks me in front, so I lose the element of surprise. But since she is still my best option at escape, I take a couple of quick steps forward then lunge back using my shoulder. I hit her hard in her solar plexus. She flies back hard, and I dive for her, trying like hell to wrap my hands and the rope around her neck. I finally get her, and her arms and legs are flailing around like she is drowning. She's clawing at my arms with her nails, but I have her pinned with my legs and the rope tight to her throat. It couldn't have gone better. Just as her eyes are rolling and she is turning a nice shade of purple, the door at the other side of the room flies open, and another asswipe walks in. I'm distracted, and I loosen my grip on the rope, but she can't wriggle free. I'm using her weight and mine against her. Then I notice the gun he has trained on me.

'Let her go, or I'll shoot you right now.'

I weigh up my options. And come up with jack shit.

Right now isn't my time. But it will come. I release her neck and free my legs from around hers. Coughing and gasping she gets to her hands and knees and crawls to his feet. When she stands in front of him, he punches her right in the face. She hits the foot of the bed and then falls into a heap on the floor, blood gushing from the cut he'd caused. 'Useless fucking bitch' he sneers, as she sobs in a heap. I feel a little sorry for her then. I get over that quickly though as he comes barrelling towards me. His strength outmatches mine on a good day, but after I've exerted all my energy on trying to escape, I have nothing left. I'm thrown on the bed. He grabs my pyjama bottoms and begins yanking them down. Panic takes over, and my blood turns cold. No no no no. Not that, please. I kick out and manage to hold the top of my pants, gripping the waistband with everything I have left. I manage to get a good boot to his face, he grunts and falls back, but it isn't enough, and he keeps coming. I continue to kick my legs and make it difficult for him to manage me.

'Get your ass over here and fucking hold her down,' he bellows at the snivelling heap in the corner. I'm wild and screaming now, adrenaline pumping through my veins. I will not allow this bastard to rape me. I will die first. His first mistake is getting close to my hands with his face. I grab at his hair and yank with everything I have, while kicking and kneeing at anything I can land a hit on. Lifting my head, I bite down on his ear, my teeth sink into the flesh and cartilage and my mouth pooling with his blood as I tear and come away with the majority of his ear. Bastard. He howls in pain and surprise as he clutches at what was left of it. With him letting go I manage to knock her on her ass too. It doesn't take him long to recover though, and he hits me with a clenched fist in the side of the head, rattling my teeth. He follows that with another blow, and I feel my nose crunch and explode as he rains down, blow after blow. And then I feel nothing.

I think I'm awake but what I'm seeing can't be real. I must be dreaming. I'm still tied down, and my bottom half is naked. I'm covered in blood, and I can taste it. It's not my blood—it's the guy whose ear I took. He's lying in a heap on the floor with a hole in his head. A huge hole. His eyes are wide and staring at me. Dead. All of that I can believe, but what I can't believe, is that sitting across from blue eyes at the table in the corner of the room, is my fucking mother. It's been over sixteen years, but I would never forget that face or that voice.

'Mom?' I mumble, and she turns at the sound of my voice.

'Hello, Devon.' She doesn't smile. Doesn't move to untie me or cover my naked body. No. She just stares at me, like I'm a piece of meat. And all I can do is stare back.

'How long has she been healing?' she asks blue eyes.

'Well, after her initial injuries she was healing quite well—'

'Daniel. Did I ask if she was healing well? No. I asked how long?'

'Sorry,' Daniel says. 'Healing has been a few days, but she was in a very bad way when she arrived, and then he—' he points to the guy dead on the floor, '— had another good go. I'd say she heals at least three times faster than we do.'

'Well, that is good to know.'

'What the fuck do you want?' I asked on a squeak. Wow, my throat fucking hurts. Come to think of it everything hurts. I need to get myself sorted and get a plan. Fast.

'Why am I here?'

'Why?' my mom laughs humourlessly. 'Because you are my blood,' she says matter of factly. Like that piece of info cleared everything right up.

'Gee, that explains everything. I think I'll sleep better tonight for knowing that.' She walks over and smacks my face. It feels like she hit me with a brick. My teeth rattle and I'm sure they're loose. Not from the power of her slap but because I'm in a real bad way. If I had it in me, I would smack her right back, but I don't, and I'm still tied up. Instead, I glare at her like I'm shooting daggers from my eyes. It's moments like these that you wish comic book heroes were a thing. But I was shit out of luck. I spat in her face instead. It was mainly blood, so I got the satisfaction of it smearing down her cheek as she wiped it away.

'If you wanted a mother-daughter talk you could have just asked?' I sass her, but deep down I'm terrified. I'm naked, beaten, and possibly raped. Although everything down there feels okay—please let me be okay. I can cope with everything this bitch throws at me but not that.

'This isn't a reunion, Devon and we have no need for a chat. You are simply a tool in a war I wish to win. You are a hybrid, one of my bloodline. I intend to make more just like you, and then no one will be able to stop me from taking what is mine.'

'What?'

'Oh, come on Devon. You were made for this purpose. We've been watching you grow. Watching as that bumbling idiot trained you to keep all of your natural instincts hidden. Well now that all changes, you are a kitsune-wolf hybrid, and you have already proven that you can infiltrate the enemy, which I am very happy about. However, we have bigger things to do, this small island has nothing I want, so we leave tonight. You will infiltrate the North American Pack, just like you have this one, and you will kill the alpha.'

'Are you high?' I ask in disbelief. 'Cause it sure sounds like you're high as a kite right now.' She slaps me again. I spit more blood. 'I will never help you. Ever.'

'Oh, but I think you will.'

I shake my head vigorously clenching my teeth. 'Never.'

Daniel walks up with an I pad and opens a screen. There, tied up and beaten bloody is Maiya. It's a live feed, and she's slumped over struggling to breathe.

'You bastards,' I scream. 'Let her go, you fucking bitch. I'll kill you. I swear to fucking god I will END you!' I'm thrashing around, desperate to be free. I need to be free. 'How can you do this? You were supposed to love me!'

'Pshh. Don't be ridiculous. I was completing a task. I made you and left you with him so you would learn his ways, and now here you are, a little disappointing, but since you've inserted yourself so well in this pack, you should have no problems doing it again.' I continue my struggle with the ropes, but it's futile. I am locked down tight, and all I'm achieving here is more injury to myself. I stop struggling and slump back. Fuck. My eyes glaze over, and I put my poker face in place. I.WILL.NOT.GIVE.IN.

'How about we start on the other part of the plan?' Daniel says a huge grin on his face. 'I'm not shy. You can watch? Make sure the job's done.'

'It doesn't seem that she is in her fertile time right now, Daniel, so I hardly see the point.' Fertile time? Oh shit. Inside I am screaming to get free, but I'm showing none of my inner panic. They'll have no satisfaction from me. I'll wait this out.

'Well, how can you be sure she even has a fertile time like a kitsune? Being a hybrid and all. Maybe wolves don't?'

*I* don't even know if I have one. Shit. Think, Devon for fuck's sake. My mind is racing through every conversation I've ever had with my dad—I come up with nothing. Chances are I could be fertile at any time, and he is gonna rape me and make little hybrid pups. Well, he is going to try. He will have to kill me first. My mother is thinking on his words. Then she walks up to me and squeezes hard on my breast, to the point of pain,

'It's highly possible that she could be fertile year round.' She shrugs. 'No harm in trying I suppose.' I cannot believe that my own mother is going to stand by while this bastard rapes me.

'You sick, twisted fuckers,' I spit as she pulls my tied hands up above my head and holds them in place. Daniel is unzipping his jeans.

He pushes them down and his filthy cock springs free. Bile rises in my throat as he grabs my legs. I kick out at him, hitting him in the face but he grabs me hard, and his fingers dig in, making me scream out in pain.

'Come here and help him,' my mother screams at the woman on the floor.

'Hold her leg there,' he tells her as she grabs one leg and pulls. He's struggling to get my other leg still while he pushes his fingers inside me. Please, someone, help me. Please don't let this happen to me. I'm fighting with all I have. And he's almost there now, he's at my entrance with his cock, and I scream for all I'm worth while wriggling and thrashing. I buck upwards, and they each pull on a limb as I'm stretched so wide it's painful. I feel him there. I thrash and bite at my mother's hands. She yelps and I feel her fist crunch my cheekbone. Blackness descends. The darkness takes hold, and all hope leaves me. I pray I don't wake up. I pray to die before he gets inside of me. *I'm sorry, Jared. I love you.* That is my last thought before I'm swallowed whole by the darkness.

# chapter
## TWENTY-THREE

*Jared*

RAD MANAGES TO WORK A stroke of genius with his hacking skills and traffic cameras, and he's called me with the good news. I park my bike about three hundred yards away. Howard and Zoe are half an hour out, and I told them I'd wait, but when Brad narrows down the location to two possible places I can't wait any longer. The first one checks out—she's definitely not been there. So this is it. It had to be. In my heart, I knew she was in here, and holding back was churning me the fuck up. I decide to change and sneak up to the cabin to see how many we were up against. I found a closer spot and stripped. Gritting my teeth I made the change as fast as I could, trying not to make a sound.

Padding up towards the place, I hear screaming. My heart stutters, before hitting the pit of my stomach. Devon. I run full out and crash through the door, and up the stairs towards the noise. The door is open, and the sight that greets me almost stops me in my tracks. Almost. The bastards have her tied up, battered, and half-naked on a bed. An older woman is holding her arms above her head, and another is holding her leg. A man is between her legs with his cock in his hands. Fucker.

They start to flee as I burst through the door. I see red and launch myself through the air just as the bastard's head turns and recognition dawns on his face. He drops to the floor with that same look, as I rip his throat out in less than ten seconds flat. My body is jacked up on adrenaline, and I search the room for any other threats. One woman—now in the corner cowering—the other long gone. There's another body in the room, but it's been dead a while. I assess my options. Deciding it's more important to check Devon's state, I change, quicker than I've ever done before. It is fucking painful, but it doesn't register. What does is the bloody mess Devon is in. Her face is barely recognisable—she is so swollen. I'm not sure where to touch her— where to even begin cleaning her up. I untie her hands and feet and cover her up. I check her airways and lay her in the recovery position. I'm frightened she'll choke on her own blood. I reach to grab my phone—I need Zoe here, now. Fuck. I don't have my clothes on, and I can't afford to leave her to go and get my phone. The woman in the corner is still cowering and crying, and she screams as I step towards her.

'Gimme your phone.' I snap my fingers at her because my words aren't sinking in. 'NOW!' She jumps and finally pulls a phone from her pocket. I dial the landline at home—it is the only fucking number I can remember. When Brad answers, he puts me in a three-way conversation with Zoe. Devon is still out cold, and I have no fucking idea what to do next.

'Where are you?' I snap, my patience with this shit is gone, and I need her to be okay.

'We're five minutes out, tops.' I growl my frustration and hear her tell Howard to floor it.

'I need you *now*, Zoe. I don't know what the fuck I'm doing, and she's a mess. Jesus fucking Christ, I can't lose her.' After talking me through checking her pulse and pupils she hangs up and no sooner has the call ended when she walks through the door. I sag with relief when I see them with her medical bag. Zoe runs straight to Devon's side, and I see the shock and fear cross her face before she puts her game face on and gets to work. I watch as she checks her out from head to toe. I'd covered her bottom half with a throw from a chair in the room, but when Zoe pulls it back and when she realises she's naked from the waist down her eyes meet mine, and I see sadness there. I swallow the bile that rises, and shake my head, indicating that I didn't want to talk about it. If he's raped her, I will drag the bastard back from hell just to kill him again. The thought alone makes me sick with rage. I can smell him and the woman all over her, but the aromas mixed with her blood and theirs means I just can't tell. Howard is watching the female still snivelling in the corner—she is clutching her knees to her chest, rocking slightly. As a rule, we don't kill women, wolf or human. But I think I'd make an exception for this kitsune. Zoe finishes examining

Devon, and her eyes met mine. With my heart in my throat, I wait for her to speak and it feels like a fucking eternity.

'I've done everything that I can do for her here, but I can't see if she's healing yet.'

When we get hurt real badly, we don't always heal without a bit of help. If she's at that point, then she's hurt really fucking bad.

'When will you know? How long?' I ask.

'Well at this point I don't really want to move her in case there is anything internal going on, but I'm weighing that against how safe it is to stay?' Her eyes move to the woman on the floor. It's time to get some fucking answers. We need to stay alert for any further threats, and there are only three of us. Zoe needs to stay with Devon. I don't want to leave her, but I have no choice. I give Howard the choice. Guard duty or interrogation.

'Well, since you've already got your junk out, I'll take the bitch while you run guard? Yeah?'

I agree.

'Anything changes with her, you holler, okay?' I tell Zoe, motioning to Devon. 'Do what you've gotta do with her.' I lift my chin toward the bitch in the corner. 'Whatever it takes,' I tell Howard. He doesn't answer—just gives me a small nod. He knows what I mean, and he's okay with it. We needed answers and numbers, and she would have to give us what we wanted. We knew four guys had taken her and only two were here now, both dead. So we were at least two missing because this female definitely wasn't in the footage we saw and neither was the older female. I kiss Devon gently on the lips. 'I'll not be far, baby,' I tell her before I drag myself away.

An hour passes, and I'm getting edgy. I've run the same circle around the boundary of the property and haven't come across anyone or heard anything from Zoe. The female Howard is interrogating can be heard from my vantage point, but what I want to hear is Zoe. Another few minutes pass and I can't wait any longer. I make my way back into the house, passing Howard and the bitch tied to a chair. I wander up the stairs, changing when I reached the top.

'Tell Howard to run guard while you watch her downstairs,' I tell Zoe. Every minute that passes and Devon is still unconscious is fucking torture. I kneel at her side and hold her hand. Whispering in her ear, for her to come back to me.

# *Devon*

'Baby, please wake up and come back to me. You're safe now, baby.'

I try to open my eyes, but I feel paralysed. I want to open my eyes, but they don't respond. I want to speak, but my mouth remains closed. I try to lift my hand, a finger. Nothing happens. I can hear Jared. I want to go to him. I want to see his face and remember it. Then the blackness takes me again.

'Harrison and Brad have arrived. Howard has delegated jobs, and he's with the kitsune.' I know that voice, but it's evading me.

'Thanks, Zoe,' Jared speaks now. My heart skips at hearing him, but he sounds wrong—off. Why?

'Jared, please get some rest—'

'No, I'm fine,' he interrupts.

'I'll stay with her. There's a bed made up just through there for you.' She's pleading with him.

'Zoe, do what you need to do with her, but I'm staying.'

Blackness.

My head hurts. I crack my eyes open and take in my surroundings. I'm still on the bed. I'm not tied though. I move my hand slightly, and pain shoots up to my shoulder, making me grit my teeth together. I'm so stiff. I feel like I have rods attached to my limbs. My hand feels so heavy and hard to lift, but I need to get out of here. Just opening my eyes fully takes so much effort. Turning my head slowly so I can assess the rest of the room, my heart stops when I see Jared, in a chair covered with a blanket, his head resting against the wall. I smile at the sight and recall jumbled conversations that I thought I'd dreamt. I need to touch him—to know that he's real, but I can't move enough.

'Jared.' Shit, I don't even sound like me. A pathetic sound no higher than a whisper comes out, but Jared is up on his feet and in motion before he's even opened his eyes. He kneels by me and holds my hand. My eyes fill with tears, and I can't help but let them flow.

'Don't cry, baby. You're gonna be fine. You're healing. You're doing so fucking good, baby. I'm so sorry this happened.' He's babbling at me, and I just want him to hold me. I can't even tell him how glad I am to see him, how much I need him right now because my voice won't work. I feel like I've been mowed down by a truck. I've never felt pain so severe and debilitating. Jared shouts for Zoe, and she comes in with Howard in tow.

'Hey, good to see you awake. You had us worried there.' I attempt a smile. It's good to see her too. So fucking good. 'Listen, I know you probably have a lot you wanna say just now, but your healing process is really slow at the minute because you were in such bad shape. So, I need you to stay where you are and try not to speak, okay?' I lift a hand to my throat, why can't I speak? Zoe has a sympathetic look on her face. 'It looks like you've taken quite a few bad blows around the larynx, so your voice will be strained, and it's really best that you speak as little as possible. We need to help the healing process along rather than hinder it further.' I nod my agreement. But already questions are swirling around in my addled brain. Where were the kitsunes? How had they found me? How long have I been here? I'm so thirsty.

'Water?' I croak in a whisper. Jesus this is already getting lame. Zoe goes to fetch me some, and I reach out for Jared's hand. He has stubble at least a couple of days old, and he's wearing dirty crumpled clothes. He's a hot mess, but a gorgeous sight to behold. God, I love this man. He sits quietly with me, just stroking my hair until Zoe comes in with a bottle of water. At the sight of it, my mouth suddenly feels like the Mojave Desert. Jared takes the bottle from her and brings it to my lips. I gulp it down greedily, and then I'm coughing and spluttering at the sudden influx of water, which sent my throat into spasm.

'Easy, baby. You need to sip it slowly,' he cajoles. His eyes are full of concern, but he doesn't look so good either. When was the last time he slept or ate a meal? I want to ask him. Damn it, this is so frustrating. I try to mime it instead, pointing at him and putting my hand on my cheek, head to one side and closing my eyes. This makes him chuckle.

'You must be getting better if you're ordering me about already.' I widen my eyes at him in mock shock, making him chuckle again. Howard chuckles from the corner of the room. I had forgotten he was there. And it shocked me to no end hearing him sound amused.

'She's right, Jared. You haven't slept in days. Now she's awake you should catch some zzz's.' I nod enthusiastically before wincing as the pain registers. This is no fucking fun.

'I'll sleep properly when you can lie in a bed beside me. Until then, me and this chair have become close friends.' He throws his thumb over his shoulder towards the crappy excuse for a chair. Howard sighs in resignation.

'We do try, Devon, but he's a stubborn asshole who never listens.' I snicker as Jared turns and has the audacity to look offended. Howard is so on the button that no one can deny it. Howard ignores him and continues. 'The sooner you get up and about the better. It's been like trying to tame a fucking grizzly bear while you've been out, sweetheart.'

Sweetheart? Howard called me sweetheart? I must have taken a huge knock to the head because Howard is a mean, sullen asshole who never cracks his face. And he hates me. This is weird. I pinch myself. Just checking this isn't all some cruel, sick dream. Nope.

The next day is better. I can speak, and I'm able to get myself up and out of bed. I wake that morning to find Jared asleep in the chair. He looks so uncomfortable, and I feel guilty that he's stayed that way for me. I make my way over to him, and he cracks his eye slightly—a small smile at the corner of his lips—and pulls me into his lap. It was gently done which doesn't go unnoticed.

'I'm all better,' I tell him with a mischievous note to my voice. He raises his eyebrows, that small smile of his growing slightly. And it wasn't the only thing growing. I could feel his cock hardening under me as his lips found mine in a hungry kiss. I love Jared's kisses in a morning. And Jared loves morning sex. He pulls me up and off his lap though.

'Come on, let's get the fuck out of here,' he says, standing me on the floor. 'You need to clean up before we hit the road?' Umm, yeah. I guess I do. I'm still reeling from the rebuff. I nod, and he takes my hand, leading me into the bathroom. 'I'll let you get showered. I'll go and grab some stuff for you that Zoe has spare.' And then he just walks away. I turn on the shower, pull off my top and get in. Then the tears start. He's rejected me. He's never ever passed up an opportunity to fuck me. No matter where we were. And that stung. Maybe he didn't want me anymore? Maybe all the trouble this had brought wasn't worth it. Maybe he was finally giving in to his father's wishes. Oh my God, I don't think I can bear this. What if he can't be with me anymore after what they did?

# chapter
# TWENTY-FOUR

## Jared

I FILL ZOE IN ON Devon's improvement and check on the guys to make sure we are still clear of any problems. Zoe gives me some clothes for Devon, which I set on the vanity in the bathroom. The room is full of steam and the sound of running water. The curtain is pulled across so I can't see Devon, but I have a bad feeling, and I want to get moving as soon as possible, so I pull the curtain back slightly to tell her to wrap it up. I find her sat in the tub with her arms wrapped around her knees, sobbing. Fuck. I reach in and shut the water off, and I wrap her up in a towel and lift her from the tub. I carry her over to the chair and sit with her in my arms. Fuck. I will rip every one of those bastards apart for this. Every. Last. Fucking one. I hold her close to me and I stroke her wet hair. I feel like a total bastard too, for getting a raging hard on with her sat in my lap. Who the fuck does that in situations like this? Jesus Christ. It must be fucking mortified her after everything she'd been through. What the fuck have they done to her? I have to swallow back bile and clamp my jaw tight to hide the rage at what she must be feeling. Devon starts to shiver. I stand up and sit her in the chair while I move to get her clothes.

'Come on, baby. Let's get you dressed and warmed up,' I tell her, rubbing her arms under the towel. 'Do you want me to get Zoe in here to give you a hand?' I don't want to leave her but if I'm making her uncomfortable, I will. Her eyes meet mine, and they fill again with tears. I fucking hate that she feels like this around me. It cuts deep, but

I understand why. So, I go to the door and shout for Zoe to come up. When she arrives, I leave them to it. It kills me, but I do it.

Howard has questioned the female and hasn't got much more than first names from her. I know we are missing at least two guys and I want them all, and this bitch is unaware as to what lengths I'll go to to get them. I don't want Devon to see any violence from me toward a female. So I will wait and do what I need to do behind closed doors. For now. Though it wouldn't harm to talk to the kitsune. I walk in, and her head snaps up. Fear is clear in her eyes even without the stench permeating the room. It is written all over her.

'By now you know what I want?' I ask. She doesn't reply. 'I'll take your silence as a 'yes'.' Her eyes follow me as I walk slowly closer and around her chair. She's pissed herself, and it stinks. 'I wouldn't normally harm a female,' I tell her and watch as she holds her breath for my next words. 'But for you, I will make an exception. Unless you want to tell me in the next, let's say ten seconds, what I want to know.'

I watch as both fear and determination cross her face. Determination to live or to die, I'm not sure yet. I count slowly. One…elephant. Two… elephant. When I get to ten, she's squirming but still not talking. So, it appears she wants to die. 'Listen, I get it. You don't want to rat on your boss, alpha, or whatever you assholes call each other. But, let me give you a piece of advice. I will get the answers I want, and after what you and your gang of rapists did to my female, I will make sure that what you experience at my order will make that look like child's play if you don't give me what I want.' Her lip curls up in a snarl, and she spits at my feet.

'I will never betray my alpha.'

I lash out and slap her face so hard her head lolls forward like a rag doll, and I feel no remorse for it. If she weren't already unconscious, I would have hit her again. I roar out my frustration and hit the wall. Harrison comes in. 'Errr everything okay, boss?'

'Get that fuckin bitch bound and gagged and in the back of the truck before I kill her. Make sure there's nothing in it that she can use as a weapon or to escape. And don't fucking leave her till I get there.' I storm out and up the stairs to find Devon trying to brush her hair with a travel comb. Her frustration evident in the way she's tugging at the clumps the comb won't go through. I offer to help, but she glares at me, in a 'don't you fucking dare touch me' way. So I hold my hands up in surrender and sit on the bed instead. I need to fix this but until the bastards responsible are six-feet under, I can't make it right for her.

I'm a patient man, but I can't wait for this. It needs to be done now. I need Devon back to her carefree self. No fears and no worries. And I have to keep myself in fucking check too. No fucking early morning wood to freak her out. Jesus this is going to be hard. But fuck me, I will do anything to make sure she gets back to herself.

# *Devon*

The ride home is exhausting, and I sleep most of the time. Jared and Zoe ride in the truck with me, while the others follow on their bikes. It's so good to be back, despite the fact that I'd not wanted to stay at Jared's—where Kristen was. Now I find myself not wanting to leave. I've always prided myself on being a strong woman. My dad always encouraged it to a degree. But right now, I feel like I need a crutch to hold me up, and my crutch is Jared, and his home. I don't want to leave the house at all. I want to stay put and just be with Jared. He's avoiding me though, in all ways sexual, and I'm beginning to feel like things may have changed between us.

I wake up to find Jared had got in the shower again, for the third morning in a row—after coming to bed late the night before. I'd know he slept with me, only because I woke in the night tucked under his chin with his arm wrapped around me. I'd gone to bed naked, in the hope that he would want me. He's told me he loves me, which had gone some way to ease my worries, but why won't he touch me? My mind is working overdrive, and I'm coming up with all sorts of idiotic reasons. I shake my head and get out of bed. This is ending right now. I open the bathroom and make my way over to the shower. He turns when he hears me, and the first thing I notice is his hand wrapped around his hard cock. A look crosses his face, but it's fleeting, and I can't make out what it is. I step in through the door and replace his hand with mine. His eyes close and he gulps hard. I let out a sigh as I move my hand up and down his solid length. His head falls back against the tiles, and he moans. I smile and get to my knees—his eyes open, and he looks down at me. I see panic for a moment, but as his eyes meet mine, it's pure lust and need reflecting back at me. I open my mouth and slide my tongue around the head of his cock before I slide him in. I make small circles, flicking and flattening my tongue, I play and enjoy the taste of his pre-cum. By the sounds he's eliciting, he's definitely enjoying himself. I take him deep, flattening my tongue, sheathing my teeth with my lips and opening the back of my throat up to take him as far as possible. I squeeze his ass, prompting him to fuck my mouth just how he likes it. I close my eyes and hum, knowing the vibrations get him off, but he pulls out and has me up and in his arms in a second.

'Shit, baby. I want to be inside you so fucking bad right now.' He kisses me with such ferocity it's almost violent. I pull on his hair ending the kiss and watch as his hazed look rakes over my face.

'So fuck me already,' I tell him, yanking on his hair. He looks relieved, then worried. And I feel myself losing him again. No. Not happening again. 'Jared, if you do not fuck me right now so help me God I am gonna—' I don't get to finish the sentence before he has me up against the wall and has thrust his cock deep inside me. YES! Finally, this time *my* head lolls back against the tiles. I'm clinging to him like a limpet. But he doesn't move. He's shaking. And his head is down. No no no. What's wrong? Shit.

'Jared?' He looks up and fear flashes in his eyes. 'What's wrong?' I ask, desperate to know, and desperate for him to carry on. I need this so badly. He's still solid inside of me, so he does want this, and he's told me he loves me. He shakes his head before he speaks, 'Baby tell me this is okay? This is what you want? That you're not just doing this for me. Because I can wait. I need you to be ready.'

'Jared, you've been hands off ever since you found me and quite honestly it's pissing me off.' He's taken aback by that I can tell. I shove at his chest. He pulls out and lets me down. But as I try to walk away he holds me against the wall of the cubicle.

'Devon, I never meant to piss you off. Fuck, I've been taking care of business every morning like this because I've had a permanent hard on for you. I *always* fucking do.'

'So why with the games, Jared? Why are you keeping me at arm's length all the time?'

'Because I don't know what to fucking do! I didn't want to drag all that shit up for you or hurt you, and I wanted to respect you and wait till you were ready!' He's pissed now.

'Ready for what, Jared? Have you forgotten we fucked like rabbits before?' I'm shouting now. This was not how I wanted this to go.

'Of course I haven't fucking forgotten! Jesus, it's on my fucking mind every damn minute of every day, but that was before they—' he falters, and he makes a little hiccup sound as he chokes back his words. 'I don't want it to bring shit up for you. I want you to be with me one hundred fucking percent when we make love. I can't bear the thought of you hating being with me because of what they did. It scares the shit out of me.'

Whoa. Back the hell up a minute. 'Jared I wasn't raped.' His eyes meet mine for a second, and then he sags in my arms. The relief I see there is virtually tangible it almost takes on an entity of its own.

'I was sure they had because you were naked and he...and you were so badly hurt, but I couldn't ask you. I didn't want you to relive any of it.'

I take his hand, and we leave the bathroom. I put on a towelling robe, and he wraps himself in a towel, and we lay on his bed.

'I'm not going to lie to you, Jared, they did try, but I fought back.' And I didn't feel like I'd been raped. 'They beat the shit out of me until I blacked out, the next thing I remember was you.' A small sympathetic smile crosses his face.

## *Jared*

'You don't have to worry about that motherfucker. I put him in the ground myself.' And thank fuck I got there when I did because unconscious or not, it was obvious what he was trying to do. Bastard.

I can smell bacon from the kitchen, and I'm so fucking hungry right now, but I need to make love to my female, and I'm not going to keep her waiting a minute longer. Just as she's about to speak, I devour her mouth, and I let go. I've been holding everything back for days, and I want to make up for all that lost time. I pull the robe tie and push it aside, revealing her gorgeous pert tits. Treating each one equally, I grope and flatten my tongue across both nipples, sucking and nibbling at each one, making her groan. I fucking love the little squeaks and moans she makes when she's turned on and loving what my mouth does to her body. So. Fucking. HOT. Swirling my tongue up the side of her throat, I kiss across her jaw, reaching her mouth as I suck on her tongue. Bliss. As I kiss her like a dying man, I find her pussy with my fingers and dip into the sweetest wetness, and her body arches into mine. I finger fuck her for all I'm worth until she's coming apart in my arms, and the way she kisses me almost has me coming before I even get inside her. When her jaw clamps shut and she cries out her pleasure, I push inside her and feel her walls contract around my dick. I have to recite in my head all the old ladies names in my pack to stop me from blowing my load in the first ten seconds. When I regain my composure, and I get her through her orgasm, I fuck her like our lives depend on it. It's hard, fast, and fucking amazing. I can't manage slow. I can't speak as my balls slap against her ass and her shouts of 'yes' get louder and wilder. Her nails dig into my arms as she holds on, and I fucking love it. I pull her legs up and put them on either side of my head, bending her so I can go even deeper. She's building again, and I'm almost there, panting with every thrust. As she screams out my name, I come. It hits me so fucking hard that I rock on my knees and an explosion of white lights set off a display behind my eyelids. Euphoria. It's a few seconds before I regain the ability to move. Sex with Devon is fucking awesome every damn time. Whether it's hard and fast, slow and sensual, a quickie, or hours in the sack. We were made for each other. The fact that she's prepared to get down and dirty with me any time or place does wonders for a male's ego. I've never had better, and I knew from the minute I saw her, she was it. Thank fuck she's finally agreed. We lay there until my stomach rumbling breaks the silence, making her giggle.

I want to ask her some questions, but I don't know how to start. I'm pondering on what I should say, then, as if she reads my mind she answers.

'I don't really remember much at all, Jared. I remember them taking me... I remember fighting and them holding me down while he tried—' she shakes her head pursing her lips holding back her tears. 'Jared, my mother was there.' I tense up. I'm not sure what look crosses my face but whatever it is, has her looking down like she's ashamed.

'Baby, what do you mean your mother was there?'

'She—she—held me down so he could rape me...'

I jump up to my feet and start pacing. I'll fucking kill that cunt. Why? What the fuck kind of mother does that? Devon is mumbling now. I stop and kneel in front of her.

'Baby, it's okay. We don't need to do this now.'

Her face pales and her hands go up to cover her mouth as her eyes fill with tears. Oh, Jesus, she's remembering.

'Maiya!' she cries out. 'They have Maiya, Jared!' What? Why?

'Devon, are you sure? Why would they have Maiya?'

'Because they want to use me. She made me, Jared. I'm just a pawn in her war. My mother played my dad. She knew all along what she wanted—a hybrid. Me. That's why she left. I was supposed to live as a wolf—learn their ways. Then she was going to use me to infiltrate her enemy pack. She said 'this island has nothing she wants'. She was planning on taking me back to North America, Jared.'

Fuck me, this can't be for real?

'Jared, they were using Maiya as leverage to get me to cooperate. Because I refused, the other part of their plan was to use me to make more hybrids.'

'Fucking hell, baby.' I rub my eyes and face, what the fuck? I need the rest of the pack in on this. We need to wipe these cunts off the face of the earth. I want revenge, but more importantly, I need them gone so this fucking idiotic plan they've formed won't ever come to fruition.

'Listen, I wasn't planning on telling the pack about you not being full blooded, but I think they just moved the goal posts on us, baby. I think they need to know the truth behind why you were taken. So we can go head to head with these bastards and not be at a disadvantage.'

She nods.

'I agree with you, Jared, but I'm scared they'll see me differently.'

'Listen, they know you. It changes nothing—they'll see that. They have to.'

Again she nods, but she's chewing on the inside of her cheek. Nervous.

'Baby, I need you to know that whatever happened there, you can talk to me about it, you can talk to me about anything, you feel me?'

She nods her head. I call the meeting.

*Jared*

I HAVE EVERYONE SAT AROUND the table. Devon, Zoe, and Imogen to my left. Howard, Logan, and Brad to my right. Harrison, Jacob, and Dom have joined us at my father's request. They are excellent trackers and have the skill set we need in finding these kitsunes. My father has given me the green light to find and take them out. I can't help but feel like it's a test to see how I deal with it. But whatever, I'll do it my way. I look at Devon, and she has a look of terror on her face. I'm about to reveal her secret to the table. I'm nervous, but I have faith in my pack, so I'm hopeful they will all be open-minded and accept her for who and what she is. Kristen is absent. No one has any idea where the fuck she is—she's been out for days. I rap on the table with my knuckles to get everyone's attention.

'Okay, so as you all know, we need to make plans to move on the kitsunes.' There are mumbles of agreement around the table and a clear, 'Fuck, yeah, we do,' from Brad. I chuckle at his enthusiasm, but I get back to business when I turn and lock eyes with Devon. She's shaking. I fucking hate this. I pull her hand into mine and lace our fingers.

'I'm not going to beat around the bush here. There is something you all should know. But before I tell you, know this—I've known for a long time and chose to keep it from you all. That's on me. I've accepted it and want you all to do the same, but it's something you'll need to decide on your own.' I look over at Devon—she's almost drawing blood she's biting her lip so damn hard. Everyone else is looking at each other, wondering what the fuck is going to come next, but they all stay silent, which is my queue to carry on and get this the fuck over with. I take a deep breath. Here goes nothing. I squeeze her hand in mine as reassurance. She slides in closer to me.

'So there's a reason the kitsunes took Devon. It's not what we thought originally. It's not to get to me or dad. I believe that if they had achieved their goal, we wouldn't have heard from them again because they're not local, not even from this country. They followed Devon here, and it's her they want.' Devon is like a rod next to me, so stiff she could snap. I haven't even got to the why yet. Again heads are turning, but all I see is confusion and anger on some faces. No one has spoken though or questioned me—they're all waiting me out.

'The reason they want Devon is because she's different to all of us.' Again, I look into a lot of very confused eyes. Brad starts to crack a joke, but one look from me and his mouth snaps shut. It's not the time. Howard is the only one who knows what's coming next.

'Devon isn't a full blooded wolf. She's a wolf-kitsune hybrid.' Gasps and shouts erupt around the table.

'Fuckin' hell.'

'Jesus fuckin Christ, Jared?'

'Is that even fuckin' possible?' Someone else asks.

Brad chimes in then, 'If they have a wet hole to stick a dick into then yeah, I'd say anything is possible.'

'Oh my God, Brad. You're a disgusting pig, seriously,' Zoe tells him. The girls sit with a wide-eyed look of shock on their faces, but they don't say anything, Devon has tears in her eyes, and I can feel the thrum of her body as the need to flee takes hold of her. Everyone is talking and questioning what I've just told them. I turn to Devon and kiss her lips.

'It's gonna be okay, baby. I promise.' She doesn't answer me, just nods her head minutely before looking back down at her feet.

'I've got a question,' Brad addresses me.

'Shoot.'

'Why the fuck are we only just finding this out?'

'Because I didn't think it was important before but now I do.'

'Are you fuckin' kidding me?' Jacob chimes in. 'You didn't think it was important to tell us that we have a fuckin' kitsune among us?'

'No.'

'Well, that says it all, doesn't it! Fuckin' 'ell, Jared. You could have your pick of females, and you bring a fuckin' kitsune to get your dick wet with.'

I move pretty damn fast—so quick he doesn't see my fist coming until it's too late. I floor him—hovering over him to give him another if he dares to spout any more shit about my female. When he raises his hands in defeat, I step away and wait for him to return to his seat before I take my position next to Devon again.

'Like I said earlier, Devon is a hybrid, not a fucking kitsune,' I say, glaring at Jacob. 'But not a full-blooded wolf either. So she's no more one than the other—'

Devon interrupts me by placing a hand over mine and starts to look around the table. 'I just want to tell you all that I grew up as a wolf, with my dad, I'm naturally drawn to my wolf side. It's the more dominant of the two. I also want to say that I had no idea that I was different or why until I had already met you all, and as soon as I knew, I told Jared. That's… that's all.' She talks like she is on trial and has to defend herself. Which pisses me off.

'Look, as far as I'm concerned, this doesn't change a fucking thing. Devon is my female, and I protect what is mine. So no matter whether you agree or don't agree, I'll be finding these cunts, and I will be putting an end to them. So all I need to know is if you are with me or not. I'll give you until the morning to make up your minds.'

'Jared, what about the alpha? He may not want us doing this if he knew the truth,' Harrison speaks this time.

'My father knows everything, and he accepts that Devon is my female and will be treated as such. The only reason I am giving you the facts now is because it's the reason for this whole fucking mess. Otherwise, you would all be blissfully un-a-fuckin-ware, and we'd be fighting these fuckers to the end, so go and do whatever it is you wanna do tonight and be back at this table for nine am—no later. I want an answer then.'

'Jared, I don't need time. You know where I stand,' Howard says,

'Thanks, man. I do, I do.' I stand grasping his shoulder. That's what I want from them all, but I need to give them time to process what we've just told them. I needed a day or so too when she told me. But if they didn't want her here, they can go and take a long walk off a short fucking pier. No, they won't need the walk. I'll show them the end of the pier with my size fucking tens up their ass. Let's just hope they all make the right decision in the morning. If they don't, they can fuck off and find another pack.

I take Devon out into the woods. I want some peace away from the house. We sit on a felled tree. I can tell she's terrified about what the guys back at the house are thinking through. No doubt bitching about too. But it is what it is. They would either have to step in line with me or step out and fuck off.

'You okay, baby?' I ask her. She's been quiet ever since we left and she's in her own little world, staring out into the trees. At my question, she turns, and I can see it on her face. She's scared. 'Talk to me?' I want to be her shoulder to cry on, her sounding board, and her best friend. I want to be all that and more.

'I'm okay. This is all just so much, you know. Asking them all to fight for me when they hate what I am. Hate everything about me. It's a lot to ask of them, Jared.'

'One, they don't hate everything about you. They fucking loved the bones of you before they knew this shit, and I'm fairly confident they still will, and two, we're a pack. It's not a lot to ask of them. This is what we do for each other, and especially for those we love.'

'Yes, but has that ever been a kitsune?'

'Granted no it hasn't, but listen to me, stop referring to yourself as a kitsune. You're just as much wolf, so stop beating yourself up over something you have no control over, okay?'

'I used to hate my dad you know, as a kid. I hated that we moved so much and that I wasn't allowed to be myself. He would recite our rules over and over, every night before bed, so I would go to sleep thinking about it and wake up with it in mind. But now I know why he was that way. Imagine if they'd have found me sooner...' I can't even contemplate that. 'My mother did say that I was no good to them unless I was brought up as a wolf, so I guess they wouldn't have taken me much sooner, but I'm guessing my dad had a good idea they were sniffing around because coming here without him was a real sudden decision.'

'Maybe we should give him a call. Clue him in?' I ask. Maybe he would have some info that we didn't. A way in. Anything would be good at this point.

'No, I'd really rather we didn't worry him, Jared. He's only just let me out of his sight, and this happens. He'd be on a plane in minutes.'

I disagreed, but I'd go with it for now. Whatever she wanted. I nod as she carries on.

'What do you think they will be doing to her, Jared. I can't stop thinking about it.' Her eyes fill with fucking tears again, and I don't know what to say to her. It kills me that she's hurting over this.

'I really don't know what they'll do to her. She's human, so I can't think what they would want her for except—' I stop. I don't want to upset her more by telling her the sick fuckers might rape her friend. 'I think they'll keep her alive for leverage over you.' I actually don't know if she'd be better off dead. This girl doesn't mean shit to me, but my girl is hurting badly, and she will have to live with whatever guilt comes with this shit, and I'm not going to let that happen. So we will get this girl back and at the same time kill every last one of them. I put my arms around her and slide her up onto my lap—not in a sexual way, I just want to comfort her. Fuck me, a month ago I would never have given a shit about a woman's feelings. But I'd kill for this one. I *will* kill for this one. When I get my hands on them.

# chapter
# TWENTY-SIX

## *Devon*

NINE A.M. COMES AROUND QUICKLY. I'm a mess. I've never, ever felt like this before—never making friends, forging bonds or attaching myself to anything. Now, in such a short space of time, I've come to love Jared and all that comes with him. I feel like I've found my place finally and found a group where I fit in and belong and all that could disappear in just one conversation. I feel sick. We walk into the kitchen, and everyone is already seated at the table. It's quiet, and I can't help but fear the worst. I can't look at anyone as I sit. I don't want to see the look in their eyes. I want to turn and leave, but I feel Jared's hand on mine, and as he squeezes, I look into his eyes and see resolve. He's confident. I'm glad. But I'm still so unsure.

'Okay, so I'm not here to give a speech, and I'm not here to hear one. Let's just get on with it. A simple yes or no will do.' I melt beside him. His no-nonsense attitude is so fucking sexy. I could jump on board and ride him right there, except this is seriously not a good time. Obviously.

'Howard, I know your answer.' Howard nods. 'Brad?'

'I'm with you.' He smiles at me and winks. 'You're one of us, Devon.'

Jared moves around the table, and it's unanimous. I sag in relief. The girls move to give me a hug.

'It was never in question, Devon,' Zoe whispers in my ear.

'So let's get down to the real issue here, Jared. What's the plan?' Brad says, and everyone stops murmuring. They all sit back down, and all eyes are on Jared. His chest expands as he inhales a long breath, and I'm overcome with emotion. I love him so much, and his pack has accepted me. I literally have to hold back the tears. I think Jared senses my emotion because he looks to me.

'Baby, you don't have to stay for this part. I can handle it if you need to leave?' I nod and move to stand.

'I'll come with you.' Zoe stands, takes my arm, and hooks hers through it. We leave the kitchen and go into the library room. I head for the window, and Zoe closes the door behind us.

'Are you okay?' she asks. She's looking really glam as always—wearing red heels with jeans and a red top. She doesn't even have to try and look good, she just does. Her hair is always perfectly done and never out of place. She's naturally beautiful, inside and out. I crumple into the chair at the window, and I cry. 'Aww, sweetie don't cry. It all worked out just fine.'

'I know. It's just all so much to take in, Zoe. I'm so relieved, but I'm shit scared too.'

'Devon, all you need to know is you are one of us, no matter what, okay?'

I nod as I wipe the tears from my face with the back of my hand and snort in an unladylike way so I don't snot all over myself.

'Thank you, Zoe.' She purses her lips and shakes her head.

'You have nothing to thank me for, hon. Friends have each other's backs, and we're pack sisters now,' she tells me grinning as she pulls me into a hug.

'I'm so grateful for you, Zoe. I really am.'

'Ditto. I feel like I've known you forever.' I hug her back with all I've got. She's definitely a keeper. Now we just need to get Maiya back, and all will be right in the world.

'Come on, let's get you cleaned up and go back to see what they all have planned.' She takes my hand, and we go up to Jared's room where I sort myself out in the bathroom while she waits. I can't describe exactly how I feel at this moment, but I'm happy and confident that we'll find Maiya. I can only hope and pray that Maiya comes out of this whole. I wash up and try to make my face look a little less puffy and red. It doesn't work. Zoe decides makeup is the best way forward and she drags me into her room where she does a full makeover on my blotchy face. Then tells me I look beautiful when she's done. We head back into the kitchen, and everyone is still around the table just as we left them. Jared puts his hand out to me, so I walk straight to his side, where he tucks me under his arm and kisses my head like he's missed me.

'I think we've covered everything for today, so let's get to it. You all know what your jobs are?' Murmurs of, 'Yes, boss,' echo around the room as they all filter out, Brad takes Zoe with him, no doubt giving her the details so she can do her part, and then it's just me and Jared. He lifts me onto the table in front of him and slips his arms around my waist.

'You okay, baby?' he asks as his hands caress my ass. My eyes flutter closed as I lose myself in the feel of him. He chuckles, bringing me back to the moment. He's smiling up at me. I rest my forehead against his and smile back. Letting him know I am, in fact, okay. I move my hands up into his hair and do my own caressing. He lets out a little rumble from his chest, which makes Niagara overflow at the pure need I hear in it. His fingers tighten and grip at my ass cheeks. Jeez, I want him to take me right here. He growls and sighs deeply. 'Baby, we have a lot of shit to get through today, and if you carry on like this, only thing that's gonna get done is you, on this table.'

It sends a shiver down my spine, and it takes all I have to pull away from him and let us get on with the job at hand. He's reluctant too, but he lets me go.

'What do I need to do, Jared?'

'All you need to do is stay safe here. Don't go anywhere without me, or whoever I place on you okay?'

'What about school and work? I have to go.'

'Taken care of, you won't be going.'

'What? What do you mean taken care of?'

'Exactly what I say, Devon. You aren't going. I've spoken to the office at Uni and cleared your time off, and I've spoken to whatever his name is and told him you aren't gonna be at work any more.'

'So you just decided that? All on your own?' This man is so infuriating. How can he do that without even speaking to me about it?

'Devon, you were fucking kidnapped and almost raped. Do you think you're gonna be leaving this house any time soon, let alone fucking working for some prick who couldn't fight his way out of a paper bag?'

I scoff at him. 'You have no idea what he's capable of Jared. Maybe he's a really good fighter for all you know.' I was making a stupid argument, I knew it, but couldn't help but be stubborn.

'Baby, whatever you have to say next is irrelevant. You ain't leaving this house unless absolutely necessary, and you're certainly not to go and work, so get used to it.' I stamp my foot like a two-year-old. He is so God damn annoying.

'I needed that job, Jared. I don't have an infinite bank account. I need to earn money!'

'You are *my* female, and I will take care of anything you need.' He turns away like that's the end of the discussion. Gah. I growl out a kind of high-pitched sound, and he turns back toward me.

'Don't fight me on this, Devon, I'm keeping you safe. If you do anything to jeopardise that I will spank your ass so fuckin hard you won't sit for a week—you feel me?'

I gasp, stunned he isn't joking. There isn't a hint of a smile on his face. Yes, he's seriously serious. No one has ever spoken to me like that before, and although it's absurdly caveman-ish, my body is limp with need for him. I am totally turned on by what he's just said. I also feel a strong need to submit to him because he's being the alpha male. I don't get a chance though before he is taking my mouth in a punishing kiss. I relent and give myself over to it. I need this. I need him. In every way. It was stupid to think we could walk out of this room without settling the sexual tension between us. Jared pulls me up into his arms and cups my ass. I wrap my legs around him, and he pushes me up against the wall beside the door, thrusting his hard cock up against the seam of my jeans. His hands move up under the front of my t-shirt, and he pops my boob out of my bra, pinching my nipple. It causes flood warnings to go off in my pants. His mouth devours mine like he's a starved man. I take what he gives and give back just as much. Our teeth clash as we become even more desperate. I move my hands down to his jeans, trying and failing to free him while holding on and not breaking the kiss. As if on queue, and in typical Brad style, the door flies open, and Brad struts in with a stupid grin on his face. Jared releases my mouth, slides me down the wall and adjusts himself, before turning to face a smirking Brad.

'Fucker. I swear you're on a personal mission to cock-block me. What the fuck do you want?' Jared growls. Brad laughs still staring at us.

'I just want food. You know the stuff we keep in the kitchen? Me, cock block? Nah, not me, man.' He turns away chuckling at himself.

'If you don't need anything, get the fuck out while I see to my female.'

'Errr, this is the kitchen, in case you've forgotten. Where we eat. I don't think you two should be—'

Jared launches a loaf of bread at Brad's head, and then they're wrestling on the floor. Jared has Brad in a headlock. It's all in fun, and I find myself in hysterics at their banter as they jab at each other.

Eventually, they give in and end the whole silliness with them both sitting on the floor, backs to the cabinets, breathing heavily.

'Get back to work, fucker,' Jared tells him, grabbing Brad's hand and heaving him up.

'You too, man, but *please* not in the kitchen.' His last word almost squeals out as Jared kicks him up the ass and he runs out through the door laughing so hard he can't speak. Jared grabs my hand and pulls me through the door mumbling something about fucking his female where no one will disturb him, turning me on even more. Jesus Christ, how does this arrogant caveman get to me so easily? I dutifully follow as he drags me by the hand to his bedroom. He kicks the door open, turns and picks me up by the waist, throwing me onto his bed. I squeal and crawl up the bed, trying but not really, to get away from him. He snags my ankle and yanks me backwards. I'm sprawled face down, and Jared crawls up and over me, anchoring me between his knees. He lifts my t-shirt up and over my head, yanking it off and onto the floor. Then he unclips my bra, pushing it roughly off my shoulders. I manoeuvre a little, in order to slip it from each arm. He pushes down on my lower back as his hands slip teasingly around my waist. He fumbles with my zipper and button, before gripping my jeans and stripping them from my legs. Leaving only my thong in place. My face is stuffed up against the pillow. I whimper as his rough, calloused hands work up along my calves and thighs and linger a little as he reaches the apex between my legs. He hovers there—its torture. He runs a finger under the thin slip of material, and along my ass crack. I shudder at his touch, needing more. I try to move so I can touch him, but he splays his fingers over my lower back and presses me down hard. His mouth finds my ear and his tongue flicks out.

'Don't move. Stay right there,' he whispers, and I feel the effect it has between my legs. Flood warning!!! I don't move a muscle. I'm shaking with anticipation. Then I feel his hot breath at my calf and the back of my knee. He flicks his tongue along the crease, and it sends shivers through me. I wriggle, and his hand presses down against my back. 'Still' he orders. Gah, his sexy, bossy voice has me quivering. I bite down on my lip and hold back the moan bubbling up my throat. As his talented mouth works its way up one thigh before moving across to the other, and his hot breath fans across my butt cheek, I clutch at the sheet below me. Biting harder on my lip. I squirm again, wriggling trying to touch him. SLAP.

'Ouch, what the—'

He cuts me off with a kiss, thrusting his tongue into my mouth. The position is awkward, but he manages perfectly. His hand rubs delicate circles over my stinging ass cheek.

'I said still,' he says against my lips. 'I mean it.' I lick my lips, basking in his taste. He moves back down my body, and then I feel his breath against my ass. My clit is throbbing, and my entire body is desperate for him. He slides his fingers up and under the small piece of material at my hips and maddeningly slowly he removes them. His fingers tracing every inch of my legs as he pulls them down and off. I'm practically panting with anticipation and need. He moves up my legs again, and I moan this time, and then his hands are at my waist, and he pulls my ass up into the air, so my legs bend up beneath me. I'm on all fours. I look back at him, and I see desire reflected right back at me. It's killing me that he's taking his time, but God, it feels so damn good. His hands trace my hips, and up my back. He's positioned behind me, but he's still fully clothed. He puts pressure between my shoulder blades, making me rest on my forearms, lowering my upper body to the bed with my ass in the air. Oh my God, his mouth. He laps at Niagara, and I feel the first tingles of orgasm run through my body, leaving tingles of heat in its wake. He flicks his tongue so expertly, tasting me and hitting my clit just right. I mewl, unable to hold back, and he slows his pace as if realising I'm close. I squeal out in objection, and he slaps my ass again. This time, I don't flinch or object, I moan long and low at the pleasure radiating through to my clit. I'm losing myself completely. His fingers find my core, and he slides in effortlessly, not surprisingly. He thrusts his fingers inside as his tongue laps and flicks against my clit. I'm building, again, and I start to chant. 'Yes…Oh yes.' He removes his fingers and thrusts his tongue inside me.

'Mmmm,' he mumbles against me, as his fingers travel. I feel him pull my ass cheeks apart and before I can say or do anything his tongue is there. At my most sacred untouched place. I want to pull away. I want to feel disgusted by what he is doing but all I feel is pleasure, and I want more. His tongue moves back to my clit, and he massages my ass with a finger. The anticipation alone almost has me going over again, but he senses it, and he slows. If I could string a sentence together right now, I would give him both barrels. He's killing me here. Then I feel a small amount of pressure at my rear and instinct has me tensing up.

'Relax, Baby. I won't hurt you.' I try, and then his finger pushes just inside the forbidden place. I hold my breath as he does.

'Relax, baby.' I do, and he pushes a little further as his tongue laps at my clit, and he uses his other hand to thrust inside me. I start to tremble all over. I can't move away from him as my climax hits because my head is now pushed as far up the bed as I can go. I climax with such force that I almost pass out. I'm stuck, unable to move, and he is fucking me with his fingers relentlessly. I cry out, my mouth so dry from screaming. But he doesn't give up. I reach a point where I am just coming down from the first orgasm when another tsunami hits. I worry momentarily he could actually drown, but that thought is fleeting. His cock thrusts inside me—balls deep on the first thrust. I hear him groan out above me, but I'm like jello. I can barely hold myself up on my forearms, and he is pounding into me like it's been a year since he fucked me.

'So fucking good, baby,' he pants out as his hands reach around and he cups a breast in each one. His squeezing just adds more and more sensation to my already over-sensitized body. The noise that rips from my throat surprises me. I sound like a wanton slut faking an orgasm. Except this is so fucking happening right now, and I can feel every inch of his hard cock inside me. I explode again, and my body seems to go into spasm. I squeeze him so damn hard I worry that it might snap off. He clearly enjoys it though. He comes, thrusting in like a piston, three more times before he collapses onto my back with a grunt. We don't speak—both panting and breathing heavily, catching our breath. I close my eyes; I can't fight it any longer. They close of their own accord. He'd literally fucked me to the point of exhaustion. I'm so sated. I feel him pull out and climb off me, going into the bathroom. I should get up, and go and clean up but I really don't have the energy right now. When he comes back in, he's freshly showered and smelling awesome. I am still star fishing and naked. He kisses my shoulder blade and gives my ass a light tap.

'You hungry, baby? We all missed breakfast.'

'Mmhmm.'

He laughs hard and low. Mmmmm, so sexy.

'You want me to feed you in bed?'

'Oh my God, you are so perfect.'

He laughs again and my heart bursts for him.

'I'll take that as a yes?'

I nod. 'Definitely, yes,' I tell him. He moves around the room getting fresh clothes, and I notice something in his face that wasn't there a moment ago. He has a serious expression that has me suddenly worried. I sit up,

'Jared?' He turns to me then, and his face softens a little. 'What's wrong, why are you tense?'

'Nothing, baby. I'm just thinking about what we need to do to finish this business, you know?'

'And get Maiya back?' I say, my head down, feeling guilty that I had forgotten for a while that she is still missing.

'Baby, listen to me for a minute, okay?' I search his eyes for something that will give me a clue to what is coming next. But I get nothing. 'My goal is to find and kill these fuckers and end this so they can't come for you again.'

'And get Maiya back?'

He sighs, and I panic.

'Jared, do you know something? Please tell me, have they found her already?'

'No, baby, not yet, and I know she means a lot to you, and that's why we will do what we can to find her. But I need you to know that you are the priority here, okay?'

'What do you mean?'

'I mean that if an opportunity presents itself where they can all be taken out, I'll take it.'

'But—'

'Baby, I'm sorry, but *you* are my priority. I need you safe, and the only time you will be is when they are all in the ground.'

'Jared, please. Please, I can't... I need her to be okay. Jared, I couldn't live with myself, please Jared, I have to get her back.'

## *Devon*

'W E HAVE A LEAD,' BRAD says, walking through the kitchen door. I'm filling a plate for Devon, and he tries to snatch some toast.

'That's for Devon, dickhead. What lead? Walk and talk—she's hungry.'

'You know that warehouse off the motorway with the big yellow for sale sign?' I can vaguely recall it. 'The one about halfway home?' he continues.

'Home, home? Ranmore?'

'Yeah, home. Knob—where else would it be?'

Smartass.

'Get to the fucking point, Brad.'

'Okay, so just before you hit Surrey. This warehouse has been up for sale for-fuckin-ever, and now it's sold.'

Jesus Christ, so what?

'And?'

'What?'

'And what's the fucking point, Brad?'

'Well, it's been bought up by an American buyer. Anonymous to anyone who doesn't know where to look.'

I grin, now he's getting to the fucking point.

'And you know where to look right?'

'Pfft, like you have to ask? From what I can tell and from what Devon has told us—it looks like it could be her mother.'

Woah. This is good.

'I'll be down in fifteen. Have everyone ready to go. I want the women, you and Harrison to stay here.'

'What? Why can't I go?'

'Because you're the tech guy, Brad, and I need someone I can trust with Devon.'

'Ahh come on—'

'Brad, train someone else to do as good a job as you, and then we can discuss you coming with. Until then you stay, and you watch my female.'

He isn't happy. Brad can fight and take care of pack business as well as the rest of us, but he has a talent the rest of us don't. His expertise was in surveillance—hacking and tracking through any means necessary via technology. Without it, we wouldn't be able to do half of what we do. So if he says Devon's mamma bought that place, then she fucking did. Brad walks away bitching, but he knows I'm right, and he'll watch Devon like a fucking hawk.

'Baby, I didn't know what was best to bring you—' I stop in my tracks. She's up and dressed stuffing shit in a bag. 'What are you doing?'

'I'm going with you.'

'Like fuck you are.'

'I heard you talking, Jared. If Maiya is there, I want to be there for her.' This female is going to be the fucking death of me. I look up to the ceiling in the hope I'll find some patience there.

'Devon,' I growl out. 'We only had this conversation less than an hour ago. You are not going anywhere near there, you feel me?' I slam the plate on the bedside table and turn to face her. She's dressed in jeans and a tight black t-shirt that's low cut in a V, and her tits are pushed up and centre. If I weren't pissed, I'd motorboat those babies. But I am. Her hands are on her hips, challenging me, and she has a fucking cute pout on her face.

'You said I couldn't go out unless I was with you or someone you put on me. So if I'm going with you, what's the problem?' *What's the fuckin problem, she says.*

'Oh, I don't know Devon. Maybe the fact that these bastards are here for YOU, and maybe delivering you to them would be a STUPID FUCKING IDEA?' I snap. And instantly feel bad for it. But I'm not backing down, and she isn't fucking coming. She looks like she might cry, and I feel like shit.

'Baby, I need to be on my A game, and if you're there, I won't be. I need you to be safe so I can concentrate on the job I have to do, okay?' I have a bad fucking feeling about this. I'm thinking she won't listen to a word I'm saying because she's a stubborn ass. But she shocks the shit out of me when she agrees to stay put, and I convince her to eat breakfast. I snag some bacon and a slice of toast and chase it with a glass of milk from my fridge. I'm ready to go. I'm just uneasy about leaving her. Not because I think she isn't safe with Brad and Harrison but because she is a stubborn female and will fuck Brad over the minute I leave.

'Baby, promise me you will stay put? Because I'm not above locking the door and taking the key with me.'

She gives me a sexy little glare. Which does nothing to reassure me. So I raise my eyebrows telling her that I mean business.

'Okay, okay, I promise I'll stay here like a good little female,' she sasses, making me chuckle. So fucking sexy, my dick throbs. I pull her to me by the nape of her neck and take her mouth in a hard kiss. Releasing her too quickly for my liking but duty calls and I have some kitsunes to kill.

'I love you, baby,' I tell her, pulling her in for another hug. I tug on her hair so her eyes meet mine, and she bites at her bottom lip.

'Eat and relax. Maybe take a bath or whatever you do to relax. Just stay put, okay?'

She stretches up on tiptoes and presses her lips to mine. Despite my handful of her hair restricting her movement, she manages it. I look deep into her eyes. And I see a resigned look there. Good. She's going to stay. Thank fuck for that. I leave her in my room and head back to the kitchen where everyone else is ready and waiting on my order. I take Brad aside.

'Devon is in our room—do not let her out of your sight, Brad. If she goes to piss, you sit right outside the door. She's fuelled by guilt right now, and I have a bad feeling she's going to disobey me and make her own way to the warehouse. You cannot let that happen—you feel me?' He nods then breaks out in a grin.

'Would love to be a fly on the wall if she does disobey you,' he sniggers.

'Well, if she succeeds, Brad, you won't need to be, 'cause I'll fucking bury you in it.'

'Harsh man, real harsh.' He shakes his head at me in mock disbelief. Fucker. I slap him on his back and signal for the rest to suit up and head out.

It's dark. We've scoped the place out for the entire day, and I'm certain Brad's intel is spot on. Howard and Logan have maintained a close proximity all day, while the others have fanned out around all sides. We can see all the entry and exit points between us. We have com radios and enough weapons to take down a small country. This isn't about how nicely it's done—it's about speed and accuracy. I want it over with. As for Maiya, I owe it to Devon to at least see if she's being held here. I can only hear male voices and they are muffled at best, possibly soundproofed walls. We've watched as the guys take turns in their guard duty. They are sloppy and stupid, making for easy targets. We move in, leaving Logon on sniper duty. Howard takes the two men nearest us out in about thirty seconds, not even slowing in his stride. We enter through the side door and signal the rest to do the same. They all enter and get in position, leaving only Dom outside running perimeter, Logan watching his back. I move silently, gun in one hand and my knife in the other. I'm not stopping to ask questions. These fuckers are going to ground today.

Howard moves to clear one room, while I stop and listen as I hear muffled voices in another, arguing. I strain my ears but even with my wolf hearing it's hard to catch the gist of what's being said. I pin myself up against the wall and listen as the voices come closer and become much clearer. I'm dressed all in black, and my face is covered, camouflaged. My adrenaline is pumping through my body, and I'm fixing to get this done. Itching for a release. Another minute passes and I get my chance, in the form of two kitsunes, small, but well built. I slice the first one's throat clean and through to the oesophagus. I leave him to flail and flap like a fish out of water while I deal with number two. He's shocked at my sudden appearance, I can tell, but I don't give him time to shout for help, pummelling my knife into his heart. The only noise he makes is a gurgle and a gasp before he also crumples to the floor next to idiot number one. Howard catches up to me, and I smell blood on him too. He signals with his fingers, two dead. Total so far, six dead. I move further down the corridor until we meet Jacob—all clear on his side, he signals, three dead. Totalling nine. Fuck, and we thought this was just a small problem. As we clear the last and only corridor left I smell it, and my stomach turns. Death.

Human and female. We round the corner, and I fear the worst, I can't make out any other scent because the stench of death is so strong.

The room at the end has a mattress in the middle of the floor and on it lays a broken body, bloody and at least a day old. I can't make out who it is, so I move closer. Howard holds up a hand. I stop in my tracks. He walks around the mattress looking for any signs of booby traps—there are none. So I move the blonde hair from the face. It's so swollen and bruised I can't tell if its Devon's girl. Whoever it was, died a fucking horrible death. These bastards are sick and twisted. From the smell alone, I know she's been raped by multiple men, and the torture she faced is just warped. Sick bastards doesn't describe what they are well enough. The poor girl has been through so much hell I bet she was grateful for death. I feel sick, and I want to kill the motherfuckers all over again.

Howard steps up beside me. 'Not Maiya, she isn't here.'

Relief floods me, and I realise just how much I want to find her, for Devon.

'She was here. I got her scent in another room, but she was alive when she left.'

'Boss?' Harrison says over the com in my ear

'What is it?'

'I think you need to come out and see for yourself.'

Howard and I look at each other, and I know it's something fucking bad. I make my way through the warehouse and out the back where Harrison is in the treeline. As soon as I walk towards him, I get the scent on the wind.

'Fuck,' Howard spits out. I can't form the words to go with how I feel. I'm just hoping it isn't what I'm thinking. Because if it is, we have a fucking traitor in our pack.

We bury the girl in the surrounding woods, giving her a small bit of decency. Her family, wherever they are, will never know how she came to her end, and I know that will forever haunt me because everyone deserves peace, but I can't give it to them without putting all of us in the frame, and putting us on the police radar was not good practice. We had to stay clean. Always. So we always cleaned up any mess. And this was definitely one big fucking mess. We burned the mattress, the bodies, and all other evidence that anything had happened, while I sent Harrison on a mission following the scent in the woods. After a couple of hours, he was back and very pissed. He'd followed the scent for six miles before it disappeared at a fuel station. He'd spent a while backtracking, trying to find it again and came back with nothing. So it was a bust. But not over. I'd been on with Brad, and he was hacking every CCTV in the area—we needed to know for sure. Being a traitor carried the death sentence, no exceptions. So we couldn't be half-assed about it, we needed hard evidence.

We arrive back, and Devon comes straight to me. Brad has a grim look on his face, telling me he had something. First though, I need to speak to Devon. I sit her down in the library.

'We didn't find her, baby, but she'd definitely been there.'

She sags in her chair, with a look of desperation on her face.

'We will find her, baby.' I just wasn't sure if we'd find her alive, but I didn't say that out loud.

'What did you find there? Were they there?'

I nodded

'We killed nine more, so this is bigger than we initially thought. They didn't come unprepared.'

She just sits in a trance, her eyes glazed over, not really with me, but not completely elsewhere either. 'Devon?'

'Hmm?'

'It's not over. I've got Brad and the others all working on leads. I won't stop until they're all dead.'

She nods her head, but she's still distant.

# chapter
## TWENTY-EIGHT

## *Devon*

I'M SO RELIEVED THEY ALL made it back in one piece. I'd been so worried they wouldn't. The relief of seeing Jared walk through that door was immense. For a minute I forgot about Maiya, and then the guilt came crashing in like a tsunami at a tidal barrier when he told me they hadn't found her. This was all my fault. They'd taken her to persuade me to do what they needed me to do. And I had escaped and left her in the shit. I would never forgive myself for that. Ever.

'Devon, did you hear me?' I nod not really sure if I did or not. 'Baby, there's something else.'

I snap my head up and stare into his eyes—what else could there possibly be?

'What?'

'I think Kristen is working with them.' My head span. Holy fucking shit balls. No way?

'I can't even wrap my head around that, Jared. I'm so confused. I thought you and the kitsunes hated each other? An age old grudge?'

'We do, and I can't believe it either, but the scent was there along with theirs. Kristen had been there.'

'And you're sure it was by choice and not by force?'

'I have Brad working the CCTV in the area, to be sure.'

I nod my head. 'Why me, Jared?'

'I don't know, baby, but I do know they are sick fuckers and are getting nowhere near you ever again.' His choice of words has me reeling. You don't use 'sick fuckers' unless you saw things that made you sick to the stomach.

'What did you find, Jared?'

He shakes his head. He doesn't want to impart that info obviously. 'Jared, tell me?'

I wasn't going to give up on this so he may as well just spill and spare me the back and forth.

'Nothing you need to hear about, baby.'

'Jared, this is because of me! I do need to hear it!'

He sighs long and low. 'Baby, they kill for the sake of it. Not because they need to but because it's fun to them.' I stop my whining and just look deep into his green orbs. He was cut up over this. And he felt bad. I could tell.

'Jared, share this with me. It's not your burden to bear—its mine.'

He shakes his head.

'They are twisted sick fuckers who need putting down. I'm not giving you details, Devon—you don't need that shit in your head.' He gets up and walks out of the room. I'm left feeling bereft and guilty. I'd made him relive whatever he found there tonight, and he'd left me and walked out because I wouldn't leave it alone. I'm and idiot. I find him in the kitchen with Brad. They're muttering in low voices. I can barely make it out, but I hear Kristen's name.

'I'm going to call my dad,' Jared announces. 'This changes things.'

I walk up to meet him as he comes toward me, and I take his hand. His face is grim, and that means one thing. Kristen is a traitor.

Mr Stone arrives, and the house is full—there are men in every room, and every single one of them looks like they do this every day. They have an arsenal of weapons. I can't say I've ever seen guns like these and I'm the only American in the house. Guns are illegal here, and they have enough to arm a small town. This is ridiculously scary, and I'm to blame. I'm standing in the kitchen as three men dismantle and clean several guns spread out on the table. It's like a bad dream—everywhere I look there are more men, more guns, and more testosterone.

I can't breathe. I need Jared, and I can't see him anywhere. I'm tingling all over, and my head is spinning out of control. Pain—my chest hurts I can't catch my breath. Pain. *Help someone, please. I can't breathe*. Jesus Christ I'm going to die surrounded by men I don't know, in a room full of illegal weapons. I feel a sharp pain in my knees as I hit the floor. I'm so dizzy that I can't see straight—my vision starts to blur, and I see black spots.

'Shit!' I feel arms around me. 'JARED, SOMEONE GET JARED, NOW!' *Yes, yes I need Jared.* I want Jared. Darkness.

# *Jared*

'Devon, baby, wake up,' I beg, it has been fucking hours, and she is still out cold. This can't be normal. She fainted— a panic attack is what Zoe called it—but why the fuck isn't she waking up?

'Zoe, check her again.'

'Jared, I know what I'm doing. She's fine, and all her vitals are okay. She just checked out, that's all. She needs to rest. She hasn't properly recovered from her own ordeal and then she's faced with all this. It's a lot for anyone, Jared, but she's practically a human, never being brought up in a pack. It will have been a huge shock.'

I mull that over and decide she's right.

'Shit.' I can't believe I left her alone to deal with all that—it never even crossed my mind.

'She feels guilty too like this is all her fault. She was talking about it being her fucking burden to bear, fucking hell and I left her alone. I'm a prick.'

'Jared, she's going to be fine,' Zoe berates me, 'and you didn't leave her alone, she was here with all of us. None of us realised—'

'It's not your job to realise. It's mine, and I fucked up. Too wrapped up in this shit that I forgot to take care of my female.'

'Jared, don't be stupid,' Zoe says, but I don't pay her any attention because Devon's eyes start to flutter. Thank fuck for that. I don't know if I should be quiet and let her sleep or if I should talk her into waking up. Fuck it.

'Baby, you okay?' Her eyes snap open fast, and she sits up, looking around her. I've put her in our bed. I can see the panic in her face as she wakes up. She's done that every day since she was taken, but she hasn't mentioned it. So I've left it alone. One day we will talk about it though. When she no longer has anything to fear from them. I hate seeing it on her face—in her eyes when she thinks no one is watching. It's eating her from the inside out and seeing what is left of that girl today only makes me realise just how fucking lucky I was to find her in one piece. I just hope to fuck we find her friend before it's too late. I don't think Devon would cope with the alternative, and I don't want her to have to. Finding Maiya isn't an option—it's a necessity. The guilt Devon is feeling over this shit needs to stop. The only way that will happen is if we get her back. So we get her back. No matter what.

There's a knock at the door. Zoe moves to answer while I sit stroking Devon's hand, trying to calm her down. 'Devon?' I ask. 'Are you okay?'

She nods and gives me a small smile.

My dad walks up to the other side of the bed. 'Quite a scare you gave my son,' he says. Great! Cheers, dad. I look over to him and am going to give him a look to shut him up, but when I do, I find him looking at Devon with something close to kindness. Well, fuck me!

'Yeah, I guess I did, I'm sorry—' She starts to apologise, but I don't let her.

'You've nothing to be sorry for, baby. You've had a rough time of it,' I tell her making sure she doesn't place more guilt on her shoulders. Fuck that. Zoe moves in and starts her blood pressure machine for the millionth time. And my dad looks at me and then rolls his eyes to the door telling me he wants to talk. I make my excuses, and tell her I'll be back in a minute. Devon smiles, and Zoë assures me she's in good hands before shooing me out of the room. I follow my dad downstairs into the kitchen where I find Jedd, Kristen's father, sitting at my table looking grey. My dad starts up the questions immediately.

'Your daughter is a traitor, Jedd. Do you expect me to believe you had no idea?' Jedd flinches at the word traitor, and the look on his face tells me he really didn't have any idea his daughter would be capable of it.

'I didn't know, Harry. I'd have stopped her. I wouldn't have allowed it. I swear to you.' My dad looks unimpressed. I'm not sure what angle he's playing here, because if Jedd didn't know, he didn't know. Meaning this is pointless.

'As a father, I make it my business to know what my son is up to, Jedd. And what I do not know, I find out. Why? You may ask,' Jedd looks to the floor, 'because, Jedd, I am his father, and he is my son, and I want to make sure he forges the correct path. Not, shall I say, walk down a treacherous one.' I can't help but feel my dad is being a little unfair here, after all, I am watched and kept safe, twenty-four seven because I'm the alpha heir. Kristen isn't, and it's a little hard to keep tabs on someone from miles away. I'm about to suggest that when he speaks again.

'How often do you speak with her?'

'Everyday.'

My dad nods, pacing up and down the length of the table.

'And you last spoke to Kristen?'

'Four days ago,' Jedd mumbles.

'So four days go by, and you didn't think that was strange?'

To be honest, it didn't occur to me as strange because she always stays out, granted not for this long. I didn't really care enough to notice I guess, as shitty as that is. Jedd's chin starts to wobble, and his eyes fill up.

'She was devastated' he growls out. Looking right at me. 'You broke her heart.'

I fold my arms across my chest and look right at him.

'If that's what she told you, Jedd, she was a good fucking liar.'

'She was your intended—this is all your fault,' he spat like he was talking to some scumbag piece of shit. That's when my sympathy for the guy ran out.

'Listen carefully. That was never going to fucking happen. And before you spout any more shit about her being heartbroken or whatever, you need to take off the rose-tinted glasses, Jedd. She is a power-hungry bitch, with a cold heart. She probably screwed her way through half the men in this town, so don't spout crap at me about how I caused this shit. No one made her do jack shit. She did this all on her own.'

He glared at me like he wanted to kill me.

'You should never have allowed this union, Harry. He was meant for Kristen, and you allowed that... that...'

'Be very fuckin careful what you say next, Jedd. Very fucking careful.' If he thinks I will let him slate my female he is very fucking wrong.

'She's not even of pure lineage.'

'AND?' I roar in his face. He flinches, and his eyes go to his feet. Fucking pissant coward. The room is silent, and everyone is looking to me, waiting to see what will happen next. My dad is leaning against the far end of the table looking rather amused with the situation. I'm just fucking mad. I walk over to Jedd and whisper in his ear,

'You ever say one wrong word about my female, I will cut your balls off and feed them to you through a fuckin straw, you feel me?' He nods. And I'm done. He doesn't know anything worth a damn, and he's just trying to save Kristen's skin by placing the blame at my door. Fuck him and fuck her. Waste of my time. I seek Brad out, leaving my dad to do whatever the fuck he wants with Jedd.

'Anything?' I ask when I find him in the room with all the security monitors.

'The bitch is clever, but I'm better. I've narrowed it down to about a six-mile radius.'

'That's a lotta fucking ground to cover, Brad. You can't narrow it down more?'

'My name's not Jesus. I don't work fucking miracles.' I grin at his tone. I've touched a nerve.

'Well shit, and there was me thinking you were the dog's bollocks.' I slap him on the back.

'Fuck you, cocksucker,' I laugh hard and leave the room.

'Find me when you've found something, Jesus,' I yell over my shoulder. I hear something hit the back of the door, and I laugh some more. In the kitchen, I gather the guys up and, give them shifts in threes. I want everyone out and searching within that area. We don't have a lot of time now and every minute that ticked past was another closer for Maiya to end up like the poor blonde girl. I won't have that on Devon's shoulders. Howard catches me as I'm walking up the stairs.

'I'm staying with you, Jared.' I nod.

'Okay, who's on first shift?' We've agreed that we would split off into teams of three. One team patrolling the grounds at all times, and another team within the six-mile radius searching for Maiya. We've collected some of her clothes and distributed them among the men so they could find the scent.

'Some of the guys who came with your dad.' Fair enough. I nod.

'Erm, is Devon doing okay, Jared?' I stop and turn to face him, and shake my head no.

'She's been through a fuck load of shit and not finding Maiya is making it worse. We haven't really gone into detail about what happened while she was gone, but seeing that girl, I don't know what to fucking think. I just hope to fuck we find her for Devon's sake.'

'What about Kristen?'

My face turns up in disgust.

'When we find her, she'll pay for her part, however small. A traitor is a fucking traitor.'

'I didn't see that coming, Jared. I got to tell you—that was a fucking shock.'

I nod. 'Me neither, brother.'

I'm eager to get back to Devon, but I stop and turn to Howard at the doorway.

'Thanks, man,' I tell him. He looks at me like I've grown an extra head. 'For having my back.' He grumbles something about always having it no matter what, as he turns and walks away. I shake my head and walk in to find Zoe sitting on the bed holding Devon's hand. My eyes find Devon's and my heart drops.

'What's wrong?'

I instantly look to Zoe. I want answers. What's wrong with her? Is she in pain? They don't answer, and I can't take it. 'Will someone please fucking answer me?' Zoë's eyes widen, and she looks to Devon, for what? Permission? I'm literally going stir crazy with this shit when Devon finally opens her mouth to speak.

'Zoe, can we catch up later?'

'Sure, no problem. I'll be in to check on you in a while, okay?'

'Tell Howard to check in with Brad will you?' I ask as she closes the door. When she's gone, I take up Zoë's position on the bed holding her hand. I can't take this.

'Devon, talk to me, baby?'

'It was nothing, Jared, honestly, just girl talk,' She's lying through her back teeth. Clearly not realising I can already read her like a fucking book. I grit my teeth, and I feel my blood heat as my patience wains. I do not want to upset her anymore, so I'm walking on eggshells, but between this and Jedd, plus Kristen on the loose, my patience is stretched pretty fucking thin.

'Girl talk that has you crying?' I look at her with wide eyes daring her to lie to me again. She plays with her hands in her lap and doesn't look at me.

'Devon, if you don't fucking tell me and stop with the bullshit, I'll spank your ass.' She sighs and I can tell I've got her.

'Jared, it wasn't anything really. I was just telling her my feelings about everything.'

'Oh well, that helps a fuck load!'

'There's no need to get all snarly with me!' Snarly? She hasn't seen fucking snarly yet. I close my eyes and take a deep breath. I count to five before I open them again.

'Baby, whatever it was, please tell me about it. I don't want you keeping things from me that upset you.'

'Why do you keep things from me then?'

How the fuck did this shit get turned on me?

'I don't?'

She closes her eyes and sighs again.

'Jared, we were talking about the fact that I feel responsible for what's happened to Maiya and Zoe was explaining what the kitsunes are like. Pretty much what you said earlier—they kill for fun. She then talked about the girl that had been found. Dead.' For fuck's sake. 'Zoe assumed I would know, Jared because the whole house knows, but obviously, you didn't feel that I'm important enough to know.'

Jesus Christ. Why? Why the fuck did I choose a female that would fight with me on every God damn thing?

'Devon, you may wanna get down off your fucking high horse. Isn't it obvious why I didn't tell you that?'

'It's something I needed to know! Something YOU should have told me.'

'Why? So you could beat yourself up some more? Carry even more guilt? Fuck, only a few hours ago you were passing out unconscious in the kitchen because you couldn't fucking deal with this shit!'

Her face changes. She looks like I've slapped her. Fuck.

'I didn't mean it like that, I meant—'

'You don't have to explain yourself, Jared. It's fine. I'm too delicate—too stupid to cope with all of this—'

'Now you are being fucking stupid. Don't put words in my mouth! That's not what I said, and you fucking know it.'

'I'd like to be alone for a while,' I growl out my frustration at her request as I get up and walk towards the door. But I turn at the last minute.

'Has it made you feel better knowing that a girl died? That I had to fucking bury her and cover up her rape and murder? That her parents will never know the truth?'

Her gasp is answer enough. I've made my point. 'Nah I didn't think so.' I slam the door behind me. I find Zoe outside. A guilty look on her face. She starts to speak, but I don't want to know. 'Don't,' I warn as I walk past her.

I don't go upstairs for the rest of the day, and I take my shift with Howard and Logan patrolling the grounds. Logan stays in human form with a cache of weapons on him while Howard and I run in wolf form. I'm not sure anything will ever happen here, but with Kristen gone over to enemy lines, we have to expect anything. I need this time to clear my head. I said some shit to Devon that I shouldn't have, but I'm about ready to snap. I'm trying my fucking hardest to keep her safe and sane, and I have no clue what I'm doing. I've never had to deal with a female's feelings or worry about hurting them. I gave zero fucks about who I pissed off or why, before Devon. And it pisses me off that I go to all this fucking effort and for what? So she can throw it right back in my face. Fucking females.

Our shift is over, and another team have taken our place. I'm just getting my jeans zipped up when I hear Howard come through the brush.

'You okay?' It pisses me off that he's even asking.

'Fucking super, you?'

He snorts back a laugh, as I pull my t-shirt over my head.

'What's crawled up your ass?'

I slip my feet into my boots and tuck in the laces. I can't be arsed with tying them right now.

'Fucking females,' I tell Howard in answer. He laughs out loud this time and doesn't try to hold it back.

'Why do you think I don't have one?'

''Cause you're too fuckin ugly to get one?' I reply, taking the piss.

'Fuck you—I get plenty. Just not the same one twice. Too much fuckin trouble.'

I thought about that for a minute, and yeah, I had been happy passing the time and getting down with a different woman whenever I wanted, but I wasn't complete. It wasn't until Devon that I felt whole. Like I had a purpose. I've never felt that need to be with someone before. Not once have I ever felt that with anyone else. And it was instant—not even after I'd tasted her or been inside her. It was before I'd even set eyes on her. My nose knew she was mine—that she was meant for me.

'You'll know one day. You will find that one person that makes you feel like a fuckin king.' Howard laughs so hard he bends over.

'If she makes you feel like a king, why the fuck are you out here bitching to me instead of up there feeling like a king?'

'Fuck you, smartass.' I smack him in the arm. He laughs some more. We make it through the treeline, and I look up to my bedroom window. Devon is standing there with my white t-shirt on. As soon as I look up, our eyes meet. As I get to the back door, she disappears out of sight.

# chapter
# TWENTY-NINE

## Jared

I HEAD ON STRAIGHT UP the stairs and go to her. I've had my fill of this shit, and I'm putting a stop to it now.

I open the door finding her sitting on the end of the bed. Her eyes meet mine, and I don't see sadness. I see resolve. I walk over to her. I don't want to talk this shit out. I just want to feel her. I pull her face up in my hands and meet her lips with mine. I'm not gentle. I'm taking what I need, and giving her what she needs. I am going to fuck the angry right out of her. I lay her down and pull the tee up and over her head—she has no bra on. I stop at her wrists and twist the material on itself creating a binding. I hook it over a piece of the headboard to keep it in place. It's makeshift, but it works. I lean back and take in the view—she's squirming a little under my gaze, but I take in every piece of her. I've fucking missed her today. I tease her tits with my mouth, and I drag my tongue along her ribcage and down to her belly button. I dip my tongue in, and she whimpers. I move further south, and I know she is desperate to get her hands in my hair, and knowing that makes me smile. I flatten my tongue and pushing her knees up and her legs wide, I pull my tongue through her wet pussy lips. Tasting her cream, from the bottom up, until I get to her clit. Mmmm, fuckin beautiful. Her face is flushed, and it's spreading down her chest. I hook her calves over my shoulders, and I lift her ass off the mattress, spearing my tongue inside her. The little moans and whimpers I elicit from her make it all that much fucking better. I tongue-fuck her pussy like my life depends on it. Her feet are like a vice on my back, squeezing me closer. I move to her clit, and I feel her legs twitch just a little. That's my girl. I circle a finger around her lips, spreading her juices, and then I push in with my middle finger, hooking it inside and stroking that little spot that drives her wild. I've tasted a few pussies in my time, but nothing ever comes close to this. Not even on the same scale. I wouldn't normally give unless I was receiving because it was never about making them feel good, it was about taking what I needed from a one-night stand. But I could eat this pussy all day long and not get bored, especially as she is always this receptive. I fucking love it. I push another finger inside and fuck her with my fingers, flicking and sucking on her clit. I circle a third finger through her wet lips and spread it up and around that little forbidden fruit. I feel her tense as I do, but it drove her wild last time, she just needs to relax and enjoy it. I circle it and hook with my other fingers, all the while teasing her clit with my tongue. I feel a small tremble as she clamps down with her thighs, and as I slide that third finger just beyond the entrance, she comes apart. I guide her through the orgasm and just when she is coming down I pull my third finger free, and she goes again, letting out a long low moan. It's beautiful. I'm still fully clothed, but I can't wait to get inside of her.

I unzip my fly and don't waste time—she cries out as I fill her, stretching her. I take her mouth and swallow her moan as I pull back and thrust forward again. Her tongue slides into my mouth, and I let her set the pace of the kiss. It's desperate and greedy, and it turns me the fuck on. I'm going to blow my load if I'm not careful, and I don't want to end this just yet. She is clinging to me with her legs pulling me in close, and I'll come in minutes if I don't pull back. I need to regain my self-control—something I've learned is almost impossible when fucking Devon. I pull out, and I feel like I've been kicked in the balls—like my dick has a mind of its own and is screaming at me to get the fuck back in there. But I need a minute, or it will all be over too soon. Devon cries out in desperation, as I pull myself from her warm tight pussy. I pull her hands free and flip her over. If she touches me, it will be game over. Pushing her face down onto the bed, I have her ass and pussy up in the air, just begging to be fucked. It's a sight to behold. And I take a second to appreciate the view. I pull her ass cheeks apart and before she can complain I have my mouth there, just teasing the entrance. She moans and pushes her ass out toward me. I slide my fingers into her pussy again and keep the same rhythm as my tongue fucking her sweet little ass. I don't take it too deep, I don't want to put her off, but I'm absolutely out of my mind happy that this is doing it for her. One day soon, I'll take her ass completely.

Her legs start to shake, and I feel the beginnings of another orgasm. I work her through it, slowing down, but not stopping until she's pulling away and can't take anymore. That's when I thrust in hard, and I have no intentions of stopping or slowing until I've filled her with my cum. I have visions of coming all over her body and rubbing it into her skin—marking her in every way possible—as if my bonding scent isn't enough. I want to make her fat and round with my babies. Yep, multiple babies. I want to watch her, barefoot and pregnant in our home. All this flashes through my mind as I fire my load into her greedy pussy, and she milks me for every last drop like she's been starved for me.

Fuck me. If we can make up like this every time we have an argument, I'll be sure to piss her off at least once a day. I'm still feeling the last of my seed pump through me when I unclench my jaw and open my eyes. I look down to see she's turned her face to the side so she can look at me. She has a gorgeous grin on her face. I'm holding on tight to her hips, and honestly, I feel a bit like jelly. Without breaking the connection, she pushes up on her arms, and I fold onto my knees where she ends up sitting with my help, holding her in place. This is a real good position, I note, hands on tits as she bounces up and down, taking what she needs. She would be in control. Of course, I could also dictate the pace by holding her hips. Fuck me I can feel myself swelling again. She turns her face to mine and takes my mouth in a kiss. This time it's different, slow, not teasing. But showing me her love.

## *Devon*

Three days has passed since the pack started its search within the six-mile radius that Brad narrowed down. I've mostly been holed up in Jared's bedroom, with the exception of meal times, and even then sometimes Jared brings up food for me because he knows how I'm feeling. I just find it hard to be around everyone right now. I know all of this is my fault and I know none of them would ordinarily be looking for someone they didn't know or care about—someone that isn't even part of their pack, or even a wolf. And I know that Jared is only doing this for my benefit, so I appreciated it all, but the fact I can't take part—can't actively search—makes me feel like I'm a burden.

Jared wakes me from another fitful night's sleep. He has a strange look on his face. Worry? I sit up and rub the sleep from my eyes, licking my lips as I realise I really need a drink. Jared seems to read my mind, and he hands me a cool drink of water from the side table. I smile and take it.

'What's up?' I ask as soon as my mouth is wet and I'm able to form words.

'There are some police officers downstairs and they want to speak to you.' He looks scared. Yes, that's the look. *Oh shit, what's wrong?*

'Why? What's wrong? Why are they here? What did they say? Is it my dad?' I fire off all these questions while throwing clothes on, barely noticing what I'm putting on. But I'm in motion, and that's all that matters. I head for the door, but he pulls me back toward him.

'Baby, hang on. They're here about Maiya. People have noticed she's missing—that you've been missing too. They want to check on you and also ask you some questions.'

'Okay, let's go—'

'Devon. You can't tell them anything.'

I stop in my tracks and meet his eyes.

'But they could help find her? Maybe they will have a better chance?'

'Devon, please trust me on this. We take care of our own business. We can't involve the police.'

I take a breath and realise that he's right. I knew this already, but my sleep-deprived brain is not thinking this through logically.

'I know. Yes, you're right. I won't say anything. What do they know?'

'I'm not a hundred percent sure right now, but they need to think you've been here the whole time. That you packed a bag and had no reason to go back to the dorm. You didn't know she was missing, and you haven't kept in touch because you weren't great friends. Okay?'

'Yup, not friends, been here, haven't left, got it.'

He nods, and we make our way down the stairs and into the kitchen, which is surprisingly empty, considering this is the hub of the house. Weird. Where is everyone? The only person in there is Howard. And he's talking about his university course while making a coffee. Wow, this is surreal. Howard is having a full-on conversation with the cops. It's more than I've ever heard him speak to anyone!

'Hey, here she is. You want a cup, Devon?' Howard asks, grinning. Grinning? Like it's an everyday occurrence. Someone needs to pinch me. I nod, accepting the coffee, while the two officers turn to greet me,

'PC Turner, and my colleague PC Hendow, Miss Hathoway.' I shake his hand.

'Nice to meet you both—what can I do for you?' I ask, trying and hopefully succeeding in nonchalance.

'Well, we have had a missing person's report filed for your roommate.'

'Maiya?' I ask in a shocked tone,

'Yes, Maiya Middleton. She's been missing for some time now, and we were hoping you could give us some information about the last time you saw her? Did you talk about anything in particular? Did she tell you about anyone she'd met or any plans she had?'

I think on it a little while, and the last image of Maiya on the I-pad screen pops into my mind. I scramble to remember the last time I saw her before then. It was when she was sweetly comforting me from my nightmare. It seems like an eternity ago.

'I can't honestly remember the last time I saw her. I've been staying here for? How long have I been here now, Jared?' I ask him, unsure of what my answer should be since I've completely blocked out some periods of time.

'Around about three weeks, maybe more, I'd say,' he responds. I look at PC Turner and agree. I can see his beady eyes assessing me, and the female officer—I can't remember her name now—is busy assessing what Jared has to offer. Bitch. I hold out my hand for Jared, and he quickly threads his fingers through mine. I watch her closely and see disappointment flash in her eyes, but she recovers quickly. *Mine*. I tell her as if she can read it in my eyes. I see Howard in my peripheral vision, smirk and turn away, washing his cup up in the sink.

'Yeah, that sounds about right,' I agree.

'Well, it's been at least two weeks, maybe more, that Miss Middleton has been missing. We can't determine the exact timeline because there have been messages sent to her parents but no actual contact with anyone.' So they had been clever and used her phone.

'How many of you live in this house?' Pc 'wandering eyes' asks.

'Seven.' 'Eight,' we answer at the same time.

'So which is it?' the officer asks looking directly at Jared this time.

'Eight, including Devon,' he says smiling at me.

'Seems you have a lot of transport in the driveway for just the eight of you.'

I look at Jared, but it's Howard who answers.

'Like I told you, we had a get together last night, and being responsible we don't want people drinking and driving,' he says, winking at her. She clears her throat as if he's affected her and redirects her eyes to Jared and me.

'What was the occasion?'

I stay quiet. And Jared just laughs.

'Do students need an excuse to party?' He grins as if that's all we do.

'I guess not,' she says smirking at him. Oh my god, I'm right here!

'So is there anything else I can do for you?' I ask sternly, moving into her line of sight, which just so happens to be in front of Jared. His arms, as if on queue come around my waist and he pulls me into him. I smile up at him, and he gives me a knowing look, busted! He caught me. Oh well, as long as she gets the memo that he's taken, then it's all good. PC Turner clears his throat. He'd been taking notes. I'm not sure on what because we'd said zilch that would be of any help to him. In fact, he'd probably imparted more info on the situation than we had. We knew they had nothing—not even a correct timeline. So we were good. But I was clearly a puzzle to them, and one they intended to crack.

'Someone informed us that you had disappeared around the same time as Miss Middleton, Miss Hathoway, so you can understand how glad we are to find you safe and well. However, you must also agree that it seems a little strange that she should disappear around the same time you move in with your...?' He looks toward us for confirmation, which Jared provides eagerly.

'Boyfriend,' he states clearly like he's making sure everyone in the room is clear on that fact. Even though it's pretty damn clear from the way he's been stroking my hips for the last few minutes. Again, it makes me smile. Stick that in your pipe and smoke it, bitch. He's mine. I hear Howard stifle a laugh. The cops in the room won't have caught it with their inferior hearing, but I did.

'Well, I guess that's a coincidence?' I ask. When they say nothing I continue, 'I feel bad—like I should have spent more time there, but in honesty, she never seemed to lack in the friends department. I figured she'd be glad to have the room to herself.'

'Well, we may need to speak to you again, so I have to ask that if you have plans to travel anywhere, that you inform us before you do?'

'What? Why?'

'Because you are possibly the last person to have spoken to her face-to-face—we haven't determined that yet—and until we do, you need to stay in the area so we can contact you again.'

'You could just use the phone,' I state a little obnoxiously, knowing damn well I wasn't going anywhere but hating the fact I had to ask permission first.

'That's no problem, Sir,' Jared informs him while squeezing slightly at my hips, telling me to back down. Howard walks them to the door and PC 'eye fuck' admires Howard in the same way she had Jared only moments ago—desperate much? I roll my eyes as Howard obviously flirts with her. Then when the door closes, he drops his smile and heads for a seat at the table. Jared's face is serious, and they both look at me.

# chapter THIRTY

## Devon

'WHAT?' I ASK, NO CLUE why they are looking at me like that.

'I'm trying to figure out exactly what they do know?' Howard says first.

'Well, we had Brad take all the digital shit off the grid after we found Devon,' Jared tells him, 'so they don't have that to go on. And they have no evidence whatsoever that you were the last person to see her,' he tells me. I nod my head. This is all running through my mind at breakneck speed, and it's a little hard to organise my thoughts right now. I want to get this all straightened out.

'We just need to find her guys. I need to know what's going on with it. Jared, I'm sick of sitting in the house. I need to be doing something. Right now I want to be out there with the rest of you looking for her.'

He starts to protest, but I cut him off. 'Jared, please. I can't stand it. I need to go out. I promise I will do everything you tell me too, and I won't do anything stupid or reckless.'

He looks glum, but I can see him cracking.

'It could be good to get her out there, Jared. It could potentially bring them to us?'

Jared suddenly looks furious, and he turns on Howard, practically biting his head off.

'You're not using her as fucking bait! Are you fucking MAD?'

Howard shrugs his shoulders, 'Think about it. We have had no sign of them any-fuckin-where. We have what they want. We could set up the perfect trap, and they would come to us. On our terms, not theirs.'

'You're out of your fucking mind. If you think I'm putting *her* anywhere near them fuckers...'

I sit and listen to what they are both saying—my head going back and forth like I'm watching a game of tennis.

'Jared, they won't even get close to her.'

'I know they fucking won't 'cause she isn't doing it.' He gets up from the table and starts pacing. Howard looks at me and shrugs his shoulders. I stay quiet. But I have plenty to say. I will wait until we're alone though and try to convince him that it's a good idea.

'Jared, you need to get past thinking that she's delicate and needs protecting. She's a part of this pack, and if it were any other female, you wouldn't give it a second thought. They would be planted and in place in minutes.'

'Listen up, fucker. Don't tell me I need to get over it. You don't lie next to her at night and listen to her fucking nightmares! You don't see her wake up every morning thinking she's still there. Yes, she's part of this pack, but she wasn't born into one and has no fucking clue yet how this shit works! So spare me the fucking lecture, Howard—she isn't doing it. Get that through your fucking skull and leave it the fuck alone.' He walks out, slamming the door, and I'm left sitting at the table with Howard. I fiddle with my hands on the table—really not sure what I should do. Do I follow him? Does he need a minute? I didn't even realise he knew those things still haunted me at night. He'd never mentioned it. Howard sighs, exasperated, and flops down on the bench at the far end of the table from me. I still don't say anything. But I can tell he's itching to.

'You know I don't want to put you in danger right? That I wouldn't let anything happen to you, any more than I would let someone cut my throat?' Urgh, what an analogy. I look around the room, not really sure how I should feel about this whole situation. I mean Howard and I don't really talk that much at all. He is expecting an answer though. I know I should answer, but my mind is still reeling from what Jared had just said.

'I know you mean well, Howard, and you are right—' a knock on the inner door interrupts me, and Imogen pokes her head around it, 'We all clear to get breakfast ready?' she asks. I nod and smile, as she comes in followed closely by Logan.

'Good, I'm starving,' Howard states. 'What are you making?'

'The usual, times about a hundred, to feed everyone,' she says rolling her eyes. 'If we're lucky we may get finished just in time to start on lunch.' She laughs, and I can't help but laugh along with her.

I've never seen so many men stay in one house together. They had a tough job.

I use that moment to slope off from the conversation with Howard, and I slip silently through the door and up the stairs. I find Jared in the shower. I don't join him because I need a clear head for the conversation we need to have. So I wait. I decide to send my dad a text. I don't expect to hear back from him yet, so I'm shocked when it buzzes almost immediately.

Hey, sweetheart. You don't call, you don't text. What am I to think?

What the hell? My dad doesn't speak to me like that? I reply with a simple

Dad?

Of course. Sweetheart. Who else would it be?

I'm not convinced—it doesn't feel right. I'm just about to call him when Jared comes from the bathroom looking all fresh and tasty, rubbing his hair dry with a towel with another slung low on his hips. He hasn't noticed me sitting on the bed. His eyes brighten when he sees me, and he comes directly to me. I still have my phone in my hand, and I must still have a look of confusion on my face because he picks up on it right away.

'You okay?'

I purse my lips and frown at my phone.

'It's probably nothing but...' I show him my phone.

'Okay?' he asks, prompting me for more information.

'It's just my dad never speaks that way. He never calls me sweetheart and doesn't really joke—it's out of character.'

'Maybe he's particularly happy today? You haven't really spoken to him much since he went home right?' I nod in agreement. I hadn't really, and now I felt bad about it. 'Well, maybe now he knows we are bonded, he knows he doesn't need to worry so much?'

'Mmmm maybe, but I still don't like it. I think I'll give him a call.'

'Okay, but I think you're overreacting.' He kisses me, and I forget for a moment what I was about to do as he pushes me backwards onto the bed, letting his towel fall to the floor and begins crawling up my body, in all his naked glory. I want him, but then my thoughts come back to the conversation downstairs, and I suddenly feel the need to talk it out.

'Jared?'

'Mmmmm,' he replies as his teeth tug at my nipple through my t-shirt. Arrgh my eyes roll, and I almost give myself over to the moment. But I don't.

'Jared!'

He sits up, looking at me, questioning my firm tone with a small frown on his face.

'Overreacting?' I ask, and he looks even more confused. 'You said I was overreacting?'

He nods. 'Devon, where is this going? I can think of so many other uses for our mouths right now—'

But I don't let him distract me. 'Jared, I think you are overreacting too.'

He sits up fast. And groans. 'Baby, let's not do this now, okay?'

'Okay, if not now, when? After we've fucked? During? Or should it wait until I'm ready to leave for a shift today?'

'Shift? What are you talking about?'

'I want to go out. I think Howard has a valid point, and I want to be active in looking for Maiya.'

He gets up and wraps the towel back around his waist.

'NO.' He walks back into the bathroom, but I'm not done, so I follow him.

'How am I ever going to be capable of taking care of myself, of being able to contribute to this pack, if I'm locked away while everyone else is cleaning up my mess?'

'Cleaning up your mess? You're being stupid, and I'm done with this conversation.'

That just plain pisses me off!

'Oh, you're done with it? So, that's it. I'm supposed to shut my mouth and stay quiet?'

'Chance would be a fine fucking thing,' he mumbles, but I hear him just fine.

'Okay, so I know I'm not real clear on the caveman rules of the pack, but I didn't sign up to be a mouse who does as she's told. If that's what you want, TOUGH SHIT!' I shout at him and proceed to the bedroom door. I snap it open, and I'm just rounding it when he comes growling after me. Naked. In the hall. He grabs me by the arm, spins me around, and frogmarches me straight back into the room. I pull my arm free, and he closes the door, filling the width of it, with his arms folded across his chest. His cock is huge and very erect, bobbing up and down from the movement. My body betrays me, and I get wet, but I could absolutely kick myself because my eyes zero in on the pure beauty of him, and I know that my arousal is clear in the air, just like his is. But I want to be mad. I am mad. And he does this to me every single time. I put up my hands and ward him off like you would a wild animal. I know if he gets another inch closer I am a goner. He has an arrogant little smirk on his lips.

'No,' I warn, as he steps toward me. 'No!' He takes another step. 'Jared!' Another step. 'Sto—'

He smashes his lips to mine in an aggressive kiss. He picks me up from the floor and throws me up and over onto the bed. He has a feral look in his eyes—one that tells me to shut the fuck up and do as I'm told. He stalks over to me, caging me in with his arms and legs before he takes my mouth again in an unrelenting kiss. He isn't giving me a choice. He is proving a point to me—that he is the alpha male and he's the boss. Arrogant ass. We'll see. I push back and slide my hand between us, grasping his rock hard cock in my hand. I swallow his moan as I spread his pre-cum around the head of his cock. He stills for a minuscule moment as I move up and down his shaft, and that's all it takes for me to push him over onto his back. He's submitted, and he doesn't even realise. I move down, kissing at his chest as I go further south. I place a kiss on the head and move right on past. I feel it kick up in my hand in protest, and I can't help but smile as I work my way down his, leg flicking out my tongue and tasting his freshly washed skin. He grumbles low, and I almost relent. That sound calls to my very core—it's like turning on a faucet. My vagina gushes at the simple sound. I moan at the heat and need in my core. I am almost humping his leg when I realise he's chuckling.

'You ass,' I tell him,

'What?' he asks feigning innocence.

'You know *what*!' I slap his chest in mock horror.

'You mean I'm topping from the bottom?'

I frown. 'If you mean that you're just letting me think I'm in charge, then yes, topping from, whatever. Anyway, you're an ass.'

'Well, I may be an ass, but I was really enjoying letting you think you were in charge, so do carry on,' he says waving his hand toward his still fully erect cock. I shake my head in disbelief.

'Has anyone ever told you what an arrogant asshole you are?' I ask grinning at him.

'Umm, yup all the time, in fact, if I remember rightly, you told me that the first time we met.'

'Yes, I think I did. Well, it's still true!'

'Fair point, Now, how about less chatter and more sucking?' he says, mocking me in his bossy tone. I laugh. I can't help it. And he has a very tasty cock. Before he says anything else I lick around the swollen head, and am rewarded with more pre-cum. I'm still clothed, and as I take him into my mouth and lap at the small slit, I feel his hands slipping into my pants, unbuttoning and pushing them over my hips. Once they're at my knees, I release him, and shimmy out of them, taking him deep again the moment they are off. Then I feel his fingers bunch up the bottom of my tee and he pulls me up, and his dick pops out of my mouth with a pop. It's so fucking sexy. He pulls my tee up and over my head and unhooks my bra in the beat of a second, and I scramble back onto him like his cock is a lifeline. But he stops and turns me, so my knees are perched on either side of his head.

'Sit,' he orders, 'and ride my face while you're sucking my dick.' He thrusts my ass down towards his face and his tongue pushes into my wet core. And oh my god. I almost come apart at the first stroke of his tongue. DIVINE. I ride his face so hard I don't know how he can breathe but I can't stop. I'm squeezing his cock in my hand, and I keep losing my rhythm because I can't concentrate. I want to make him come like this. I want to come with him, like this. I want to tell him I'm almost there, but my mouth is full, so I hum the words as they catch in my throat, and I swallow him as far down as he can go, and I feel the hot jets of his cum, hit the back of my throat, just as the heat from my orgasm hits the bottom of my spine and spreads, working its way through me, and rocking me to my core. He has his fingers inside me, and his tongue works magic on my clit, and I explode so intensely that I see colours flash over my closed eyelids. I try to pull up and away from his face as I jerk out the remnants of the orgasm, but he holds me tight, clamping his arms around my legs as he sucks and laps every drop of my cum from me. I turn to jelly as my body jerks in his arms. And I can no longer hold myself up.

'BREAKFAST, BITCHES,' comes screeching through the door courtesy of Brad. And Jared laughs against my now extremely sensitive clit. I fall forward off his face and catch him licking his lips and fingers.

'Uurgh.' I screw my face up.

'What? You didn't mind when I had my face in your pussy so why when I lick your pussy juice off my fingers?'

I shrug, not really knowing the answer. After all, it doesn't make sense.

'It tastes fucking beautiful, baby. Come here, and try some.' He pulls me in for a kiss, and his tongue invades my mouth like he's waging war in there. He pulls back to look into my eyes. 'See?' he says matter of factly. 'Best taste in the world,' he says as he saunters off for the bathroom. I lay on the bed a little while, basking in my post orgasm state, when Brad comes again, this time hammering on the door. Jared comes flying out of the bathroom, sensing the urgency that I could hear in the way he knocked. He wasn't playing—something was up. I wrap myself in the towel Jared had earlier dropped, and he pulls some pants on as he opens the door. Brad looks grey, a pretty hard feat for a black man.

'We have her, Jared. You need to come fucking quick man. I dunno if she's gonna last much longer.' I'm up and in motion before my mind registers what he's actually just said. They've found her.

*Devon*

WE GET TO THE KITCHEN, and on the table, where Imogen and Logan would normally put breakfast, there's a body. It can't be her. They've got it wrong—this isn't Maiya. No no no no. Please no. There is barely any hair on her head from what I can see. Her face is unrecognisable—she is black from the bruising and has what look like burns all over her skin, which look infected. And the smell. Oh my god, this cannot be happening. All her fingers look broken and deformed, and she has a bone sticking through her lower leg. Zoe is tending to her, but she looks way out of her depth on this one.

'We need a doctor! Has anyone called an ambulance?' I ask, stunned at everyone standing around.

'We can't,' Brad informs me.

'What do you mean we fucking can't. She'll die, look at her?'

I feel in my pocket for my phone—it isn't there. 'Shit, someone give me a phone. We need to call the emergency services. I can't believe you're all just standing here.' I'm ranting and looking at everyone to hand over their phone—no one does.

'Jared, I cannot let her die. Please, *please,* someone help her!'

'Baby, we are. Look, see, Zoe is working her magic. We can't call an ambulance because the police will come and we'll be in the frame. Think about it, baby.'

Right then and there I didn't give a rat's ass about me or anyone else. Maiya looks like she has about a second to live. This isn't right!

'We need blood,' Zoe informs the room, 'but I don't know her type.'

Brad steps up and offers his arm. 'So use mine, I'm type O.'

She works fast and soon has blood from Brad in a drip bag and on a trolley that seems to appear from nowhere. She is just putting in an IV when a thought suddenly flashes in my mind.

'Wait! She's human!'

Zoe looks grim, as she nods. 'Devon, we don't have a lot of choice right now. She could die from this. It's a risk, but if we don't try she is going to die for sure.'

I nod, resigned to the fact that this has to happen. I don't know what the side effects will be—if there are any, or if this has ever been tried before. But I hope to god it works, and she pulls through. Wolf blood couldn't do any more damage than was already done.

'Zoe, call the pack doc get him up here asap,' Jared tells her.

'Already dialled him,' Brad says with his phone up to his ear.

## *Jared*

I eye the boys and jerk my head—we need a meeting now. We get to the library.

'Where's my father?' I ask

'He left for home early this morning. He said something had come up, and he was needed. He'll be back as soon as possible though.' Harrison filled me in. I nod. This is my rodeo anyway.

'Howard, explain what happened.'

'We had just gone on to shift and were doing our first lap of the outer property lines when I found the scent on the air. Smelled like death, and we thought she was gone, but then Harrison found a heartbeat. They obviously dumped her there for us, or the police, to find.

'Where exactly was she?'

'To the right of the big oak—just outside of the property line. Literally just outside, too,' Howard continued. Fuck me, right where we bury our dirty laundry.

'Jared, my guess is they thought she was dead. So they're either sending a 'don't fuck with us' message, or they were banking on the police sniffing around and finding her,' Harrison chimes in. And I hated to admit it but he I thought he was fucking right. Why else would they dump her there of all places? This was Kristen. If the police found Maiya, they'd dig deeper and find more. Fuck. I still can't believe Kristen would sell us out.

'I want these motherfuckers found and in the ground TODAY!' My patience with these bastards has run out, and if they have Kristen's intel on our dirty work, this needs to end quickly. I can't fucking protect Devon if I'm arrested and locked up, and I won't survive that either, no wolf could. 'Brad, I want you to stay with Zoe and Maiya. I want updates. Howard, Harrison—find Dom and Jake. We're going hunting.'

'Fuck, yeah.' Harrison pipes in. Howard stays quiet, as does Brad. Until Harrison leaves the room,

'What about duties here?' Brad asks.

'Logan and Imogen will be here. Gather all the rest of the pack. We'll split it down the middle. I don't want anyone left unprotected.'

'Okay,' he agrees and leaves the room.

'Fuck me. Am I in an alternate universe?' I look to Howard for an answer

'Huh?'

'When does Brad ever just agree?'

'He's been acting weird since we brought that girl in.'

'She is a fuckin mess.' I shake my head. 'Just hope she makes it— Devon will never forgive herself if she doesn't.'

'She shouldn't be shouldering the blame.'

'Try telling her that.'

He rolls his eyes

'Nah man, that's your territory. I ain't going there.' He chuckles but it's soon lost. The situation is grim, and we need to end it fast.

I find Devon in the same place I left her. She's helping Zoe wrap the girl's arms in cling film or some shit. It still stinks to high heaven, but the smell of disinfectant is blurring the lines with the burnt flesh and death stench. My head already feels woozy from the potency of the disinfectant they're splashing about. I never did like that smell. Always has pain attached to it, and right now that pain is clear for all to see on Devon's face. I put my hand on her shoulder, and as I do, Maiya starts convulsing on the table. Fuck. Devon screams and Zoe goes into action. Brad seems to appear from nowhere, and Zoe barks orders at us. I pull Devon away from the table and help Brad to get Maiya into the recovery position. Zoe checks her airways while we do our best to hold her still so she doesn't hurt herself anymore. It's a fucking horrible task. She's choking on her tongue and foaming at the mouth. Zoe manages to get to grips with it and stop the choking, but her body is still doing its own thing. I can hear sobs coming from Devon in the corner, and the need to comfort her is strong, but I can't. The seizure eventually stops, and we all look at each other while Zoe checks her vitals.

'When is the doc arriving?' I ask Brad,

'He was leaving when I rang, so I'd say an hour if he's driving fast. Hour and a half, tops.'

'Good, Zoe keep working your magic till he arrives. Brad, I need you to check all the outer perimeter surveillance before we leave. You up to that after giving blood? I want to know if we got a look at any of the fuckers faces.'

'On it,' he says and runs from the room. Devon is still crying, but she pulls herself together as she comes over and puts her arms around my waist.

'You okay?' I ask. She nods her head into my chest.

'Baby, I'm going out with the boys, and we're gonna bring you their fuckin heads. I promise.' She nods again, wiping at her eyes. She swallows and looks me in the eye.

'You make sure you come back, Jared. Just promise me you will come back?' I take her face in my hands and press my lips to hers. It's not the time for a passionate kiss, but I need her to know that nothing will keep me from her. Her eyes close, and she moans a little before pulling back and looking me directly in the eye.

'Say you promise.'

'Baby?'

'Jared, say it! I need this.'

'Devon, you are my reason for breathing. I will always find my way back to you.' Her eyes close. I didn't promise, but she seems pacified. I would never make a promise like that. One that I would have to break if the Reaper came for me.

'Okay, so listen up. Brad, Logan, and Imogen will all be here staying with you guys, and I have a team of guys that came with my dad, staying too. So you are protected.'

'What about you who is going with you?'

'Don't worry. I have men with me too, plus Howard and Harrison. We'll be fine,' I tell her, stroking her hair. Pushing it behind her ears.

'Okay,' she mumbles, 'but be careful.' This is something she would get used to in time. This is what we do. We've gone to war with other packs, and we've gone to war with the kitsunes before too—this is no different.

'Always am,' I tell her, grabbing a handful of her ass and pulling her to me. Her arms go up and around my neck and her lips touch mine. I let her lead since we're in the presence of her sick friend and Zoe, but she doesn't seem to care. Her lips open up, and I feel her tongue flick out and taste my lips—an invitation I won't refuse. I slide mine in along hers, and I kiss her until she's gasping for air. 'God. I fucking love you,' I tell her honestly.

'Love you too,' she smiles against my lips, and I let her go.

I meet Brad in the surveillance room. We have images of them but no faces. There were four in total. One looked to be a lot like fucking Kristen. I meet the guys where Maiya was found. Howard has rallied everyone up and given my orders. I saw the team that were staying as I left and now all that was left to do was find these fuckers and kill them all. Harrison, Dom, and Jake are our best trackers, and they found a trail to follow in wolf form, so we followed with weapons and clothes in our backpacks. Although I was certain on the CCTV that Kristen was among the four that dumped Maiya, her scent was not easy to determine, which pissed me off. We track a few miles through the woods before we come to a more public area so the guys have to change and get dressed before we can carry on. It is more time consuming this way but it was never good for us to be seen in wolf form—people tended to freak the fuck out.

We come to a road. The guys are stopping intermittently to sniff the ground because that's where the scent is strongest. From someone else's point of view, we just look like a bunch of guys who can't tie their fucking shoelaces very well. We come to a garage and the scent disappears. I have the surveillance on my phone, thanks to Brad, so I walk into the shop and straight up to the counter. Howard stays with me. I ask the clerk if she was on all night or if she's just started. She smiles and tells me she gets off in fifteen minutes. Great, she thinks I'm flirting. I seriously aren't, but it could work in our favour. 'Can you do me a favour?' I ask and grin at her.

'Sure, handsome.' I grit my teeth a little, but I don't falter. I take my phone from my pocket—Brad has sent me stills too. The faces aren't clear, but you can see their build. They all have caps and hoodies on.

'Can you look at these and tell me if you remember seeing them get into a car here?' She leans over, and her tits practically spill out over the counter.

'Oh yeah. I remember them alright. They fuelled and ran. I got their registration and reported it to the police. Is that why you're here? You want my statement?' She grins at me again, and I almost roll my eyes.

'Yeah, we're looking for them for another crime they committed. Did you get a good look at them?'

'Yeah, I have a monitor right here under the counter. There were three big guys and one woman.'

'Can we take a look?' I ask smiling my best smile.

'Sure, come on back, just lift the flap there, that's it,' she says as I lift and go behind the counter. She does something with the control and up comes a still of the car with the registration perfectly clear. Then another still and there in the back seat of the Nissan Patrol is Kristen. Clear as a bell. Bitch. There is a guy next to her who isn't clear, but the guy in the passenger seat and the one at the pump are both clear as a bell too. We've fucking got them!

I get on the phone and text Brad the details, and what do you know, he gets a name and an address in minutes. Chances are it won't be that straightforward, but it's a fuck load better than what we started with.

# chapter THIRTY-TWO

## Jared

SOMEONE NAMED TRAVIS WELBORN OWNS the Nissan, and he resides on a fuck load of land with a house at the end of this drive. We've spread out. Howard is by my side. Harrison a few feet in front. Dom is at my back, and the others have fanned out to check out the property. I'm waiting on the signal for 'all clear' then I'm walking through the front fucking door. I'm done playing games with these fuckers. I get the yip, and then another, and three more follow that. It's go time. As we near the place, all I can hear is some heavy metal shit playing through an even shittier sound system. It makes my ears bleed—who even listens to this crap?

I don't bother trying the front door. I just boot it. Once is all it takes and the piece of crap plastic folds in on itself. I follow the screaming and wailing of the speakers. Howard kicks another door open and bingo, I find Kristen on her knees giving the blowjob of her life to fucktard number one, while fucktard two and three are having a three-way with some prostitute-looking bitch.

All clearly too fucking arrogant to expect trouble—let alone prepare for it. This is going to be like taking candy from a baby. I aim my gun and watch as Harrison and Howard do the same. I grin knowing that this is going to be a fucking good day. I pull the plug on the sound system, and for a second the moaning from the three-way continues until they all realise it's gone quiet. Everything seems to go in slow motion. Fucktard number one's head snaps up, and the blissful look from his blowjob disappears real quick as he fumbles for his weapon. Fucktard number two pulls out of the woman's cunt and turns to look at me, with his junk on show. I grin, aim and fire. He writhes around on the floor, screaming all kinds of hell while he bleeds out from the hole his dick had filled. Meanwhile, the prostitute who was being banged at both ends tries to run and cover. Not happening. I shake my head, and she sits on the makeshift bed, covering her tits. Her eyes as wide as fucking saucers. Fucktard one and three, who moments ago were both being sucked off, are now looking at each other with a gun to their heads. Not mine, though. No, mine is trained on Kristen who looks very pale, like the reaper just came knocking. I move Kristen over to the two guys, and I pat them down for weapons. Howard grumbles at me—he doesn't like me getting up close and personal, but it's just the way I like it. Especially when it comes to these bastards, and fucking with what's mine. When they are searched and weapons removed, I move to the idiot rapidly losing blood on the floor.

'I'd say you have a few more minutes before you black out. Your heart is beating real fucking fast right now, trying to keep the oxygen flowing through your body, and when that slows, you're in big fucking trouble, so, here's the deal. I want information—you need a doctor. You scratch my back, and I'll scratch yours. You feel me?' His eyes are wild, and he looks pretty fucking pale. But he nods. Good.

'Okay, I want the kitsune. The American woman—the one calling the shots. Where can I find her?'

He swallows and tries to speak.

'Keep your mouth shut, Bri—' Fucktard three shouts, but he's cut off by a blow to the head, thanks to Harrison.

'Brian is it?'

He nods his head, and his eyes start to roll. Fuck. I'm losing him. I look to Howard, and he shrugs his shoulders.

'We have two more, and her,' he says curling his lip at Kristen. I nod, we should move. During my search, I found the keys to the Nissan, which is parked conveniently outside. I finish off the guy on the floor, and we load the other two and Kristen into the truck. Harrison and Howard come with me, leaving the rest of the team on clean up. I drive, Howard insists. He's like a fucking woman. Always nagging. But I've got to give it to him. It's his job to protect me at all costs, and he does that. Not just because my dad would kill him if he did a shit job, but because he has my back. He's my best friend. He and Brad always have been.

It doesn't take long for us to arrive back at the house. It's no surprise to look up and find Devon sitting in the window, watching for us to return. What is strange though is that she's in Brad's room, not ours, and I don't fucking like that. I wave, and she smiles. It makes my stomach flip a little. Fuck me, I'm turning into a pussy, but I'll be damned if that isn't the best fucking feeling in the world coming home to see her smiling down at me.

I watch as she leaves the window and I turn my attention to the two pricks in the bed of the Nissan. Tied real nicely, thanks to Harrison's strange obsession with different types of knots. They are restrained like a couple of double-jointed contortionists. It's quite a sight, to be honest, and they are clearly in a lot of pain. Good. Harrison has no sympathy as he hoists one up and over his shoulder like a pig on a spit roast. Making him squeal like a fucking pig too. I pull Kristen out of the back seat—she is also nicely tied up, although not quite as tight as the kitsunes. Her face is impassive like she doesn't have a fuck to spare over the whole situation. That would soon fucking change. Traitor.

I'm pushing her up in front of me when the door bangs open, and Devon comes barrelling through it. I'm thinking I'm going to get some lip action, but she walks right up to Kristen, pulls her arm back and socks her one right on the fucking jaw. I have hold of her by the rope, but I don't stop the fall she takes. And I don't stop Devon going in for a second hit either—this time splitting her cheek open. As bad as this sounds, Devon throwing down, turns me way the fuck on. I'd say I could watch her all night, but that'd be a lie. I would rather take her to our room and fuck her right now. Brad follows, and he's the one to stop Devon going all out. I'm just looking on like a horny teen with a semi. Brad snaps me back to the here and now though when he pulls Devon by the arm.

'Hey,' I tell him. 'Hands off.' I push him away. It's childish, and I know it, but she was in his bedroom, and now he's here putting his hands on her? Fuck no.

'Jesus, man, calm the fuck down. It's me, man?'

I don't realise I'm growling and baring my teeth until Devon steps between us. I feel instant calm when she touches her hand to my cheek. I look down into her big browns, and everything else slips away for a second. All there is is her and me. Her lips are moving, and I'm trying to let it seep into my brain, but it seems the only thing working is my dick. He's very alert and wants in.

'Jared! Let him go!' What? I look at her properly now, and the haze falls away. I've got Brad by the scruff of his neck and Devon has pushed her way in between us. She has her hands on my face, and I'm an inch away from kissing the shit out of her, but she's right, I have Brad in a stronghold. Jesus Christ. I shake my head, letting him go, he straightens out his t-shirt and flicks me the bird.

'You need to get a handle on that shit, Jared.'

'I'm sorry.' I shake my head again. 'I wasn't thinking straight.'

'Oh, well clearly! Fuck me. I thought you were gonna rip my fucking head off.'

'He's a bonded male, idiot,' Harrison walks back toward us. 'You don't fuck with a bonded male's female.'

'I wasn't!' Brad shouts back.

'I know that,' I tell him. 'I don't know what that was.'

'I fucking do. It was your dick brain and not your actual brain thinking!'

'Brad, I didn't want to fuck you,' I tell him with a smile on my face, slapping him on the back as we get to the back door. Harrison has taken Kristen from me and was securing her in the lockup downstairs. Lucky for us we had four lockups, and this was only the second time we'd had more than one occupied at the same time. Brad was prattling on about how anyone would want to fuck his black ass when there was a blood-curdling scream followed by a shit tonne of crashing about coming from upstairs. We all fly up there pretty damn quick, getting to Brad's door we open it to find Maiya wielding her drip trolley at Zoe. How she's even standing with all the injuries she's sustained is beyond me. Clearly, this little waif of a human is stronger than she looks. Her arms and legs are all wrapped up, and her face is still a mess, but she looks a little better than when I left earlier. All good signs. Zoe steps forward and tries to calm her down, but it only seems to make her worse. She's fucking hysterical, screaming all kinds of shit, most of which is incoherent babbling, but one thing is clear, and she says it over and over.

'Your fault, you freak…'

Devon's whole body sags and even from behind I can tell her face is screwed up and she's holding back tears. Maiya crumples to the floor mid hissy fit, and she's out cold. Brad and Zoe lift her to the bed again and secure her drip. All my attention is on Devon. She's trying to hold it together, but I can see through that. I pull her into my arms and hold her against my chest.

'She'll be okay, baby,' I try to reassure her. 'She's pumped full of drugs right now and doesn't know her arse from her elbow, but she will be okay.'

I feel her nod against my chest, and I decide now is a good time to take our leave. 'Come on, let's go.' I don't take her to the bedroom as I'd first planned on doing when we got in the house. Instead, I feed her. Imogen has cleaned up in the kitchen and as always has prepared a shit tonne of food in the fridge. I take out a ham hock, some butter and bread, and I make us sandwiches. Devon sits, watching me prepare from the table.

'You just gonna stare at my ass all day?' I ask trying to lighten the mood.

'Well, it's a very fine ass.' She giggles.

'Glad you think so.' I wink at her and carry on with slicing the ham. I take the plates and sit beside her at the table. The room is normally packed full, but everyone has a job to do at the moment, so it's quiet for the time being. 'Are you okay?' I ask knowing the answer already. She isn't okay—that much is obvious, but she's trying to put on a brave face.

'I guess I just wanted so much for her to wake up. I didn't think about what would happen when she did. I just expected her to be Maiya.'

I slide my arms around her waist and pull her into sit between my legs on the bench.

'I can't imagine what they did to her, Jared, and it's all my fault.' And there it is. I fucking knew it. I close my eyes and shake my head.

'Devon, none of this is your fault. You didn't make them do what they did. You didn't ask them to come for you, and you sure as fuck didn't ask them to take her. This is all on those sick motherfuckers. I want you to get that shit out of your head right now, okay?' She smiles a small smile that speaks fucking volumes. She's not going to get over this guilt anytime soon, but she'll accept what I've said just to please me. Fuck's sakc.

## *Devon*

I CAN'T SLEEP. KNOWING THAT the kitsunes that held me, and left Maiya for dead are in the same house is bad enough. But hearing what Maiya said to me is on a loop in my head, killing me inside. I never expected her to blame me. In my mind, some ill-placed fantasy, I saw her waking up with relief on her face that she was with us, safe—that I was there for her. But the reality was much different. *All your fault, you freak.* Each time it gets louder and louder in my head until I can't stand it any longer.

I get up from the bed. Jared must be exhausted because he doesn't even stir at my movement, or when I got dressed and opened the door. I want to go to Brad's room, to check on Maiya but I knew that isn't a good idea. For Maiya or Brad, after the way Jared acted toward him. I smile a little, thinking about the caveman act he pulled. At the time it wasn't funny at all—it was scary. But looking back on it, I can't help but let the smile spread across my face. I'm thinking about that as I opened the cellar door. I've never been down here before, and I didn't know why I was here, other than an urge, an itch I needed to scratch. I found myself face to face with a man, recognition flaring in my brain as a memory came flashing through like a movie playing in front of my eyes. He'd been one of the guys to beat me, strip my clothes from my body and piss all over me, like I was a piece of shit. He'd also tried to stick his dick in my mouth while I was unconscious, but when I came to, I fought him, and he obviously wanted to keep his dick attached to his body because he didn't try that again.

At that moment I don't feel fear. As I look upon him, strung up in a strange and painful looking way, I don't feel pity or any kind of sympathy for him. The only feeling I have is pure hatred. I want to cause him pain and torture him like he'd done to Maiya. The feelings surging through me at that moment have my wolf standing up to attention. I feel her at the forefront begging for some action—begging to be let loose. I search for the other side—the mostly dormant kitsune. How does she feel? Does she want to act on these hateful feelings? Against her own kind? She seems so indifferent. I expected some feeling of kinship, like I feel with the wolf pack, but I feel nothing from her like she doesn't give a crap if I torture a kitsune or anyone for that matter. In the next cell, I can't make out the man's face, but I know his scent. He's also strung up from the ceiling in a very creative way—there is no room for manoeuvre, and definitely none for the change they would have to undergo if they wanted to escape the ropes. It was beautiful really, very cleverly tied and looped. The knots were not just for binding, but to cause pain. Knotted at pressure points, making sure the slightest movement caused maximum pain. This one had his eyes open, well, in so much as there was a small amount of iris showing through the very swollen lids. He tries to say something but even the mere action of opening his mouth causes him severe pain. I chuckle as he shrieks against the pain. The more he screams, the more I smile. I'm elated. If I could open this cell and walk in, I would poke him, just to hear him howl some more. I drink it in like a soothing medicine. I look for a long stick, a pole, anything that would reach far enough. Then I hear a whimper, and I look to the right, Kristen. She's tied but not so tightly nor is she strung from the ceiling, but there is no room for a change in the way her legs and arms are bound. I feel a small amount of anger at the fact she isn't suffering the same wrath. I want that. I stare at her for a minute, wishing her pain. A slow death. If only she could feel what I am wishing right now while I watch. I feel Jared enter the room, and I search his eyes to gauge how he is feeling about me being here, his head tilts to one side, questioning, unsure? I smile reassuringly. And his whole demeanour changes. He comes to me and pulls me to him.

'I woke up, and you were gone,' he says sleepily.

'I needed to see this,' I tell him honestly. His head tilts to the side again.

'Why isn't she strung up like them?' I ask, and I almost want to bite my tongue off because I sound annoyed. I am annoyed.

'I didn't request that any of them be tied in a specific way. It's probably Harrison subconsciously not treating a female so badly?'

I purse my lips and frown. 'She doesn't deserve his sympathy.'

'No, she doesn't deserve anyone's,' he tells me matter of factly. 'Come on let's go back to bed. I can think of a better way to spend the night, if we have to be awake, than staring at these dead fuckers.'

# *Jared*

If I'm honest, I'm looking forward to spending a bit of time down in the cells today. But, I'm currently lying in bed after an amazing session followed by an amazing sleep. I'm wondering how the fuck I'm going to explain to Devon what I have to do today. I think she knows what has to happen, but I'm not sure if she agrees with it, or if she'll like the fact that I like to take care of pack business. I'm thinking about how I should explain it when she stretches out next to me, and all the blood rushes to my dick, making him rise immediately. I don't know what the fuck happens to your brain when your dick gets hard, but when I'm near Devon like this, my brain doesn't fire on all pistons. It's as if all the oxygen in my brain leaves on the express train straight to my dick, losing all normal rational thoughts on the way. All I can think about now is sticking it in her sweet, sweet pussy. But she's not waking—she only stirred. Maybe I can give her a nudge, or my dick can. He's definitely up for that challenge. I turn on my side and face her. She's on her back, so I let my dick rest on her thigh while my hands do a little exploring. I find her breast, and tweak her nipple, which elicits a small moan. I move to her other and give that a small pinch. She arches her back, wanting more, but she's still asleep. Pulling back the cover, I take one perfect mound and cup it in my hand, bend my head and run my tongue over it before sucking it into my mouth. Her back arches up again, as I pinch the nipple between my teeth and run my tongue around it.

'Mmmmm.' I lift my head to see her smiling down at me. Perfect. I move down, kissing her stomach and dipping my tongue into her navel. Her hands go to my hair, and she helps me on my way down, practically pushing my head in between her legs, so fucking eager, even after our session last night. I've never found a female that I wanted to fuck more than a couple of casual times. But this female has me by the balls. My dick and balls are hers. Fact. I want her pussy like nothing else. I want HER like no one else. I fucking love this female so goddamn much. I'd do anything for her. Scary but so very true. Never thought I have a chance at this. Never thought I'd ever find my true mate. Yet here we are, and I'm about to eat out the best fucking pussy I've ever tasted. I can still smell myself inside her, and I love it.

It makes me even harder, and my dick even more impatient to get inside. Devon's practically twitching already, and I've not even touched her pussy yet. I widen her legs and lift her ass for better access. I go straight for her clit. I'm not easing her in. I go all out. I want her orgasm quickly, and then I'm going to fuck her until I get at least a couple more. Only a minute or so later and she's crying out, biting into the pillow to stifle her scream. I want to tell her to pack that shit in and stop trying to hide it, but she gets embarrassed when the rest of the pack take the piss. Me, I couldn't give a shit. They can hear everything, but only I get to see it.

I bring her down gently before I push inside her—my dick already weeping with pre-cum. If he could talk, he'd be cussing me out right now. Telling me, it's about fucking time too. I laugh at the way my thoughts are going, making Devon look at me with a frown on her face. I shake my head and circle my hips—her eyes close and she groans. That sound is so damn sexy and beautiful, and it's all mine. Only for me. I pull out and thrust back in, circling my hips, and she does it again, fuck yes. Her hips come up to meet mine on every thrust, and as I circle she groans even louder. I'm going to explode way too soon if she carries on. I groan myself as she circles her hips, and I have to stop her. Her hands are gripped tight onto my ass, and she's thrusting up, topping from the bottom. Fuck me—I can't. I need to take back control, or this will be over too soon. I pull out and flip her over, pulling her ass up and pushing her head down. I pull her hips against mine, and my dick is home once again. Fuuuck she's so fucking tight this way, and I'm balls deep. I hold her still and savour that feeling. Closing my eyes, I count to ten, and then I thrust in and out, grunting on each one.

'Aaaaah, aaaaaahhhhh, Jared.'

'Come on, baby. Give it to me, let it go.'

'Mmmm. Jared, don't stop. Don't you dare sto— Oooooooh sooo gooood.' She comes, hard. She can't even hold herself up. She's gone to jelly. I hold her ass up in the air and go for my life until that warm, fantastic feeling grasps my balls and my stomach. I thrust it out as I come inside her wet, greedy pussy, and she takes it all. I collapse to the side, bringing her with me, and we lay spooning with me still inside her. I feel so fucking content at that moment. Fuck everything else, it can wait.

I take breakfast up to Devon in bed, and I'm sifting through my wardrobe, choosing what I'm going to wear when Howard knocks on the door.

'Hey, J,' he says awkwardly as he comes in and sees Devon still in bed. I beckon him over to me as Devon mumbles a hello. He's dressed in dark jeans and a dark tee—dark clothes that blood doesn't show up on so much. Probably best considering the job we have today. But I want to see the progress I've made. Or more like the pain I've inflicted. So I choose a white tee with regular denim jeans. I wouldn't normally consider any of this shit. I'd just throw on an old top and be done with it. But every decision I make lately is with Devon in mind. If I'm honest, it has to fucking stop. I can't make pack decisions based on my fears or feelings where Devon is concerned. I just have to hope to fuck that she gets used to that side of things and accepts it. It's that simple. I don't want to hide anything from her, but at the same time, there are things that I don't want her to see. Like the lengths I go to, to get what I need. And the things I will do to get what I need from the fuckers downstairs. Kristen included. Although her fate is a decision my father will make because he's the alpha—even though on this land and in this house and for this whole rodeo, I am alpha, it's still down to him to decide. The fact that she will die is a given. You do not betray your pack. But the how, where, and when is his decision. So I have to hold off on that.

'Just came to let you know that we're all set.' His eyes roll toward Devon as he says much quieter, 'Downstairs.' He's on the same page. It's not keeping things from her—it's more shielding her from the ugly shit. At least that's what I'm telling myself anyway.

I'm about an hour in, with nob jockey number one, when I sense Devon's presence. I turn towards the door and see her coming down the stairs. Fuck me. When I saw her down here last night I wanted to pick her up and carry her out, like the dirt from all the shit that's gone on down here would somehow contaminate her innocence. But she's looking at me now with excitement? I'm not sure why, but I don't fucking want her seeing this shit. I want her as far from this as possible. I don't want the way she sees me to change. Ever. If that means keeping this shit under wraps, then that's what I'll do. I make my way out of the cell and stop her on the stairs.

'Baby what are you doing down here?'

## *Devon*

'I want to question her, Jared—'

'Baby, come on, you don't need to be seeing this shit,' he tells me wiping the blood from his hands and onto his now ruined t-shirt.

'Jared, it's not about what I need—it's about what I want, and right now I want to go in that cell, and I want to get answers from her.'

'So you're telling me it's personal?'

'Damn straight it's personal!' I yell back. Sighing he pushes me backwards toward the stairs.

'Baby, that's not the right way to go into something like this. Just go back upstairs and leave this to me and Brad.'

That's it. I'm done trying to seek his permission. I'm doing this, no matter if he likes it or not. I fold my arms over my chest—he has his hands on my shoulders, and his eyes are pleading with mine to just do as I'm told. I've never done it before, and I'm not about to change a habit of a lifetime. I raise an eyebrow and pout my lips, at which point, he knows I'm going nowhere. So now it's just a case of how far he will back down. Will I get to do some questioning? Or will he at least just let me in the room while he does it? He sighs in resignation.

'Devon, I don't want you to see this part of what I do. I don't want that look in your eyes to change. I couldn't live with that baby.'

Well, what's a girl to do with that?

'So don't show me? Let me go in there with Brad?'

'You always have a fucking smartass answer don't you?' he says with a smirk on his face.

'So? Do we have a deal?'

'Huh oh, female. Not so fast. I ain't finished.'

I puff my cheeks and blow out the air, frustrated. He grabs my chin with his thumb and forefinger and pulls my face up, so I'm looking into his eyes.

'Maybe I don't want to see you do that shit either,' he tells me. I growl out my frustration.

'Jared, seriously. I was the one they took. I was the one they tortured. ME! I could have ended up like Maiya! I want this, Jared! No, hell, I NEED this. I couldn't sleep last night, Jared, you know why? Because all I could think about was them down here, and when I came and saw them, all I wanted to do was kick the shit out of them all. I understand you don't want me in there with them, Jared, but please, please, don't take this away from me.'

I was bordering on hysterical. I don't think I even took a single breath throughout that whole speech. But I saw a shift in him. A look in his eye that told me he had taken in every word.

# chapter
# THIRTY-FOUR

## Jared

W ELL, WHEN SHE PUT IT like that, I could hardly fucking argue could I?' I would give her just about anything she wanted, but if she NEEDED this, to sleep at night, who the fuck was I to take that from her? She was right. She was the one that went through it, not me. And I would have to let her into this shit some time. I just wanted her to remain pure—untainted by pack brutality. The truth behind our success as a pack was our capability to extract information, and it backed up our right to own the reputation of the strongest pack in Europe. It had been tried and tested many times, and we'd always come through on top. We've had casualties but nothing like what any opponent has suffered at our hands as a consequence. And I am set on a course to make sure we remain that way. I want a safe and happy home for my pack, but most of all for Devon, and the family I want to have with her. And when we do decide to have one, they will be safe in the knowledge that no one will harm a hair on their head. I bow my head and rest my forehead to hers. I'd lost this battle, and I was giving her what she wanted. But. How I was going to give it, I still wasn't sure.

'Okay, baby, you got it. But I want to talk this over first, okay?'

She nods and smiles. I fucking hate the thought of her going in there without me, but I don't know if I can do what I need to do with her watching me either.

'Brad?'

'Sup?' He comes out of the cell and over to me.

'Put the lights back on and crank the sound up. I'll be back in ten.'

He nods and walks back into the cell we were working in. We have the UV lights set up, and the sound cranked high in their earphones. Sleep deprivation, the easiest and yet one of the worst forms of torture. It fucks with your head. Howard and Harrison are at the far end of the corridor. They nod as I take Devon up the stairs. She has a look of confusion on her face, but I don't question it. I just want to keep her moving in the direction further away from this shit. I get her to the library. I sit her in the chair and look on the shelves for a book. It's a particular book that teaches ancient torture methods, used over the years, right up to the modern day. I find it and hand it to her. Frowning, she takes it from me and seats herself in the winged back chair that she seems to love. I will let her have this if she really wants it, but she needs to know what happens when I go down into those cells. I watch as her face scrunches up as she turns the first page, and she slowly flicks through the book. Her lip curls up and her eyebrows scrunch down as I see the disgust on her face. I get a glimmer of hope. But then she looks up at me,

'Why rats? That's really gross,' she says as she closes the book.

'That's it? That's the only question you got? From the whole book? Rats?'

She smiles and places the book on the small table, as she stands and wraps her arms around my waist.

'I would cave immediately if someone put rats on my stomach,' she says in a mocking tone.

'Ah well, Now I know your weakness.' I laugh. 'Seriously, though, looking through the book is one thing, being a part of and doing that shit is a whole lot different. You get me?'

'Jared, I didn't ever think I would be kidnapped and beaten the shit out of, but I was, and I got through it. I didn't have a choice in that. My only choice was to survive and get through it—this is my choice, and if I regret it later that's all on me. I want to do it. I deserve to.' I nod, taking in what she's saying. I still wasn't happy about it.

'Okay, baby. If that's what you want. But for the record, I still don't fucking like it.'

'Thank you.' She kisses me like I just gave her a fucking gift. Yeah, the gift of nightmares for the rest of her life. I still haven't decided if I want her in there with me, or if it's best to let her go in with Brad. I'm still feeling a bit territorial where he's concerned, and I know it's stupid, but I'm weighing that over letting her see me go to work on these fuckers? The latter isn't something I want her to see.

But then what if she freaks the fuck out and can't handle it? I need to fucking be there for *her*. Fuck me. I'm like a fucking woman—worried about feelings and shit. Right! Decision made. I take her hand and walk back toward the cells. Devon doesn't say a word. So I don't either. I'm worried that if I speak anymore, I'll change my mind and march her right back out. Harrison is pacing the corridor when we get to the bottom of the stairs.

'You okay, man?'

'Want to get in there,' he says pointing to the first cell. He's twitchy as fuck and practically shaking with adrenaline.

'Harrison, we aren't ready for that yet.' He was the best in the game and loved it too—definitely a bit weird in the head. But if we let him loose on them now, they would cave or die quickly. We wanted them to suffer, and we all wanted to have a pop at them first. He didn't fuck about, and no one else would ever learn shit if they didn't have a chance. I walk Devon right past him, and he continues to pace. I shake my head and shout for Brad. He pops his head out of Kristen's cell at the end.

'C'mere, I have a job for you.'

'For fuck's sake. I want to get in on this shit! Always left behind, never doing the good shit,' he moans, and I shake my head.

'Listen, dickhead. I'm not pulling you off this. I'm just adding a duty.'

He frowns and looks from me to Devon and back again. She's smiling like she just got the lottery win. Fuck me.

'Devon wants in, and I think it's best she goes in there with you, not me.'

He frowns a bit deeper. 'Why?'

'Does it fuckin matter why? Just take her in with you for fuck's sake,' I tell him, my patience with this now gone. I walk away from them both, and I know I need to be down there for her, but I need to get away from it. I don't like her doing this shit—number one. I don't like her being in there without me—number two, and I don't like her alone with Brad—number three. As fucked up as it is I need to let her do this without me because I can't handle that she's doing it. And it's something she needs. So I leave the house and head to the forest. I strip and feel the first tingles and shooting pains that the change brings about. I'm ready to lose myself in my inner wolf and let go of my emotions. I take off running as my body finalises the change and I feel nature calling to me.

# *Devon*

I walk into the cell with a very confused Brad. But he doesn't question me. He simply starts to crank a wheel on the wall and the guy dangling from the very beautifully tied ropes starts to descend. He hits the lights, and the very powerful strip lights turn off, leaving me blinking, trying to make my eyes adjust to the now much darker cell. Then he pulls the buds that are blasting out noise from his ears. The asshole is panting—he's soiled himself, and he stinks. Brad pulls him up and throws him into the far corner. He isn't capable of doing anything—he's a mess. But Brad doesn't turn his back. Instead, he points to a chair and asks me to get it. I do, and I put it in the centre where he points. There are metal rings attached to the cell floor, and I briefly wonder what they are for but then Brad does something with the rope, and I get my answer. The asshole is now attached to the chair and to the floor. Nothing quite as beautiful as the knots that were tied before but it works. The asshole's eyes have obviously adjusted because they widen at the sight of me. And my anger flares.

'Yes, asshole, remember me?' I ask through gritted teeth. 'I bet you didn't think you'd see me again so soon, huh?'

He scoffs a little, trying for bravado, but I don't fall for the pathetic attempt. I can smell the fear oozing from him. It acts like a drug to my wolf. And I can feel her pulsing under my skin. The stench of fear making my body want the change. But I've had years of practice, keeping it under wraps, so I manage with no problem at all. I stare at the piece of shit and let all the hate bubble to the surface. I lash out and punch him in the face. His head snaps backwards, but he doesn't make a sound. And that upsets me. I want to hear him suffer. I bring back my arm and punch from my shoulder, once, twice, on the third he groans and mumbles for me to stop before he passes out. I look to Brad who gestures to the asshole with a 'go for it' look on his face. I suddenly feel alive. Like I've waited for this my whole life. I'm taking my revenge for everything they have done to Maiya, and me, I let my brain clear and my wolf come to the forefront of my mind. I'm careful. I don't want to change, just to let her think freely in this form.

'What do we have?' I ask Brad. He looks confused, so I elaborate. 'Methods? What can I use?'

'Oh umm, pretty much anything you like? I can get it set up, or you can carry on how you are?'

'I want a table and lots of water. And a cloth please.'

His eyes widen a little, but he gets it under control quickly.

'Waterboarding?' he asks seemingly surprised.

'Umm hmm,' I think that's what they called it in the book. But whatever.

'Howard, Harrison?' Brad shouts, and they come through the door.

'Waterboarding. Devon wants it set up in here.'

Howard leaves the room, and I notice the look on Harrison's face as he looks at the asshole in the chair. I'm confused by it. I look harder and just as I realise what it is he looks directly at me and smiles. Longing, that's what it is. I take all of him in then, and I notice the twitching of his hands the tick in his jaw. The rapid blinking of his eyes. Either he's high, or he's desperate for some action in this room. The way he's studying the guy, I'd say it's the latter. Howard comes back with a barrel and a hose. The hose is attached to the main supply somewhere, so I'm wondering why the barrel? Then he places it behind the chair and pulls the chair back on its two back legs. He secures it on a lean so it won't move. Perfect. So easy. Harrison is still pacing, but I like his presence here. I'm fairly sure the asshole will shit his pants at the mere sight of him. That's what I want. Howard and Harrison turn to leave, and I can see in his face the craving he has for this.

'Harrison?' he turns to look at me, with a tense jaw and lifts his chin in answer. 'Please, can you stay?'

'Errr, Devon. We ain't at that point yet,' Brad jumps in, but I don't take my eyes off Harrison.      This is who I want in the room. This is who will show me what it's really like. I don't want a watered-down version. I want the dark, the gritty, the violent, and dirty, all of which I can see in his eyes right now. If I were to meet him in a dark alley, I would run screaming for the hills just from that look. Cold hard killer. And he is on my side.

'You said I could have any method I want?'

Brad scrubs at his face. He looks worried.

'Yeah, but this is not what I had in mind, and I'm pretty sure Jared wouldn't let you watch Harrison at work.'

'Jared isn't here.' I tilt my head and raise my brows, challenging him.

'Fuck me. He'll go bat shit crazy.'

He looks around. Howard is hovering at the door. He nods to Brad, and Brad lets out a resigned sigh.

'Right, okay, whatever you need. Fuck. But if he goes nuclear—'

'I'll deal with it,' I cut in.

He nods and heads to the door.

'Bring my kit,' Harrison speaks for the first time, the excitement clear in his voice. Brad mumbles several more curses as he leaves the room. Harrison grins at me when we're alone, just the unconscious asshole between us. I smile back, knowing it's a thanks for letting him loose.

'How do you usually work someone over?' I ask, genuinely curious.

'Depends,' he answers looking over the guy with assessing eyes.

'On what?'

'On who's been at them first. I don't usually get time to play,' he says still looking at the guy.

'You enjoy this obviously?'

He nods, grinning.

'Good, let's start then shall we?'

He doesn't give me an answer. Instead, he walks straight to the guy, lifts the hose and flips a switch—the water trickles out onto assholes face. Just a little.

'Wakey wakey, cocksucker. It's playtime.' He hovers over his face, and when the guy opens his eyes, he yelps and starts to struggle in his bindings.

'Ah, there you are. I was beginning to think you'd checked out, fucker.' I watch as he places the cloth over his face, then, as the water gathers speed he places the hose over his mouth and nose. Asshole coughs and splutters, shaking his head from side to side, and I get the urge to go over and hold his head. I take a step and hesitate. Harrison sees me, and his lip quirks up a little at the side. He nods his head down toward where I was headed—an invitation to do what I want. He understood just from that small movement what I needed to do. I hold his head tight. One hand in his hair, the other on his forehead, and it makes what Harrison is doing with the hose all that much easier. I visualise the mess that Maiya was in. How he made me feel. And hate fills me once again. He's choking, and Harrison lets up, removing the cloth from his face. I let go, and we watch as he hacks up all the water that's entered his lungs. He's gasping in huge gulps of air. When I think he's had enough air, I pull his hair back and hold him in position. Harrison doesn't speak. He just places the cloth back over his face and pours the water again. I count the seconds as I watch Harrison silently mouth each number. He stops again, and the asshole is hacking it all up again. I'm soaking from the water, but I don't care. I'm transfixed, and I can't look away. I'm enjoying his suffering. How sick is that?

'Now asshole. I'll ask you the same fucking question you've been asked a hundred times already. You can answer if you want? It won't be so much fun for us, but I'll give you a quick death. Or, and this is my favourite, you can keep your fucking mouth shut, and the fun just gets better and better, capiche?'

'Fuck you,' the asshole groans, making Harrison's face split into a huge grin. I feel butterflies in my stomach, and I suddenly feel nervous. Not afraid, just nervous of the unknown.

'Aww but I haven't asked the question yet, fucker. You're jumping the gun,' he says with a smile on his face like he's talking to a small child. I snigger. I can't help it. Maybe it's the situation I'm in, or the nerves I'm feeling, but I can't help it. The snigger turns into a laugh, and before I know it, I'm busting a gut laughing. What the actual fuck is happening to me? Harrison's head tilts to the side with a smile as he looks at me. I've got tears streaming down my face, and I'm trying like hell to get myself under some sort of control when he bends over double and laughs with me. I've seen infectious laughter at work before, and this was definitely that, but what a bizarre set of circumstance to be laughing like this. The door opens, and Brad sticks his head in.

'Everything okay?' he asks raising his eyebrows and looking from Harrison, to me, and back again' We nod, and I try to speak, but can't. I take a deep breath and calm myself. Harrison does the same.

'You sure?' Brad asks one eyebrow raised. ''Cause I can count on one hand the number of times I've heard him laugh' he says to me pointing at Harrison. 'Even my best jokes don't crack him.'

'That's 'cause your jokes are shit,' Harrison retorts.

'Well, fuck you, asshole. My jokes are the best,' Brad says in mock offence. 'Anyway, get back to fucking work you two,' he says, winking at me. I turn to the asshole still laid back and coughing up his oesophagus, and I get my serious face back in place. This is a serious business after all.

'You've had enough of a break,' I tell him, 'Either talk now or this gets a whole lot worse for you.' His eyes swivel my way. And just as he's about to tell me to go fuck myself, Harrison kindly fills his mouth with water, so he's cut off.

'No one ever teach you manners, fucker? This here is a lady. You don't talk shit to a lady,' he says pushing the hose further inside his mouth. Howard comes in then, takes note of me holding the guy's head back, and he kind of looks pleased. Proud? It's fleeting though because in true Howard style he says nothing. He just walks up to

Harrison and hands him a roll of cloth. No, not cloth. It's leather. In his other hand is a small holdall. Harrison stops what he's doing, taking it from him and allows asshole to cough up another lung. He grins from ear to ear, and I feel those butterflies again—the anticipation growing inside me from what he's going to do next. Harrison seems happy at the prospect of showing me too.

# chapter
# THIRTY-FIVE

## *Jared*

AFTER A RUN AND SOME time clearing my head, I go back to the house. I find Brad in the kitchen, eating a sandwich. Well, inhaling it would be more accurate.

'Where's Devon?'

I assume she's upstairs or somewhere since I left her with Brad and he's in the kitchen. But his face tells me different, and I immediately go on high alert. He looks really worried.

'What the fuck, Brad? Tell me you haven't left her down there alone?'

He shakes his head, and I wait impatiently while he chews and swallows.

'I haven't left her down there alone,' he says, and I feel a little relief until Howard walks in. And my head swings to him and to Brad again. Brad's face changes.

'Who the fuck is she with?' I ask, but I'm already heading for the stairs. This can't be good. The only other person allowed down there today is fucking Harrison. Jesus fucking Christ. I fly down the stairs three at a time, and slam the door open.

'FUUUUUUUUUUUUK! What the fuck, Harrison?' I walk into a scene from a fucking horror movie. Blood everywhere. Devon is covered in splatter. And I can't fucking believe I let this shit happen. I fucking knew I should have stayed. Harrison is looking at me like what he's doing isn't anything unusual. And I guess he's not, but my female covered in blood with Harrison at the helm of whatever you called this shit was—because there was torturing information out of someone, and then there was Harrison's twisted way of extracting information. What Harrison did wasn't fucking pretty, and it was always a last resort because he never left them any room to talk. It was more a way of killing them slowly and painfully. And Devon is smack in the middle—not fucking good! Shit.

'Jared, what's wrong?' she asks like I didn't just walk up into this shit storm.

'Devon, what are you doing? Jesus, you don't need to see this shit! Come on?' I want to get her out of this room, fast. She'll never sleep again. Fuck me. I'm an idiot, trusting any fucker but myself to make sure she was okay. Fucking Brad.

'Jared, stop. It's okay.'

I turn and look into her eyes—she's serious. I take a minute to process it all. The room, her, the asshole strung up from the ceiling, Harrison. And then it hits me. It wasn't Harrison's doing—it was hers. Devon had done this. Fuck me. No. I did this shit—not her. This was my job. This was my burden. I didn't want this for her. I wanted her to sleep happily—feel safe and never worry about this shit. But here she is. Knife in hand. Soaked to the skin. Face covered in blood and she's okay. I look at Harrison whose face splits into a grin. Devon comes over, and I pull her into my arms, her head to my chest. Harrison is giving me a fucking thumbs up behind her back.

'Got a fucking keeper there,' he tells me. 'She can come and play with me anytime.' I knew what he meant, but it didn't stop the growl rumbling up and out of my chest. He called this shit playtime. Sick? Yep. But he did it and slept like a baby. So that was that. I didn't complain. He's one of the best guys there is.

But apparently, my female has the stomach for this too. Who knew? I'm not sure how I feel about it right now, so I'll store that shit for later. What I do know is, when she wanted to kill Kristen, just the thought made her spew her guts up in the toilet. But a lot has changed. Clearly what they did has affected her more than I realised. So now I have to think about how the fuck we move forward from here. Would she feel guilt? Remorse? Sick? I didn't know. But whatever came I'd be there a hundred percent. And Harrison can go fuck himself if he thinks she's going anywhere near his playtime again.

'Baby, let's get you cleaned up.' I pull her by the hand, and she follows. And we head straight up to our bedroom. I strip her and walk her into the bathroom. She's quiet, and I'm freaking the fuck out at what's running through her mind. Probably a constant stream of visuals from that cell. Fuck me. I'll cut his fucking balls off for allowing this. I turn on the shower, and she walks in, eye-fucking me over her shoulder. She curls her finger for me to 'come here'. I frown, and she does it again. I go, obviously! Stripping my tee and jeans, I kick them off my feet and get in after her. The water runs pink as the blood runs from her hair. Her arms come up around my neck, and she pulls me into a kiss—her tongue dominating and pushing into my mouth. I lift her by the ass and press her up against the tiles. She's like a horny nympho. Jesus Christ, she reaches down between us and cups my balls in her hand.

'Fuck me, Jared,' she begs. Oh, fuck me. I love this female. I line myself up with her pussy, and I push in. *Home*. I take a moment to savour it. As always it feels fucking amazing. Her hands grab my hair, and she begins riding me, curling her lower back and ass. Eager, and not willing to wait a moment longer, I push harder against the wall to limit her movements. This is still my domain. And I will make sure it stays that way. I call the shots. I pull her up and off my dick, lowering her to the floor. She protests, and I like that. My girl has fire. I push her to her knees, and I push my thumb into her mouth—she opens and takes it. Her eyes look up at me, she's waiting for my dick. But I don't give it to her. I watch as her demeanour changes—there she is. My submissive female. I kneel in front of her and take her mouth in a demanding kiss. Leaving her moaning and breathless as I break it.

'Turn around,' I order, and she does as I ask. I push lightly in between her shoulder blades. And she bends on all fours, presenting me her very fine ass. I take in the view, sliding my hands up and over each cheek. Pulling them apart so I can see the fruit in between. I want my mouth there, but I'm impatient, so that will have to wait. Instead, I line myself up and push into her warm wet pussy. Fuck, yes. I rock back and forth a minute, not wanting this to end too quickly. Closing my eyes, I just taking in the feeling. Her pussy is clutching my dick—the best fucking feeling ever. I thrust in and out, and I'm grunting on every thrust. Devon's panting and her moans are getting louder with each stroke. She's hyped up and taking everything I give her, not even trying to hold back the noise like she normally does. And I fucking love it. She comes hard and screams out my name. Her pussy is clenching me like a tight fist, and I pump harder as her legs go stiff and the orgasm takes hold. I hold her hips up so she doesn't collapse, and she's still moaning out loud. It doesn't take long before I'm blowing inside her. A few more thrusts and I'm collapsing on her back. Fuck that was intense. I pull out and stand, helping her to her feet. And we clean up, locking lips at every opportunity. Fuck, this is good. I want this so fucking much. I need this shit over and cleared away so we can actually get on with a normal fucking relationship. Preferably one where I don't walk in on her slicing and dicing some asshole in the cellar. Suddenly my mind is back to that shit. Everyone down there is going to get a fucking piece of my mind, and probably a fist in the mouth for emphasis. Fuming isn't strong enough to describe how mad I am at them.

As Devon towel dries her hair, bending over at the waist, I think about the gleam in her eye as she looked at me with the knife in her hand and the way she's been since. Her smile. The intense fucking we just had. This isn't a broken female. No, she almost seems better than she was this morning. Happier. Chirpy.

Fuck me. Maybe she really did like it. Maybe it is what she needed. I need to take another look at this asshole before Harrison ends him for good. I get dressed while I'm still damp from the shower, making it hard to get my jeans on, but I'm in a rush, so I struggle and get pissed off. I don't bother with a shirt—can't be arsed with the hassle. I kiss Devon and tell her I'll be a minute. I make my way to the cells and meet Howard and Brad in the corridor. Howard starts to speak, but I put my hand up in warning and clench my jaw. I do not want to hear it right now. I open the door and walk down to the cell. He's a fucking mess. I go in, and the stench hits me. I missed it the first time. Piss, not the asshole's though, Harrison's. What the fuck?

'You pissed on him?' I ask in disbelief.

He shrugs his shoulders, 'What your female wanted, so that's what I did.'

What? 'Devon asked you to piss all over him?'

He nods as he spins his knife in his hand. I shake my head and take in the stinking bastard who is strapped to the chair with his arms at an awkward angle and his junk on show. He's covered in so much blood that I can't tell where he's actually cut. I take the hose from the floor and turn it on full. He's passed out, but he soon wakes up. The chair tries to move from the force, but it's tied tight. I can see now that the cuts are all small and have been made strategically, so he doesn't bleed out really quick.

'Did you tell her how to do this?' I point to the cut on the bastard's neck. A small nick in his artery had been burned, cauterising the wound.

'Nope, she's got a natural talent for this,' he says grinning. 'She didn't really need me here except for a few pointers here and there. I was kind of glad when you came, allowed me to get rid of my fucking hard on for his blood.'

Then I think back to what he said minutes ago… and my brain fogs with red mist.

'You had your dick out where my female was?'

He couldn't fucking piss on the guy with it in his fucking boxers, could he? Motherfucker. He puts his hands up in self-defense at which point I realise I'm advancing on him real fast.

'Easy there, boss. She turned away—didn't see a fucking thing. I swear.'

I growl a little, swallowing back my immediate anger. I need to dial it down. I'm shaking and ready to blow my lid. This fucking female has me tied up in knots—threatening my pack brothers, who I've trusted all my life. Now I knew why the older guys would be kicking the shit out of pissants who dared show their female any attention. Jesus, I would total a fucking town for Devon. My blood boils at the mere thought of another male anywhere near her. Fuck me. I hear Brad and Howard in the corridor beyond the door. I turn my attention there and stride up to a worrisome pair.

'Who the fuck thought THAT was a good idea?' I ask pointing to the cell. They both look at each other, and then back at me. It's Howard who answers.

'Jared, she's fucking stubborn. Brad tried to tell her no and she wasn't fucking having it,' he says waving his hands around as he speaks. 'She wanted Harrison in there, and nothing we said or did would have stopped her. You weren't here, so we went with making her happy,' he says, shrugging his shoulders. I don't say anything, thinking it through. 'Look we were in a shitty situation. If we'd said no she would have been mighty pissed off and you wouldn't have been happy about that either.'

True. I sigh in resignation. I couldn't really argue with that when it was spelt out to me.

'You know she'll never fucking sleep again after that shit show?'

'Hate to break it to you, bud, but she seemed pretty damn comfortable in there,' Brad chimes in, smiling.

'Fuck you,' I tell him and turn my back. I had a bone to pick with the bastard before Harrison put the finishing touches on his masterpiece.

'Okay. So now is the time for talking. This game is called show and tell, fucker. I show you how much pain you get if you don't fucking tell. You feel me?' He groans. 'Okay, so I have a question, and you are going to TELL me the answer. Why did my female want my brother here to piss on you?'    He grins at me. Motherfucker. But I have my answer. He tries to speak and chokes a little, no doubt on the blood running down his throat. But then he tries again.

'I…I'm…ex…expecting…to…choke…on…hi…his…cock…next .' He grins as he speaks and that red mist descends. I roar out my frustration, and I don't think, I act. I punch him in the face until it caves in. I end up on the floor. The rope has snapped or possibly his arm, but the chair is no longer, holding him up. I'm covered in bits of him, but I keep going. I don't want this fucker in one piece. Only fucking moments ago did I have Devon on her knees in front of me, ready for me to push my dick in her mouth and she— FUCK.

'Motherfucker, you motherfucking CUUUNT!' I roar out like he can still hear me. He's long dead. I stand and take a knife from Harrison's leather case, and I stab the fucker's dick until there is nothing but mush left there too. I walk out panting and straight up the stairs where I find Devon asleep on the bed. I fall to my knees beside her. Why didn't she tell me? Why didn't she tell me what that cunt had done to her? I hold her hand as she sleeps, smearing his blood all over her and the sheets, but I need her close. I move onto the bed next to her, and she stirs, then her eyes blink open as she realises I'm back. She sits up really quick looking at me.

'Is he dead?' she asks. I nod, unable to get the words out of my throat for the clogged up feeling I have there as I fight the tears.

'Tell me,' I manage. Her eyes close and I know then. She doesn't need to speak the words. What the bastard said was true—he made her choke on his… fuck me I can't even…Fuck.

'I didn't want to tell you, Jared, because I didn't want us—this—to change. You had already stepped back from me so much. I couldn't bear the thought of losing you.'

'Baby, you can tell me anything—any fucking thing, and you will never lose me.' I clutch her face in my hands and make her look me in the eye. 'You and me are forever, Devon. No matter what, You feel me?' She nods. 'I need you to know that no one will ever touch you again.' She nods and her arms come up and around my neck. I pull her in for the hug. 'Ever,' I tell her. When she pulls back she has a mischievous smile on her lips—she's once again covered in blood.

There is more between us now than I thought possible and that smile is where my eyes are glued.

'What about you?' she asks, all sassy.

'Well, that I can't promise because, no one, not even you can keep me away from what's mine.'

'Is that right?'

'Damn straight,' I tell her as I drag her up and into the shower once again.

# chapter THIRTY-SIX

## *Devon*

I WAKE UP FEELING FRESH and content. There's something about clean bedding and the man you love beside you that just makes you sleep so much better. I haven't slept properly in ages.

Maiya hadn't wanted to see or speak to me, but the police had been informed that she was not missing after all. I don't know the specifics, but I know that Brad dealt with it all and he is currently in charge of her care and everything that goes along with that. He doesn't seem too happy about it, but he was obviously doing a great job. I really want to see her, but over the last couple of days Brad had warned me off. I'd been biding my time, and right now Brad was in the kitchen, and I can't smell Maiya in there or see her through the crack in the door, so I decide now is as good a time as any to risk seeing her, while Jared is in the basement.

I head up the stairs and listen outside of Brad's bedroom door. I can only hear Maiya, and I think she might be asleep so I crack the door, as I do, her eyes open and she takes me in. A look a pure undulated disgust fills her eyes, and I almost shrink back and close the door again, but I've never been one to quit. So, I square my shoulders and walk in, closing the door behind me. We're alone. For now.

'What the fuck do you want?' she spits full of venom. I ignore it and walk forward until I reach the end of the bed. I take a deep breath and square my shoulders once again.

'I wanted to see how you are doing. You look much better.'

She scoffs.

'Well, appearances can be deceiving can't they?' she says with an accusing tone.

'Maiya, it's not like I could just tell you—'

'That you're a freak?'

I bite my tongue because I know she's hurting and I can't really blame her for being mad at me. I'm the reason this all happened to her.

'Maiya, I can't tell you how sorry I am—'

'Save it for someone who gives a shit.'

'Maiya. Please don't be this way. Don't shut me out. Talk to me.'

'Talk to you? Why would I want to fucking talk to you? You've ruined      my      life—do      you      understand      that? YOU.HAVE.RUINED.MY.FUCKING.LIFE!' She moves toward me, and I hear metal hit metal as she struggles to sit up. I step forward, and she growls at me. I move the blanket and watch as she struggles against cuffs that are fastened to the bed sides. So she can't get up. I look into her eyes, and I realise then that she is no longer the carefree, up for anything as long as it made her happy, Maiya that I knew before. This Maiya is cold and empty—a shell of what she once was. I can't bear to see her this way. Her flesh is marred from the burns she sustained at the hands of those evil creatures. She had been beautiful, but her face is now sunken and sad. All things that werewolf blood can't heal. Only she, with our help, can fix that look in her eyes. And I will help her in any way I can—even if she hates me for it.

'Do they hurt?' I ask pointing to her wrists.

'In comparison to what exactly? The rest of my fucked up body?' she asks, revulsion clear in her voice. I ignore her tone and move toward her again. I can't see a key, but I will sure as hell find it if she's uncomfortable.

'Do you want me to remove them?'

She looks at me then. Trying to work out why I would take them off I think. Trying to weigh up if I really mean it.

'I can't leave anyway, can I?' she asks.

I shake my head no. 'This is the safest place for you right now.'

She sighs

'Yes. So everyone keeps telling me. Funny how I'd rather be anywhere but here with a bunch of fucking freak shows.'

'Oh, now come on, Maiya. You know you love us really?' Brad chimes in as he walks through the door. 'I mean, what's not to love?'

I stand stiffly at the end of the bed knowing I'm in for an ear bashing. I can't believe he's messing with her right now.

'Fuck you, pig,' she snarls at him before turning her head away from the both of us and closing her eyes. Brad gives me an 'I told you so' look.

I know she hates me and I understand why completely, but it still smarts when I hear her speak to me like that. I just want her back to normal. *Us* back to normal. But if I've learned nothing else in the last few weeks, I've learned that you may not always get what you want, but you have to make the best of what you have. And that's what I will do with Maiya. I wasn't giving up on her, and she would realise that and have to accept it sooner or later.

'Baby?' Jared speaks from the door. I turn and look to find a sympathetic look on his face. I go to him, and he wraps his arms around me. We walk together and sit at the kitchen table. I still feel cut up by what Maiya said.

Jared's father walks in. I'm shocked because I didn't know he was back.

'Did I hear correctly that you had a pop at Kristen? Nearly killed her?' He doesn't mince his words and gets straight to the point. I look at Jared, who stiffens beside me. Zoe puts her cup down, and everyone stops what they are doing to turn to look at me, waiting for my reply. Jared gives a slight nod, telling me I should answer. His dad is the alpha—although that barely means shit to me. I sit up straighter and nod my head. Mr Stone addresses me again. 'Well then, that's good, because today is her last and you've just got the job.' Jared stands up before I can say anything.

'Can I speak to you in private?' he asks his dad.

'Jared, I hardly see why that's necessary,' his father answers.

'Well I do, so shall we go to the library?' Jared doesn't really give his father room to think about an answer he simply walks to the door and raises his hand in an 'after you' gesture. His father's face is like stone when he walks toward the door. Jared's isn't too dissimilar as his eyes meet mine before he too leaves the room, leaving all eyes on me.

'What?' I snap. Logan shakes his head, and everyone turns back to what they were doing. I slink out of the kitchen door, walk around the house, and sit on the swinging chair on the deck. And that's where Jared finds me about thirty minutes later. His face is pale, and he is shaking—anger, nerves, I'm not overly sure which. He just sits down next to me and puts his arm over my shoulder. I instantly feel at ease, and I place my head on his shoulder and wait for him to tell me whatever it is he needs to tell me. And I don't have to wait too long.

'My father thinks it's best that you carry out Kristen's sentence. I don't agree, obviously.'

'Why?' I ask

'Because he's an idiot.' He's misunderstood my question.

'No, I mean why don't you agree?' He looks at me like I've slapped his face.

'Devon, taking a life isn't something that everyone can deal with. I've done it when I've had to—when I'm left with no other choice, but it's not fucking pretty, and it's not fun. I don't want that for you.'

'Has she given up any information?'

He shakes his head.

'Just keeps telling us that I betrayed her before she betrayed us.'

I sigh in frustration.

'I guess I can see where she's coming from—a woman scorned and all that.'

'It's not like I fucking cheated on her. We weren't together, never have been, and she knew long before you came along that there would be no relationship between us! It was the power that she wanted that came with the status. She didn't give a fuck about me!'

'I know, but then I guess when I came along she had that status stripped even if it wasn't you that she cared about.'

'What the bitch does keep saying though, is that we will never find your mother. That she's too fucking smart for us—and she keeps laughing, telling us it is far from over.'

'What does that mean? Do you think they'll try and get to me again?'

'From what Kristen and the other cunt isn't saying and their little taunts I think that's a definite. And she's saying that she has something to tell you, but she won't tell anyone else, only you.'

'So let's go and find out what she has to say then?'

I move to get up, but he pulls me by the hand. I stop and look him in the eye.

'Baby whatever it is, she will be taunting you, trying to rile you up, so you snap. She knows she's got nothing to lose, and that she's going to die today. So bear that in mind, okay?'

'Okay.'

We walk around the house and head down the stairs. As we walk through the door, I can smell the blood, and as we pass the first cell, the stench is rancid even though the cell is now empty. The next one I pass, houses asshole number two, who Howard is working over. I feel that thrill run though my entire body again, at the prospect of working over Kristen. And then I come to a stop outside of her cell. She's a mess. Someone has had a really good go at her this morning already. Although her face is swollen and distorted, her face splits into a grin as she sees me. Her teeth have a coat of red on them, and there are gaps where teeth have been extracted from her mouth. Something that Harrison was going to show me yesterday, before Jared had intervened and put an end to it.

Despite the fact she is hanging from the ceiling and can barely move, she looks at me like she holds all the power. It unnerves me for a second, but I don't let that take root. Instead, moving into the cell, I poke a finger into what looks like an infected wound on her shoulder. She squeals in pain. I smile as I poke it further, and she grits her teeth while she blows snot and spit out on a breath. She exhales, trying to keep the noise to a minimum. There is a container of salt on the floor in the corner. I eye it, knowing it will sting like a bitch if I apply it liberally to her wounds. Jared looks to where my line of sight has gone, and he moves to get it. I think he's going to give it to me, but instead, he keeps it at his side.

'Spit out whatever the fuck you have to say to Devon.'

She hasn't taken her eyes off me, and she grins until she notices what Jared has in his hand, then the smile falters a little. I look her in the eye, and I demand her to submit. Her eyes lower and I know I have the upper hand, mentally as well as physically. Suddenly her eyes snap up again, and she glares at me, and that crazy-as-shit smile is spread even wider now. I don't waver in my dominance though. And I lift my chin, telling her to get on with it. She barks out a humourless laugh.

'I could be pregnant you know?' she says. 'With your niece or nephew.'

'Not possible,' I tell her

'You of all people should know it is possible. I mean you're a mongrel, just like this one will be.' I ignore her snipe at me.

'It's entirely possible that you are pregnant, but it's no relative of mine, and besides, you won't be alive long enough to know if you are or aren't.' I watch the look of panic in her eye, and I smell the fear oozing from her pores.

'Listen to me. I have information that I know you will want. If you kill me, you'll never know,' she pleads.

'By the sounds of it, I'll never know anyway because you haven't told us shit so far, so why should I wait. Why not just kill you now? I've been itching for it since the last time.' I walk around her, and she pulls at her restraints, causing her to howl in pain. I laugh at her attempt to get free, and then I step in front of her. I ask Jared to lower her with a flick of my eyes to the wheel on the wall. He does, and I step up close and slide my fingers around her throat. I meet her eyes with mine, and we are nose to nose. 'Why don't I just kill you here and now—get it over with. Damn, I'm sick to death of seeing you already.' I squeeze until her eyes start to bulge and she makes a noise between a gasp and a choke. All that registers in my head at that moment is how pathetic she sounds, but I like that the whites of her eyes start to turn red. Jared clears his throat behind me, and I loosen my grip. She is head down and gasping for air.

'What information do you have that's so important we should let you live?' Jared asks from behind me.

'You have a brother,' she blurts out in a raspy voice.

I sigh in boredom. 'I gathered that when you told me you might be carrying my niece or nephew. And I don't care if he's knocked you up. He's on the other team, just like you, so quit the bullshit, Kristen. You die today. Tell me something worth knowing or die slowly.'

'Wow, you really do think you're the alpha female. Look at you, acting the big I am. It won't last—you're weak.'

I slap her face as Jared pours salt over her back and she screams in pain.

'I'm weak?' I laugh. 'Says the girl strung up from the ceiling at my mercy.' I smile.

'Let me down, and we'll fight. That's tradition, you mongrel piece of shit,' she spits at me. 'But you wouldn't know that because you're not even part of the pack.'

'That's where you're wrong,' Jared tells her through gritted teeth.

'They'll never stop coming for her, and you'll regret what you've done to me, Jared.'

He scoffs. 'I've done shit to you. You brought all this on yourself.' He pours more salt in her wounds, and she wails. I love the sound, and it makes me smile. I watch as she writhes in pain.

'They will get you, and they'll fuck you, and fuck you, and fuck you until you're no longer of use. Just a bucket to fuck and give birth.' I don't bite, but her words have an effect, and I feel sick. Jared responds with an uppercut to her chin, knocking her out for a few seconds. He looks at me, and his face is full of concern.

'You know that shit won't happen. I'm gonna get every one of those cunts before they even get near you.'

I step into his embrace, and I believe he will do just that. The trouble is, in the meantime, I'm stuck on twenty-four-hour lockdown with security around the clock. I nod, and he kisses me.

'Come on she's got nothing worth sticking around for.' I say. We start to walk out of the cell when she says something indistinct. Jared

FORBIDDEN LOVE

ignores her, but for some reason, I need to hear what it is she's said. I move from under Jared's arm and walk toward her,

'What did you say?' I ask. Her chin is swollen, and her lips are split open. She speaks with a mouth full of blood,

'vay hab yow fabber.' It doesn't sink in what she's saying. I'm trying to decipher the words.

'They have your father...' Jared repeats. 'You better start fucking talking right fucking now, Kristen!' he demands.

## *Jared*

Devon is standing there with huge eyes, and fear all over her face. Kristen spits blood at me.

'Got your attention now, huh?' she croaks out. The fuckin bitch.

Devon has her phone in her hand, and she dials her father. I can see her shaking hand as she brings the phone to her ear.

'Hello, sweetheart. I wondered when you would eventually call.' I hear over the line. It's clearly not her father because it's a female voice. Devon gasps as the blood runs from her face. Shit. I catch her as her knees buckle, and she almost hits the floor. I take the phone from her hand.

'Who the fuck is this?' I shout into the phone.

'Now now, none of that, kindly put my daughter back on the phone.' Devon seems to come to herself again, and she grabs the receiver from me.

'If you hurt him, I will kill you,' she screams,

'There is no need for any of this, sweetheart. Come back to me, and I will let everyone else live,' the crazy bitch says.

'WHERE.IS.MY.DAD?' Devon speaks through her anger and if she clenches her jaw any tighter I'm thinking she'll break a fucking tooth. I pull her to me and turn her away from Kristen's smug fucking face. She has bought herself some alive time, but it still won't end in any way other than death, and a painful one if I get my way. I take the phone from Devon and speak calmly.

'You want a war? You hurt what's mine, and I will come for you, and I won't stop till I have your fucking head.' I cut the call and Devon is looking at me like I just signed her dad's death warrant. Kristen is laughing, thinking she's got one over on us.

'You wanna quieten her down before I do, baby?' I lift my chin toward Kristen. Devon doesn't even hesitate—she's in motion and striking out before I've even finished my sentence. Kristen's head flops forward, and blood runs from her mouth, effectively ending her shit show.

## Jared

I HAVE BRAD CHECKING ALL areas he can from the security room. He isn't happy that I've pulled him from Maiya. A complete fucking turn around, considering he threw a bitch fit when I gave him the job. I conceded and told him he could do both jobs as long as he remains effective.

'I can't find a fucking thing on the bitch, so I have no fucking idea when she left the country. She isn't using her married name or her maiden name. I've got jack shit,' he tells me.

'Well, keep fucking looking.' Devon's dad's mobile phone pinged up on the radar in Salem, Oregon. But he says that doesn't mean shit— he could be anywhere, and until he finds the bitch on the flight she took, he won't know for sure. Devon is freaking the fuck out, and I don't know how to fucking help her. I have Harrison down in the cell working on Kristen. Either she doesn't know shit, or she is one tough nut to crack. I'm tempted to just end it, but I'm worried she does know something. On that thought Harrison comes into the security room where we're scanning a shit tonne of flight registers, trying to find something.

'She talk?'

He nods. But doesn't look too happy about it.

'She says the dad is a lost cause—dead already. That she's only trying to use it to lure Devon back and that he was dead the moment they picked him up. They have him on ice somewhere.' Fuck. I scrub my hands across my face. I don't know how I'm going to break this shit to Devon. She's currently upstairs, in pieces, pulling her fucking hair out. Harrison grips my shoulder in his hand. 'Send Devon down to me. It'll help.'

I shake my head. That's not what she needs. I can't let her do that and then regret it.

'How sure are you that the bitch is telling the truth?' I ask holding a tiny bit of hope. He shakes his head.

'Jared, he's dead. I'm a hundred percent.'

Devon chooses that very fucking moment to walk in the room. She stands in the doorway, with no emotion on her face. I can't read the look at all. All I can do is stare at her, with sympathy all over my face. I feel fucking useless as I move around Harrison and take her into my arms, but she's stiff and doesn't go with the hug.

'Baby, I'm so sorry.' Her eyes are trained blankly on the wall behind me, and she doesn't speak. Harrison moves from the room and then Brad is hot on his heels. I swivel his chair and sit her in it. 'Baby talk to me,' I plead. I need something, anything from her. I can't do anything with nothing. She takes a deep breath in through her nose, and I look up into her eyes. She doesn't meet mine when she speaks.

'I am going to end them, Jared. All of them. I'm not going to stop until they are all gone.'

Fuck me—had our roles reversed?

'Baby, I'll get them, all of them. I promise you, not one will survive. I'll get every single fucking one.'

She shakes her head, no.

'No, Jared, I will. I have to.'

Jesus. Do I argue? Do I give her what she needs while she's grieving? Fuck me, I want to lock her away until this shit is sorted, not set her on a course to go to war with the kitsunes.

'Okay, baby, whatever you need,' I find myself saying although I nearly choke on my fucking words. She stands then, and I straighten up with her. 'What do you need right now? What can I get you?' I need to fucking do something for fuck's sake.

'Take me to the basement.' And I know what she wants to do. I sigh and remember Harrison's words. *It'll help.* God, I fucking hope so.

## *Devon*

I walk down the stairs, and the stench hits me. I breathe it in like a healing tonic. I want it to heal me from this pain I feel. I need to act—

need to make it go away. I want to kill them, take their lives like they took my dad's. Like they ruined Maiya's, and are ruining mine. I need to let this feeling free—let it out and never let it back in. I see my dad's face smiling at me as I walk into Kristen's cell.

Harrison stops working and turns to me.

'Your call?' he says

'Let her down. Help her heal and feed her,' I tell him. Jared looks at me and to Harrison in a split second, and then I'm out of the room and walking into the next. The asshole in this cell is stinking the place up so bad he could already be dead, but I can hear his heartbeat. Faint but still there. I study him, tilting my head slowly from side to side. Assessing the best way forward. I feel Jared enter behind me, and Harrison a second later.

'Please lower him,' I ask. And Harrison cranks the wheel. This guy is a full-blooded kitsune, and in my opinion, they all need to be purged and wiped off the planet if this is what they are, what they do. I want to rip his heart right out of his chest. But I don't. I watch his chest rise and fall as the grunt leaves his mouth when he hits the floor. He isn't healing very fast—maybe that isn't a trait of the kitsunes. He has missing fingers, toes, teeth, and only has one eye. Looking at him, I notice an ear missing too.

'Cauterize his wounds so he doesn't bleed out—clean him up and let me know when he's healed up enough to leave.'

'What the fuck, Devon?' Harrison says, clearly pissed and feeling robbed. I know because I understand that feeling too. He'd planned their deaths, and I want them healed.

I move into the kitsune and speak into his only ear.

'I am feeling generous, and I'm offering you a chance. I'll get you fit enough to leave, and here's the thing—you will get a fifteen-minute head start, and then you are fair game. Maybe you'll get a message to my mother, maybe you won't?'

'What's the message,' he whispers,

'Oops, I almost forgot, the message is, 'Run bitch run,' because she just started a war, and I'm coming for her.' I walk past a slack-jawed Jared, and Harrison, who has a knowing smile on his face. I leave the cells and have no intention of talking to anyone. So I go straight to Jared's room. I throw myself onto the bed and let my heart break.

The pain is overwhelming. The one constant in my whole life is gone. Just gone. He lived his whole life for me, knowing what I was. He protected me, over and over again—leading a lonely life, never having friends or women. Never living. Just taking care of me. Always. And for what? *'So you could live.'* I hear his voice in my head, chastising me. It's so unfair, and I can't get my head around the injustice of it all.

At some point, Jared comes in, and Zoe stops by to check in on me. But I don't get out of bed for anything other than for a bathroom break. My mind is racing, and I'm covering all the different possibilities of my father's death. It's like my own personal torture. I never knew hate could be just as powerful as love. The hate inside me right now is so strong that I'm scared it will overtake me. Swallow me whole. Suck me in so deep I won't be able to get out. I'm really hot, and I fling the comforter off me, pulling at my t-shirt. It's constricting my breathing. I need it off, and I can't get it off quickly enough. I yank at the neck instead, and I heave in a long shaky breath. It isn't enough. Jesus why is it so hot? My hand starts to tingle, my fingers and then my arm. Oh my god, I can't breathe. I hear a tearing sound, and I feel cool air across my face and back. I heave in another breath, then another—each one becoming easier than the last. My t-shirt is torn down my back, and the window is wide open. I look up to find Jared fanning me with a notebook. He looks worried, almost like a lost child. What's wrong with him?

'You okay?' I croak out.

He frowns and his head shakes a little bit.

'Am I okay? Baby, *you're* not okay! What can I do?' he asks. And I don't know what to say to him. What can he do? What can anyone do? Nothing. There is nothing to do.

'I can't even bury him, Jared.'

He drops his head to my shoulder.

'I'm so fucking sorry, baby,' he tells me, and that's all anyone can say. Even though they have nothing to be sorry about. It isn't their fault my mother is a sick, twisted bitch.

'If I had known—'

I place my fingers to Jared's lips to stop whatever he was going to say. It is pointless.

'Nothing you could have done, Jared,' I tell him. I feel guilty. I should have known my mother better, but my memories of her were so few and very poor. I have to be thankful of that in some way too. He holds me against his chest, and I know without him, I would be completely empty.

'I just can't believe it, Jared. I can't believe he's gone.' He holds me tighter, and I have to choke down a sob.

It's been three days since I found out about my dad. At least that's what Jared says. I've barely left the bedroom. I've eaten bits but not a great deal. But as Harrison knocks at the door, my heart flutters a little. I hope he has news from the basement.

'The kitsune is ready. Any healthier and I'll be fucking annoyed, so he needs to go as soon as possible.' His voice is devoid of emotion, but I see a glint in his eye. He's excited for this. And what do you know—my mood lifts at the prospect too.

'Who is going?' I ask, looking at them both. Harrison rolls his eyes Jared's way, and he shrugs his shoulders.

'I was going to ask you the same question, baby.' He half smiles. And I smile back.

'Well, I guess it depends on who wants the hunt?' I ask, making Jared choke a little, and Harrison grins so wide it almost reaches his ears.

'I'll ask the question, but I doubt there will be many men left to guard you and the house. I think everyone will want in.' I frown at his words.

'I'm going, Jared.'

He shakes his head no.

'I AM.'

'Devon, this isn't up for discussion. You've barely eaten and barely slept in days.' I look at Harrison, and he turns his head away. Fuckity fuck. I thought I could count on his vote.

'Fine! But only because I want to be at my best for Kristen, and I don't give a flying fuck what you have to say about that, Jared. SHE is MINE!'

To my amazement, he doesn't argue. So I take that as a win. Ha! I hear Brad through the open door and turn to find him standing in the frame. He smiles a little at me before looking Jared square in the eye.

'I want in on that bastard. I'm not staying in on this one, Jared. I want in.'

'Fair enough,' Jared concedes, and Brad nearly falls backwards from the ease of his agreement.

'Is my father back?' Jared asks and is told that he's still not back from his business. Meaning the helm was still his. Not that I think he would object to our plan. I think he'd appreciate it and take part.

The asshole is set free, and it takes less than an hour for Jared to come back and find me in the kitchen. He's still naked from his change, and he's covered in blood. I jump up from the bench and frantically check him over. No one else comes in with him, but we still have plenty of men on guard. Harrison, Howard, Brad, and Jared chased the kitsune and he clearly never made it off the grounds. I take in Jared's face, and the blood covering the lower half and his chin. I smudge my thumb through it, and I smile a little.

'He's gone?' I ask, already knowing the answer. Jared nods and still has that look in his eye—the one he gets when his wolf is still lingering at the surface. It's beautiful and powerful and all alpha male. I knew what comes next. What always follows that look. And the happy feeling that one less kitsune walks the earth has me in the same mindset. I feel, more than hear, the rumble of his chest as he pulls me into him. Before I know it, I'm hauled over his shoulder, and he is taking the stairs two at a time. He doesn't slow, only stopping to look at me for a moment when he tosses me on the bed. He starts with my jeans and begins dragging them down my legs. When he is done with those, he tears my tee over my head, and I catch a glimpse of his wolf again, in his beautiful green orbs. He flips me over then and pushes inside me. Although he's taken no time to prepare me, my body always seems ready to encompass his cock. He slides inside with little effort and the moment he sinks balls deep, he groans out like an addict who's just plunged on the needle. He's greedy though and doesn't stay still long. He pounds out his need as he clutches my hips and bites into my shoulder. He cums on a roar, and I join him seconds later.

*Devon*

THE DAY HAD COME. KRISTEN was up on her feet, and I was ready to take her out. Jared had grizzled about letting her heal all the way, and so we had compromised on a few days. I wanted her able to fight back, so I'd wanted to wait until she was fully healed.

'Devon, this isn't a fight. It's an execution. I already don't like that you are doing this—don't make me change my mind,' he told me. Oh hell no. He wasn't taking this from me.

'Jared, if it was you fighting another male, would you want them injured?'

He growls his impatience.

'Completely fucking different, Devon. Like I said. NOT.A.FUCKING.FIGHT.'

'An execution. Yeah yeah, I know! But I want to win fair and square.'

'Baby, listen to what I am saying. Okay?' I nod. And smile in amusement. 'You are not going out there to have a fight. You are going out there to execute a traitor—nothing more nothing less.'

'So when she fights back you're still gonna call it an execution? Still not a fight?'

He stamps his foot, and I laugh at his frustration until I see the seriousness in his face, then I stop.

'If you think I'm going to stand back and let her hurt you, you are waaaay the fuck wrong.'

'Jared, have you forgotten. I almost took her out last time? If you hadn't stopped it—'

'Don't fucking remind me,' he grumbles.

'Jared, I'm not afraid of getting hurt. I want to fight her, and I want to win. I will win.'

He shakes his head, sighing and sits on the bed. He runs his fingers through his hair as I pull on my jeans.

'She'll be desperate—she's got nothing to lose, and she's going to die anyway. She will go all fucking out to take you with her!'

I shrug my shoulders, and turn my lips down in a 'so what?' gesture.

'Fuck, Devon. I can't stand the thought of her hurting you anymore. I wish you would just let me deal with this shit,'

'Sorry, buddy, not a chance,' I tell him, trying to lighten the mood.

'I'm serious.' He purses his lips which makes me smile. I walk over to him and wrap my arms around his neck, putting his head at boob level. I only have my bra on, and he is suddenly preoccupied and stops with his pep talk.

I walk out of the kitchen and into the waiting crowd outside. Jared's father is there. He grins as I walk to Jared's side. And I see Harrison, dragging along Kristen, looking much better than the last time I saw her. My lip curls immediately when our eyes meet. I can smell her fear—not so clever now she knows it's the end for her. I take comfort in that. I can feel how tense Jared is. He's made it clear how he feels about this, on too many occasions today. I really should make this swift if I'm going to keep him happy. But I also want her to suffer. If I remember rightly, I was quicker on my feet than she was, more nimble, agile. I will use that to my advantage and prolong her death. Drag it out and injure her as much as possible before I deliver the fatal blow.

I shake myself back into the here and now and look at Jared. He's so tense. I hate seeing him like this, but I have to do this my way. I have to, or I will regret it my whole life. I'm doing this for me, for my dad, and for Maiya. The crowd is eager for blood. I can feel it buzzing. Jared's father steps up and quiets the crowd with a simple raised hand.

'An execution would normally be carried out in human form, swiftly, but this execution is somewhat different. I believe that my son's mate deserves to carry out this execution in any way she sees fit.' The crowd cheers and lots of eyes meet mine. 'Devon has lost a lot because of this traitor, and so I am handing over the gavel, so to speak, so that she can exact her punishment.' With that, he gestures that the floor is mine. Kristen is on her knees in front of me, with Harrison at her back.

'I want her in wolf form,' I tell him, and he gives me a nod before dragging her to one side of the crowd and cutting a hole through. Jared and I walk through, and he takes me to the kitchen. I watch through the window as Harrison puts a chain around Kristen's neck. Jared closes the blind, and I start to strip down. There is no time to be skittish about changing form in front of him, so I just get on with it. As I kneel down, he comes with me. I realise then he had undressed too. He holds my face in his palm and looks me in the eye. We don't speak—he just kisses my lips before dropping his head to start his own change. The pain is less than usual, and it seems to come much quicker. I don't wait around. As soon as it's over, I make my way to the open door. Jared is at my heel, and as we leave the kitchen, the crowd parts for us. Jared walks around the edge of the circle, backing the crowd up.

I see lots of friendly faces now, Brad, Zoe, Howard, Logan, and Imogen and so many more as they all take a step back. Then I hear Harrison cussing and see the crowd part as he drags a struggling Kristen by the chain around her neck into the centre of the circle. Jared stands by my side, and his father stands to his right. He nods his head minutely, giving his father the okay. And then he steps in front of me, once again quieting the crowd with a small rising of his hand. There is a moment of silence as Kristen stops her struggle, but it passes in a second as the alpha drops his arm, his hand slicing through the air between us. Then the crowd jeers and shouts as Harrison releases the chain from around her neck. I watch her stumble, trying to track my movements as her head lifts. She whimpers and lies on her belly, but I'm not falling for that. I curl my lips and snarl. She skitters back, pathetically. I growl out my frustration. I want her to fight me. To challenge me. I want the Kristen who laughed while telling me they'd taken my father. The one who attacked me on more than one occasion. Someone throws a boot out and hits her in the ribs, sending her sprawling in my direction. I strike at her left side yanking on the flesh between her flank and forepaw. I taste blood, and it sends me into a frenzy. I forget the crowd. I want blood. Kristen's. I strike again, this time at her hind leg. I tear through the muscle there—she bites back and takes a chunk from my side. It stings, but it doesn't slow me down. I tear at her ear and yank it away in my teeth, and she squeals, making me hungrier for more. I have a shot at her throat. I don't take it. I wait until she limps up onto her feet again. Tilting my head, I take her in—watch how she holds herself. I'm sure she's playing a game, feigning weakness. But that's fine. I won't fall for it. The fear radiating from her is diluted by the excitement in the air. Then I see her. Maiya. As Brad holds her in his arms, she looks right at me and seems to nod her approval. That's all I need to end this. During the split second it takes to look over at Maiya, I miss Kristen leap into the air. She takes hold of my scruff, trying with all she has to grip on, but I side step and spin around on her, making her lose her grip. I leap onto her back and bite into the soft flesh—my teeth taking hold beneath her jaw and behind her ear. I bite down and am almost choked as her blood spurts into my mouth, hot and metallic. Kristen crumbles like a house of cards beneath me, taking me down on top of her because I refuse to let go. I plant my paws on either side of my mouth, and I rip the flesh and muscle away—and Kristen is dead. It's over.

'Baby, come and lie down. Zoe said you should rest while the stitches take.'

I'd had to have several in my side where Kristen had taken out a chunk, but I wanted to see Maiya. I couldn't stop pacing.

'Jared, Maiya watched. She was there—she looked right at me.'

'Baby, I know. I saw her. But God help me, if you don't get your ass on this bed right fucking now, you'll need re-stitching 'cause I'm gonna fuck you till you're still.'

I grin. It always comes down to that with Jared. We both knew he dominated the bedroom and if he wanted me still while he fucked me, I would be still. But we both know he will do no such thing while I'm injured because he worries too damn much. Catching my grin, he snaps his arm out and drags me onto his lap.

'Don't believe me?' he asks feigning seriousness. I roll my hips, pressing my already wet vagina into his growing erection. He groans, closing his eyes. Then pushes me up while he stands behind me. His hands taking a breast each as his arms circle me. He tweaks both nipples and then pulls away from me.

'What are you doing?' I ask incredulously as I watch him walk to the bathroom.

'Absolutely nothing. Now sit your ass down and stop fucking pushing your luck!' I sit and huff out in frustration. I lie myself back on his bed as I hear the faucet running. I'm so tired. I ache, and I realise just how much when I try and push the comforter from the bed. Jeez, I hurt almost everywhere. Jared had been right by my side the minute I'd ended Kristen's life. He'd lapped at my muzzle and cleaned me, and the minute we changed forms, he had Zoe check me over. Kristen wasn't buried—there wasn't a ceremony of any sort like I knew there had been for her uncle. Instead, she was thrown in a shallow hole and burnt. Fitting really, I guess, for a traitor.

# chapter
# THIRTY-NINE

## Jared

*Christmas day (two months later)*

I'M SITTING OUT ON THE deck. It's freezing, but it's fresh out. The snow lay last night, and it's fucking perfect. Just what Devon wanted. It's been hard on her after the loss of her father. Hard in every way, but Christmas is special and about family. We've chosen to stay behind as the others went back to their families, only Howard and Harrison stayed, but they don't really have family other than me and the pack. Brad surprised me because he took Devon's not-so-friendly friend back with him too. My father had allowed it, given the circumstances. And that meant that we practically had the place to ourselves.

I'm desperate to wake Devon this morning when the sun starts to rise. I've been like an excited kid. I just want everything to be perfect, but I've left her to sleep. She's not slept well in such a long time, and she hasn't been herself these last few weeks either. Hardly eating. And just generally being off. I want to change all that today. I want to bring her happy back. I head back into the kitchen, and up the stairs, and I find her sprawled like a starfish on the bed—the covers barely covering her at all—instead, wrapped around her legs acting like a pillow under her knees. It isn't cold in here—the heating makes sure of that, but the way she's sprawled you would think it's the middle of summer. She makes a little mewling noise, and I move closer, getting worked up thinking this is it—she's waking finally. But she doesn't, she just turns onto her side, throwing her arm out to where I would have been. When she doesn't find me, her eyes crack just a little. And she stretches. I groan as her nipples pop through the tight vest she's wearing and that gets me a fully awake and wide-eyed Devon. She crawls up onto my lap, and I kiss her lips. She's reluctant, but I force the issue. I couldn't give a shit about her morning breath that she grumbles about. I want her when I want her and brushing her teeth makes no damn difference to how I feel. I've argued this so many times I've lost count. But she still says it every fucking morning.

'I'll just brush my teeth,' she mumbles against my lips. I fucking knew it.

'No.' I pull her close as she tries to climb off me. 'Merry Christmas, baby,' I whisper in her ear. 'You ready for your present?' She squeals on my lap. 'Hell yes!' she replies. I reach over to my side table draw and pull out the gift. It's a large black box with a fucking big ass bow that Zoe made me buy. Fucking pointless if you ask me. But she is a female and insisted Devon would love it.

'Wow!' And she was right obviously. Her face splits into a huge grin as she pulls at the ends. She opens the box and pulls out the underwear I've chosen. When she's finished oohing and aaahing she realises there is another box. She looks at me for confirmation that there is more. I smile, nodding my head. I hope to fuck she likes the rest. I chew on my lip, the apprehension getting to me now as she pulls open the box and pulls out the envelope.

'Open it, baby.'

Tearing at the envelope she pulls out the tickets.

'OH MY GOD, JARED! PARIS!!' She almost falls off the bed, she's so excited. 'Oh my god. I can't believe it, Jared. This is too much! Jared, how much have you spent?' Typical. For fuck's sake.

'Devon just open the damn presents. It's not about money,' I tell her straight. I have a lot of money. Not everyone knows, and I don't flaunt it like some pricks do, but I've invested well, and it's paid off. Devon obviously knows this and being the stubborn fucking female that she is, still insists on finding a job when we're off lockdown and this whole situation is put to bed. I don't like the idea and will argue that point to my last dying breath but being the pussy that I am when it comes to her, she will no doubt end up with her own fucking way. As always.

I'm pussy-whipped, as my pack brothers like to call it. And didn't I fucking know it! But if it makes her happy, who the fuck am I to complain. As she gets to the last box, I take it from her hands and get down on one knee. Her face is a picture, and her eyes are wide as saucers. Her shaking hand moves to cover her mouth as I snap the box open.

'Devon, you are my bonded mate, and we are sealed in this life together in every way but this.' I clear my throat as her eyes fill with tears. 'Devon Hathoway, will you marry me?'

She waves her hand in front of her face as she sobs. Then she throws her arms around me and almost bowls me over. She kisses me all over my face as she cries, but she still hasn't said yes.

'Baby, don't keep me hanging.' I chuckle, but I'm nervous as fuck. I still have the ring box clutched in my hand, with my arms wrapped firmly around a sobbing Devon. Jesus this was supposed to make her happy. Then she swipes at her eyes with the back of her hand and looks me dead in the eyes.

'Yes, Jared. I will marry you. Of course, I'll marry you!' she squeals. And I'm fucking elated—on a high. I spin her around and kiss her with everything I've got. She said fucking yes!! I'm practically dancing with her in my arms when she suddenly covers her mouth with her hand—she looks green. I put her down, and she runs for the bathroom. Shit. She's hanging over the toilet, throwing her guts up. I hold her hair back as she pukes, reaching when nothing more comes.

'Sorry, baby. I didn't mean to make you sick.'

She slaps my leg. 'Don't be stupid,' she chastises me. She flushes, brushes her teeth, and washes her face.

'Where is my beautiful new ring?' she asks like a giddy kid. I slide it on her finger. It's a Tiffany Princess something or other that Zoe helped me choose. And it fits perfectly. Thank you, Zoe. I mentally high-five her.

'I love it, Jared. I love you.' She strokes my face and then looks a little nervous. Probably feeling sick again. Shit.

'You okay? You don't look so hot?'

She swats at me, but I'm serious. 'Baby, really. Maybe you should go back to bed?'

'Hell no. It's our first Christmas, and you haven't had your present yet!' She reaches over and into her side cupboard and pulls out a box with another stupid fucking bow on it. She pushes it into my hand, and she looks almost scared.

'Is it gonna blow up with glitter or some shit?' I ask, laughing as I pull the end of the bow. It falls apart, and all I need to do is take the lid off. I look over to her. She's biting on her bottom lip, apprehensively.

'Devon, I love it.'

She frowns at me. 'You haven't even opened the damn thing—you don't know what it is yet?'

'I know I'll love it—that's what matters.'

Her head tilts and she kisses me. 'That's so damn sweet, but for the love of God, open it please!'

I lift the lid, and my breath catches in my throat. I swallow, but I can't get the lump to move as I pull them out by the ribbons. I look up—she's becoming out of focus as my eyes fill with tears. I look past the little booties and into Devon's eyes.

'You're gonna be a daddy,' she confirms. And fuck me if I don't cry like a fucking baby. I put my hand to her stomach, and I'm so happy at that moment. I can't wait to watch her belly swell with my kid. I lay her down and lift her vest. I shower kisses all over her belly.

'Hey, baby. This is your daddy speaking. I love you so much I can't fuc— Ouch—'

'No cussing around the baby!' Devon tells me as she swipes me across the head. I have everything I wanted right here in this room. Love. Family. Happiness.

### THE END

This is the end of Jared and Devon's story, but only the be
Brad and Maiya. If you want to read more look out for Co
Love, Book two in the Stone Pack series releasing spring

Thank you so much for reading. Authors rely a lot on reviews so if you
enjoyed this book, please leave a review on Amazon and/or Goodreads
if you can ☺ Much Love Harper x

# Find me:

**Website -** www.HarperPhoenix.com
**Facebook -** www.facebook.com/HarperPhoenix16/
**Instagram -** @HarperPhoenix2016
**Twitter -** HarperPhoenix1
Or drop me a line @HarperPhoenix2016@gmail.com

Printed in Poland
by Amazon Fulfillment
Poland Sp. z o.o., Wrocław